The Thirteen

Hannah Hooton is
novels for adults ai
writing in a variety of genres from
equestrian romance to paranormal
mystery. *The Thirteenth Hour* is her first
venture into the war drama genre. She
also writes for an ongoing television
series and has had a smattering of short
stories published in collaborative
anthologies. Alongside her writing,
Hannah is a teacher and former
screenwriting lecturer, and lives in
Cambridge, UK with her grumpy cat,
Atticus.

Also by Hannah Hooton:

At Long Odds
The Aspen Valley series:
Keeping the Peace
Giving Chase
Share and Share Alike
Making the Running
Chasing the Wind
The Messenger series (as H.R. Aidan):
Girl Missing
Calix Puritatis

Television:
Jackplot
Peckham Mix

The Thirteenth Hour

Hannah Hooton

ASPEN VALLEY BOOKS

Dear Maureen & Debbie,

With best wishes,

Hannah Hooton

ASPEN VALLEY BOOKS

First published in 2024

Copyright © Hannah Hooton, 2024

All rights reserved
The moral right of the author has been asserted.

No part of this publication may be reproduced, stored in a retrieval
system, or transmitted in any form or by any means without the prior
permission in writing of the publisher. Nor be otherwise circulated in
any form of binding or cover other than that in which it is published and
without a similar condition including this condition being imposed on
the subsequent purchaser.

All characters and events in this publication, other than those clearly in
the public domain, are fictitious and any resemblance to real persons,
living or dead, is purely coincidental.

978-0-992-9853-7-0

Published by Aspen Valley Books, 2024
www.aspenvalleybooks.com

For Michelle, a great author, editor, and most precious friend.
(1969-2021)

Prologue

T'ime is an illusion…'
  Rain battered harder against the window pane and the late afternoon light filtering inside weakened a few more watts. The dingy hotel room was lit by a weak blue light that cast shadows over the budget furnishings. At the dressing table sat Simon Hayes, the glare of his laptop screen reflecting off his spectacles. His dark hair was askew, roughed by many a finger-trawling. His eyes never left the screen.

  '…*Time dilation is the difference in elapsed time measured by two observers. A clock that is moving will tick slower than a stationary observer's clock. The faster a clock travels the slower it ticks…*'

  '…*To travel backwards, time essentially must slow to a negative value, requiring such extraordinary speed as to travel faster than the speed of light…*'

  Simon frowned at the screen. 'So, what if…'

  He typed '*brain wave speed*' into the search engine, and his heart began to thud as the results loaded.

  '*The brain operates on five different speeds – Gamma…; Beta…; Alpha…; Theta…; Delta…*'

  Simon chewed his thumbnail. Brainwaves didn't travel at the speed he hoped they did. He thought for a second then clicked back to the search engine and typed in '*brain waves: altered state of consciousness, past life regression*'.

  He scrolled down the results examining epileptic seizures, hallucinations, and such like until one caught his eye.

  '…*Under hypnosis and regressing to former life states, we bypass the critical consciousness and enter the subconscious and semi-conscious. Through a heightened sense of all three conscious levels, the brain operates on a number of different frequencies, culminating in Sigma, a wave-speed faster than the speed of light…'*

A bang on the door sent Simon leaping in his chair. He shook himself alert and rubbed his dry eyes behind his glasses. For a moment longer, he stared at the screen. '*…Sigma, a wave-speed faster than the speed of light…'*

He wasn't crazy. This was real. This was possible.

His step-brother, Nick, strode in as soon as he opened the door and began pacing the room. 'I wanted to get here before Amanda. Do not go shooting your mouth off about this to her or we'll end up with her packing it all in and ruining everything we've already done. It was all I could do to convince her to come this afternoon.'

Simon closed the door behind him and leaned against it. 'I've been doing some homework, some research, and it's not as fanciful as you might think.' He stepped forward, desperate to convince Nick, desperate to be believed. 'We *can* change things. We *can* change history. We *can*… save Catherine.'

PART ONE

1

Amiens, France – Tuesday, 21ˢᵗ May, 1940

57 Rue des Jardins stood pock-marked with bullets, its elegant walls blackened by the smoke that hung over the city, darkening the dawn. Shredded curtains billowed through the broken windows, a dull flap amidst the eerie quiet.

A peasant family in front of the house restacked a cart with their belongings. A young boy of no more than ten balanced atop the precarious load while his father passed him items of fallen furniture and tinkling sacks of belongings. They worked in silence, only broken by the abrupt but hushed whispers of the father directing his son's efforts. A whimper broke the quiet, and the father darted an intense frown to his wife standing to the side with a baby in her arms. She nestled the infant to her chest, bouncing it in comfort and it soon settled. Not even the soot and dirt that stained her face could disguise her anguish.

Suddenly, 57's front door was thrust open, and Catherine, a girl in her late teens, emerged and ran into the street, her flimsy shoes pat-patting on the cobbles. The peasant family leapt in surprise, and the boy had to grapple with the ropes to keep his balance. From such a luxurious house, she was strangely unkempt. She stopped in the middle of the street, her eyes wild, her thick dark hair twisting about her face. Her gaze wavered over the peasant family then continued across to settle on the rubble and devastation that was once the street she'd played on. A low rumble was carried up the road by a cool smoke-laden breeze, and Catherine turned to the lorry idling at the bottom – the thing that had caught her attention from the upstairs window. Amidst the belching exhaust, the dark figure of a man helped others into the back of the vehicle.

Catherine's eyes widened. 'Papa?' she whispered, then sprinted down the street. Shadows of people, skulking in the darkness, turned in fright to see what she was running from. Catherine panted to a stop behind the lorry just as the last person was pushed inside. The man heaved a luggage trunk over the tailgate, his strong shoulders and willowy figure so familiar to Catherine.

'Papa?' she gasped again. Her hope shattered when the man turned around. He didn't look anything like her father.

His eyes softened, and he held out his hand. 'Do you need help?'

Catherine shook her head and stepped back. 'I'm looking for my father. Benoit Jacquot.'

The man turned to the inhabitants of the lorry. 'Benoit Jacquot?'

Catherine searched the miserable dirty faces observing her from the dark confines of the lorry, but none responded. Their expressions barely altered. Their eyes seemed dead, the shock of the attack still resonating.

Catherine clutched the tailgate to lean in further. 'Has anyone seen him? He is a doctor. Dr. Jacquot.'

A few heads shook, but most just continued to stare at her. Catherine pushed away from the lorry in despair. The peasant family trundled past, and Catherine darted over to the man pulling the cart.

'Have you seen my father? Dr. Jacquot?'

Not stopping, the man kept his eyes averted.

Catherine reached out to stall his wife. 'Have you seen him? I'm looking for my father. Please!'

The woman clutched her baby tighter to her bosom and shook Catherine off to hurry away.

Catherine watched them go in mounting hopelessness.

'Mademoiselle.' The lorry man touched her arm. 'Amiens has been taken. The authorities are directing us to Paris. If your father is a doctor then it is possible he has been drafted there.'

Catherine turned to face the pity in his eyes. How could

Papa have left her? The man bolted the tailgate shut and unravelled a dirty canvas to cover the back of the lorry. He skirted around to the cab and held the door open for her.

Catherine hesitated. She couldn't leave. Papa had told her to stay put, he'd come back for her. But he hadn't known how severe the attack would be. How could she stay? Amiens was destroyed. She could see that from here. If her father was still here, he would have come back for her by now.

She clutched the necklace at her throat, a pendant fashioned into a Star of David and inset with a fat blue gemstone. Uncertainty prickled her every nerve-ending like an electric current.

The man gestured one more time for her to get in.

Catherine looked back up the street to her home. Black smoke, more visible as the sky lightened, billowed above the city. With a deep breath, she turned to the man then clambered into the cab.

Catherine awoke with a jerk of her stiff neck. The midday sun, beating through the lorry's cracked windscreen, was stifling, and her skin was slick with sweat. She reached instinctively for the necklace burning the base of her throat. Her dirty fingers crept around the sun-warmed gemstone, comfortingly counting the six sharp edges of the star. She shifted her aching limbs in the squashed space. On her right, smelling less than savoury, were a woman and a man, bedraggled and dirty, the sort Catherine would once have crossed the street to avoid. Squashed on the man's lap was a toddler, fractious and tearful in the heat. To her left was the man she had mistaken for her father, and in the harsh sunlight she could see there was no resemblance beyond his black hair. He was a good fifteen years younger than Papa even with the stress and dirt that was rutted into his skin. He was busy rolling a cigarette on the steering wheel.

The lorry moved at a funeral pace, stopping often then stuttering forward. Outside, an endless line of people trundled along the road. Some in cars but most on foot, dragging carts and even prams piled with possessions. Catherine stiffened as she spotted a fracas further up the road – rifles lifted high, military uniforms. She relaxed again when she saw the square *kepis* and khaki livery of the French army, a battalion struggling against the tide of refugees. Where were they going? More importantly, where were they now? Outside were vast swathes of flat agricultural land and skies, wide and white with heat.

'Where are we?'

The driver glanced over at her and cracked a yellow smile. 'You're awake! We're just past Beauvais.'

Catherine knew Beauvais – a city almost halfway to Paris. She had visited on a school trip once and walked around the cathedral – an alien but fascinating experience for someone who had only ever worshipped in synagogues. How she had marvelled at the Gothic spires and colourful stained glass windows!

Catherine swallowed to soothe the dryness in her throat. She had no water to drink, and Paris still seemed a lifetime away, given the pace they were travelling at.

The man seemed to read her thoughts. 'Are you thirsty? We may as well stop here for a break.'

Catherine climbed gingerly down from the cab after the man and stretched out her limbs. Her head swam, and she clutched the door for support. The man banged his fist against the side of the lorry to signal to the others that they'd stopped. He flicked a match with his oil-ingrained sausage fingers and cupped the flame from a listless breeze. He handed Catherine his flask. It was grimy and hot, but she was past caring. She swallowed the tepid water greedily, revelling in its sustenance, until she felt the flask being pried away.

'Leave a bit for me.'

Catherine had the grace to blush, but the man didn't appear to mind. Instead, he pinched his cigarette between his teeth and held out a massive hand.

'Duras.'

'Catherine.'

Catherine's hand was gruffly shaken. She gave back the flask and watched the slow trundle of people pass them by. They dragged their feet along the ground, their shoulders heavy, their heads down. Some sat on the roadside, taking cover beneath their cart or the occasional tree. People of all ages, the very old and the very young, of all classes – she noticed the peasants' sacks and the wealthy's leather suitcases – of all nationalities too it seemed. She was sure some of the murmurs of conversation that drifted over were Dutch and Belgian French.

'Who are all these people?'

'Refugees.' Duras grinned at her. 'Like us.'

Catherine was taken aback for a moment. Was she really a refugee? She couldn't be. Soon she would find her father, and they would go home. Refugees were people who had no home to go to, people who were dependent on others for their safety and subsistence. Catherine stopped herself there. Was she not dependent on Duras for both of those things? Temporarily, perhaps, but when he helped her find Papa he would be rewarded handsomely, she was certain.

Duras continued to grin at her. 'We are all trying to escape the Germans, yet what we should be doing is climbing one of those hills.' He pointed with his crooked cigarette to a small humpback cluster of hills across a broad stretch of wheat. It was the only rise in land on the horizon.

'Why?' If she was being dim then it was because of dehydration and lack of sleep.

'The Germans hate hills.' He laughed heartily at his own joke.

Passersby roused the energy to lift their heads to stare at Duras. What man could possibly have anything to laugh about?

'Where are they all going?'

He shrugged. 'Paris like us, maybe? Hitler is pushing us all south. It is up to him how far we must go to escape.'

'And to them,' added Catherine, pointing to the battalion wrestling their way through the exodus.

Faces flushed from overheating in their uniforms and

backpacks, they yelled in frustration at the oncoming crowds who slowed their progress, slowed their chances of curtailing the enemy's devastation of their homeland.

Duras shook his head and dragged on his cigarette. 'Such young boys.'

Catherine looked again. Yes, she supposed they were quite young; some perhaps even her age: eighteen. She tried to imagine being one of them, of running towards the danger, to fight, to defend, to be brave. She shuddered. She was none of those things.

'Boys that yesterday had their mothers do their washing but today are sent to protect us all.' He sighed. 'So, your father is a doctor?'

'Yes. He left to help at the hospital.' Catherine tried to keep the pitifulness out of her voice. His abandonment still stung.

Duras nodded, his eyes suddenly solemn, but he blinked away whatever it was he was thinking. 'Then, like I said, if he's a doctor then he'll have been drafted to Paris. If he's any good, of course.' His eyes twinkled.

'The best,' Catherine assured him. A lump rose in her throat as she thought of her father. He would be worrying about her. Instinctively, she reached for the Fleur de l'Alexandrie, the necklace at her throat, remembering his last words to her. '*Pray. Be brave.*'

Duras motioned to her necklace. 'I would keep that hidden if I were you. It won't be just the Germans who want to be rid of the Jews. People will do crazy things when they are frightened.'

Catherine's fingers locked around the pendant in sudden fear. Every refugee around her suddenly felt like a threat. Hurriedly, she unclipped it and slipped it into her dress pocket. Duras nodded his approval and took a last satisfying drag of his cigarette.

'Time to move on. We will have to find fuel from somewhere before long.'

Fuel shortage hadn't occurred to Catherine, and she stared

at him, wide-eyed. 'What will we do if we run out?'

Duras shrugged. 'We walk.' He laughed again at her shocked expression. 'It is no more than fifty miles away. Fifty miles won't kill you.'

As his laughter faded, Catherine became aware of another sound. A hum. A swarm of bees? A frightened murmur rippled through the refugees. The hum became a growl. Duras shaded his eyes and looked into the blue horizon. Catherine followed his gaze. An aircraft engine, two, no, three, more maybe. She saw the little black specks in the sky. A fresh sense of urgency swept through the people and they ran for cover. But where to hide? There was nothing to hide behind. People latched on to the soldiers, crying to them for protection. The soldiers shrugged them off as they knelt and readied their rifles. A sense of relief gushed through Catherine. They would be okay. They had the army with them. How fortunate were they?

The planes dived; a high-pitched whistle then a *rat-a-tat-a-tat* as they opened fire. Catherine's relief was brushed aside by fear. The sound of gunfire had her rooted to the spot, just like before.

'Get down!' Duras shouted at her.

He pushed her to the ground, knocking the air from her lungs, and they squirmed towards the lorry's undercarriage. Catherine gasped for breath under the weight of Duras, cried out as bullets spat up a line of dusty red dirt near her head.

It was over as soon as it had begun. The growl and angry chatter of the planes drifted away, leaving Catherine's ears ringing, but was replaced by the pitiful wail of the wounded. Duras still lay atop her.

'Duras,' Catherine whispered. 'Duras?'

With no response, she tried to wriggle free. Stones bit into her back and tore at her dress. With a last shove, she rolled Duras aside and scrambled to her feet. Duras stared up at her, his laughing eyes lifeless, a thin watery trail of blood seeping from the corner of his mouth. Catherine trembled at the sight. Black pools spread out from under him and Catherine felt the world tilt again. She looked down and saw her own dress stained with blood, moist and cool against her skin. Her blood? She patted her body frantically. No pain. No, it couldn't be hers. Duras's. The thought made her want to run, screaming. She needed help. Duras had been her saviour, she had had absolute trust he would deliver her to her father. But now she was alone again, not only alone, but in the middle of nowhere. Papa would never find her here.

She looked around in panic for someone else to depend upon. The soldiers! She gasped. Most of the battalion lay dead, their rifles held in limp bloodied hands. More bodies littered the road. A pram lay on its side, its wheels still spinning, the only animation in an otherwise lifeless scene. An old peasant lady cried over a young man's body. No, they weren't all dead. She saw others crawling out of the ditch. But they all looked as terrified and helpless as she felt.

Catherine's knees quaked. What if they came back to finish them off? Her breath caught in her throat at the horrifying thought. She had to get away. But to where? The road would surely be a primary target. But everywhere else was open country. She would be picked off just as easily there. Her eye was caught by the small huddle of hills in the distance. Duras had said the Germans hated hills!

Without a second thought, Catherine leapt from the road into the field of wheat and sprinted towards the hills.

2

Amiens, France – Monday, 8ᵗʰ August, 2016

Like a child raiding the cookie jar whilst he still had the chance, Simon gazed greedily upon her face, smooth and tanned, as she lay, unaware, on the chaise longue in his hotel room; at the tendrils of dark auburn hair framing her face, the small crease between her eyes where she frowned, the spidery legs of mascaraed lashes twitching over her upper cheeks. Pinheads of sweat glistened on her upper lip, and Simon had to stop himself from reaching out and stroking them away. She was so beautiful, so uniquely perfect. He wanted to hold her in his arms and take away the pain, blot out the horrors she had witnessed.

A kick to his chair jerked him out of his reverie. Nick stood beside a cine-camera set up on a tripod and motioned to Simon to get on with things. Simon realised who he was looking at – not the vulnerable Catherine Jacquot, but the snarky, though nevertheless still beautiful, Amanda Woodbine. He raged inside at his own weakness. When they played back the recording and Amanda saw him all gooey-eyed over her, she'd never let him forget it.

'Three – you are becoming more aware of your surroundings; two – the sounds and smells of your surroundings are getting stronger; one – and you're awake.'

Amanda's eyes fluttered open, and her nostrils flared as she sucked in a great lungful of breath. Her sapphire eyes darted between Simon and Nick. 'It worked, didn't it?'

'You okay?' Simon asked.

Amanda pulled herself upright and stretched out her stiff limbs. 'I – I think so. Better than Catherine at any rate.'

'Nothing we can do about it now,' said Nick as he flipped

closed the camera's viewfinder and began to pack up the equipment. 'But it's exactly what the documentary needs. We just need to find a few other cheap and willing subjects to really back up our theory.'

'Nicholas Taylor, I might be willing, but I am not cheap, thank you very much. If Catherine's story checks out, won't that be enough?' Amanda looked put out.

'Sorry, darling,' Nick drawled. 'Yours is an interesting story though so we might lead with it. Unless, of course, we find Genghis Khan or Napoleon's soul festering in someone else's body.'

'Or Hitler?' suggested Amanda.

Nick laughed. 'That would be a bit too much of a coincidence, don't you think? A French Jew and Hitler all in the same study?'

'My past life was from the same era,' said Simon with a shrug. 'Daniel Barrow could only have been a few years older than Catherine.'

'A: he was British, and B: we haven't exactly been able to confirm the guy ever lived, have we?'

'You think I made him up?'

'No, but there isn't a lot of evidence to suggest he actually existed. He didn't seem to vote or even have a birth certificate. Nothing that could be used to prove reincarnation is real.'

Simon cleaned his glasses. 'I'm just saying coincidence happens. It would be some experience, going back and embodying the world's most hated psychopathic dictator.'

'Rather you than me,' said Amanda with a shudder. 'Seeing what Catherine went through was disturbing enough.'

'No thanks,' Simon added. He caught Nick's look of annoyance and realised their thoughtlessness. Nick hadn't even managed to go under hypnosis, never mind discover a past life. It had been an inconvenience given the initial plan for their documentary had been to follow the three of them. It was still workable with both Simon and Amanda reliving old lives but then, of course, Simon's past life, while real enough to him, couldn't be authenticated. Now, with just Amanda left they needed to find more subjects and do more research into historical case studies, which would gobble the meagre production budget Nick's grandfather, Joe Taylor, had allocated them.

Everything boiled down to money in the end. Even the most fantastical experiments that looked to reach beyond the realm of reality and touch lives long dead as if they were happening right now, to prove existence was not just restricted to the boundaries of consciousness, to prove there was life after life, all depended on the sordid tangible question of money.

The thought of money sent an icy shiver of unease down Simon's spine, and he pushed it away. 'Let me get you something to drink.' He went to fetch Amanda a glass of water.

'Fuck that,' said Nick, zipping the last of the equipment into its bag. 'Let's go get a proper drink down at the bar.'

The next morning, Nick and Simon walked through a set of glass doors into the air-conditioned respite of the Bibliothèque d'Amiens Métropole, the city's primary library. The cool thin smell of mouldy carpets and stale coffee made Nick all the more aware of his hangover.

'Microfiche?' he suggested.

Simon shrugged. 'I guess so.'

Nick looked about at the unending rows of bookshelves, surprisingly modern given its old-fashioned exterior, but couldn't see anything resembling a microfiche or computer in sight. 'What's microfiche in French?'

Simon gave him a heavy-lidded look of disbelief over his glasses. 'You're kidding, right?'

Twenty minutes later, Nick half-heartedly flicked through a microfiche, a Styrofoam cup of lukewarm coffee beside him. He was bored already. It was a waste of time going through all the old newspapers; he didn't even know what they were reporting on. All he could do was look out for the name Jacquot, which was making his headache even worse.

A wave of resentment surged through him. If he had to work in television, he'd much rather do music videos. They'd be so much more fun, less researching in stuffy libraries, and the cast couldn't be any more temperamental than Amanda. But it was too late to back out now. He would look even more of a failure to his grandfather if he quit. And with old Joe Taylor approaching his mid-seventies, he didn't want to upset him unduly. It wouldn't be long before he could do whatever he wanted.

He glanced across at Simon. He was glued to a computer screen beside him, his eyes hungrily scanning the screen, his glasses reflecting the pale blue light. Simon had always been a swot, all through school, all through university. Which had been great for Nick; he'd just paid Simon to do all his assignments, but it could still get tiresome.

Simon fumbled for his inhaler without taking his eyes from the monitor and took a quick puff. Nick watched him with more interest. Simon didn't use his inhaler unless he was anxious or excited.

'You got something?' he asked.

Simon wheeled his chair to the side to make room for Nick and pointed at the top of the screen. 'That necklace Amanda mentioned, the Fleur de l'Alexandrie. I think I've found it.'

Nick's heart thumped into life in his chest. If it was, then it was another confirmed fact from Amanda's past life regression session. He took the mouse and clicked on the accompanying link. It was a New York Times article from a few years back.

'*"At a private auction in New York, a Jewish pendant necklace known as the Fleur de l'Alexandrie was sold for a reported \$21 million to an unnamed buyer by movie mogul and tech billionaire, Bernie Costa…"*'

Nick started in his seat. 'Bernie Costa?'

'What?' Simon looked at him warily.

Nick shook his head. 'It's nothing. Just a coincidence. Bernie's big mates with Joe.'

'Seriously?'

'Weird, huh? Twenty-one mill's a fair old price tag for just a necklace. Bernie must be cracking open the champagne.'

"'...*The sapphire necklace is believed to date back to 1798 when Napoleon Bonaparte invaded Egypt. Upon seizing the city of Alexandria, the stone was found and subsequently named the Fleur de l'Alexandrie, or the Flower of Alexandria. After the abdication of Napoleon in 1814, the necklace fell into the hands of the new king Louis XVIII who had the stone fashioned into his ceremonial sword. It is not clear how the Fleur de l'Alexandrie found its way from a Roman Catholic king's sword into a Star of David necklace, but many historians believe that the sword was passed down to his brother and heir, Charles X, who had been exiled in Italy during the French Revolution where he was rumoured to have had a Jewish mistress and to whom he gifted the stone. From there it found its way into the Costa family, where it has remained for many generations.*"'

Nick stumbled over the last sentence. 'But that's bullshit,' he murmured. 'It belonged to Catherine's family. In France.'

Nick and Simon exchanged uncomfortable glances. Had they got it wrong? Was this the first chink in their reincarnation armour?

'It could be wrong,' said Simon. 'It does speculate quite a lot.'

'Yeah, but the Costas would know how long it's been in their family. Surely.'

'I guess we could always ask since Joe's pally with Bernie Costa.'

Nick shifted in his seat. Such a request probably wouldn't fly with Joe. Even to the CEO of Taylor Made Television, Bernie was someone only disturbed for the most important of matters. Nick had no doubt his grandfather and the mighty Bernie Costa would consider his reincarnation documentary too trivial to bother themselves with. 'Maybe Catherine's necklace is a different one.'

'Amanda was quite specific. She called it by name.'

Nick agreed grudgingly. Amanda wasn't the sort of person to know such historical details otherwise.

'What do we do now?' Simon asked.

Nick considered the impossible – that his big project to

impress his grandfather had failed before it had barely got off the ground. 'We keep going. There's bound to be a few inconsistencies here and there.'

Simon was still for a moment, his eyes behind his glasses considering him carefully. Then he nodded. 'You're right. Let's keep going.'

Simon printed off the article nevertheless and returned, resting his chin in his palm, focussed once more on the screen. Nick turned back to his microfiche search, a cold dread seeping through his gut. What would he tell his grandfather? It had taken a lot of convincing to get him to fund the project to begin with. Would Nick now have to return with his tail between his legs and admit the whole thing was a bomb? His gaze flickered back to Simon. It was his fault. He was the one who had sworn by the theory. He'd gone under hypnosis on more than one occasion and had been adamant it wasn't his imagination. In his silent attack on his step-brother he noticed Simon's demeanour change. The asthma inhaler made another appearance.

'You okay?' Nick asked.

Simon darted him a look before returning to the screen. 'Yeah. Just…' His voice was breathless. 'Forget the necklace. I think I've found her.'

'Catherine?'

'And her father. Look. "*Jacquot, Benoit. Surgeon*",' he read aloud. 'That could be them, couldn't it?'

Catherine had said her father was a doctor when she'd been trying to find him at Duras's lorry. Nick wheeled his chair closer as Simon clicked on a thumbnail image. They held their collective breath as a picture slowly loaded. It was a black and white scanned photograph, grainy and tattered, of a tall, wiry Jewish man and a teenage girl with thick, dark hair, dressed in a modest cotton dress, standing in front of a grand château.

'She's beautiful,' murmured Simon.

Nick was too captured by the accompanying caption to roll his eyes at Simon's romantic notions. "*Amiens surgeon Benoit Jacquot and his daughter, Catherine, at the family's Château de*

Pierrecourt." It's got to be them!' Nick gave Simon an excited half-hug then snatched the mouse from Simon. He scrolled down to the next paragraph.

"'*Benoit Jacquot, death recorded 16th March, 1942, Aushwitz-Birkenau, Poland.*'"

The pair exchanged regretful looks. Even though Nick was the first to admit he was more interested in proving his theory of reincarnation than he was in the actual stories, he had to admit he'd hoped Catherine would find her father. With a sober realisation, he concluded there weren't many happy endings during World War Two. "'*Catherine Jacquot, detained 22nd May, 1940…*'" Couldn't have been long after she left Amiens with Duras.'

Simon looked distraught. He took off his glasses to clean them and rub his bloodshot eyes. 'Been staring at the screen too long,' he mumbled at Nick's questioning eyebrow.

Nick was too distracted to tease him. He turned back to Catherine's write-up. 'Dead, do you think?'

Simon shrugged. 'She had to die at some point.'

Nick gave a dry chuckle. 'Otherwise we wouldn't be blessed with darling Amanda.' Honestly, that girl treated them all like she was already Meryl Streep, rather than a drama graduate getting her first gig.

Simon scrolled further down the page. 'Doesn't say anything about her reaching Paris. Only that she was "*detained on the 22nd of May, 1940 by Sturmbannführer Heinrich Schneider.*" But nothing on where or how or what happened next.'

The name zapped Nick's brain like an electric shock. This was getting too weird. But there had to have been thousands of Heinrich Schneiders in Germany; he was being stupid.

'Nick?'

'Perhaps Amanda can fill in the blanks,' he replied hastily.

'And we should probably check out that Château de Pierrecourt.' Simon clicked on the print symbol and got up to collect his printouts.

Nick watched him go for a few seconds then drew his chair

in closer to the screen. He clicked on the hyperlink on Sturmbannführer Heinrich Schneider's name. Slowly a photo loaded, like a magician's measured revelation of his trick, from top to bottom – the outstretched silver wings of the Imperial Eagle on an officer's cap tilted on a wide forehead, blond brows and piercing eyes, a straight nose and flat cheekbones, down to a small vindictive mouth and strong jaw, a crisp collar with an "SS" badge on the right wing and a pattern of four diamonds on the left. The hairs on Nick's neck stood to attention.

'Sorted,' Simon said, reappearing with the printout.

Nick sucked in a lungful of air, realising he'd stopped breathing and hit the backspace to return them to the original page on the Jacquots. He beamed up at Simon. 'Great. What say we go grab some lunch and a bottle of the old vino to celebrate?'

3

Amiens, France – Tuesday, 9ᵗʰ August, 2016

Still full from his cheese baguette, Simon fiddled with the two tripod cameras set up around the chaise longue by the window in his second-floor hotel room. Outside, the sun slanted off the gothic spires of Cathédrale Notre-Dame d'Amiens jutting above the red-brick buildings that lined the street from their hotel. What must it have been like for Catherine the morning she came out and saw her world had been obliterated? Somewhere north of here, not far, but out of sight from his viewpoint was the Somme River, linked inextricably with the slaughter fields of the Great War. So much bloodshed, so much brutality, so many wasted lives.

Simon's arms prickled with emotion. He glanced at his watch. Nick and Amanda were due any minute. He unzipped an old leather overnight bag slumped in an armchair and rummaged through it for his audio recorder. He should probably change the batteries before they began. Delving into a side pocket for spares, he instead withdrew an old dog-eared photograph. He glanced quickly at the door then sat down to study the photo. He must have put it in there during a holiday in his youth and forgotten about it. Discoloured with age, it showed a skinnier twelve-year-old version of himself, his bony arms wrapped around the waist of a thickset moustachioed man, his father, John Hayes.

Simon traced his fingers along the outlines of the image, stopping at the ragged edge where the photo had been torn. Only a few wisps of curly blonde hair reaching across the tear gave away the fact that a third person had been there. They stood in front of a red Peugeot 406, now so old-fashioned, but Simon could recall how thrilling the feeling had been at the time his father had bought it, how flash the car had seemed, how cool he felt when they drove around London in it. He could even recall the low hum of the engine as they drove. A muscle jumped in Simon's cheek as the engine noise flooded his memory.

London, England – Monday, 21ˢᵗ March, 2005

A door jingled open from somewhere below the Hayes' London flat. Twelve-year-old Simon skidded around the landing corner, his school rucksack slapping against his mother's wall pictures, brown eyes alight with excitement at the prospect of the coming weekend and his cheeks flushed from an afternoon playing football with his friends down at the sports centre.

'Dad?' he called. He poked his head through the kitchen door. There was no-one there. Darting a quick look around, he whipped a biscuit out of the tin then continued his search.

'Dad! You've got cuftomers in the fop!' he called, spitting crumbs on the threadbare carpet. 'Dad?'

Simon wrenched himself back into the present. That memory made him nauseous. He could even taste the ginger biscuits in his mouth still. He considered the photo once more then fetched his notebook to place it in for safekeeping. Instead, he was met with the printouts from his and Nick's library excursion that morning. He unfolded the printed black and white photo of Catherine and her father and smoothed out the central crease. They looked so devoted to one another – proud father and doting daughter. He gazed at Catherine's photo, not so much in admiration of her beauty but in sorrow at the loss of such youth and innocence.

'Christ, I'm sorry,' he muttered.

He turned his attention to Benoit's grainy face. The man had a friendly smile and kind eyes – the sort you'd expect from a doctor. It seemed so desperately unfair that a man who dedicated his life to saving others should perish under such brutal circumstances. He wondered what it must have been like, being shuffled into the gas chambers. Were they told they were just going to bathe? Did Benoit know he was walking to his death? Did he fight? Was he scared? Relieved? The thought of welcoming death made Simon glance back at the picture of him and his father. He held the two photos side by side to compare. Catherine smiled shyly back, immortally fixed, forever eighteen years old. He looked at his own image, feeling very much like he was stuck at twelve years old as well.

A sharp knock on the door startled him, and he dropped the photos. 'Coming! Hold on.'

He stuffed the photos into the notebook and hurried to open the door. Amanda waited, an uninterested pout on her face.

Simon tried to act nonchalant. 'Hi.'

Amanda sauntered in, leaving him to close the door behind her. 'Where's Nick?' she asked.

'Late.'

Amanda stood in the centre of the room and looked around, hands on hips. 'You have a better view than me,' she said.

Simon's gaze shifted to the notebook on the table, and for reasons he didn't quite understand, he picked it up and slipped it into his overnight case, out of sight.

'We can swap if you like,' he suggested. An image of Amanda sleeping in his bed flashed through his mind, and blood surged to his groin.

'No. Mine's closer to the lift. Closer to the bar.' Her eyes twinkled. 'And we're only here for a few more days. You got a minibar in here?'

'Over there.' Simon pointed to the other side of the bed.

'How'd it go at the library?' she said into the fridge as she surveyed its contents.

Simon tried not to look at her bottom. 'Yeah, good. We found a few things.' He clasped his hands, hating being so evasive when all he wanted to say was: 'She's real! You're her! It really works!'

'Like what?' Amanda swivelled on the balls of her feet to look around at him. She looked interested for the first time, and it was tempting to tell her, just to keep her that way, engaged in him and what he had to say.

He looked down at the worn Persian rug and brushed his toe over a ridge that had formed, smoothing it down. 'Well, I – I can't really say. Telling you would be – I mean, I *want* to tell you, but I can't. The authenticity of the experiment – it would be compromised. It needs–'

'And it needs to be authentic.' Amanda rolled her eyes. That same glaze of apathy seeped back, and he desperately tried to think of something fascinating that would recapture her attention, but once he'd voided Catherine Jacquot and the reincarnation experiment from potential conversation topics, there was nothing. Christ, he was pathetic. And boring.

Amanda poured herself a glass of wine. 'You want one?'

Simon shook his head.

'God, Simon, you need to live a little.'

'We've got work this afternoon.' He didn't want to add she shouldn't be drinking either since she was the one scheduled to regress. He wondered if her drinking would affect the critical authenticity of the study.

'He's got to be the laziest person I know,' Amanda said.

'Who?'

'Nick, of course.' She walked over and sat down on the chaise longue. 'Not like you and me.'

Simon sat as well, chiding himself for feeling so ridiculously thrilled to be considered united with Amanda on anything. Still, loyalty to his step-brother pushed its way to the fore. 'He'll be here soon.'

'You and me, we *work*,' said Amanda.

Simon regarded her doubtfully. She had barely scraped through her drama degree and had taken great pride in the fact that she'd passed many of her modules by sleeping with her lecturers. 'Nick doesn't have to work,' he pointed out.

'Why do *you* though?' asked Amanda. 'Doesn't your family share its dosh?'

He examined his fingernails, unable to meet the challenging and, dare he say it, mocking violet of her eyes. 'We're not *family*-family. They're Taylors and I'm a Hayes. It's Taylor money.'

She snorted. 'You're mad, Simon.'

He regarded her for a moment, tempted to explain just how complex their situation was, why any financial charity from Nick's family would only ever be blood money to him, but he doubted whether she'd care, even if she did make the effort to understand.

'Maybe,' he replied, 'or maybe running a pawnbroker's shop has taught me the value of money.'

'Like how?'

'Like seeing people bring in their most prized possessions in exchange for a bit of cash. Seeing that anguish and then seeing the pride if and when they're able to buy it back. It teaches you to value the small things in life.'

'That doesn't make sense,' said Amanda. 'If they're breaking their hearts over selling materialistic things, doesn't that make them shallow and the opposite of what presumably you're saying you are?'

Simon shifted awkwardly in his chair. Of course, it would be nice to have enough to cover the bills every month, he wanted to add, but Amanda thought little enough of him as it was.

'No, I didn't mean it like that. I just mean... I don't know. I just don't see the appeal in having lots of money. That's all.'

He was saved by a quick knock on the door. He got up to let Nick in.

'Where've you been?' demanded Amanda. 'We've been

waiting ages.'

'Nowhere.' Nick ignored her accusing glare. 'We all set?'

4

Amiens, France – Monday, 20th May, 1940

The crunch of marching soldiers' boots drifted through the Jacquots' living room window, through the heavy taffeta drapes that billowed inward. Catherine's father, Benoit, stood to the side of the window in the half light of dawn to peek outside. His face was gaunt with worry, his body tense.

Catherine watched from the other side of the room, her fingers nervously playing over the brocade of her father's favourite armchair. 'Papa?'

Benoit darted a sharp look in her direction and held up his hand. To placate her? To dismiss her? To quieten her? Catherine didn't know what she was to do.

The rhythmic thwack of jackboots grew louder as they turned into Rue des Jardins. Catherine picked up another sound, a low growl. Suddenly a burst of tinny machine gun fire erupted outside followed by terrorised screams. Benoit flinched away from the window, but Catherine remained frozen with fear.

'Catherine, lie down! Lie down!'

But still she couldn't move.

The deafening staccato clamour of gunfire filled the morning air, but all Catherine could hear was her own breathing, hoarse and shallow. Bending double, Benoit hurried across the room to her, long lanky legs covering the oak floor in the barest of time.

'Come Catherine, it's time for us to go.' His tone was gentle, a well-educated voice that had calmed many an anxious patient, but there was a breathlessness to him that unsettled Catherine. His dark eyes burned into hers, and his neck muscles were pulled taut. He grasped her arm, making her gasp. She remembered she had a piano lesson that afternoon with Madame Bonnet.

'Where–'

The windows shattered in a terrible crash of glass and ripping of material. Ornaments on the mantelpiece exploded into dust. The Degas portrait of Catherine's grandmother in her youth battered against the wall as the canvas was shredded by invisible bullets.

Benoit threw himself over Catherine, and they hit the floor with a cry of extinguished breath. The gunfire was replaced with angry German voices, and Catherine looked fearfully at her father.

'Papa?' She hated to sound so helpless and weak, but her precious upbringing had neither prepared her for such an onslaught nor even warned her of the approaching threat of the Nazis.

'Come, there is no time,' he said. He pulled her to her feet and, shielding her body with his own, hustled her out of the room and away from the assault. Catherine yelped as the Degas painting fell to the oak floor with a heavy gilded crash. In the hall, Benoit snatched up his black leather medical case and hastened Catherine downstairs.

He forced open the heavy cellar door, spilling light down the dark, damp steps. Catherine's teeth chattered with fear, and she clutched his hand tight as they hurried down. The muted light glinted off tall racks of bottled wine and Benoit swept one last cautionary look up at the cellar door before sliding across one of the racks to reveal a hidden room. He grasped Catherine by the shoulders.

'Now, you must be brave. You must not cry. You must keep very quiet. Understand?'

The sudden realisation that he did not intend to join her in the secret room filled her with wild fear. 'No, Papa! No! Don't leave me! No, Papa! Don't go!' She fought against his attempts to push her inside, even hammering on his chest.

He gave her an abrupt shake and gripped the tops of her arms until she cried out. His desperate eyes searched hers in the dim light. 'I will come back for you, I promise. But the hospital will need me now.' He reached out and held the necklace at her throat between his fingers. 'Pray. This will keep you safe.'

'No, Papa. *I* need you. Don't leave me! *Please!*' Her voice was drowned out by the rattle of bottles as the door was slid shut again, leaving her in dark isolation.

Catherine awoke with a dry gasp. 'Papa!'

It was dark, so very dark, and chillingly silent. Her right hand ached, and, when she opened her fist, the Fleur de l'Alexandrie slid down the clammy contours of her palm until caught by the chain entangled with her fingers. She rubbed the area where the peaks of the Star of David had pressed into her skin.

The horrors of the day slunk back into her consciousness like shadows stalking her. Of Papa pushing her into the cellar, of losing him, of taking that momentous leap of faith to go with Duras, the heat of the endless exodus of refugees, the chaos and clamour of the German air attack, of Duras's lifeless eyes staring up at her. Then running. Running here.

Catherine shifted on the dirty ground, looking about her. She took in the smell of diesel fumes, of dust and mould and the whiff of pig manure, and, as her eyes adjusted to the darkness, the tall flat-shaped face of a beat-up tractor looked down upon her. She jumped as a loose cladding board knocked against its neighbour on the wall. Stiffly, she climbed to her feet. Her head throbbed, and her bones ached. But worse than that, her throat was so parched! And her stomach twisted itself into painful knots searching for food to digest.

She slipped her necklace into her pocket for safe-keeping then carefully opened the rickety door of the outhouse in which she'd taken refuge. The wood scraped against stone, deafening in the silence. She caught her breath as a dog barked in the near distance. When it had quietened, she gingerly stepped out into the night.

It was much brighter outside. Alder trees, bathed in moonlight, shivered as an asthmatic breath of wind blew over from a silvery expanse of wheat. Crickets whistled in chorus from everywhere around her, and a solitary frog croaked out a baleful invitation for company.

Catherine proceeded across the farmyard, as silent as a shadow. There had to be water somewhere. She ducked through a drunken fence and gave a strangled yelp as a great black bulk snorted away from her, long ears wheeling like antennae. Catherine stumbled away from the mule in terror, falling over the baked, pockmarked ground in her fear. She'd never been a great one for animals. Anything bigger than a cat sapped the strength from her knees.

She rounded a barn and hesitated. Up on the rise of the hill stood a small stone farmhouse, windows alight. Catherine was torn. On the one hand, it looked such an inviting vision; safe, secure, sheltered from harm. But on the other, it represented the unknown; an ominous threat, strangers in a world upturned who could be foe as easily as friend. No, she couldn't risk it. What had Duras said? *'People will do crazy things when they are frightened.'* She must find somebody else, somebody she could trust to help her get to Paris.

Catherine looked around at the dark night, a cold fear seeping into her gut. She was all alone. Again. But worse, she no longer had the sanctuary of home to reassure her. She didn't know anyone in Beauvais. For a moment, she wished they'd detoured east towards Verdun where her grandmother's château was, like she and Papa had done on so many trips to and from the capital, but she realised the pointlessness of the wish as soon as she'd thought it. Château de Pierrecourt had been leased to tenants since Grandmaman's death. She didn't know them. She couldn't trust them.

She took a deep breath in an attempt to quell her panic. Château de Pierrecourt was out of the question, going back to Amiens was pointless, she didn't know anyone in Beauvais. Her only option was to walk to Paris. Duras had said it wouldn't kill her, it was only fifty miles. She looked down at her shoes, scuffed and dirty leather lace-ups. The stitching between the leather and the wooden heel was already frayed and misshapen from when she'd stumbled, running through the wheat field. Would they last fifty miles? Perhaps on decent roads, but they weren't walking shoes by any means. Her feet would be shredded by the time she got to Paris. *If* she got to Paris. She couldn't risk another event like the previous afternoon. Duras's death was a frightening reminder of just how much danger she was in. She daren't trust anyone, so she must move at night, under the cover of darkness like the heroines in her books. She would hide in buildings and farmyards like this one by day.

For a moment she wondered what she would do for food and water, but cast it aside. She would find a way, and if not, perhaps fifty miles wasn't as far as it sounded. With Papa and the car, they would leave after breakfast and be in Paris before lunch. Of course, she was fooling herself that she could walk it that quickly, but surely such a short drive couldn't mean a terribly long walk? And if it really was that bad then when she got to Paris, Papa would be there to nurse her back to health.

As she contemplated her plan, she suddenly became aware of the distinct sound of liquid drip-dropping onto tin. She darted another anxious look at the lighted farmhouse, but her need for water outweighed her fear of being discovered. She hurried about, turning this way and that, pausing to listen for the next drip, turning again until she was dizzy, the sound ever louder, ever more enticing.

At last she found the source, collapsing beside a bucket outside another ramshackle outbuilding. There were only a couple of inches in it, but Catherine scraped her fingers against its rusty base to scoop up as much as she could. It tasted revolting. Goodness knows what had been in the bucket before or for how long it had been there, but the soothing moisture against her lips and the walls of her throat was too gratifying to stop. Unable to scoop any more out with her hands, she upended the bucket to drink from its brim. The last of the water trickled through her lips followed by a sludgy silt. She gagged. Spluttering on the diesel-flavoured slime, she dropped the bucket. It clattered to the ground, its tinny echo reverberating about the farmyard.

Catherine froze, her gag reflex overpowered by fear. The dog barked again, more insistent. Someone would surely come to investigate now. She crept along the side of the outbuilding towards an adjoining barn. She could take cover in there then make a run for the wheat field.

Heart hammering in her chest and her skin chilled with perspiration, she skirted around the wall against which leaned rickety piles of apple crates, keeping to the shadows. The click of a rifle hammer brought her up short. A man stood in her way, moonlight glancing off the barrel of the shotgun he pointed at her face. She gasped in fright and stumbled backwards. Her foot became wedged in a crate and she fell.

'Who are you and what are you doing?' he growled in precisely paced, lethally charged tones.

'I – I – I–' Her lungs felt as if they'd shrunk to the size of seed pods. There was barely enough air to breathe, let alone talk. She held up her grimy hands and winced away from the sight of danger. 'I'm just looking for water.'

The man pushed the cold muzzle of the gun against her cheek, prompting an inadvertent whimper of terror from her, then he darted an anxious look around. 'Are you alone?'

Catherine nodded fervently. 'Yes. They killed Duras. He was taking me to Paris. I'm looking for my father…' Her voice became a pitiful squeak as listing the trauma of her day out loud became too much, and a hard, painful lump rose in her throat. Through the sparkles of her tears, she saw the man half lower his gun.

He looked at her suspiciously. 'You were in the air raid?'

'They killed Duras,' Catherine wept. 'He was going to help me find Papa.' Sobs convulsed her body, and her head and shoulders hung in pitiful surrender. It was her fault Duras was dead. But the guilt of that responsibility was only a small part of her shame. She was more overcome by the fact that now he was gone, she had no one to protect her, and her own selfishness and inadequacy disgusted her.

The man sighed and uncocked his shotgun. With a sniff, Catherine wiped her stained face with the back of her hand and looked up at him. She saw now that he was a portly man, moustachioed, perhaps a little younger than her own father; not as refined or elegant as Papa, but his face was free of malice. He held out a large stubby-fingered hand and helped her to her feet. She became uncomfortably aware of her dirty appearance as he looked her up and down. He pointed to the dark brown blood stains on her dress.

'Are you hurt?'

Catherine shook her head weepily. 'Duras…'

'You had better come with me,' he said reluctantly and began to stride away.

Catherine's instinct to flee surged to the surface, but she wasn't quick enough.

He retraced his steps and took her by the arm. 'My family will be worrying where I am,' he said in a gentler voice. 'It has been a frightening day for us all. What is your name? I am Monsieur Gromaire.'

The kindness of his words tilted Catherine's emotions from flight to utter dependence, and she clutched his words of friendship like a drowning swimmer to a raft. 'Catherine Jacquot. I am looking for my father, Benoit…'

Gromaire led Catherine up to the house, kicking dirt at the dog chained outside the backdoor when it snarled at her. Inside a generous stone-clad kitchen, Catherine squinted against the light even though the hurricane lamps hanging from the walls were soft and inviting.

A tall, broad woman with salt and pepper hair tied in a tight bun sat at the kitchen table stripping runner beans. The bowl clattered, and her chair fell back as she stood up, startled by Catherine's appearance. She rushed across the room to shield two young children playing with a mongrel puppy. The puppy growled.

Catherine tried to smile, but she too was afraid. She couldn't get Duras's words out of her head. '*People will do crazy things when they are frightened.*' The woman looked wide-eyed from Catherine to Monsieur Gromaire and swallowed nervously.

'Maman, we have a guest for dinner,' said Gromaire cheerily.

'Who is she?'

'She was caught in the raids this afternoon.'

Presented as she was, Catherine's upbringing switched her to autopilot, and she took a tentative step forward while keeping a wary eye on the puppy. 'Good evening, madame. I apologise for my intrusion.'

'Catherine Jacquot, please meet my wife, Agathe, and my children, Octave and Hélène.'

The children peeked out from behind their mother's sturdy legs.

'Louis!' said Agathe. 'What are you doing? You don't know who she is!'

'She is just a girl.' Gromaire set his rifle down in the corner of the room alongside a multitude of boots, rods and oil bottles. 'I couldn't just leave her out there.'

Catherine took in the fear and distrust on Agathe's face and backed away. 'I – I should not stay…'

'Nonsense!' said Gromaire. 'I can't possibly allow a young girl to wander around at night amid all this unrest. You must stay. Maman?'

Agathe Gromaire's pinched lips disappeared into a stern line. From behind the thick hem of her skirt, the young boy, Octave, peered at her on his hands and knees. He couldn't be older than Catherine's eleven-year-old cousin, Michel. His expression lit up and he pointed at Catherine's dress. 'Is that blood?'

At the prospect, Hélène, maybe a couple of years younger than her brother, hugged the puppy closer to her.

'She could be anyone!' Hélène's whimpers sparked a fresh wave of dissent from Agathe. 'We do not need trouble, Louis. What are you doing putting your children at such risk?'

Gromaire's face grew sombre. 'We must do our part, Maman. Besides,' he added, looking at Catherine doubtfully, 'she does not look dangerous.'

Catherine gulped and tried her best not to look suspicious.

Agathe turned her hard dark eyes on her. 'Are you a Jew?'

Catherine's hand instinctively went to her throat to feel for the Fleur de l'Alexandrie before she remembered it was safely in her pocket. A moment's relief, a moment's hesitation, and she shook her head. 'No, madame. I am just trying to get to Paris to find my father.'

Agathe folded her arms and looked no more sympathetic than before.

Gromaire gave her a placating look. 'At least let her stay for dinner. I found her scuffling for food in the dark.'

Catherine held her breath, waiting for the woman to chivvy her out of the house with a broom. Agathe's shoulders relaxed in defeat and, after giving her husband a final dirty look, returned to her runner beans.

The expected relief at being allowed to stay didn't come though. A cold shiver ran up the back of Catherine's legs and up her spine to the nape of her neck. She didn't feel any safer here than earlier on the road beside Duras's body.

5

Amiens, France – Tuesday, 9th August, 2016

Simon strolled along the pedestrian street, Rue des Trois Cailloux, enjoying the warm sun on his neck, listening to the soft murmur of French voices around him, and admiring the pastel-coloured buildings rising up on either side of the street with their pretty Juliet balconies and overflowing flower troughs. He tried to imagine what it must have been like for Catherine before the war. Had she walked down this same street looking up at the same buildings, arm in arm with her father? Certainly, the modern shopfronts of Gucci and BOSS seemed so bizarrely out of place. How much of the art deco architecture had been destroyed and recreated?

He imagined her walking alongside Benoit, skipping every few steps to keep up with his lanky stride, her cotton dress swishing around her calves. Would she have worn cotton? By all accounts, the Jacquots were a rather affluent family with a château and fancy townhouse, so perhaps she would have worn silk. Yes, a modest but stylishly tailored silk dress, perhaps a scarf over her thick dark hair.

A voice inside Simon's head murmured that head scarves hadn't come into fashion until probably much later. Jackie Kennedy was the earliest person he could recall wearing a headscarf as a fashion accessory. Amanda was a fan of headscarves, primed with large dark sunglasses. Simon stood and screwed his eyes shut. It was too easy for Catherine and Amanda to morph into one being. Two bodies, two such very different lives, yet one consciousness, one soul.

He opened his eyes again to see a young couple cuddling and laughing on one of the sun-drenched benches along the centre of the walkway, sipping soft drinks and eating fresh food no doubt bought from one of the innumerable cafés spilling out onto the street. He couldn't help but imagine himself as the young man whispering in his partner's ear and sending her into fits of mischievous giggles. He tried to imagine her as Amanda, but his fantasy wavered. Amanda had none of the girl's innocence; she was too aware of her own charms to be caught up in the magic of unfettered love. But Catherine... Simon's fantasy blossomed as the beautiful Jewish girl took Amanda's place. He saw himself whispering into the thick wave of hair that covered her ear, inhaling the lemony scent of her skin, finding pleasure in the faint blush that pricked her cheeks, the cool sensuous feel of her silk dress beneath his fingers.

'*T'as besoin d'aide?*'

Simon jolted back to reality at the Frenchman's sarcastic tone. The couple were staring at him, the girl with affront, the young man with undisputed territorialism.

'Pardon,' Simon mumbled and hurried on, bumping into a couple of German tourists who muttered at him. His ears burned with embarrassment. What kind of fool fantasised about a woman who'd been dead over seventy years, a woman whom he'd never known?

Simon reached for his inhaler and took a puff. He stopped outside a jewellery store called Camille's and stared up at the corn blue sky. He exhaled in despair. But he *had* known her, he was sure. Perhaps only through Amanda, and perhaps his own feelings for Amanda were clouding his perception of her, but no earthly reason could convince him that there wasn't some connection between them. Yes, it was more... *spiritual*.

God, how Nick and Amanda would laugh at him if they could read his thoughts. Amanda would most likely mock him. But was it so impossible? So many stories he'd heard, so much of the literature he'd read claimed that some souls returned to one another life after life. Not always as lovers, but often as other family members, friends... *soulmates*.

Might it have been more than a mere coincidence that he and Amanda had met at Fresher's Week? Simply thinking of how she'd chosen him over any other guy must surely have more to do with destiny than just luck? And even if their relationship hadn't exactly lasted very long, their paths had continued to cross all through uni, and now, as graduates, here they were again, by chance, taking part in Nick's documentary. Maybe 'by chance' was pushing it a little. He had, after all, suggested her inclusion to Nick. But, Simon argued with himself, she'd still had to agree. Which she had, so to that extent, it was chance that had brought them together again. Destiny even.

But if he and Amanda were soulmates, then who had he been to Catherine during her short life? No, it couldn't have worked, not if he'd really been that womanising rat, Daniel Barrow. He didn't want to think of the two of them being soulmates. Anyway, he had been English and she'd been French, and there had been a great big bloody war to keep them apart.

Simon ground his teeth in frustration, trying to keep his thoughts from spiralling. He glared at the jewellery storefront. Why couldn't he get back what he and Amanda had shared during those first few weeks at university? What had he done that had been so wrong that she now treated him with such disdain? She teased him, made him feel pathetic. It was all an act, he was certain. It had to be an act. For Nick. She was always meanest when Nick was around. She didn't despise him. She couldn't. She'd agreed to take part in this documentary study, after all.

He took a deep breath and squared his shoulders. He had to stop being so pathetic. He had to show Amanda that he was a man worth her time, a man she deserved, a *real* man. And a real man treated his true love with respect and bestowed upon her fine gifts that exemplified his status as an alpha male deserving of her affections.

His eyes alighted on a gold necklace with a sapphire pendant in Camille's window. Yes, that was it! He would buy her a necklace just like Catherine's Fleur de l'Alexandrie. Perhaps not quite so lavish, he didn't want to bankrupt himself, but something that would characterise Amanda just as the bejewelled Star of David had defined Catherine. The sapphire would bring out the striking blue of her eyes, and the delicate cut of its design would befit her beauty.

He squinted at the price. Okay, it was a bit more than he could probably afford, but it wasn't outrageous. It probably wasn't a real sapphire then. But it didn't matter. She didn't need to know that. All that she needed to know was that he, Simon, could afford to buy her presents *that at least appeared* worthy of her. He pushed open the door to make his purchase.

Nick and Amanda waited at an outdoor café overlooking the Somme.

'Wish he'd hurry up,' Amanda grumbled without conviction.

Safe behind his sunglasses, Nick looked across at her, stretched out on her flimsy metal chair, soaking up the loving warmth of the sun. She reached for the chilled glass of Chardonnay that he'd bought her and took a long luxuriant sip. She was so obviously enjoying herself. Nick found it endearing that she should try to hide her pleasure behind that mask of derision. He wondered what it would take for her to drop the act and show her true self.

'France suits you,' he said. 'This,' gesturing around to the sunshine and the novelty of their unfamiliar surroundings, 'suits you.'

Amanda didn't react. He wasn't even sure if her eyes were open or closed behind those huge dark glasses.

'We're tourists, Nick,' she replied at last, 'sitting in a café whose menu is written in English, drinking cheap plonk that I dare say is less than six months old. Once Simon has graced us with his presence we'll return to our budget hotel. Then next week we'll take the train back to London and back to the same old struggle.' She tilted her face so she could see him over her sunglasses. 'When I'm spending a couple of months a year on a yacht on the Côte d'Azur, drinking sixty-year-old champagne, and topping up my tan before flying on a private jet back to my beach condo in Santa Barbara for my next award-winning movie, then that will suit me.'

Nick considered telling Amanda sixty-year-old champagne would most probably taste like vinegar after so long, but decided against it. He grinned, unfazed. 'And the award for Best Porno Actress in an XXX feature film is Amanda "Woodsucker" Woodbine.'

Amanda gave him a droll look and lit a cigarette. 'Wouldn't that be a film you'd like to watch.'

Nick held her gaze. Neither looked away.

'Hi, sorry I'm late.' Simon's arrival broke the intensity.

Amanda took a long drag of her cigarette and blew it in Simon's direction.

Nick took a giant gulp of his Merlot. Amanda certainly knew how to unsettle a man. His throat was tight and he coughed. 'You get lost?'

'No, just… sidetracked.'

Back at their hotel, Simon breathed a sigh of relief as they walked through the foyer. The sun was lovely, but it was stinking hot. The concierge hung up the phone and waved at them.

'Monsieur Taylor! A package has arrived for you. Express delivery.' He ducked behind the desk and reappeared with a DHL box.

'You expecting something?' Simon asked.

'Oh, I'll collect it later. Thanks,' said Nick with a nonchalant wave of his hand. '*Merci.*'

But Amanda was already on her way over to the desk. 'What is it? Who's it from?'

Simon read the sender's label. 'Looks like it's from Joe.'

'Why's your grandfather sending you stuff? I thought you wanted to do this on your own? Couldn't it wait till you got home?'

Nick looked unusually annoyed. He snatched it from their curious eyes. 'It's just a couple of books I asked him to send, okay?' He rolled his eyes at their surprised faces. 'It's for the documentary, that's all. Look, let's meet up later.'

Simon nodded. 'Sure.'

Amanda gave him a look that clearly said, 'Whatever.'

'Sorry, I've got a headache,' Nick muttered and walked away to the lifts.

'What's eating him?' Amanda said once he was out of earshot.

'Probably Joe interfering. He can be a bit pushy.'

'Do you want to go for a drink? I don't fancy holing up in my room.'

Simon felt a wave of heat rise up from beneath his collar. 'Yeah, yeah, of course. Downstairs?'

The pair walked down to the restaurant-bar in the basement. Moodily lit, there weren't any tables occupied. The only activity came from the little stage where a couple of men were setting up sound equipment and from behind the bar where the barman was drying glasses.

Simon ordered their drinks and idly looked around. A poster on the wall advertised a band playing at the hotel for the next three nights. He paid for their drinks and carried them over to the table Amanda had secured.

Too aware of the jewellery box burning a hole in his pocket, he listened with only half an ear to her bemoaning the lack of opportunities on offer to actresses over twenty-two.

'How the hell did your mother manage it?' she said in exasperation.

'She ran off with her producer,' Simon replied dispassionately.

'Oh yes.' She took a sip of her wine and gave him a coquettish smile. 'So, would you recommend that route for a budding actress?'

Simon swallowed hard. She was testing his masculinity. He had to man up. He'd had over ten years to get used to what his mother and Joe Taylor had done. 'Not if you wish to keep the love and respect of your son.'

Amanda's smile faltered for a moment. 'I won't have kids.

Pregnancy ruins the body.'

'She gets the roles, but he's a bastard to her.'

'We all have to make sacrifices.'

He took a puff of his inhaler but it did little good. 'Would you sacrifice love for fame?'

'Isn't that the same thing? With fame comes the adoration of fans. Who could be more loved?'

Simon couldn't take it any longer. 'Amanda.'

'Yes?'

He fumbled in his pocket for the box, which now didn't appear to want to come out. 'I saw this today and thought of you.' He whacked the box onto the table a little too hard. His courage wavered. 'I mean, it's nothing really. Just a – a…'

Amanda opened the box. A smile lit her face. 'Why, Simon…'

A tiny spurt of courage mixed with adrenalin filtered back into his gut. He tried to look at her, but every time his eyes met hers, he was jolted with terror. He settled for looking at his drink mat instead. 'Actually, it's not nothing. It's special. *You're* special. To me, I mean. *Still.* I just wanted you to know that.' She could run off with a rich producer if she wanted, but God help him if he didn't make her aware of his feelings first. He hazarded a look at her. Her smile wavered for a moment but broadened again when she looked at the necklace.

'Isn't that a sapphire?' she asked.

Simon cleared his throat and tore off a piece of the drink mat; tried not to blush. 'Yeah.'

She took the necklace out and slipped it around her throat.

'Do you need a–' Simon's belated offer to help was met by a shake of her head.

She picked up her mobile and lifted it high, pouting up at it. The camera clicked and she examined the selfie. 'Gorgeous.' She reached across the table and squeezed his hand. 'Thank you.'

Electricity shot through his body, and it was all he could do not to yank his hand away. 'You're welcome,' he muttered.

Simon walked her back to her room after they'd finished

their drink. Buoyed by his consumption of alcohol on an empty stomach and Amanda's response to his gift, he leaned in to kiss her. He was a man, a man taking control of the situation.

Amanda jerked her head back. 'Er – what are you doing?'

Simon's brain felt like a multi-car pile-up on a spaghetti junction. 'I thought – you and I – like I said earlier, I care about you. I gave you that necklace…'

Amanda gave him a scornful look. 'That doesn't mean you get to paw me outside my room.'

'I know. I didn't mean that.' Simon's face was on fire. 'I just thought–'

'Well, you thought wrong.' Amanda unlocked her door and slammed it in his face.

Simon suddenly felt very sober. He leaned against the wall and sighed. That had not gone as he'd imagined it would.

Two doors down, Nick tore open the box and took out the three leather-bound journals, dog-eared and yellowing. His heart bounced into his throat, and his fingertips left small moist imprints on the cracked leather covers.

A note fell out, and he picked it up.

'Don't know why you need my father's journals so suddenly, but look after them with your life. Grandpa.'

He opened up the title page, which read, in careful, bold handwriting: *'Das Tagebüch des Sturmbannführers Heinrich Schneider'* then he flicked through to the ink-stained journal entry for the twenty-second of May, 1940.

6

Amiens, France – Tuesday, 9ᵗʰ August, 2016

Later that afternoon, driving to Beauvais in a hire car with Nick, Simon contemplated sharing his failed move on Amanda with his step-brother. He decided against it. Nick might laugh, and Simon wasn't sure he could survive more humiliation. He hoped Amanda wouldn't tell him either. He hated the thought of the two of them sniggering behind his back.

The air conditioning in the car didn't work, and the afternoon heat was stifling, so they stopped off at a corner shop in Beauvais to get a couple of Cokes. The woman behind the counter was elderly, her dark skin as crumpled as an old leather bag.

Simon paid for their items then paused. '*Pardon, madame.* Have you lived in Beauvais for a long time?'

The woman said something scathing in French then turned away. Simon blinked at her rudeness and was about to leave the shop when a much younger woman appeared from behind a shelf.

'I'm sorry, please excuse my grandmother. She doesn't speak English.' She smiled, brown eyes sparkling behind long sweeping lashes and a pixie-cut fringe. 'You are visiting here in Beauvais?'

'Actually, my friend and I–' Simon pointed out the window to Nick stretching his legs outside. '– we're trying to track down a family who might have lived here a few years ago. Around Nazi Occupation time.'

'*Grandmaman,*' the young woman said, but the older woman had already recognised the words.

She babbled something in French.

44

'My grandmother wants to know who you are and why you're asking questions?'

Simon hesitated. 'We're filmmakers. From London. We're – er – making a documentary on people who lived through Occupation. We believe a family called Gromaire owned a farm in these parts?'

'Gromaire?' said the old woman sharply.

'Yes. Did you know them?'

She looked blank, and Simon looked desperately to her granddaughter. She patiently translated, and the old woman nodded cautiously. Simon's stomach flipped over. Another fact proven correct!

'The Gromaires are still living here,' said the granddaughter.

'What? We couldn't find anyone in the telephone directory.'

'Haha, *oui*. Octave and Hélène. They live there still. I don't believe they have a telephone.'

Simon reeled at the mention of their names. According to Amanda's last past life regression session, they'd been small children clinging to their mother's skirt. 'But they must be…'

'*Old*. Yes. Neither of them married. There are no children. They live in that old farmhouse by themselves. Goodness knows how they manage.'

'Do you know where exactly the farmhouse is?' Simon was desperate for his inhaler, but it was in the car.

'Of course.'

Simon and Nick exited the hire car and picked their way across the shabby unkempt grounds to the farmhouse's front door. All the shutters, once a vibrant green but now peeling and faded, were closed. The faint whiff of dog excrement and chickens hung in the hot air, making Simon loath to knock and be subject to smells from within.

He was about to knock again when he heard the faint clip of movement beyond. The door opened with a plaintive whine. A small, elderly woman stood on the threshold, leaning hard on a cane.

'*Oui?*'

Simon hesitated. He and Nick hadn't discussed what to do if the Gromaires didn't speak English.

'*Bonjour, madame. Parlez-vous anglais?*' said Simon in his best and only French.

The woman's brow furrowed deeper. 'Who are you?'

Simon sighed with relief and beamed at her. 'Thank you. Are you Hélène Gromaire?'

She looked at him suspiciously.

'Madame, we are so sorry to bother you,' said Nick, oozing charm. 'My name is Nicholas Taylor. I am a British filmmaker, and this is my brother, Simon.'

She gave them a small, polite smile but remained uncertain.

'We were hoping you could help us in our search for a woman who might have stayed here.'

'We do not do lodgings,' said the woman.

'You are Hélène Gromaire though, aren't you?' Nick asked.

The woman nodded.

Nick smiled at her and took her hand warmly between the both of his. 'Madame, it is such a pleasure to meet you.'

Hélène's uncertainty seemed to abate beneath Nick's charm offensive. 'Who are you looking for?'

'Her name is Catherine Jacquot – *was* Catherine Jacquot,' said Simon.

She shook her head after a moment's thought. 'I'm sorry. I don't know anyone by that name.' She began to close the door, and Simon stepped forward to stall her.

'Please! It would've been a very long time ago. During the War.'

Hélène paused. Simon dug through his bag and took out the photo of Catherine and Benoit standing in front of Château de Pierrecourt. Hélène hooked her glasses over her ears and peered at the photograph for a long moment. The frown on her face suddenly disappeared as recognition dawned. She looked at Simon, mouth agape, milky eyes wide.

'That girl? Catherine?'

Simon's heart palpitated in his chest. Here, at last, was someone who had really known Catherine; not through some library records or hypnosis recollection, but had met her in person.

'I haven't thought of her in years!' said Hélène. 'How do you know her? Why are you looking for her?'

'We're making a documentary about her,' said Nick. 'We would be honoured if you would be a part of it.'

Hélène hesitated. She looked past them to the driveway and licked her thin lips nervously. 'I don't know...'

Simon noticed the shabby living room behind Hélène – the crumbling stone walls and rotten wood beams. 'We would compensate you for your time, of course.'

Simon and Nick set up an unobtrusive camera in the living room and fiddled with the white balance to compensate for the poor lighting. Meanwhile, Hélène went to change her shawl and make some coffee. She reappeared with a tray, the ancient cups and saucers clinking beneath her unsteady hand and a woven pink shawl now covering her hunched shoulders.

Simon hurried over to help her with the tray. He placed it on a stained and scratched side table but was ushered away when he tried to pour the coffee.

'Sit down. You are my guests,' said Hélène. 'We do not have many of them these days. So, how you do know Catherine? I used to wonder what happened to her. Are you family?'

Simon and Nick looked at each other.

'No,' said Simon slowly.

'We were told about her by a distant relative,' added Nick.

Hélène looked delighted as she passed them their coffee. 'So, she survived the War?'

'Unfortunately, not,' said Nick.

Simon took a sip of his coffee and nearly choked. It was bitterly strong. He smiled in appreciation nonetheless at Hélène, but she wasn't paying attention. Her face fell and she sat down in her armchair with a deflated bump.

'Oh. I so hoped she had lived. I would have been only eight or nine years old then…'

Simon discreetly switched the video camera on. Hélène looked into space, her cup half-raised from its saucer. 'Octave was older, he probably remembers it better than me. He is out now doing his deliveries. Ah, Catherine had the prettiest hair, long, and dark, and thick.'

'So Catherine really did hide on your farm?'

'Oh, yes. I remember that night well now. I think… there had been an air raid on the road close by earlier that day. Papa was so nervous. Then he found Catherine outside looking for food. Maman was not happy about it.' Hélène blinked and took a sip of her coffee. She smiled apologetically. 'It was not Maman's fault. You must understand, it was a very frightening time. The Germans were all around, and we didn't know what they might do to us. I was too young to understand, of course, but there was much uncertainty for our future. We were not Jewish, but we knew Jewish sympathisers were not treated kindly.'

'How long did Catherine stay with you?' asked Simon.

'Just the one night. A Gestapo officer arrived the next day and…' She hesitated. '…he *found* Catherine and arrested her.'

'Do you know where he took her?' Simon asked. He shot Nick a pleading look. Strictly speaking, Nick should have been doing the interviewing, but he didn't seem terribly interested in Hélène's answers.

'No,' she replied. 'A camp maybe, but it was still very early in the War. I don't believe there were many camps set up that soon, in France at least. I used to wonder what became of her.'

'Is there anything else that you can tell us about Catherine that you can remember?' Simon said. 'Anything at all?'

Hélène shook her head. 'I'm sorry. She was only with us for the one night. She stayed in the attic. The Gestapo officer warned Papa–'

She was interrupted by the front door opening. An old man with a thick white moustache and thatch of silvery hair beneath his faded flat cap stood silhouetted in the doorway.

'Octave!' Hélène cried. 'You are home early.'

Octave replied in French then threw a look their way. Hélène introduced them in French, and Simon noticed the slight tremor that had seeped into her voice. He picked up his and Nick's names and Catherine's being mentioned. Octave couldn't have looked any less impressed. Hélène smiled appeasingly at her brother and poured him some coffee. Octave ignored the offer, remaining stiffly by the door, forcing Hélène to put the cup back on the tray.

'I was just telling our guests how the Gestapo officer didn't arrest Papa or anything when he found Catherine in the attic. Yet, a couple of years later, we had a British airman hiding with us. He stayed much longer… Clive. That was his name, I remember! Ah. He was so tall and handsome. He helped Papa with the harvest.' A smile spread across Hélène's face. 'I fell head over heels in love with him, but Octave did not love him so much!' she said with a chuckle.

'It was too dangerous,' snapped Octave.

Simon eased the camera around to face Octave. 'Too dangerous?'

Octave's lips clamped shut again in a crooked grimace.

'He was discovered,' Hélène said sadly. 'I don't know how – I suppose the Nazis had their ways, didn't they? They were very powerful, very influential. They locked him in the back of a truck.' She sighed and took an unsteady sip of her coffee. 'And then the officer came back and shot our father for collaboration.'

Simon gasped. 'They killed him?'

Hélène nodded. 'Dear Papa. He only ever wanted to help people.'

Simon looked at Octave for his reaction. The old man glared stonily back. His sense of mistrust was obviously mutual.

'It is time for you to go now,' said Octave. 'We are busy today.'

Simon was jolted by Octave's rudeness. However, he

switched off the camera and smiled sympathetically at Hélène.

'We're very sorry for your loss. But thank you for your time and for telling us so much about Catherine.'

Hélène saw them out of the house and into the putrid heat. She patted Simon's hand with affection. 'Will you visit again? We do not have many guests. Maybe I can tell you more about those years next time.'

Simon felt sorry for her, being shut up in that crumbling old house, obviously living under the thumb of her sour brother. 'Thank you, yes, I'd like that.' He shot Octave a quick look, noting the older man's stony glare. 'I'll try.'

They waved goodbye and made their way back to their hire car.

'What do you make of that?' asked Nick, once they were out of earshot.

'I don't know. I think Octave knows a lot more than he lets on.'

Nick nodded in agreement. 'He totally ratted that airman out to the Germans.'

Simon puffed out his cheeks. 'And got his father killed.'

They reached the car and stowed the camera and tripod safely in the boot and got in.

'I wonder why that Gestapo officer who took Catherine – what was his name again?'

Nick shrugged. 'Dunno.'

'Schmidt? No, Schneider, that was it. I wonder why Schneider didn't kill Louis Gromaire for hiding a Jew?'

'Maybe it wasn't such a big deal back then,' suggested Nick, starting up the car and doing a three-point-turn.

'He still arrested Catherine. It must have been a fairly big deal.'

Nick put his foot down and they roared down the narrow rural road back to Amiens. 'Maybe he wasn't that bad a guy.'

7

Beauvais, France – Tuesday, 21ˢᵗ May, 1940

At the Gromaires' kitchen table, Catherine tried to retain some semblance of table manners in the face of her voracious hunger. The glass of creamy milk and rich stew coated the parched walls of her stomach, but soon the ecstasy of eating and tasting for the first time in at least two days gave way to cramps and a not-so-subtle rejection of her gut to the stew.

Catherine slowed down, looked for a napkin to pat her mouth. The Gromaire family tucked in, hunched over their meals, elbows territorially folded around their plates. Catherine thought how appalled her grandmother would be by such dining etiquette. Louis Gromaire was fully focussed on the task of cleaning his plate. His wife, Agathe, similarly so, although by the tension in her neck and vicious movements of her knife and fork, Catherine was sure her every move was being watched peripherally. She longed to feel for the Fleur de l'Alexandrie in her pocket, to feel the painful pressure of the star's points in her palm to reassure her, to strengthen her faith that finally she was safe. With the exception of Agathe, the Gromaire family appeared unthreatening; had invited her to their dinner table to share their food, but they were strangers. She could not know what they might be thinking, and, as Duras had said, people would do crazy things when they were afraid, unpredictable things, things that would test their ethics if it meant protecting their family.

Catherine caught Hélène's eye and the little girl sniggered into her food. Agathe sent them both ominous looks. Octave took the opportunity of his mother's distraction to discreetly rid his plate of beans. By the retching sound under the table, the puppy wasn't so keen on them either.

The meal over, Catherine sat with the food churning uncomfortably in her gut, waiting to be thrown out again. Perhaps it would be for the best. It would at least rid her of this simmering mistrust. On the other hand, what awaited her outside but more danger, more uncertainty, more darkness, hunger and thirst?

Agathe rose to clear the table and Catherine hurried to help her. She would take her chances inside. Agathe's lip curled in distaste as Catherine neared her.

'The water from the children's bath is still in the tub,' said the woman. 'It is cold by now, but you are not staying here smelling like a peasant.'

Red hot heat swept over Catherine's ears and filled her cheeks. Then she realised what the woman had relented to. 'Thank you, madame! Thank you, monsieur!'

She grasped Agathe's cold hands, but they were pulled out of her grasp. Catherine turned to Louis and held her hands to her chest. 'Thank you, monsieur.'

Louis beamed from his seat at the head of the table, his moustache widening across his lip.

'You cannot stay long though,' said Agathe, clattering the plates next to the sink. 'We do not have food enough for ourselves, never mind a stranger.'

Catherine shook her head. 'No, no. I do not intend to, madame. I must find my father. He has been taken to Paris, I think.'

Agathe's eyes narrowed in suspicion. 'Are you sure you are not Jewish?'

Catherine darted a look at Louis, hoping for his alliance, but he too looked curiously on. Again, she shook her head. 'My father is a doctor. He has been drafted to help in Paris.'

'That is fine then,' said Louis, wiping his mouth on his sleeve and getting to his feet. 'Octave and Hélène will set up some blankets for you in one of the bedrooms.' Agathe shot him a venomous look and he hesitated. 'Or perhaps the room in the attic would be more comfortable for you. The bedrooms are very dusty.'

Catherine nodded. She'd never slept in an attic before, but she would take it over one of the bedrooms any day. The further away she was from Agathe when she was sleeping, the better.

Alone in the attic, Catherine towel-dried the thick coil of her dark hair over her shoulder. The water hadn't been especially clean and not at all warm, but she felt much refreshed. She had scrubbed herself until her skin was a smarting pink, but the traumas of the past couple of days still stained her mind.

The floorboards creaked as she walked over to the narrow iron bed in the far corner towards the front of the attic. At the opposite end was a large window that overlooked the back yard. The window had been forced reluctantly open to let the fresh air in, and through it she could hear Agathe on the kitchen step below chastising the dogs as she fed them scraps.

Lining the walls were piles of wooden crates and dusty green bottles. The heady odorous mix of apples and burning paraffin from the lamp was reassuring. Her dress, that she'd feebly washed until her knuckles were rubbed raw, hung from a wall hook next to the bed.

She wondered where her father was now. Had she been too hasty in leaving Amiens? Perhaps he had never left. Perhaps he was home now, and had found her gone; was anxiously searching the city for his only daughter. She should have left a note. But that wouldn't have been possible. Duras hadn't been about to wait for her. He'd barely given her a minute to decide to leave or not.

She tried to blame him, imagined telling her father that she'd been given no choice. Fear would provide her with a million excuses to show Papa she hadn't meant to worry him. But blaming Duras, after all he'd done for her, was unforgiveable. She remembered the glassy stare, the red dirt rubbed into his stubble, the thin watery blood trickling from his mouth.

Catherine sat down on the bed and squeezed her hair with

the towel, pulling painfully on the roots. She closed her eyes.

'*Hashem*, please take Duras into your house. Like your Son, he sacrificed his life so that others may live. I am here now only because of his act of selflessness. *Hashem*, give me the strength and courage to be worthy of his sacrifice. Blessed be He who lives forever and endures to Eternity; Blessed be He who redeems and saves; Blessed be His name–'

A creaking on the steps leading up to the attic stopped Catherine in her reverential whispers. The door-hatch, positioned in the centre of the long room, opened a couple of inches towards her, and two pairs of large curious eyes peered in at her. Catherine smiled.

'Hello?'

The hatch opened wider, and Octave and Hélène clambered up into the room, carrying blankets. Hélène balanced a rag doll atop her blanket.

'Octave says you escaped from the German soldiers. Did you?'

Catherine didn't really know what she'd escaped from but the Germans sounded as good a reason as any. 'You could say that.'

Octave dumped the blankets on the bed and turned to the much more important task of examining Catherine's dress on the wall where there was still a faint residue of Duras's blood. Hélène shuffled closer to her, picking at the woollen braids on her rag doll.

'That's a very pretty doll,' said Catherine. 'What's her name?'

'Francoise. Would you like to hold her?'

Catherine took the doll and stroked the coarse fabric. 'Nice to meet you, Francoise.'

'She can sleep in your bed tonight, if you like,' said Hélène. Her cheeks flushed pink at her daring. 'She usually sleeps with me.'

Catherine's pleasure wasn't put on for effect. 'Thank you, Hélène!' She knew how generous it was to give up one's most precious doll, and to a stranger like her made it even more of a privilege.

'You have beautiful hair,' said Hélène, gazing at Catherine's long mane dampening the old nightdress Agathe had grudgingly lent her.

'Thank you. So do you.'

Hélène squirmed and twisted a finger in her thin blonde pigtails, obviously not as enthused about her own. 'Can I plait it for you?'

'What's this?' said Octave. He held up the Fleur de l'Alexandrie that he had found in the dress pocket.

Catherine gasped and lunged towards him. 'Put that away! You're not to touch it.'

Octave smartly side-stepped her and held it up to the light, letting the gold chain dangle between his grubby fingers. 'Why? This is the Jewish symbol. I thought you said you weren't Jewish?'

Catherine froze in fear. Panic flooded down to her feet like a wave of hot water. 'I'm not. I – give it to me!' She made a swipe for the necklace, but Octave was too quick. He whipped it out of her reach and laughed.

'Please! Give it back! You mustn't tell–'

The boy skipped out of the way of her desperate lunges while Hélène looked on in bemusement.

'Are you Jewish?'

'No, I'm not!'

'Then why do you have a Star of David?' said Octave.

'Octave!'

The door-hatch whined open again and Agathe's angry face appeared from below. 'What is going on here?'

Catherine's knees went weak. 'Madame…'

Octave bounced on the bed, making the iron frame squeak in objection. He waved the Fleur de l'Alexandrie about his head like a lasso. 'She's a Jew, Maman! She's a Jew!'

'No!' cried Catherine. 'He's lying! Give it back, Octave!' She made another grab for him, but he sprung off the bed towards the hatch to show his mother the necklace. Agathe's face turned puce.

'See? I'm right, aren't I, Maman?'

'Please, madame...' Catherine pleaded.

Agathe turned her iron gaze on the children. 'Come, Octave. Come, Hélène. Out of here now. Quickly!'

'Madame, it doesn't mean anything.'

'Why, Maman?' said Hélène with a tremulous quiver to her lip. 'I wanted to plait her hair.'

'Now, Hélène! Get away from her.'

Hélène didn't argue. She slid through the hatch after Octave, sending Catherine a watery glare as if it was all her fault.

'Louis! Come here!' barked Agathe down the hatch. She turned her accusing gaze back on Catherine. 'You selfish girl. What do you think you're doing?'

Catherine opened her mouth to speak, but she had no answer. What *did* she think she was doing? Lying about her faith to get her out of trouble, and to what purpose? How did being Jewish make her any different to anyone else? A hard ball of indignant tears swelled in her throat. How pathetic and fickle she was to have prayed to her God for courage when only minutes later she was denouncing her faith, begging these prejudiced people to give her food and shelter when she should be wearing her Judaism proudly.

Louis Gromaire's appearance forced both adults into the attic. The room suddenly felt much smaller, and Catherine backed away until her calves touched the cold metal of the bedstead.

'What is going on in here?' demanded Gromaire.

Agathe shook the Fleur de l'Alexandrie at him. 'She is a liar! She said she was not a Jew. What do you call this?'

Gromaire frowned at the necklace, turning it over so the dusty light of the paraffin lamp caught the gold lines of the star and reflected off the blue stone cut into its centre. He looked at Catherine and she hung her head, unable to withstand the disappointment in his eyes.

'Is it true?' he said, but he needn't have asked.

'She cannot stay here!' said Agathe. 'She is putting us all in danger.'

Gromaire hesitated and Catherine clung to the man's wavering expression.

'Monsieur, I'm sorry. But please don't send me to the Germans. Don't send me out there again.'

Agathe's nostrils flared, and she opened her mouth to speak, but Gromaire raised a sharp finger to silence her, his eyes suddenly angry. He stepped across to Catherine, and she flinched away, waiting to feel the hard strength of his hand against her ear. Instead, he grabbed her wrist and pressed the necklace into her palm.

'You will stay here for as long as you must.'

Catherine was hit by waves of relief and disappointment. She grasped his hand in gratitude and babbled unintelligible thanks.

'You're letting her stay?' Agathe's tone was enraged.

'This is how we show who we are and what we stand for.'

Agathe sent her husband a furious look and stomped out of the attic, letting the hatch-door slam closed behind her. Gromaire sighed in resignation and, opening the hatch again, followed her down, leaving Catherine alone.

Clutching her necklace, she collapsed on the bed. She pulled her knees up to her chin and closed her eyes and moved her lips in prayer.

8

Beauvais, France – Wednesday, 22nd May, 1940

Catherine had made up her mind by the next morning that today she must move on to Paris. With each passing day, Papa's concern for her safety would be mounting. Besides, she was not welcome here by Agathe. She couldn't trust her.

Dressed and washed, she was folding her blankets away when she heard the rumble of vehicles outside the farmhouse. The Gromaires' dog barked and snarled. Whomever it was, they were not being welcomed. Catherine's blood ran cold. She'd known she wasn't safe here, yet she'd chosen to ignore her instinct. She tip-toed to the hatch but stopped when she heard an abrupt rap on the front door. Through the cracks in the floorboards she watched the Gromaire family gather in the living room below. Agathe pulled the children into her skirts. Louis unbolted the door.

'Good morning, monsieur,' said a deep heavily accented voice.

Catherine couldn't see the owner of the voice, only Louis Gromaire's tight-lipped smile lit by the early morning sunshine radiating through the open doorway.

'I am Sturmbannführer Schneider. I am with the authorities. May I come in?'

Catherine's heart leapt into her throat. This was it; her worst fears realised. She should never have trusted Agathe! But when she angled her view through the floorboards to the woman, Agathe appeared just as frightened as she.

Gromaire looked over his shoulder at his family. His gaze swept up towards the ceiling, and Catherine was panicked to see the fear in his eyes. Then, quickly, he assumed a neutral expression and turned back to Sturmbannführer Schneider.

'Of course. Please come in. How can we help you?'

The man stepped into the front room and Catherine caught her first glimpse of him – a tall, imposing figure who had to bow his head to enter through the doorway. He removed his cap and tucked it beneath his arm, revealing a head of short blond hair styled just as precisely as his tailored Gestapo uniform. He walked around the room, large blunt fingers tapping the pistol on his belt, nodding politely to Agathe and the children. Each deliberate footstep of his polished boot heels thudding on the floorboards sent a spasm of fear through Catherine's body. Her teeth began to chatter. She held her breath as he passed beneath her. She thought of how Agathe had wrinkled her nose at her the previous evening. Could this man smell her too? She'd had a bath, but the water hadn't been terribly clean. Could he smell her fear, just like her father had always told her that dogs could?

'You are aware of the air raid that happened yesterday, I presume?' said Schneider.

'Yes, we heard it,' replied Gromaire in a pinched voice.

'The strike was targeting military opposition; a battalion of soldiers heading north towards Amiens.' Schneider stopped pacing and rounded on Gromaire with frightening pleasantness. 'There is a chance that those soldiers who escaped fled to your farm.'

'You can check, but there's no one here.' Gromaire gestured out the window towards the farm outbuildings, but his arm trembled so obviously, that he quickly returned it to his side.

Catherine winced. She willed him to be calm, to show just the right amount of nonchalance to subdue the German officer's suspicions.

Schneider took a step towards him, bemused. 'You say that with the authority of a man who knows differently, monsieur.'

Gromaire stood his ground, muscles tensed, while Schneider continued his slow pacing of the room.

'Do you know there are two types of people in this world that I have little patience for?'

Gromaire looked jerkily across at the German, eye ticcing. Schneider completed his perimeter walk and stopped inches from Gromaire. The farmer took a shaky step backwards.

'Hmm?' Schneider raised his eyebrows and Gromaire shook his head. 'Jews. And liars. And you,' Schneider said, poking Gromaire in the chest, 'I am beginning to suspect, are one of the latter.'

The German looked about at the Gromaire family, smiled apologetically and stepped out of Gromaire's personal space. His eyes settled on Octave. 'You know I have a son – Josef – not much older than you, young man.'

Octave shuffled closer behind Agathe, his eyes wide at the imposing Sturmbannführer in his living room.

'He is young,' Schneider continued, 'but he is smart. He knows when to tell the truth. Yet your father here appears not to.'

'There's no-one here–'

Gromaire was interrupted by Schneider spinning on his heel and striding towards him. In a flash he grasped the farmer by his shirt lapels and pressed his pistol beneath Gromaire's jaw. 'Don't lie to me, monsieur.'

Agathe screamed, and Hélène began to cry. The barking outside rose to a frenzy. Catherine leapt in fright as the hollow crack of a gunshot rang out, hurting her ears. She muffled her cry with her hands and peered desperately through the crack at Gromaire. But the man didn't fall. Catherine became aware of an uneasy silence. The dog had stopped barking. She pressed her hand to her mouth to quell the whimper of alarm that rose in her throat.

'You are a fool, Monsieur Gromaire,' snarled Schneider in his face. 'Why do you put your family in danger like this? Where are they hiding?'

Catherine felt awash with hopelessness and fear, drowning in it, choking on it, enveloped by its unmerciful might. She knew Gromaire would give her up before harm would come to his family, but she didn't have the courage to do it herself, to save the Gromaires.

'There's no-one here,' said Gromaire again in a strangled voice.

'You are lying!' bellowed Schneider. He shoved the pistol deeper into the farmer's neck.

Gromaire blinked the sweat out of his eyes but said nothing. A muscle leapt in his jaw. Schneider released him roughly then strode over to Agathe. Before she could react, he had her in a vice, his arm across her chest and the gun digging into her temple. Agathe whimpered, and her knees gave way. Only Schneider's iron embrace kept her from falling.

'You are willing to sacrifice your family for deserters and criminals?' said Schneider to Gromaire.

'There is no—'

'What? Speak up!' shouted Schneider. He pushed Agathe away and followed through by whipping the pistol across her face. Agathe crumpled to the ground with the children cowering over her, crying her name.

Schneider sent them sprawling with one kick of his shiny black boot and pulled Agathe to her feet. 'Where are they?'

Catherine bit her lip. She knew Agathe must give her up. Blood poured from the woman's temple into her eye. Buckling at the knees with Schneider's arm about her bosom and her steel grey hair falling from its tight bun, her humiliation was complete. But her thin lips remained firmly sealed. Her defiant eyes turned from Schneider to Gromaire.

A wisp of hope curled through Catherine's heart.

The German growled and cocked the pistol, pressing the barrel deeper against Agathe's skull.

'Maman!' cried Octave from the floor.

'WHERE ARE THEY?'

Catherine willed Louis and Agathe to keep their silence.

'In the attic!' screamed Octave. 'She's in the attic!'

9

Amiens, France – Tuesday, 9ᵗʰ August, 2016

Amanda flinched on the chaise longue, her brow furrowed and her breath shallow. 'The officer is surprised,' she murmured. 'He's asking Octave who he means by "she".'

A rivulet of sweat ran down Simon's face as he struggled to fill his lungs with air. He desperately needed his inhaler, but he couldn't tear himself away. He looked down at Catherine's photo scrunched in his fists. This was it. This was the moment he'd been dreading. But what would become of her? He couldn't bear to think of the atrocities that would befall her, the fear that she'd felt.

'Sturmbannführer Schneider is going to find me!' whimpered Amanda.

'It's okay, Catherine,' Simon wheezed.

Nick, behind the camera, mouthed 'Amanda,' at him with an amused grin. By the look on his face, he was thoroughly enjoying the drama being relayed by Amanda. Simon felt sick in comparison. He forced himself to read the caption beneath the photo again: '*detained on the 22ⁿᵈ of May, 1940 by Sturmbannführer Heinrich Schneider.*' But such impersonal words did nothing to describe the nightmare Catherine had lived through.

'He's asking Agathe how to get into the attic.'

Simon tried to draw in a breath. There'd been no record of Catherine in any camps so what had Schneider done with her after her arrest? What other horrors must they relive? Simon wished he could have done something to stop it instead of sitting here in the safety of his hotel room, spying on her misfortune, uselessly, seventy-six years too late.

'He's coming!' Amanda cried.

The photo tore in Simon's fists. He couldn't. It was too much. 'Run, Catherine! Get out of there! Run!'

Amanda's sapphire eyes shot open in surprise, and she sat bolt upright.

'What the hell?' said Nick.

Simon snapped out of the moment. They stared at him, and he slouched back self-consciously, aware of the burning heat flooding his face. As if his earlier humiliation hadn't been complete.

'Sorry,' he mumbled into the shredded ball of paper that had been Catherine's photo.

'What the hell happened?' said Amanda.

Nick switched off the camera, laughing to himself. 'He shouted at Catherine to run.'

Amanda turned murderous eyes on Simon, who shrank in his chair. 'You *what?*'

'Hey, I'm sorry. You were taking us closer and closer and… and I – well, I just got a bit too absorbed, that's all.'

Amanda stood up, over him. 'Are you out of your mind, you fucking psycho?' she hissed. 'You know how dangerous that is.'

Simon glared in her direction but couldn't make eye contact. Now that she mentioned it, he remembered the risks. Risks that he'd explained to her before the study had started, had her sign a contract that had said the study would take no responsibility for the harm past life regression could have. He gestured feebly at her. 'You're fine.'

'No thanks to you!' Amanda waved her arms.

'Wait, what are you guys talking about?' said Nick.

'It's nothing.' Simon got up and went to his dressing table to find his inhaler.

Amanda laughed humourlessly. 'Why am I not surprised? Nick, did you even read the contract you and Taylor Made Television got me to sign?'

'Course I fucking didn't. You know me better than that.'

'Tell him, Simon. Tell him the danger you just put me in

with your little stunt.'

Simon puffed on his inhaler, tried to clear his airways. 'The mind can get muddled if it's not brought out gradually. The consciousness can get confused as to which life it's in.'

'Leaving me with a dual personality,' added Amanda.

'Well, you're not talking French,' said Nick.

Amanda glared at him. 'For once in your fucking life, will you take this seriously?'

Nick wagged a finger at her. 'With language like that I'd say there's no trace of our good little Jewish friend, Catherine.'

'Nick!' Amanda's nostrils flared, and her eyes flashed.

'Strictly speaking, it would be dissociative identity disorder,' muttered Simon. 'D.I.D. You wouldn't be half Amanda, half Catherine. You would either be one or the other.' For a crazy moment, Simon wished that she would be Catherine. He tried to smooth out the French girl's crumpled photo. His fingernails had ripped right through her face. 'You would switch between the two.'

Nick's humour began to fade. 'Seriously? But how can she become Catherine when we're not even conversing with her? We're just looking. Besides, she's dead. How can you become a dead person?'

Simon sighed. Amanda was never going to forgive him now. 'What we're doing in these PLR sessions is hacking into the psyche; it's not as simple as just "looking". It doesn't matter if the person's dead or not. Consciousness doesn't die, but it does need a body in which to reside in order to manifest itself. Think of the body as being like a filing cabinet full of files that together make up the consciousness. Each file represents a life. So, we're using Amanda's body to access the archives of her consciousness and pulling up Catherine's file. If you close the filing cabinet too quickly you mightn't have time to put Catherine's back in place and pull up Amanda's.'

'Then can't you just open the filing cabinet and put the old file away and bring out the right one?' asked Nick.

'Sometimes. Sometimes not. The psyche is a bit more…'

Simon paused. He wanted to say 'temperamental', but Amanda was still shooting him murderous looks. '...*complex*.'

Nick looked Amanda up and down. 'Well, if you don't mind me saying you are definitely the sexiest filing cabinet I've ever seen.'

Amanda glared for a moment longer then relented. 'Dickhead,' she said fondly.

'Great. Glad we've got that sorted,' Nick replied. 'Why don't we forget about work for the rest of the day and go downstairs for a drink?'

Under Amanda's sneering gaze, Simon wanted to melt through the floor. 'You guys go ahead. I – I'll pack up here.'

Amanda flounced out without another word, and Nick followed, fluttering his hands and saying in a deep Southern drawl, 'Run, Forrest! Run!'

Simon sighed in relief as the door clicked shut. He made his unsteady way to the bed and collapsed onto it. He stared up at the ceiling. His chest felt crushed in with embarrassment. Amanda would never take him seriously again. But more heart-breaking than that was the thought of Catherine Jacquot being dragged out of the Gromaires' attic by Sturmbannführer Schneider to her death. How terrified she must have been. What more had such an innocent soul had to endure before it was put out of its misery?

Amanda had been upset, but not about Catherine. She'd been upset about the danger Simon had put her in. It was always about her. Tears of frustration, of embarrassment, of resentment, rolled into his hair. Amanda didn't deserve Catherine as part of her.

It was late but the Bibliothèque d'Amiens Métropole was still open. Only for another twenty minutes or so but that was plenty. Simon hurried over to the computers and typed in the website where he had found Catherine and Benoit's photo. It loaded slowly, revealing, bit by bit, first the Disneyesque conical spires of Château de Pierrecourt, its circular towers, and narrow arched windows which, to Simon's limited knowledge, seemed more in keeping with German architecture; then, in the foreground, Benoit's gaunt but intelligent features and finally Catherine, smiling shyly, grasping her father's hand. The printout hadn't done her justice, and Simon took a moment to simply gaze upon her.

'*La bibliothèque fermera dans dix minutes.*' A demure voice came from hidden speakers around the building.

Simon glanced at his watch. He had ten minutes until closing time. He did a quick search for the Fleur de l'Alexandrie, hoping to find more details on Bernie Costa's involvement with the necklace, but nothing showed up. It was as if it had never existed. A hard ball of unease swelled in his stomach. Perhaps the website they had found last time had been taken down. It had to have been. He couldn't find it anywhere. He deleted the Fleur de l'Alexandrie from the search bar and looked for Bernie Costa alone. Multiple websites came up, but none that mentioned the necklace. A pity he hadn't brought along the printout of that article whereupon he could have got the exact web address. If it had been taken down then they could still contact Bernie Costa and ask him about it. Joe Taylor was at least good for some things.

Simon took off his glasses and rubbed his eyes. He returned to the photo of Catherine and her father and clicked Print. He paused for a moment to drink in Catherine's face before closing the page and getting up.

Nick and Amanda sat at their table in the dimly-lit restaurant-bar and watched that evening's one-man band. Nick wasn't impressed. The guy could barely hold a riff on his guitar and couldn't hit high C even if someone twisted his nuts. He had tuned out Amanda ranting about Simon and how he'd accosted her earlier and was now taking his revenge by endangering her mental health, but then the solo artist stopped for a break and he was forced to listen to her.

'You know this can't happen again, don't you?' she said.

'You need to control your step-brother or whatever he is to you. I'm putting my life in your hands.'

Nick twisted his tongue inside his mouth to prevent himself from telling her to stop being so dramatic. 'He won't do it again. Trust me.'

'Why? He's not... *stable*, Nick. You don't know what he's going to do next.'

'He's fine. Seriously, Amanda. Yes, we both know he's got a bit of a crush on you, but that doesn't make him a nut job, does it? I mean, on the contrary, he would be crazy not to have a crush on you.'

Amanda smirked. 'It's hardly a crush though, is it? It's been going on since we first started uni.' She took a sip of her wine, looking off over Nick's shoulder into her memories, then shook her head. 'It should never have happened.'

'Why did it happen? I mean, you're obviously not attracted to him. Why did you hook up?'

'I don't know. I was drunk that first night. Looking for a good time. Simon was easy enough.'

'But it wasn't a one-night stand. You were together for a couple of months after.'

'Five weeks,' Amanda corrected him. She fiddled with the stem of her wine glass then sighed. 'I saw sense.'

'He's not such a bad guy,' Nick said, thinking of the heartbreak he'd seen in Simon after Amanda had dumped him, of the way she still treated him like dog shit on her shoe.

'I've got dreams, Nick. Big dreams.'

'And what, you think Simon's too small to fit into them?'

She shrugged. 'He owns a pawnbroker's shop and sits up in his flat meditating and reading all day.'

'I've heard meditation is quite hip in the Hollywood Hills.'

'You know what I mean.'

Nick reluctantly agreed. Simon was never cut out to be an A-list celebrity or even the partner of an A-list celebrity. He didn't do glamour. Besides, Amanda would walk all over him. Watching her, he could understand his step-brother's obsession with Amanda. She was beautiful, certainly, but lots of women were beautiful. It was her arrogance. The way she held herself, the way she convinced others that she was worth more than everyone else in the room. Waiters fell over themselves to serve her drinks, men fought to open doors for her. And she accepted their subservience as her rightful due. Nick had a compulsion to seduce her and experience that strength and conviction of self as a lover and then toss her away like she'd done to Simon. The more he thought of Amanda naked on top of him the hornier he became. He took a gulp of his wine and tried to think of something else.

'Why is Simon doing this?' Amanda asked.

'What?'

'The study. Working for you and your grandfather. I know how he is.'

'He needs the cash. The shop must be struggling. Olivia gave up a long time ago trying to give him money, so she and Joe hatched this plan to employ him instead.'

'It wasn't your decision then?'

'No.' Doing a documentary hadn't been his idea either. Again, Joe had strongly implied that if he didn't get his hands dirty he could kiss goodbye to his inheritance. 'I don't mind though. It was Simon who came up with the idea for investigating reincarnation. He's apparently already "visited" his former life a couple of times by himself. Sounded pretty cool.'

'He hypnotised himself?'

'That's what he tells me.'

Amanda rolled her eyes. 'He is a psycho, you know that, right?'

'He's okay.'

'Why do you stick up for him like this?'

Nick shrugged and took a swallow of his drink. 'He's the closest thing to a brother I've ever had, even if, strictly speaking, he's my step-uncle.'

'That's fucked up, you know.'

'Show me a family that isn't.'

Amanda conceded the point with a roll of her eyes.

'Besides,' he went on. 'I feel like I owe Olivia.'

'Simon doesn't think so. He hates his mother.'

'So would you if she left your father for some decrepit but loaded TV producer and pushed your father to suicide.'

'I don't know. Having a rich TV producer for a step-father would come in mighty handy.'

'Yeah, but you want to be an actress. Simon's not like that.'

Amanda laughed. 'No, he's certainly not.'

A pang of disloyalty for speaking about Olivia so disparagingly lingered in Nick. After having had forced upon him the hordes of au pairs and nannies in his childhood, mostly wannabe actresses who'd either wanted a leg-up in the film industry or a leg-over old Grandpa Joe, when Olivia had appeared on the scene when he was twelve, she'd become the one constant in his life. He fiddled with the menu on their table. Revealing to Amanda such intimate details of his childhood would only serve as ammunition for her if they ever fell out, but at the same time he didn't feel comfortable making Olivia out to be the devil incarnate. A gold-digger certainly, no fresh-faced beautiful woman would settle for an arsehole twice her age if he didn't have a fat bank balance, but not the devil.

'Olivia's not so bad,' he said. 'She was more of a mother to me than my own.'

'What about your mother?'

'She was never the maternal sort.' Nick looked around, trying to find a point of interest that he could change the subject to. The hotel maître d', M. Fourrier, was visiting the tables, smiling and exchanging small talk with the guests. Nothing really to spark a diversion, and Amanda was looking far too interested in his dysfunctional family to be distracted.

'Is she still around?'

'Somewhere. I guess,' he replied. 'We haven't heard otherwise. Last I saw her I was about seventeen.' Nick took another glug of his drink. It made talking about his childhood much easier, and although not something he particularly liked to do, it did feel quite therapeutic to tell somebody about it. His mother wasn't exactly Joe's proudest achievement, so any attempt to talk to him about her in the past had usually been blocked.

'And your father?'

'Don't know. He was just a fling that my mother had. Apparently, he was a drummer in some German rock band. She was their groupie.'

Amanda's eyes widened. 'Cool. Your life's so much more interesting than mine. And you do have quite Germanic features.'

Nick gave a mirthless laugh. 'So they tell me.' If only she knew the whole truth.

'So, what's worse – never knowing your father or finding your father's suicide?'

Nick had to laugh at Amanda's audacity. Subtlety was hardly her forte, but she had no shame. 'It depends on who you are, I suppose. I've never loved anyone like a son is supposed to love a father, so if I were to find my father dead, I don't think it would affect me hugely. Simon, on the other hand, had that love, idolised his father. He was devastated when he found him. Olivia had Joe shelling out for all the best therapists in London for him.'

'Didn't do much good,' said Amanda with a disdainful pout.

'It's an improvement on what he was before. Since he moved out and started up his dad's old pawnbroker's shop, he's been much happier. Even if a lot more broke.'

Amanda shook her head. 'I don't understand him.'

'To be fair, I don't think he understands you much either.'

Amanda sent him a coquettish look. 'So, do you think you'd feel the same devastation if you found the body of someone you *did* love?'

'To be honest, the first thing I'd do was make sure I couldn't be implicated in their death.'

'Nick! How very cold!'

He grinned. 'Not cold. Sensible. You've all the time in the

world to grieve later. All I know is that I'd rather be grieving in the comfort of my own home than in a jail cell.'

Amanda laughed, but, before she could reply, M. Fourrier arrived at their table. Like a true professional, their host remembered they were British.

'I trust you are enjoying your evening, monsieur? Madame?'

Amanda fluttered her eyelashes and raised her almost empty wine glass. '*C'est magnifique.*'

M. Fourrier reacted instinctively. 'Perhaps a bottle of wine on the house?'

'*Merci,*' murmured Amanda.

Nick looked at her in admiration. It wasn't even charm, it was something more magical, more primitive, that she exuded. And she was an expert on using it to her advantage.

'Say, how do you go about booking your entertainment?' Nick asked.

'You are enjoying tonight's performer?' beamed M. Fourrier.

'I perform in London.'

'London?' echoed the maître d' looking far more impressed than he should. 'You have a band?'

'No. I'm a solo artist. Like tonight's performer. Although perhaps you might say I have a little more experience.'

M. Fourrier nodded knowingly. 'We like to encourage new talent as well as hiring more experienced musicians.'

Nick thought about his guitar sitting up in his room, about the gigs that he was missing in London because of this documentary. He thought about his grandfather telling him that being a musician could only ever be a hobby. To hell with it. 'We leave next Wednesday. Do you have any open slots?'

The maître d' hesitated. 'Well…'

'Oh, he's very good,' gushed Amanda. 'He's one of the most sought after solo performers in London.'

'Your name, monsieur?'

'Nick Taylor.'

The name, understandably, didn't register with M. Fourrier,

and Nick could see their host was in a quandary. On the one hand he didn't want to hire some useless amateur who claimed to be able to perform. On the other, here was Amanda working her magic on the man like the snake in *The Jungle Book*.

'You have heard of Nick's father, Roger, haven't you? He was a drummer.'

M. Fourrier's eyes widened to the size of cymbals. 'Of course, Monsieur Taylor!' he said clapping his hands together. 'Would Sunday night be acceptable to you?'

'Very good.' Nick shook his hand.

M. Fourrier turned adoringly to Amanda. 'I will go to see about that wine. Good evening.'

Nick and Amanda tried not to laugh too hard at the poor man.

'I didn't know you played.'

'I didn't know you could be so persuasive.'

'You'll have to play for me.'

'You'll hear me on Sunday.'

Amanda gave him a sultry look. 'But I've already recommended you. It could damage my reputation if you turn out to be one of those losers on *Britain's Got Talent*.'

Nick met her gaze, knew what she wanted. 'My guitar is in my room.'

Amanda smiled. 'Let's go, then.'

They got up from their table, walked purposefully towards the exit. They passed their waiter along the way and Amanda smoothly relieved him of their complimentary bottle of Merlot as she passed by.

In his room, Nick drew up a chair and settled his guitar on his lap. Amanda took possession of his bed, curling up on her side with the bottle of wine.

'What do you want to hear?' he asked.

'What do you want to play for me?'

There was an edge in her voice, a challenge. Was he a big enough boy to take her on? A flurry of fear and excitement fluttered through his body. Yes, now he could understand Simon's obsession. It wasn't that he didn't notice the disdain that she treated him with; it was the fear this disdain aroused in him that was the turn-on.

Nick adjusted the capo and fine-tuned the strings. Right. Here goes. 'Give me that.'

Amanda stretched over to pass him the Merlot and he took a healthy slug. It trickled down his chin, wet and cold, and he wiped it away and passed the bottle back. Unable to look at Amanda, he plucked at the strings and began to sing 'Black Magic Woman'. Slowly though, his confidence grew and he raised his gaze, running it up her bare folded legs to where her dress had ridden up her thighs, up to the hint of cleavage and the necklace about her throat that brought out the ethereal blue of her eyes. He met her gaze and kept it, accepting her challenge, even smiling to himself. She thought she could out-seduce anyone. Well, he was going to show her.

Amanda broke the look to take a swig from the bottle. She slid off the bed and began to dance around the room, swaying to the music, moving her hips from side to side, lifting her dark auburn hair so that it tumbled down over her shoulders. The muscles in Nick's lower abdomen spasmed, and the pulse of arousal began to throb beneath his guitar. It was all he could do to keep on singing, to keep on playing. Actually, it was probably a good thing he had something to focus on. Without it, their clothes would already be on the floor.

Amanda swayed mesmerically before him, arching her back, lifting her arms so her dress rose up. Nick refused to capitulate. He focused on the guitar solo. She took a last slug from the wine bottle then put it aside. Slowly, she took the hem of her dress and ruched it together between her fingers, all the while dancing, revealing red lace knickers that barely justified the term, up over her smooth brown ribs to her matching red bra. She lifted the dress over her head and cast it at him. Nick smiled and tossed it aside to keep playing. She had a body like a mountain nymph. He refused to fall under her spell. Not until he was good and ready. As he began on the last chorus, Amanda straddled him, making it impossible for him to continue. She took his hand and placed it on the coarse material of her knickers. Nick's guitar thudded to the floor with an indelicate twang. He smiled up at her. This was going to happen on *his* terms.

It was past midnight by the time Simon arrived back at the hotel. He'd stopped off at a bar to mull things over with the aid of a few beers. Stumbling up the stairs to the second floor, he decided he should apologise to Amanda before telling Nick about what he'd found or what he hadn't found, to be precise. Amanda was right to have been mad at him. He *had* endangered her by telling Catherine to run. He hadn't done it on purpose, of course, but he was culpable, nonetheless. He reached her door and knocked. It remained stoically closed.

'Amanda? It's me, Simon. Please, I just want to talk.' He knocked again, louder this time. 'Amanda? Are you in there?'

He couldn't hear a thing. With a sigh, he turned away to knock on Nick's door. Maybe Nick could help him untangle his feelings for Amanda.

He paused a couple of feet from Nick's door. A 'Do Not Disturb' sign hung from the doorknob. Maybe Nick had had enough of Amanda no doubt bitching about him and had retired to his room to get away. He reached out then stopped. He swayed a little. The doorknob went in and out of focus.

Simon was transported back to That Day. He paused on the landing, mid-crunch through his ginger biscuit, to listen for his father. Only then did he hear the low hum of an engine coming from beyond the door leading into the garage. His earlier bounce dissipated as he approached the six landing steps that led down to the door. His tennis shoes bent over the lip of the first step. His rucksack slipped from his shoulder to his elbow with a tug. A faint whiff of pollution.

'Dad?' he called again, less certain of his father's response.

The low hum seeped through the crack around the door.

Unease prickled his arms as he descended the steps and reached out to twist the doorknob. The door opened with a familiar squeak. The low hum of the car engine increased to a fraught growl, and he was overcome by the acrid smell of exhaust fumes.

Simon pulled his hand away from Nick's door with a sudden gasp and staggered backwards into the corridor wall, coughing uncontrollably, dislodging a picture frame. He tried to breathe. Deep. Slow. Deep. Slow. Deep. Slow. God, he was a fool. Getting drunk and upsetting himself, allowing himself to go back to that moment. He'd talk to Nick in the morning. He'd apologise to Amanda in the morning. He pushed himself away and staggered back to his own room.

10

Amiens, France – Wednesday, 10ʰ August, 2016

Simon awoke with a throbbing head. Nevertheless, he couldn't allow himself to linger in bed. He got up, swallowed a couple of paracetamol and had a quick shower before heading back down the corridor to Amanda's room. He stopped short of her door. It was only 8.40. Knowing Amanda, she was probably still asleep. Maybe it wasn't such a good idea to wake her up, even if it was to apologise. Instead, he headed over to Nick's room where the 'Do Not Disturb' sign still hung on the doorknob. He hesitated, but it held none of the ominous memories that it had the night before. He knocked. He could hear Nick moving around inside.

'Did you order breakfast?' he heard Nick say.

The door swung open, and Nick stood in his boxer shorts, his blond hair askew. He looked somewhat startled to see him.

'Sorry, I know it's early,' Simon said. He peeped around the door at the messy bed. 'You got company?'

Nick blocked his view. 'Yeah, you know, just met a girl – a local girl – last night. Now's not a good time–'

'I know. I'm sorry. But I just had to tell you something.' Simon peeked over Nick's shoulder. He could see steam seeping out from beneath the bathroom door. 'I went back to the library last night–'

'Can this wait?'

'I did another search for the Fleur de l'Alexandrie, but that article we found last time about Bernie Costa owning it has been taken down!'

'Si–'

'There's no record at all of him having it. So we might have to tap Joe for a favour. How good a friend is he of Costa's? Do you think…' He was interrupted by some hotel guests passing by and looking Nick over in his boxers. Hastily, he stepped into the room.

Nick cleared his throat and glanced back at the bathroom.

Simon lowered his voice to a conspiratorial whisper. '…Do you think we could get an interview?'

'Simon, look, can we talk about this at breakfast maybe? I'm not even dressed.'

'You said they were friends…' Simon's words died on his lips as his eye was caught by a glint of sparkle on Nick's bedside table. His throat tightened and he stepped closer. 'That's… what's Amanda's necklace doing here?'

'Simon, let's talk about this later, okay?' Nick tried to push him out of the room.

Simon staggered back, more from shock than Nick's insistence. His knees liquidised. As if caught in a slow-motion whirlwind, his gaze flickered from the sapphire pendant on the table to the lacy underwear discarded on the carpet then to the steaming bathroom and back again. 'I gave that necklace to her,' he said dumbly.

Nick had the courtesy to look guilty. 'Shit, Simon. It isn't what you think. Not really.'

Simon backed out of the room, colliding with more guests walking past. He didn't want to know. He didn't want to hear what lame excuses Nick could come up with. It didn't matter. He knew what they'd done. And Nick knew what it would do to him. He hurried after the guests, pushing past them, ignoring their objections.

'Simon! Jesus Christ!'

He heard Nick's hushed call behind him, glanced back once to see his step-brother standing half in the corridor, reluctant to go any further in his underwear, motioning to him desperately to come back. Simon belted down the stairs, just as desperate to put as much distance between them as he could.

* * *

'What's going on?' Amanda appeared out of the bathroom, her skin pink beneath her hotel towel.

Nick leapt back into the room and closed the door. 'That was Simon. He knows.'

Amanda didn't react. She walked over to the stool in front of the dressing table mirror and began to towel-dry her hair. 'So?'

'So? Bloody hell, Amanda.'

She looked at him through the mirror as he pulled on his jeans and rummaged through his suitcase for a clean shirt. 'I'm not beholden to him.'

'But you know how he feels about you. Don't you feel any sense of remorse?'

Amanda rounded on him, suddenly angry. 'We dated for a poxy five weeks years ago when we were teenagers. We were kids! I have a right to do what I want with whomever I want without having to worry about hurting poor, little Simon's feelings.'

'And I'm his step-brother.'

'You should have thought about that last night.'

Nick bit his lip. She was right. And he had, briefly, thought about Simon but had justified his actions by telling himself he'd merely been showing Amanda what a tart she was. But now, without the persuasive influence of alcohol, he realised Simon wouldn't see it that way. And Amanda didn't appear to care less what last night made her look like. He pulled on his shoes and headed for the door.

'Get your clothes and go.'

Simon didn't know where he was going. He'd somehow picked up a hire car at the hotel and was now heading down a highway. He'd already nearly crashed twice when he'd driven down the wrong side of the road. His head was a numb mush of shock and hurt. His gut twisted in a hollow spasm of emotion that made him nauseous. He couldn't decide what hurt more – Nick's betrayal or Amanda's. He was a complete fool! Stupid for thinking Amanda might come back to him. Knowing now that she would never be his – that she'd never intended to be his – was like a grief he'd only felt once before in his life. He couldn't carry on with the documentary now. Couldn't face Amanda. Couldn't face Nick. Yes, he was broke, and he needed the money, but by God, even if he lost the shop, he still had his pride, what little, pathetic cow-pat pride he had left. He couldn't go back. He'd drive to Paris, catch the Eurostar back to London. And Nick and Amanda could sort out the mess of the failed documentary themselves. They deserved it. They deserved each other.

A lump swelled in his throat and his lip trembled. The bastards. Did they care so little for him? Tears sparkled his vision, and a car tooted at him. Simon swerved back into his lane. Shit. He could barely see. He needed to pull himself together. He tried, made a concerted effort to be a 'man', but the pain was too overwhelming. The tears stung again. He took the approaching exit and, for the first time, recognised where he was. He was just a few miles out of Beauvais. Another wave of grief crashed down on him as he thought of Catherine. With the end of the documentary, he'd never connect with her again. Damn Amanda! She'd never cared about anyone but herself.

But maybe... Simon's thoughts turned to the lovely Hélène Gromaire. She'd told him and Nick to visit again. He could connect to Catherine one last time through Hélène's faded recollections. It wasn't much, but it was enough to quell Simon's emotions. Some of the old Frenchwoman's strong coffee and nurturing attention would make him feel better.

Simon drew up outside the Gromaires' farmhouse and took a moment to compose himself. A quick glance in the rearview mirror showed puffy bloodshot eyes behind his glasses and a red nose. He sighed. Maybe if she asked, he could blame it on hayfever.

Hélène answered the door, and Simon was struck dumb by her appearance. Her cane was nowhere to be seen, and she stood straight and strong, her hair freshly permed, her clothes colourful and new.

'*Oui*?' Her milky eyes were enquiring, showing no sign of recognition.

'Hélène! You look–' Simon didn't want to appear rude by drawing attention to their last meeting, but her transformation was startling. 'You look amazing!'

'Pardon?' Still she looked quizzically at him.

Dementia probably. Their visit yesterday had been very brief. Glimpsed behind Hélène were paintings on the wall – a brilliant one he hadn't noticed before of a Spitfire, green grey camouflage, the blue, white and red roundel on a tilted wing against a bright blue sky.

'I'm sorry,' said Hélène awkwardly. 'Do I know you?'

'It's Simon. Simon Hayes? We met yesterday.'

Hélène shook her head. 'No, I'm sorry. You must be mistaken.'

'No, Hélène, we did,' said Simon gently. 'Yesterday… I came with my brother Nick. We're filming a documentary. You gave us coffee–'

Hélène's expression changed from puzzlement to annoyance. 'You are mistaken. I haven't met you before.'

She pushed the door closed, and Simon instinctively put his foot out to jam it open. 'No, wait. Hélène! You do know me. It's okay.' He fumbled in his pocket for the printout of Catherine's photo. 'You told us about this girl – about Catherine Jacquot–' He held out the picture to her, but she was too distracted to look. She tried to close the door again.

'Hélène, please! Is Octave here? He'll remember.'

Hélène's hand flew to her mouth. 'Please go! Just leave us alone.'

Simon was mortified by her distress. 'Hélène, what's wrong? Is Octave okay? Where–'

'Hélène? Everything all right?' A very English voice interrupted him from within the house, and Simon looked at Hélène in surprise.

'Gosh, I'm sorry. Do you have company? I – I just wanted to ask you about Catherine Jacquot again. I didn't to mean to upset you.'

A tall, elderly man limped to the doorway, looking like he was held together by tangled wire coat-hangers. He stood protectively close to Hélène and glared at Simon. 'Who are you? What's going on?'

Simon's bewilderment took an unsettling turn. 'I – Where's Octave, Hélène?'

Hélène's thin shoulders shook as she gave a sob.

The Englishman put his arm around her. 'I don't know who you are, but we don't want any trouble. Please, just leave.'

He began to close the door, and Simon was too confused to stop him, but Hélène forestalled him.

'No, wait, Clive. I want to know – please, how do you know of Octave?'

Simon paused. His gaze flitted between Hélène and this strange Englishman, Clive. Simon did have the right house, didn't he? He looked around. It was certainly tidier than yesterday. They'd obviously done some maintenance since he and Nick had visited. Christ, it had only been a day. Octave hadn't been lying when he said they were busy. Maybe he'd wanted them to leave so he could crack on with sprucing the place up. He'd certainly got the job done quickly. He must have hired some help.

'We met him. Yesterday,' said Simon slowly.

Hélène shook her head, and her shoulders drooped. 'I'm sorry – Simon, is it? You could not have met my brother yesterday. Octave has been dead for many, many years.'

A cold shiver ran up Simon's spine. 'Dead? But...'

'Octave was killed in the war,' explained Clive.

'But...' Simon's brain felt like it had jammed on that one word.

'He angered a German officer and they shot him,' said Hélène. 'He was just a boy, just trying to protect his mother.'

'But...'

Hélène sniffed into a handkerchief then pulled herself together. 'I'm sorry, you are obviously confusing us with someone else. Clive, please.' She gestured to the door, and, before Simon could protest, it closed in his face.

He stood, shell-shocked for a long moment, staring at the shiny brass knocker. That was senility at its most bizarre. But who was that? That was definitely not the man he and Nick had met yesterday. That man had been French. His name had been Octave. He hadn't been dead for seventy-odd years. He'd been very much alive! And this Clive character? Who the hell was he? The name caught in Simon's memory. He'd heard that name before. The airman that the Gromaires had hid; yes! Hélène had told them how she'd fallen in love with him. But she'd also said he'd been captured by the Nazis. Had he survived? He must have if that was the same guy. But even so, where was Octave?

Simon backed away from the door. A prickling of unease swept over him. There was something very odd going on. Maybe the shock of finding Nick with Amanda this morning was causing him to have some sort of weird seizure. His gaze swept across the façade of the house. Yes, it did look brighter than yesterday. The paint wasn't peeling, and the shutters hung tight to their hinges, but there was still a bit of wear and tear to it. It had been painted recently but certainly not since yesterday.

Simon stumbled back down the weedless path to the car and shut himself in. He clung to the steering wheel, trying to catch his breath. He pulled out his inhaler, dropping Catherine's photo, and took a couple of ineffectual puffs. Shit, he was nearly out. He snatched up the printout again and tried to fashion a paper bag out of it to breathe into. After a couple of minutes, his airways began to relax and he felt the tightness drift away from his chest. He flattened the paper against the steering wheel.

'What the hell's going on, Catherine?'

And it was only then that he noticed the caption beneath the new photo no longer read '...*detained on the 22nd of May, 1940 by Sturmbannführer Heinrich Schneider*' but '...*captured during the Vél' d'Hiv Roundup in Paris in July 1942. Later executed at Auschwitz.*'

11

Amiens, France – Wednesday, 10ᵗʰ August, 2016

Nick was in the hotel lobby grilling the maître d' about his step-brother's last known movements when Simon himself appeared through the glass doors, looking flustered.

'Simon! Where've you been? I've left a dozen messages on your phone.'

Simon grasped his arm. His eyes were wild and panicked. 'We need to talk.'

Nick was again filled with guilt. He had done this. But at least, thank God, Simon was here and not strung up by his neck or floating in the Somme. 'I know. I'm sorry about this morning. It wasn't what you think.'

Simon shook his head. 'Forget about it… for now, at least.'

'I was simply showing Amanda for what she is: a gold-digging tart.'

Simon's eyes flashed, momentarily distracted. 'She's not a gold-digger or a tart.'

God, when would he see sense? 'Okay, if you think so—'

'That's not important right now,' Simon interrupted. He glanced over at M. Fourrier who was tactfully going about his business but so obviously eavesdropping on their conversation. 'Can we go somewhere private?'

'Yeah, yeah. Sure.' Anything to placate him. 'You want a drink? You look like you need one.'

Simon nodded. 'I think so too.'

'Come.' And Nick led him to the stairs that led down into the basement restaurant-bar.

* * *

With two cold bitters in front of them, Nick and Simon sat in the deserted room. Simon was already halfway through his by the time Nick had taken a first sip. Perhaps alcohol wasn't the best idea, after all.

'Are you okay?' he asked. 'You seem a little... agitated. I'm sorry about–'

'Things have changed,' Simon said, wiping his mouth with the back of his hand.

Nick nodded, unable to make eye contact. Shit. His grandfather would kill him if Simon decided to quit the study. He'd want to know why, and then there'd be a whole load more aggro to deal with. 'I know, but it was a one-off. It won't happen again.'

'Not that. *Other* things. I went to see the Gromaires–'

'The Gromaires?' echoed Nick in surprise. They were the last people on earth he'd think to see after this morning. 'What for?'

'I was heading back to Paris,' said Simon with a dismissive wave of his hand. 'I was going to catch the Eurostar back home, but I ended up in Beauvais.'

'Look, Simon, we can work things out. I promise.' The reality of losing the documentary's hypnotist sent dread plunging to Nick's feet.

Simon didn't appear to hear him. His eyes were glassy as he stared at Nick. 'But when I got there... It was all... *different.*'

'Different how?'

'Everything! Hélène didn't know who the hell I was.'

'Well, come on. She's probably got Alzheimer's or something. She must be at least eighty.'

'That's what I thought at first, but it wasn't just that.' Simon leaned forward, his hands cupping his pint glass. 'I mean she didn't look as... *decrepit* as yesterday. You know? Old, sure, but her hair, her clothes, she wasn't using her cane.'

Simon looked at him expectantly, as if he should show some sense of shared disbelief. No matter how hard he tried, Nick didn't see the relevance.

'So, she was having a bad day yesterday?' he suggested. 'Simon, look, you're upset—'

'And the house! Jesus, the house! It wasn't falling to pieces like it was yesterday. It was all painted and the garden was all tidy and – and maintained.'

'So she and Octave had a gardener round.'

'Jesus! Will you listen to me? Just for a second!' Simon banged the table, making their beers jump. 'Octave wasn't there! He was…' He paused, looking wildly off into the distance. 'He was *gone*.'

Nick tried to keep the patronising tone out of his voice. It was all he could do not to pat his step-brother's hand. 'People go out, Simon. It's not that unusual.'

'Not gone out. Gone as in dead!'

That did startle Nick. 'Shit. Octave's dead?' He leaned back in his chair and ran his fingers through his hair. 'Bloody hell. He looked all right yesterday. Old, of course, but not exactly at death's door.'

'No. Dead as in dead for seventy-odd years,' hissed Simon. 'During the war. She said he'd pissed off some German officer and got himself shot.'

Nick considered him for a moment. Obviously, he'd had a shock this morning, and it hadn't helped that some mad old woman was spinning tales about her brother and upsetting Simon even more. 'Simon, she's obviously got dementia. Octave isn't dead. We saw him yesterday. Come on.'

'And there was a man there. An English guy called Clive. And there were pictures on the walls of planes, of Spitfires and stuff. Don't you remember? Don't you remember Hélène told us about that RAF pilot that her family hid? The one she fell in love with? His name was Clive!'

Nick's sympathy was wearing thin. Simon was taking things too far. For God's sake, all he'd done was sleep with Amanda, and now Simon was acting like a madman. 'Look, none of this is making much sense,' he said quietly. 'You're upset. You're confused—'

'I'm not confused… fuck! I know what I saw! And look at this…' Simon scrambled in his pocket and withdrew a folded piece of paper. He laid it out on the table, smoothing it out flat, turning it so Nick could read it. 'I printed out a new one at the library last night after – after the other one got ruined. Look at the caption!' He jabbed the paper with his finger.

Nick stifled a sigh. It was the picture of Catherine Jacquot. Christ, Simon really was getting unhinged about this girl.

'See?' Simon said. 'The original said she'd been detained by that Gestapo guy Schneider, but this one… this one says she was captured two years later and sent to Auschwitz.'

Nick remembered something vaguely along those lines. He remembered she'd been arrested by Sturmbannführer Schneider, but he hadn't committed everything to memory, unlike Simon who obviously had. He shrugged. 'So, they updated their website.'

'Don't you think it's a bit of a coincidence? First, Hélène Gromaire appears to be living a completely different life, and then Catherine's fate changes…' Simon's words faded, and he looked about helplessly.

Unease replaced the guilt inside Nick. Amanda was right. Simon was not well. 'What are you saying?' he said carefully.

'I don't know.' Simon sighed. 'I don't understand it either. But maybe…' He hesitated, and his eyes swam with uncertainty. '…I don't know, Nick. Maybe we changed things somehow… *when I yelled at Catherine to run.*'

A silence fell between them. This was more serious than Nick had imagined. Simon had always been emotional, could be a bit overdramatic when he was upset, but this was verging on straitjacket material. Now, not only would his grandfather kill him for ruining the study, but Olivia would kill him for sending her only son over the edge. He cleared his throat uncomfortably. He wasn't sure how one dealt with this sort of situation.

'You, um – you mean, *changed history*?' he said. Just to be sure. Just in case Simon meant something else, that he wasn't suggesting the impossible.

Simon's arms fell limp by his sides and he slumped in his chair. 'I don't know. I guess so.'

Riiiiight. 'Simon, listen to yourself,' Nick said as gently as he could. 'Just for a minute. Listen to what you're saying. Changing history? That's crazy talk. You can't change history.'

'I'm not crazy!' said Simon, sounding exactly that. 'I know what I saw. I'll take you to the Gromaires.'

'Come on. You're upset. It's understandable. You've been under a lot of stress lately. The shop, money, now this with Amanda. Go have a rest. We'll wrap things up with Amanda's story and we'll go back to London. You can take a break. Don't worry about money. I'll make sure you get paid for the whole–'

'Nick,' Simon said desperately. 'I'm not making this up.'

'I know you're not.' Nick couldn't quite meet his eye. Shit, this was all his fault. He'd turned his step-brother, his best friend, into a headcase. 'You're just… just…'

'We've changed things, Nick.' Simon's eyes bore into his. 'We have to do another session with Amanda. You'll see.'

Actually, that was probably the best idea. Another session with Amanda, and Simon would get this silly notion of changing history out of his head. 'Okay, okay. We'll do that. Just go rest for now, all right?'

Simon shook his head, bewildered and beaten. He got up and walked out of the bar. Nick sat back and blew out his breath. Christ Almighty. It was in the genes. It had to be. Simon's father had also been emotionally unstable. Simon was the same. Admittedly, he'd never known him this bad. Sure, Simon had had his fair share of upsets in his life, but nothing that had pushed him into this… this… was this a psychotic event? Not even his break-up with Amanda at university had sparked this frenzy of delusion.

Speaking of whom – oh, Christ, she would have a field day when she found out. He wouldn't hear the end of it. Would she agree to another session with Simon acting the way he was? Perhaps he'd best keep it to himself for now, tell Simon to keep it under wraps if that was possible.

He wondered if he should call home, speak to Olivia, but blocked the idea. For all he knew this could blow over by tomorrow. Once they'd done another session with Amanda and seen how Sturmbannführer Schneider arrested Catherine, Simon would calm down and stop going on about this nonsense of changing history. Changing history! Maybe in a few years' time they'd laugh about this. Right now, Nick had never felt less like laughing in his life.

He got up and walked over to the bar to pay. He still had to settle last night's bar bill, although that last bottle of red had been on the house, he suddenly remembered. Wow, that had been some night. For all her faults, Amanda was a terrific lay.

'Pardon, monsieur. Your card is not accepted.'

'You take Visa, don't you?'

The barman nodded and tried again. He shrugged and gave the card back to him. Nick pursed his lips. All he needed now was for his bank card to stop working. He slipped a couple of Euro notes out of his wallet and handed them over.

'Keep the change.'

Simon was engrossed in quantum physics and brainwave research on his laptop when he was interrupted by a knock on his door. It was Nick. Early for once.

'I wanted to get here before Amanda,' Nick said abruptly before he could say anything. 'Do *not* go shooting your mouth off about this to her or we'll end up with her packing everything in and ruining the work we've already done. It was all I could do to convince her to come this afternoon.'

Simon closed the door behind Nick and leaned against it. 'I've been doing some homework, some research, and it's not as fanciful as you might think. We *can* change things. We *can* change history. We *can*… save Catherine.'

This wonderful moment of enlightenment was ruined by his mobile ringing. It hadn't stopped all bloody day. He'd presumed all the missed calls had been from Nick, but here he was standing in front of him. He glanced at the screen. It was his mother.

'Get it,' said Nick, looking completely unfazed by the miraculousness of what they'd discovered. 'We have time.'

'No. Not–'

'Get it.'

'I'll call her later.'

'Simon!'

Nick was being unusually severe, and Simon hesitated. His phone stopped ringing, but a few seconds later it beeped to notify him there was a message. He was about to put it back in his pocket when he saw the look on Nick's face. He didn't want to anger him any more than he had already. He needed Nick on side.

Dutifully, he listened to his messages, first the desperate attempts from Nick that morning telling him what he'd seen wasn't what he thought. Simon sent Nick a dark look. What else would it have been? Finally, he reached his mother's message.

'Hello, darling! Just checking in to see how things are going. And to say have a good time at your show. Your father sends his best.'

'He's not my father!' Simon exclaimed and threw the phone at the bed. It bounced like a skipping stone and disappeared between the bed and the bedside table.

Nick looked up in surprise from Simon's laptop where he'd been skim-reading the quantum physics article. He was right. Simon had to calm down. At least on the outside. But what a cheek his mother had. First of all, referring to their documentary as a 'show', like some patronising adult speaking to a child and then to refer to Joe as his father? When was she going to get the message? Joe would never be his father!

'Everything okay?' asked Nick.

Simon composed himself and nodded. 'Just being her usual self.'

Nick pointed to the laptop. 'You gonna tell me what this is all about?'

Simon took a deep breath and ushered him over to the

chaise longue.

Once he had explained as best he could what he'd read online, Simon sat down and waited for Nick's response. For a long moment, all that could be heard was the incessant drumming of rain against the window.

'So, if what you're saying is true and everything is happening "now" then explain how consciousness can exist in two bodies at the same time?' asked Nick, slowly.

'The same way quantum mechanics work. Think of a single light particle being projected at a board of some sort. You punch two holes in the board and the light is seen on the wall behind that through both holes. Two pinpricks of light showing up. The particle hasn't split because the light is of the same brightness as it was before, but it's in two places at the same time.' Again, he paused to gauge Nick's response. It didn't look good. 'I know. I'm not exactly a quantum physicist either, but other scientists have proven that something *can* be in two places at once.'

'Simon—'

'It's pretty mind-bending, I'll admit, but just because we can't quite get our heads round it, doesn't mean it isn't real. The Gromaires have proved that! We've already changed things!'

'No disrespect, but I don't know anything of the sort. For all I know, she's got dementia.'

'Then let's do this session with Amanda and see what happens. I'm telling you, things have changed. We've changed them—'

On cue, there was a knock on the door and Nick got up to answer it.

'Not a word, okay? She already thinks you're batshit crazy.'

Amanda strolled in and gave Simon an innocent smile. 'Okay, Simon?'

Simon was filled once again with the dread he'd felt that morning when he'd seen her necklace in Nick's room. 'All right, Amanda?'

'Let's get this over with, shall we?' said Nick, awkwardly rubbing his hands together.

12

Beauvais, France – Wednesday, 22nd May, 1940

Catherine knelt on the attic floor, watching breathlessly through the floorboards as Sturmbannführer Schneider pulled Agathe to her feet.

'WHERE ARE THEY?'

Octave, sitting so helplessly on the floor, shouted, 'In the attic! She's in the attic!'

Catherine froze. She felt paralysed, literally unable to move, just like she'd been at home when bullets had been flying through the living room window and her father had had to shove her to the floor.

'"She"?' said Schneider, letting Agathe loose and taking a step towards the boy. 'Who is "*she*"?'

A sensation, almost like instinct but more demanding, told her to flee, to *run*. She darted a look at the attic door. Catherine sat back with a start, freed from her paralysis. It would be too late to escape through there. She could already hear Schneider's boots clopping the wooden floor below. He'd catch her before she'd even had time to get down the ladder. Her gaze swept to the open window at the back of the attic. Scrambling to her feet, she tip-toed as hastily as she dared towards it. Outside, the back garden was clear. Birds chattered in the copse of trees that separated the house from the farmyard. A cockerel called, lingering on its last proud note. Pigeons cooed from the open doorway of a ramshackle shed that was partly shrouded by ivy and bushes. An overhanging alder tree dappled its buckling roof with shade. Catherine edged the window wider. It screeched against its rusty frame and she winced.

'She's a Jew!' she heard Octave cry down below.

Catherine didn't wait around to hear the Nazi officer's

response. Her eyes set firmly on the shed, she stepped onto the apple crates that lay beneath and manoeuvred her foot through the open window. The wooden sole of her shoe slipped against the dusty outer ledge, and she scrabbled to keep her balance. The apple crate gave way as she straddled the sill. She shot one last glance back at the hatch where she could hear the ladder being drawn down. She tried to swing her other leg over the frame, but her shoe caught in the crate. She clutched the sill to stop herself from falling. She tried to wriggle her foot free, but her awkward position on the ledge made mobility impossible.

Heavy footfalls ascended the ladder and dust rose in disarray above the hatch as it was forced open towards the opposite end of the attic.

Panic lent her strength, and, with a last desperate kick, her shoe broke free from its vice, and she swung her leg over the ledge and jumped.

The ground seemed so terribly far down. She landed with an unceremonious thud. White hot pain shot through her feet and legs, and she tumbled forward onto her face, scraping the skin from her nose and cheek on the dusty baked ground. Her adrenalin was so fierce she barely felt it. She was on her feet in an instant. She ran as fast as her legs would carry her towards the shed, the image of the German officer standing at the window and taking aim with his pistol branding her mind's eye.

A soldier appeared around the corner of the farmhouse, the sun's reflection glancing off his grey *Stahlhelm* and rifle in his hands. Catherine wouldn't make the shed. Instead, she dived amongst the tangled ivy and thorny bushes alongside it and ducked down into their shade.

One eye on the patrolling soldier, she watched shadows moving beyond the attic window. Schneider's raised voice drifted over to her.

'I do not like liars!'

The soldier stopped briefly to listen. He shook his head, chuckling to himself, and lit a cigarette. He flicked the match, and it landed a couple of feet from Catherine. She couldn't take her eyes off the smouldering black stick as the soldier stepped into the shed beside her, causing a flurry of flapping wings and indignant cooing from its residents.

She cast a quick glance around. She couldn't run. He would be out in a moment and would certainly see her, yet, if he came any closer, he would see her anyway. Catherine was not so much torn as shredded by indecision. She would have to make a run for it and risk the soldier shooting at her. But where would she go? She didn't know what was beyond the outbuildings, certainly no cover. Just fields.

She couldn't run. She would surely die. She crouched closer to the ground, hugging her knees, barely daring to breathe. The soldier exited the shed, stepped closer, the crackle of dry grass beneath his boots loud in Catherine's ears. The faint acrid tang of tobacco smoke drifted over to her. The soldier coughed and spat. Catherine closed her eyes. She knew she must be seen. She would have to try to fight him; it was her only chance of escape.

Suddenly the sharp crack of a gunshot echoed around the yard. She ducked, certain the soldier had spotted her and taken fire. But it was followed by Agathe's screams, blood-curdling wails that chilled Catherine's bones.

'Octave! Octave! Oh, my Octave! My boy! Why? Why? He wasn't lying! She was here! She was here!'

Taken by surprise, the soldier hurried around the corner of the farmhouse to the front. Putrid dread obliterated Catherine's relief, plunging through her body as she realised what had happened. The officer had shot Octave for telling 'lies'. Octave was dead because of her, just like Duras. She couldn't stop trembling. The reality of the Germans' ruthlessness was overwhelming. There would be no reasoning with them, no mercy. All she knew was that she would surely be next; that she must get as far away and as quickly as possible if her fate were to be any different to Octave's.

Like a fawn startled into flight by the scent of a predator, Catherine sprung away from the bushes and sprinted away from the farmhouse.

13

Amiens, France – Wednesday, 10ʰ August, 2016

Simon held Nick's gaze as he brought Amanda out of hypnosis. It had gone just as he'd expected it to, but nonetheless he couldn't help mirroring his step-brother's look of disbelief. They really *had* changed things.

'Do you believe me now?' he said.

Amanda sat up, squinting her eyes against the light. 'Believe what?'

'Simon–'

'We've changed Catherine's fate.'

He tried to ignore Nick rolling his eyes; concentrated on Amanda. She was the one whom he needed to convince. She was their gateway to the past and Catherine's life and death.

Amanda stared at him, wide-eyed then raised her eyebrows at Nick. 'Oh. My. Fucking. God. Is he actually serious?'

They both rushed to quell her utter rejection of Simon's sanity.

'He's just confused. He's not–'

'No, I'm not confused, dammit! Stop treating me like a lunatic! I've told you what happened with Hélène. You refused to believe me then, so I said I'd prove it to you at the next session; and I have.'

'What is he talking about?' Amanda demanded. 'What happened with Hélène?'

'Nick and I went to see Hélène and Octave Gromaire yesterday–'

'But–'

'Exactly. But Octave is dead,' said Simon. 'You can vouch for that, Amanda?'

Amanda pursed her lips, unwilling to commit to anything.

'Nick? Did we or did we not speak to Octave yesterday?' said Simon. 'We've got it on film if your memory needs jogging.'

Nick sighed. 'Yes. Okay. We did. But what we've just heard – what you've just seen, Amanda – it doesn't confirm anything. For all we know, Octave was only injured.'

Simon ignored him; turned his attention to Amanda. 'So, I went to see Hélène again this morning after – well, anyway, I went to see her. And not only did she not know who the hell I was, but she claimed Octave had been killed after, and I quote, "he angered a German officer during the war".'

Amanda stared at him, not in ridicule, but in amazement. 'So, what are you saying?'

Nick sighed. 'Simon, don't, please. Just–'

'I'm saying we've changed things. When I yelled at Catherine to run, it sounds to me like she did–'

'Understandable in the circumstances, don't you think?' said Nick. 'She would have run anyway.'

'But she wasn't going to,' said Amanda. She looked at them, agape. 'She was paralysed with fear. She was going to sit there and let that Schneider guy take her. But this time, suddenly I felt… I don't know, I felt this – this overwhelming urge to get away; to *run*.'

Simon couldn't stop a grin spreading across his face. At last! Someone, and Amanda at that, believed him. She was the one who usually called him crazy, yet she was the one believing this crazy theory. 'You see! You believe me, don't you? See Nick?'

'Amanda, come on,' drawled Nick, trawling his fingers through his blond hair. 'We're talking about *changing history* here. *Time travel*. This isn't some sci-fi movie we're making.'

'Then how?' said Amanda.

Simon took a deep breath. 'Okay, bear with me. I'm not a quantum physicist, but, from what I can gather, the faster something travels the slower time moves, like a clock on a jet plane will go slower than one sitting on your mantelpiece. So if you go even faster, much *much* faster, time doesn't just slow, it takes on a negative value. It starts going *backwards*. Brainwaves work on a bunch of different frequencies and speeds depending on our state of consciousness, but something happens during past life regression that makes it speed up to something called sigma, faster than the speed of light... *fast enough to turn time backwards*. We are not time-travelling per se. Not physically. But we *are* accessing Catherine's version of "now" simply by hitching a ride on your Sigma brain waves.' He finished breathlessly and had to snatch up his inhaler.

Amanda looked bewildered. Simon didn't know whether it was because she couldn't believe how stunning the truth was or whether she thought he belonged in a straitjacket.

'And look here.' He scrabbled for his photo of Catherine and shoved it towards his new unlikely ally. 'When I printed this out originally, it said she'd been caught by Schneider on the 22nd of May, 1940. Now it says she died at Auschwitz.'

'Holy shit,' she murmured.

'If we've changed this much, we could change things again. We could save her!'

Amanda stopped. She regarded Simon from beneath heavy lids. 'You want to save her?'

'Yes. Think about it. We've been given this – this power. We *have* to use it to save her! We can't just let her die.'

'Oh yes, we fucking can,' she said, still looking agog.

Simon pulled up short. 'What?'

'You want to save her? Seriously? Have you even thought this through? What do you think would happen to me if you swooped in and saved Catherine's life? If she lives, I might not be born at all!'

Simon was speechless for a moment. No, he hadn't thought about that element.

'If a soul can only live in one body at a time and Catherine lives a long and happy life, then that soul isn't going to hop into my body in time for me to be born, is it?' Amanda went on.

Simon frowned. He'd been too busy trying to prove to Nick that they had changed events that had happened seventy-six years ago to think about such a dilemma. 'What would the odds

be of it interfering? Really? Catherine would have to live to…'
He paused to do a quick calculation in his head.

'Seventy-one,' said Nick helpfully.

Okay, that wasn't terribly old, but still… 'People didn't always live to the age they do nowadays,' he said.

'Simon!' Amanda jumped to her feet. 'She didn't live in the Dark Ages. This is *my life* we're talking about here.'

'And Catherine's,' countered Simon. 'And right now, she's gone from plain old AWOL to being a Holocaust victim.'

'Well, shit!' screamed Amanda. 'That's tough luck for her, but it's already happened. I'm here – I'm *now*. And you are *not* going to risk my life for some stranger who lived seventy-odd years ago.'

'Actually, what we've just proven is that it hasn't already happened.' Simon pulled an anguished face. He knew what he was saying required a significant leap of faith. 'You're *now*… but so is she. Kind of.'

Amanda's nostrils flared as she sucked in her breath. 'You do whatever the hell you want, but you are not playing Russian Roulette with my life.' She turned to Nick and sliced a finger across her throat. 'I'm out.'

Simon and Nick jumped to their feet in unison as she marched to the door. 'Wait, Amanda!'

Amanda yanked open the door and turned back to them. 'Tell your granddad thanks for the holiday. It's been a blast. I'll find my own way home.'

She slammed the door behind her, leaving Simon and Nick alone, with just the sound of rain drumming on the window.

Nick glared at him. 'Now look what you've done!'

'Me? What was I supposed to do? Just let the fact that we have changed history slide by?'

'Will you stop saying that?' snapped Nick. 'You sound like a bloody fruit loop the way you keep going on about "changing history". I don't know what's happened. But somewhere along the line there has been a breakdown in communication. And there is a rational explanation for all of this. It is not possible to change history, Simon!'

Simon glared back, his fists clenched at his sides. He'd never wanted to punch some sense into Nick more than he did right now.

'It is. And we have,' he said through gritted teeth. 'And now we have the opportunity to save somebody. And not just from any old death. From Auschwitz. Who knows what her fate had been before we interfered, but now she's going to the gas chambers. We have an obligation to fix things.'

'Oh-whoa-whoa. *We* didn't do anything. That was all you, buddy. And if some poor girl has suffered because of it then it's on your head. Not mine; not Amanda's; yours.'

'But, Nick… Come on. Don't do this to me. Don't leave me with this as well.' Simon suddenly felt near tears. 'I can't let this happen… not again. *Please.*'

For a moment he thought Nick was going to relent, but then he growled and marched to the door. 'Right now, I'm going to try to calm Amanda down. Otherwise, this whole documentary is going down the plughole. Do you know how much this little trip to France is costing the company?'

Simon shook his head, ashamed. He hadn't thought of the expense at all. The Taylors had so much money anyway, he doubted they'd even notice it.

'You,' Nick said, pointing at him, 'stay right here. We are going to fix this, and we are going to fix this documentary. I'm going to try to patch things up with Amanda.'

'Like you did yesterday?' Simon couldn't keep the bitterness out of his voice. 'Are you going to sleep with her again, Nick?'

Nick drew in a deep breath and said in a low, steady voice, 'I wouldn't have to if you didn't keep fucking things up.'

'We don't need her,' Simon heard himself say. 'We don't need Amanda to save Catherine.'

'What are you talking about?'

'Daniel Barrow. You can put me under. We can influence Daniel's movements. Send him to France. He can save Catherine for us.'

Nick stared at him in disbelief. 'You're seriously off your rocker.'

'But how can we just let things be when we have this *power*?'

'This "power" is about as real as a Philip K. Dick story, okay? Besides, even if it was real, and even if I did agree to go behind Amanda's back and help you influence this Daniel Barrow character, I'm not a hypnotist. I wouldn't be able to put you under.'

'It's not as difficult as you think. You've seen me do it a dozen times.' Simon paused at Nick's resolute expression. He had an idea. He hurried over to his bedside table and withdrew a box of pills. He shook it triumphantly at Nick. 'My chill pills. Even if you're the worst hypnotist in the world – which you won't be – then these will help. I've used them before when I've gone under by myself.'

'Maybe you ought to have one of those now. Take a look at yourself in the mirror. You look like you need it.' Nick turned on his heel and slammed the door behind him.

Simon sighed. He sank into his chair and laid his face in his hands. He didn't want to look in the mirror. He could imagine what he must look like and how he must sound simply by the expression on Nick's face. But that didn't mean he was insane. It just meant that he was desperate. He couldn't leave Catherine stranded like this. He just couldn't. He considered the box of pills scrunched in his hand. He could put himself under, could tap into Daniel by himself, but knowing what Daniel was like, it wouldn't be enough. He needed someone to manipulate Daniel from the 'surface'. He needed Nick's help to save Catherine.

Nick knocked on Amanda's door, and it drifted open. Amanda was stuffing her belongings into her suitcase.

'Hey,' he said. 'Where're you going?'

'Home. I'm done, Nick. For real this time,' she said, not looking up from her furious packing.

Nick caught sight of the minibar left open and a half empty wine bottle on the dressing table. 'I know,' he said, walking over to close the fridge.

Amanda grappled with her hair dryer cord and tried to pull it free from her straighteners. 'He's gone too far this time. I don't know if he's crazy or what, but I'm not sticking around to find out.'

Nick stepped in and helped detangle them. 'Slow down,' he said. 'You don't have to leave right now.'

'Yes, I do.'

'What are you going to do? By the time you get a car or a train to Paris, buy a ticket on the Eurostar, it'll be too late. You'll end up having to fork out for some overpriced hotel in Paris and having to wait till tomorrow. Just stay here. I'll drive you personally to Paris tomorrow and buy your ticket home.' That would at least give him a bit of time to calm her down and change her mind.

Amanda tugged on her case's zippers but it was too full and it caught on a blouse hanging out the side. Nick placed a calming hand over hers. 'Just wait until morning.'

'I'm not going to change my mind, Nick. I'm not going to let him risk my life a second time.'

'Come on. Yesterday's session wasn't that bad.'

She turned to him, her eyes sparkling with fury. 'I'm not talking about yesterday. I'm talking about before.'

'Before when?'

Amanda hesitated. 'Back in our first year at uni. I… He's just dangerous, okay?'

'What did he do to you last time?'

'It's none of your business,' Amanda muttered, unpacking then repacking her case.

'Did he threaten you? I can't imagine Simon ever deliberately being violent towards you.'

Amanda gave up on her case and sighed. 'Fine! If you must know, I was pregnant and… and I lost it, and I nearly lost my life with it.'

Nick stared at her in shock. Whatever he'd been expecting to come out of her mouth, it hadn't been that. 'Christ, Amanda.

I'm sorry. I had no idea.'

'It's not exactly the sort of thing you go around telling everyone.'

'Simon never told me.'

She gave him a withering look. 'Simon doesn't know. No one does. And don't you dare tell him either. It's done, it's past.'

Nick shook his head. Telling Simon that Amanda had lost his baby would likely send him over the edge. But Nick also knew that this was definitely the final straw for Amanda. He wasn't going to change her mind. His thoughts returned to the documentary. What a cluster-fuck. 'Do you – er – do you want to talk about it?'

Amanda rolled her eyes and resumed squashing down her clothes into the suitcase. 'No, for God's sake. Just pretend I never told you.'

He nodded quickly. He didn't much fancy counselling Amanda. What would he say? 'Okay. I won't say anything. But–' He was suddenly filled with compassion for what she had gone through with Simon '– just stick around for tonight. I'll keep Simon out of your way, and I'll drive you to Paris first thing. Simon and I might as well pack up too.'

'I'm not travelling with him.'

'That's fine. We'll take two cars. And he can sit in a different carriage on the train.'

Amanda stopped with a deflated sigh. 'Fine.'

'I'll treat you to dinner tonight, what do you say? Get away from the hotel buffet, try a bistro over by the river?'

Amanda sniffed. 'Okay.'

'I'll meet you in the lobby at seven.'

Back in his own room, Nick lay on the bed and stared up at the ceiling. What a God-bollocking cock-up. It had all been going so well until Simon had decided to go all *Twilight Zone* on them. Now he would have to tell Joe that it had all fallen through. He'd say Amanda's former life hadn't checked out. He couldn't tell him the truth – his grandfather would be contemptuous enough at his failure without the added bonus of Simon having a nervous breakdown, which of course he would be blamed for. Was Simon the crazy one or was he? Nick had to concede there was evidence to suggest they'd changed things, but there had to be a rational explanation. There had to be. This sort of thing just wasn't possible. He took out his phone and dialled his grandfather's mobile number.

'*The number you have called is invalid,*' came the automated response.

Nick checked it again. Maybe it was because he was calling from France; maybe it hadn't included the British country code.

'*The number you have called is invalid.*'

'Christ's sake,' muttered Nick. He scrolled through his contacts looking for Taylor Made Television's main office number, but he couldn't find it. He must have deleted it at some stage by mistake or after some argument with Joe. He leaned across his bed to get his laptop and logged on. He opened up the web browser and searched for Taylor Made Television's website. It returned over 150,000 results – Taylor Made Golf, Taylor Made Menswear, Taylor Made Music… but no Taylor Made Television. Nick frowned at the screen. A horrible feeling of unease crept over him. Too much had been out of his control today. He didn't like it. Where the hell was his grandfather's website?

He shut his laptop. Joe would find out soon enough when they arrived back in London tomorrow. Nick got a drink out of the minibar and sat by the window, watching the sun struggling to break through the thunderclouds as it descended behind Cathédrale Notre-Dame d'Amiens. He glanced at the dog-eared leather journals on the coffee table and gave a mirthless huff. Fat lot of good those had done.

Nick suddenly sat up. He knew exactly how to prove Simon was off his trolley. He grabbed the top journal and flicked through the yellowing pages to the 22nd of May, 1940. He read it again.

And again.

This wasn't right. He knew his German was rusty at the best of times, but this entry was completely different to what it had been before. This was… *changed*.

Nick stared into space, the cogs in his brain spinning. The pieces, ludicrous as they may be, began to drop into place – Simon's interference, Hélène and Octave Gromaire, the Fleur de l'Alexandrie vanishing from the Costas, the age-old stories that had been passed down through the Taylor family of how his great-grandfather had got his big break… Nick suddenly felt icy cold as he remembered how his bankcard had been rejected at the bar. He flew to his laptop, letting the journal topple to the floor, and logged into his bank account. After two false starts, his current account page finally loaded.

Blood drained from his face and black fog pulsed behind his eyes in time with his thudding heart.

'No,' he whispered. His head swam. He couldn't believe what he was seeing. 'Jesus Christ, Simon. What have you done?'

Nick had almost exhausted his minibar when there was a knock on the door. He ignored it, slumped in his chair by the window in the gathering darkness, numb with shock and vodka. The knock came again.

'Go 'way!'

'I thought you were buying me dinner?' Amanda's voice came through the door.

Nick groaned and got to his feet. The room tilted violently, and he fell against the chaise longue, kicking the journals under the table.

'Nick!'

'Coming.'

He switched on the light and opened the door to a very annoyed Amanda.

'Did you forget?' she demanded. 'My God, you stink of booze. What are you doing?'

Nick closed the door after her and propped himself up against it. 'Just… thinking.'

'You're sloshed.'

'Simon's right.'

'Here we go again.'

'I'm serious. We *have* changed things.' Nick pushed himself upright and stumbled back to his chair by the window. 'And we need to change them back.'

'Why?'

'Because by telling Catherine to run from the Gromaires, Taylor Made Television no longer exists, and I'm ten grand in debt.'

'You're joking.'

'Nope. All gone.'

'But how? What did Catherine have to do with your family?'

'You wouldn't believe me if I told you.'

Amanda sat down and folded her arms. 'Try me.'

Nick took a deep breath and felt ever so slightly queasy. 'Heinrich Schneider is my great-grandfather.'

Amanda stared then slowly, 'Shut the fuck up.'

Nick nodded sagely. 'Yep. He's Joe's father.'

'But your name's Taylor. You're English!'

'It hasn't always been that way.' Nick played with a loose thread on the chair's arm. He'd never told anyone about his heritage. No one wanted to know his great-grandfather had been a Nazi officer. 'Heinrich immigrated after the war; first to Italy, then to Britain. Anglicised Schneider to Taylor to avoid the stigma. Started Taylor Made Television. Or rather that was what was supposed to have happened.'

Amanda looked puzzled. 'But it must still have happened. You're here. You're Nick Taylor, presumably, aren't you?'

'He must still have immigrated, but Taylor Made Television didn't happen.' He flicked the thread away dispassionately. 'All gone.'

'But what would Catherine escaping have had to do with your great-grandfather setting up Taylor Made Television?'

Nick considered her for a long moment. She would probably blow her top when he told her, but right now, who cared? It was all changed, anyway. 'My whole life I've been led to believe that my great-grandfather owned some valuable antique jewellery. He sold it all to some rich Italian guy he knew from his filmmaking days before the war: Roberto Costa. And then he invested the money in the studio once he moved to London.'

'I still don't see the connection with Catherine.'

Nick sighed. 'Simon pulled up an article online the other day about the Fleur de l'Alexandrie's history and how it was valued at something like twenty million dollars, and—'

'Twenty million dollars? Oh my God, Nick!' She groaned. 'Oh, why couldn't it have belonged to me in *this* life?'

'It belongs – or did belong – I don't know which way is up anymore, to be honest – to Bernie Costa.'

'Costa?'

'Yup. We're old family friends. Bernie's mates with Joe. Bernie's father Roberto—'

'—was friends with Heinrich Schneider,' Amanda finished for him. Her mouth fell open. 'The antique jewellery he sold to Costa was the Fleur de l'Alexandrie?' Her expression suddenly changed to indignation. 'He stole it from me? He killed me and stole my necklace? Fucking hell, Nick, your great-grandfather was an asshole.'

'He didn't steal it from *you*. He didn't kill *you*.'

'But still, your family have profited from this ever since.'

'I didn't know, did I?' Nick exclaimed with vodka-fuelled passion. 'We need to change things back to the way they were.'

'How do we do that?'

'My guess is we do exactly what Simon did: put you under, have you relive the day Schneider visited the Gromaires and just manipulate Catherine into staying rather than running.'

'But what if we change things differently? What if Catherine doesn't end up in a death camp? She could survive.'

'She won't. We can make sure of that.'

Still Amanda looked sceptical.

'Come on, Amanda! How would you feel if one day you

woke up and your entire inheritance – your entire fortune – had disappeared?'

'Actually, I know exactly how that feels.'

Amanda swam before Nick's gaze. 'You do?'

Her steely expression softened as she smiled weakly. 'My dad was supposedly this great businessman. We had everything – a big house, racehorses for Mum, ponies for me, holidays abroad. What we didn't realise was that actually he was a crap businessman but a bloody good conman. Everything we thought was ours was paid for with money he'd borrowed, promised to invest, that sort of stuff. Then…' She paused, as if to edit her memories, 'he got found out, and we lost everything. So yes, I do know what it feels like.'

'Then you know you have to help me get it back.' Nick sat forward and clasped her hands in his. Amanda looked sympathetic – for him or for her own misfortune he wasn't sure – but it was a foothold. 'Please, Amanda.'

'What about me?'

Telling her she'd be doing the right thing wouldn't resonate with her. Amanda didn't do selfless. 'You help me get back Taylor Made Television,' he said slowly, 'and when it's mine I'll make you into the leading lady of every single blockbuster show that comes through our doors.'

Amanda's eyes sparkled. 'Can I have that in writing?'

'I'll sign it right now.'

'But what about Simon? He's not going to agree to this.'

Nick hesitated, but only for a second. 'We don't need him. I'll put you under. I've seen him do it dozens of times.'

'You're sure?'

'Of course. I wouldn't suggest it if I wasn't. Let's just go home tomorrow, then you and I can sort something out.'

'But where is home for you, Nick? If Taylor Made Television doesn't exist, I doubt very much whether your Chelsea flat is still there.'

Nick's unsteady plans stumbled to a halt.

'And what about your grandfather? I mean, do you even

know that he still exists?'

'Yeah, he's definitely still around. Simon got a message from Olivia saying they hoped he was having a good time. Simon got all upset about her calling Joe his father instead of his step-father.'

Amanda looked at him in shocked silence. 'Nick, I don't think she was referring to Joe. Do you?'

Nick froze and the drunken cogs in his brain bumbled into action. 'Olivia would never have left John Hayes for Joe if Taylor Made Television and its fortune didn't exist.'

'Therefore John Hayes would never have committed suicide.'

Nick gulped. 'Shit. Simon's dad is alive.' He staggered to his feet and headed for the door. He had to tell Simon.

Amanda dragged him back. 'You can't tell him, you fool,' she hissed. 'You go tell Simon that his dad is still alive, and he won't want to change anything.'

'Why not?'

'How did his father die?'

'He gassed himself in the car.'

'Do you not see a trend developing here? John Hayes dying in his own gas chamber and now Catherine going to Auschwitz? Simon once told me he blamed himself for his father's death. He'd been out playing football. When he got back, his father was dead. He thought if he'd been home he could have stopped him.'

'But that's ridiculous.'

'Try telling Simon that. Now, his intervention has sent Catherine to the gas chambers, and he sees saving her as some sort of redemption for not saving his father.'

'But if his dad's still alive—'

'He doesn't have to save Catherine. And he'll do everything in his power to keep things the way they are.'

'But...' Nick was torn. By changing things back to how they were – to get back the Taylor family fortune – Simon would lose his dad all over again. 'He's going to find out anyway when we go home tomorrow.'

'Then we don't go. We stay right here. We keep Simon here. Just until we reroute history to the way it should be.'

Nick thought of how close they'd already come to Simon finding out. 'We'd have to get rid of his phone.'

'How do we get him to stay? The way we left things – there was no coming back from that. He'll know something's up if we decide to stick around. Do you think I should seduce him?'

'What? No! Don't, please.' Nick felt guilty enough for scheming behind Simon's back without sending him straight to the asylum for being toyed with by Amanda. He thought for a moment. Sight-seeing. Exhibitions. What else could he persuade Simon to stay in Amiens for? Maybe he could persuade him that because they'd paid until the following Wednesday, they had to stay until then. No. Simon might be a little unhinged, but he wasn't stupid. Nick had a gig on Sunday! He could say they had to stay for that. Well, Nick had to. Simon didn't. Suddenly he had a flash of genius. 'Daniel Barrow!'

'Who?'

'Daniel Barrow. Simon's former life, or so he says. None of his details ever checked out. Simon wanted to save Catherine by influencing Daniel's movements–'

'He was going to go behind my back?' cried Amanda.

'Well, he couldn't have done it alone. He asked me to help. He needs me to help, to – I don't know – influence, manipulate, "speak" to Daniel through him while he's under hypnosis.'

'So, what, you're going to keep Simon here by promising to regress him?'

'I'll humour him. Even if Daniel Barrow does exist, he's English. He's on the other side of the Channel. What sane person is going to go to France when Hitler's about?'

'So, you just make Simon think you're trying to influence Daniel, and that's it?'

Nick paused. His conscience felt bruised with guilt for betraying Simon like this when John Hayes was alive. But what about himself? What about Joe Taylor? For all Nick knew, his grandfather could be dead. How was it fair that John Hayes should live and Joe should die? Nick tried to rouse the indignation and anguish of grief at such a thought, but it wasn't stirring. Perhaps it was the alcohol. He did love his grandfather. Honestly, he did. Most of the time. Sometimes. Occasionally. Either way, regardless of his feelings for his grandfather, it wasn't right. John Hayes was meant to die.

He met Amanda's gaze full-on. 'Yes. I'll lead him round in circles, I'll bemoan Daniel's lack of action right along with him.'

'And why would he believe that? Would he not suspect this about-turn?'

'I'll say I've had a change of heart. That I want to save Catherine.'

'He won't fall for it.' Amanda pursed her lips in thought. Her eyes lit up. 'We can have a very public row. We can call each other all sorts of names. If Simon sees it, then he'll believe your change of heart.'

'Shit, Amanda. You're the actor, not me.'

Amanda glowed. 'I'll do most of the shouting then.'

'Yeah, you do that.' He got up to fix himself another drink and discovered he'd finished the vodka. 'Shit.'

'When are we going to do this?' Amanda's voice rattled with excitement, and Nick just hoped she wouldn't go too over the top and throw something at him or get them kicked out of the hotel.

'Once I've had another drink. How's your minibar looking?'

'Not as depleted as yours.' She recrossed her legs and gave him a sultry smile. 'Care to join me?'

Nick gulped as his groin gave an inadvertent surge of approval. What could it hurt? Simon already knew about the first time. The second time wouldn't be half as gutting, surely.

She got to her feet and walked behind him, trailing her long nails across his neck and shoulders. 'Coming?'

Nick gave an affirmative mumble and followed her out of the room.

14

Amiens, France – Wednesday, 10th August, 2016

Nick rolled over and gave Amanda a luxuriant smile. 'You're fantastic, you know that?'

Amanda didn't return his smile. 'I wish I could return the compliment.'

He gaped in surprise. Nobody had complained before. 'What?'

She tossed off the sheets, got out of bed and slipped her dress over her head. 'I said I wish I could say the same about you.'

Affronted, Nick scrambled out of bed. 'You certainly sounded like you were enjoying yourself.'

'A girl has to hope it'll get better before throwing in the towel, hasn't she?'

'Amanda!' Nick didn't know whether to be upset or angry. 'I thought – I thought–'

'I know. You think you're such hot stuff because of who you are, but the truth is Nick, you're nobody. You're simply riding on the coat-tails of your grandfather. He's the successful one… or was.'

'Well, you're not exactly a woman of action either,' Nick retorted. 'I know what your game is. You're not as good at hiding your little JCB as you'd like to think. Now I haven't got anything to offer you, you're just going to toss me out like old laundry.'

Amanda snatched up his clothes and strode to the door, opened it, and flung out his jeans, shirt, and boxer shorts. 'Go on, get out.'

'Amanda, wait!'

She gave him a surprisingly powerful shove, and Nick, still feeling a little lightheaded from his earlier minibar raid, stumbled out into the corridor.

'You're a spoilt little turd!' she shouted.

'You weren't saying that earlier.' He snatched up his clothes to cover his crotch and looked around uncertainly, feeling suddenly vulnerable in the public corridor.

'I thought you had something more to offer a girl. But I guess I was wrong. Go on, fuck off with your poncey ego and limp dick.'

A woman came out of her room and retreated with a moan of distaste at the sight of Nick's state of undress.

'I'd had a few drinks! What do you expect?'

'A little more than you were able to deliver, clearly.'

More guests' doors were opening as people looked out to see the disturbance. Nick gathered his clothes over his groin more securely.

'You're not as wonderful as you think you are either,' he said.

'Oh really? That's not what you said just a minute ago.'

'Yeah, well, I was trying to be nice, wasn't I? Which is more than you ever are. You treat everyone like goddamn slaves, bemoaning how shit your life is. But you're not prepared to do anything about it yourself!'

'I do plenty! I'm here, aren't I? I'm doing this documentary for you, aren't I? The difference is I've been taking it seriously, while you're just playing at it. You have no idea how hard people work to be given the opportunities that just land in your lap thanks to your grandfather!'

'I didn't ask for this!' Nick shouted back at her. 'I never wanted to work in television. I wanted to be a musician! But TV's the family business, so I'm stuck with it, aren't I?'

'Oh, you poor thing. You're a waste of space and a loser,' Amanda sneered and slammed the door.

He was distracted by the chuntering of guests, now openly staring at the spectacle. And there, down the corridor was Simon, glowering at him with open hostility. His step-brother's eyes bore into his, filled with hate and betrayal. Nick looked away. Once more, in the sober light of day, he knew he had failed him again.

The lift pinged, and a couple stepped out. The woman's hand flew to her mouth in surprise at Nick's presence. The man glared at him beneath hairy grey eyebrows. Nick pressed himself against the wall and sidled down the corridor to his own room, his bottom scraping against the brittle, peeling wallpaper. Getting his keycard out of his jeans pocket was tricky without exposing himself to his audience, but with a gasp of relief he finally let himself in and closed the door behind him. His body was ablaze with anger and indignation at Amanda's rebuttal. How dare she say such things about him? What right did she have to treat him like some lowlife vermin when she had as much to lose as he? And in such a public display of humiliation.

Nick paused. The people. Simon. He and Amanda screaming at each other in the corridor. Was this what she'd intended? Was this all part of her game to convince Simon that he, Nick, was his ally? It had to be. Why else would she turn on him so unprovoked and so dramatically? He couldn't believe she could truthfully be that disappointed with his performance.

He tried to clear his mind of the humiliation and affront. Amanda was smart. Yes, that had to be the public row she'd said they must have. Nick seethed. The least she could have done was give him some warning. On the flip side, it had worked. It had worked so well that even Nick had believed it.

He pulled on his clothes and opened the door. His audience had dispersed. He strode down the empty corridor to Simon's room and knocked.

Simon opened the door. 'What?'

'You still want to save Catherine?'

Simon hesitated then nodded.

Nick pushed past him into the room. 'Then let's get on with this, shall we?'

PART TWO

15

London, England – Saturday, 25th May, 1940

Daniel Barrow stirred in his sleep and opened his eyes. His bedroom was darkened by blackout blinds, but his body clock informed him it must be morning outside. He sat up, the heat of consciousness burning away the mistiness of his dream before he could even remember any of the details. It hadn't been pleasant though, that much he knew. He had felt watched. It was paranoia, it must be. The events of the past few days were obviously weighing on him more than he realised.

He shook off the feeling and rifled through the mess of books, notepads, pens and keys on his bedside table. His fingers closed around a used condom, and he regarded it curiously. He glanced over and could just make out the vague shape of a woman sleeping beside him. Eventually, he found his box of Capstan Navy Cut and slipped one between his lips. Dammit, where was his lighter?

He got up and limped over to a chest of drawers where he always kept a spare. The dancing flame cast a golden glow about the room, and he was finally able to see the woman better.

She lay on her stomach, her bare back curving to a shapely bottom half-covered by the sheets. Blonde, which surprised him. He didn't usually go for blondes. He took a deep satisfying drag of his cigarette and turned to the chest of drawers again to search for his wristwatch. He opened the blackout blind, flooding the bedsit with light.

Modestly-sized, the room was made smaller by the accordion stacks of books piled against the walls and on the tiny counter in the corner – which his landlady considered good enough to pass as a kitchenette – Hemingway, Dickens, Stein, Wilde, and a French language collection of Voltaire's letters.

His watch was sitting atop Trotsky's *The Living Thoughts of Karl Marx*, a handsome silver device that he'd been awarded at his promotion to feature writer last September. He picked it up and held it up to the light.

Daniel's heart dropped. 'Bugger!' Cigarette pinched between his teeth, he pulled on his clothes. He inspected his creased shirt for a micro-second before flinging it away. 'No, no, no.' He dug through his drawers, squinting away from the cigarette smoke stinging his eyes, and pulled out the black shirt he was after.

The blonde turned over and shaded her eyes from the light. 'Daniel, come back to bed.'

'Not this morning...' Damn, he couldn't remember her name – '...sweetheart.'

He hopped about as he pulled on his shoes then snatched his coat from the back of a chair.

The blonde gave him a coquettish smile and patted the mattress next to her. 'Must you go?'

Combing back his oiled, black hair, he looked again at her through the mirror. He was sure it began with a vowel. Anna? Elizabeth? Ingrid? 'I'm late.' He opened the door but paused at the sound of voices on the landing then hastily closed it again.

'*Daniel*,' the blonde whined in what was meant to be a seductive tone.

He ignored her and made for the window. He heaved it open to its maximum height and swung his good leg out. He turned to grin at the blonde, cigarette still clenched between his teeth. 'Let yourself out. If you meet Mrs Reynolds on the way down, tell her I'll have the rent for her by Friday.'

'Wait!'

Daniel slipped out onto the fire escape then leaned back in and winked at her. Eleanor, that was it. 'I'll call you. See you later, Eleanor.'

He was halfway down the ladder when she appeared at the window, sheets bunched around her chest. 'It's Evelyn, you berk!'

* * *

Daniel exited Charing Cross Station and, despite the mildness of the weather, flicked up the collar of his coat. Lethargic cloud, tinged dirty yellow, mouldered over the city, so heavy it was a wonder the sky didn't collapse beneath its weight. He fell into step with a throng of black-shirted men and women marching west along the Strand, chanting 'Free Mosley now! Free Mosley now!'

A young curly-haired Blackshirt passed him a banner and grinned. 'There'll be more of us when we get to the square. You mark my words!'

'So there should be,' Daniel said, raising his voice above the noise.

With their Union Jacks and British Union Party flags held aloft, they emerged from the constraints of the streets into the wide expanse of Trafalgar Square. Waiting for them like the bronze lions that guarded Nelson's Column was a line of mounted police, and bobbies stood with their batons at the ready. Apart from that, there weren't very many other people around, certainly not the numbers of protestors they'd been expecting. Not to be discouraged, the marchers struck up the British Union Party's anthem, and Daniel sang louder to make up for their lack of protestors.

'Comrades, the voices of the dead battalions; Of those who fell that Britain might be great. Join in our song for they still march in spirit with us; And urge us on to gain the Fascist state!'

They faced off against the police, and Daniel found himself pushed nearer the front than he'd anticipated. A solid grey horse flung its heavy head and rolled its eye at him.

'FREE MOSLEY NOW! FREE MOSLEY NOW!'

'Save your breath, you lousy cowards,' shouted one of the policemen.

One ballsy lad stepped forward and raised his arm in a *Sieg Heil* salute. The gesture spooked the horse in front of him, and it flung its head. The policeman astride kicked forward, and the horse plunged over the lad. The tension between the two factions overflowed. From somewhere appeared crates of rotten fruit, vegetables, and flour bombs.

'Here!' The lad next to Daniel thrust two squidgy apples into his hands then pointed at the mounted police. 'Get 'em!'

Daniel hesitated. He didn't want to harm the horses. Instead, he hurled the apples at the foot policemen. The police broke rank and barged into the crowds, batons flying.

Daniel was shoved from behind and sent sprawling to the ground. He tried to climb to his feet, but his bad leg wouldn't hold beneath the shoves and jostling. Down on the ground again, he picked up a broken banner and used it as a crutch. As he straightened up, a bobby came at him, baton raised, yelling like a Hun warrior and eyes as fierce as every one of the foster-fathers of Daniel's youth.

He held up the banner defensively as the baton came down, and he knocked it out of the man's hand. The bobby kept coming though, rugby tackling him around his middle and knocking the air out of his lungs as they landed on the ground. Daniel kicked out, punching, pulling, grappling to free himself. He rolled away, under trampling feet, and scrambled upright.

A horse came plunging through the crowd, knocking everybody out of the way like they were tree saplings, flecks of foam spittling its barrel chest, its solid legs thrusting and rearing forward. It was coming too fast. Daniel didn't have a chance to dive out of the way. All he could do was turn his shoulder into the impact.

It was like being hit by a bus. The clash sent him wheeling, and again he found himself spitting dirt out of his mouth and wiping loose gravel from his palms. He crouched on his knees, wheezing and gasping, desperate to refill his lungs. A wayward boot caught him in the jaw, rattling his teeth and sent him back down.

'Son of a bitch!' he tried to scream, but his words were muffled and deformed. He climbed to his knees again and crawled a couple of paces to pick up a half-squashed rotting cauliflower. He flung it wildly. A bobby lunged at him and brought his baton down on Daniel's shoulder like a samurai swordsman striking the killer blow. Daniel dropped to the ground as pain electrified his arm.

'Right, you piece of shit. No more of this.' The policeman hauled him to his feet and bent his arms behind his back.

Daniel yelled in pain and anger as his wrists were tightly cuffed and he was manhandled out of the mêlée.

Daniel and the curly-haired lad he'd marched alongside were shoved into a damp holding cell beneath Canon Row Police Station. A ginger stubble-jawed man regarded them with bloodshot eyes from the bench that stretched along the one side. Daniel looked around. Not bad, not bad. It was roomier than the ones in Whitechapel. Smelled a bit too much of stale urine for comfort though. Ginger eyed him as Daniel walked to the rear of the cell, unzipped his flies and relieved himself in the bucket. Daniel eyed him back, unfazed, shook himself dry and zipped himself up again. He sat down on the bed, testing its springs. Not as comfy as it looked. Still, better than the cold, damp floor. His arm lay stiff and numb at his side, and he wondered if he'd broken anything. He lay down and watched his fellow protestor pace the cell.

'You're a coupla those Blackshirts, aren't ya?' their ginger cellmate said.

The lad turned an agitated glance at the man. 'What business is it of yours?'

'It's very much my business to know which of my countrymen are rootin' for the enemy.'

Daniel sighed. Here we go again.

'And who exactly is the enemy?' the lad said.

'There ya go!' Ginger clapped his hands on his thighs in triumph. 'Don't even know what bloody side you should be on. Bleedin' fascist. It's about time someone saw sense and locked you buggers up.'

'With you, you mean?' Daniel drawled from his horizontal position.

Ginger glared at him. 'I may not be perfect, but I know what side I should be fightin' on.'

'That's right,' said the lad. 'You're the side that wants to fight.'

'You tellin' me you fascists don't believe in fightin'?'

Daniel considered him for a long moment. He really didn't like the way the man spat out the word 'fascists' as if they were the scum of the earth. Mind, Hitler wasn't doing their reputation much good.

'That's right,' the lad said, approaching Ginger with a swagger that implied just the opposite.

Ginger laughed. 'When I seen your lot doin' "'Eil 'itler" salutes in our streets – in the streets of London – to that smarmy shicer, Mosley; when he's been over in Europe drinkin' Schnapps with the ol' Fuhrer and that bald-'eaded merchant from Italy...'

'Benito Mussolini,' Daniel provided helpfully.

'Yeah, that's 'im! *Il Doochay.* You mean to say your leader's mates with 'em all, and he don't believe in fightin'? 'Ang on! I don't think 'itler was in on that meetin'.'

Daniel suppressed a sigh. He really didn't want to get involved, but it was as Mosley said, you had to explain their ideology to people in a rational way if you were to really get through to them. This lad was all fired up and looking for a fight. He would do their cause no good.

'We don't believe in getting involved in each other's politics or each other's quarrels.' Daniel smiled at the irony. 'With us, it's Britain first. Always Britain first. All Mosley did was try to negotiate peace and save thousands of British lives.'

Ginger snorted, then belched. 'Yeah, mate, you carry on believin' that. Your Mosley don't know the meaning of the word peace.'

'But Chamberlain and Churchill do, yeah?' said the lad. 'You think they wanted peace? Like bloody hell they did. They wanted to fight.'

Ginger growled at him and wobbled to his feet, fists

clenched, but the lad didn't back down.

'First, they said it was to save Poland; now, it's to defeat "Hitlerism", whatever the hell that is. Do you know what Hitlerism is?'

Ginger looked cross-eyed. He hiccupped.

'Exactly,' said the lad. 'They're so keen to get their hands dirty, we don't even have a proper government no more. We have a "war ministry". A bunch of toffee-nosed, trigger-happy suits moving darts on a map, "strategising" how they intend to sacrifice the lives of their own British men. And for what? For a quarrel that had nothing to do with them. So, they locked up the only man who wanted peace and then did the same to us for exercising our right to free speech to protest his illegal detainment.'

Ginger spat at the lad's feet. 'Yeah, right. I saw Cable Street. You really deserve a peacekeepers' medal for that. Bunch of anti-semites, you are.'

Daniel watched from his prostrate position. Ginger and the lad were sizing each other up, and he knew despite the lad's bravado, one well-timed punch from Ginger and the boy would crumble. Daniel shifted on the thin mattress. His shoulder was beginning to throb again.

'We're not anti-semites!' said the lad. 'Hitler is the one who has a problem with the Jews. His reasons are his own; we've no interest in meddling with his political fancies. He wants to produce a country of particular qualities, and if that doesn't include Jewish people, then that's his problem and their problem. It had nothing to do with us until the Jews over here started getting involved. They made it our problem. Cable Street had nothing to do with the fact that they're Jewish. They could have been black, brown, yellow or purple for all we cared. If you're going to start a quarrel on our soil then we have every right to retaliate.'

'And you see nothin' wrong with leaving 'itler to lock up thousands of innocent people in those camps?' Ginger scoffed.

Daniel lifted himself onto his good elbow. 'Can you imagine

if we went around poking our noses into everyone's business like it was our own? If we started a fight with them if their political values didn't agree with ours? We'd never have the time or the resources to deal with our own issues, with progressing the British Empire. You believe in the British Empire, don't you?'

Ginger eyed him like it was a trick question. 'Course I do.'

'Then how is it any different to what Hitler is doing? He's simply expanding the German Empire, staking new territory, building a population of what he considers superior breeding. It's no different to what we've done to much of Africa and Asia.'

'Yeah, but we don't treat them lot like 'itler's treatin' those Jews, do we?'

'My friend, do you think the Germans are the first to use concentration camps?'

Ginger squinted at him. 'Eh?'

'This compassionate and democratic country we call our own,' Daniel went on wryly, 'was using them forty years ago in the Second Boer War.'

'Well, the Boers must've deserved it. Not like those poor Ikes.'

The lad sneered at Ginger. 'You're a prime example of why giving every man the vote's a bad idea.'

Ginger grabbed him by his shirt and lifted him up onto tippy-toes. 'Whadya mean?'

The lad, at last, saw the danger of his position, and paled.

Daniel sighed and hoisted himself up. 'It means idiots like you put idiots like Chamberlain and Churchill in a place of power,' he said. 'If you don't know anything about politics then you shouldn't have a say. I don't tell my mechanic how to fix my car or my doctor how to perform an operation. You'd think a job as important as running the country wouldn't be shelled out to every Tom, Dick and thick-headed Harry to make the decisions.'

Ginger flung the lad aside and took hold of Daniel. 'Is this what you're after, you stinkin' Blackshirts? Yeah? You preach the word of peace but go round causin' fights.'

Daniel sent the lad a sidelong look of annoyance.

Ginger took his silence as admission of guilt, and his jeering took on a more brazen quality. 'Piece of Kraut-lovin', good-for-nothin' dog shit.'

Daniel felt like he'd been winded. Instead of the slobbering ginger-haired man in front of him, he saw his first foster-father standing over him, small eyes the colour of sewage, thin lips twisted in disgust. *'Piece of dog-shitting good-for-nothing frog spawn.'*

Instinctively, Daniel head-butted Ginger. The man staggered back, clutching his nose then charged forward wielding his fist. Daniel ducked and Ginger smashed his knuckles into the iron bars.

Ginger roared in agony.

The lad cheered.

Daniel glowered at them both. He jerked his head at the lad sitting on his bed. 'Get off.'

The lad scampered, and Daniel sat down. Nursing his fist, Ginger slid down the bars to the floor.

There was a loud twanging as a policeman rapped his baton against the bars. 'Eh, eh, eh!' he shouted. 'Cool it down in there.' He looked at Ginger without compassion then pointed his baton at Daniel and the lad. 'We can make things a lot more difficult for you if you're looking for more trouble, young Führers.'

16

Amiens, France – Wednesday, 10ʰ August, 2016

Simon awoke with a serene sense of restfulness mixed with ominous doom.

Nick sat next to him, shifting something in his jeans pocket. 'You okay?'

'Yeah.' Simon sat up and put his glasses on. Nick came into focus.

They looked at one another for a long, silent moment.

Nick finally broke it. 'So, a fascist, huh?'

'So it would seem.'

'In jail.'

Simon nodded glumly.

'Sorry there wasn't anything I could do to stop it,' mumbled Nick, his cheeks pinking.

Simon was touched that Nick should feel it so keenly. He looked at his step-brother in despair. 'What do we do now?'

'Know anybody else whose former self lived through World War Two and is willing to sacrifice themselves to save Catherine?'

Simon stood up and went to the window. The rain had passed with the daylight, but there was a dampness in the air that hugged the sounds of the city closer. Cars splashed through puddles, and a foggy glow clung to the yellow street lights. He'd thought fate, if there was such a thing, had brought him to Catherine, to rescue her somehow, but Daniel Barrow... could he have been a more unsuitable saviour?

'We just have to keep trying,' said Nick.

'You want to keep going?' said Simon in surprise, turning to face him.

Nick shrugged. 'Don't you?'

'Well, yes, but – but he's in jail.'

'He's got two years to get out.'

Simon nodded, a sudden surge of energy rejuvenating his spirits. 'We could still save her. We can just go home and carry on until we get somewhere. Even if it takes *us* two years.'

'Yeah. We've got to hang around here a few more days yet.'

'Why?'

Nick bent down to retie his shoelace. 'You know, we're paid up until next Wednesday,' he said to the carpet. 'Plus I've got a gig on Sunday night.'

'You want to stay on?'

'Well, sure. Don't you?'

Simon was dumbfounded. He'd presumed they'd all be on their way back to London tomorrow. 'But what about Amanda?'

'She's threatening to go to Joe about all of this if she doesn't get a full holiday out of this trip.' He gave Simon a rueful smile. 'Some day, I'm going to have to learn how to deal with high-maintenance actresses.'

'How are we going to get away with doing these regressions with her down the corridor?'

Nick fobbed him off with an indifferent wave. 'She wants to take in all the "culture" of Amiens, visit the cathedral and what art galleries there are. You know what I mean.'

'She said that?'

'Yeah.'

'But she was packing her bags to leave just a couple of hours ago.'

'I got her to change her mind.'

Simon narrowed his eyes at him. They both knew how he'd got Amanda to change her mind. But now wasn't the time to confront him. And to be honest, he wasn't sure why Nick *had* wanted to change her mind. Regression sessions to manipulate Daniel would be a lot more flexible if they weren't in danger of having Amanda knock on the door at any minute. Simon thought of the row he'd witnessed in the hotel corridor, of Nick's lily-white ass being kicked out of Amanda's room. To a certain degree, he'd enjoyed Nick getting his comeuppance for betraying him again. But maybe Nick had persuaded Amanda to stay before they'd fought, before he'd changed his mind about helping Simon to tap into Daniel. For all he knew, Amanda might be packing her bags again. Hopefully.

'She might have changed her mind again,' Simon said.

'Why would she do that?'

'Because you and she had an all-out row in the corridor and she chucked you out of her room naked?'

'Oh.' Nick gave a little embarrassed laugh. 'Yeah. Maybe.' He patted his thighs in finality and stood up. 'I should probably go check.'

'Nick.' Simon stopped him as he went to the door. 'You're going to help me, aren't you?'

Nick gave him a weak smile. 'Sure I am, Si.'

Simon lay down on his bed after Nick had gone and breathed a deep sigh of frustration. Bloody Daniel Barrow. Why did he have to be a BUF member? Why did he have to go to some stupid rally and get himself arrested? It had been odd being inside Daniel's head, of arguing with the red-headed man in the jail cell, of believing every word that he and the BUF lad had said. The odds of manipulating any old person into going to a warzone and rescuing a stranger had been slim, but of manipulating a fascist now stuck in jail...

'I'm sorry, Catherine,' he whispered.

He'd failed her. He felt responsible for Daniel's extremist values; Daniel, after all, was a part of him. Simon shook his head. How could his former self have had such different values to him? Different times? Different ways of life? Seeing the world through Daniel's eyes he had understood, empathised, with his every belief. Perhaps this was what reincarnation was all about – the pursuit of perfect empathy; of living the lives of many, of becoming more and more empathetic as a result, becoming kinder and more compassionate until one reached the all-knowing, all-understanding position of perfect empathy.

He was surely an improvement on a fascist. Daniel didn't

seem to care about anyone but himself, whereas he, Simon, was risking everything for a selfless deed. Admittedly, he was risking Amanda too. So, did that negate his goodness? Was what he was doing akin to murder? He wasn't deliberately trying to kill Amanda. Who deserved to live more – Catherine or Amanda? He didn't want anyone to die.

Simon dug deep and asked himself the question again, forcing himself to answer with complete and blatant honesty. He realised that right now he'd prefer Catherine to live, but that was understandable, surely? Catherine was a good person, innocent and untarnished by a world skewed by capitalism and self-seeking entitlement. Amanda was arrogant, selfish, and had no reservations about bulldozing over others if it got her what she wanted.

How could Amanda be an improvement on Catherine? A terrible thought occurred to Simon, prickling his skin.

Nick let himself into his room and, ten seconds later, was interrupted by a knock at his door. Amanda stood there looking expectant.

'Well?' she demanded.

Nick hustled her inside and closed the door behind her after a last peek down the deserted corridor. 'So, we're on speaking terms again, are we?'

'Of course we are. That row was all for show.'

'Oh. Okay. Just making sure.'

'Did you think I was being serious?'

Nick wrung his hands. 'At first. I mean, you were very convincing.'

Amanda glowed. 'As you and Simon are so fond of reminding me, it had to look authentic.'

'I know. It's just that…' Nick couldn't quite meet her eye. 'Did you have to be so… *brutal*?'

'We were just acting, Nick. Well, I was.'

'So you didn't mean what you said about my… um, my performance?'

Amanda gave him a languid smile. 'Of course not. You're at least in my top five.'

'Top *five*?'

'Oh my God, I did not take you for the sensitive type. What do you want – a gold star?'

The thought of gold stars reminded Nick of his geography teacher, Miss Tennant, when he was thirteen, and the fantasies he'd had about her in which she'd given him more than a gold star. 'No, it's just...'

'Nick Taylor, you are a fantastic lay. There. Feel better?'

Nick looked at her doubtfully. 'Not really. Not when you say it like that.'

Amanda rolled her eyes. 'How did it go?'

Nick cleared his throat and tried to focus. 'Good. Very well, in fact.' He dug into his jeans pocket and withdrew a mobile phone. 'I got his phone. *And* Daniel Barrow is in jail.'

Amanda beamed at him. 'Excellent! Well done.'

Nick smiled weakly. Truth be told, he'd been nothing more than a spectator to Daniel's actions. 'And he's a BUF member.'

'BUF?'

'British Union of Fascists.'

'That's a good thing, right?'

'Did you not attend history class at all when you were at school? Yes, that's good. Fascists are bad. Fascists are Hitler and Mussolini. Fascists don't save Jews.'

'Great!' Amanda's eyes twinkled. 'So, all we need to do now is change things back to the way they were. You didn't have a problem with the hypnosis bit?'

Nick shook his head. 'Nope. I just channelled my inner Leonard Cohen and Simon went under like he was ten Stellas to the good.'

'Fabulous. Let's get going then, shall we?'

Nick looked at his watch. It was past eleven, and his hangover was already kicking in. 'Can't we do this tomorrow?'

'Nick, the clock is ticking. If we get this done now then we can go home tomorrow.'

Nick sighed and followed her over to the chaise longue.

'Oh, before I forget.' Amanda pulled a couple of sheets of paper out of her bag. 'I just need you to sign these. One for you, and one for me. Just at the bottom there.'

'What are they?' Nick took the papers and read the first line. "I, Nick Taylor, do solemnly swear to give Amanda Woodbine first dibs on all female leading roles in film and television that are produced by Taylor Made Television...'

'The contract we spoke about?' Amanda raised her shaped eyebrows at him expectantly.

'Oh, yeah. Okay. Where did you get these printed?'

'The concierge desk.'

'They do printing for guests?'

'No, I had to give him a blow job.'

Nick stared at her, horrified. He should probably get himself checked for STIs when he got back to London. God only knew what Amanda had given him if this was how she rolled.

Amanda gave him a disparaging look. 'Joke, Nick. I'm joking. I just asked nicely, okay?'

'Oh. Yeah. Of course.' He took the pen Amanda brandished at him, flashing a suspicious glance at her still, and scribbled his signature at the bottom of each page. 'Okay?'

'For now.'

Amanda lay on the chaise longue, eyes closed, hands folded over her stomach, skirt riding up her thighs. Nick sat beside her and tried not to think about how appealing she'd look lying there without any clothes on at all. He shook himself. Now was not the time. He was acting like a hormone-dictated teenager when he needed to be an adult. His future was at stake. His past was at stake. He had to concentrate. Changing things back to the way they were – telling Catherine *not* to run from the Gromaires' farm – was his priority. He tried not to think about how doing so would enable his great-grandfather to steal her necklace and allow his family to live in luxury for generations to come while at the same time sending Catherine to her death. But it had happened already, it was the way fate had dictated things. It was Simon who had meddled with things. All Nick was doing was putting things back to the way they had originally been.

Keeping his voice low, he talked Amanda through the initial steps of relaxation until her responses were nothing more than sleepy murmurs.

'There's a door in front of you and steps leading down. With each step, you're feeling sleepier and sleepier. With each step, your mind becomes emptier of all thoughts. With each step, more relaxed until it is completely free, completely detached. Emptier, clearer, step, step, freer. Your fingers and toes become light and relaxed, your arms and your legs become light and relaxed, your whole body is consumed by lightness. So relaxed. By the time you get to the bottom of the steps, you'll feel like you're sleepwalking. You'll see a corridor with doors. Do you see it?'

'Hmm.' Amanda's response was barely more than a sigh.

Nick's ego swelled. This hypnosis lark was a piece of cake. 'Now, I want you to go to the door that has a sign on it saying the twenty-first of May, 1940. Have you found it?'

Amanda gave an affirmative murmur.

'I want you to open it.' He waited, breath held, for Amanda to describe meeting Duras, the air raid, or even better, hiding on the Gromaires' farm and being found by Louis.

Amanda's brow knitted, two perfect little lines above the bridge of her nose. 'It won't open.'

Nick frowned. 'Okay,' he said, trying to keep his voice even. 'Then look for the door that says the twenty-second of May, 1940.' It wasn't ideal. For all he knew, Amanda might take them an hour past Catherine's escape from the attic. 'Have you found it?'

'Hmm.'

'Now open it.'

Amanda's lips twisted. 'It won't open.'

Nick suppressed an impatient sigh. 'Then push harder.'

'It's locked.'

'No, it's not. Just turn the handle. It will click open.'

Amanda's frown deepened. 'No. It's stuck.'

Nick rolled his eyes. 'Then give it a push with your shoulder. It *will* open. Just – just put some effort into it.'

Amanda gave an irritable sigh and opened her eyes. 'Seriously?' she said.

Nick jumped. 'You're awake. But I – I haven't brought you out properly.'

'I was never under, you pillock.'

Nick's ego deflated like a hot air balloon with a broken burner. 'Oh.'

She sat up and glared at him. 'I thought you said you were good at this.'

'Well, I managed okay with Simon.'

Amanda chewed her lip as she thought. 'It probably wouldn't have been very hard to put him under. He lives in cloud cuckoo land most of the time anyway.'

'Do you want to try again?'

She shook her head. 'It won't work.' Then her eyes lit up. 'Do you have any weed? That might help.'

'Maybe. I do become quite monotone when I'm stoned.'

'Not for you, you idiot. *Me.* Do you have any?'

'No, of course not. I'm not going to take drugs over the border, am I?'

'My God, Nick, you're as much a sissy as Simon is.'

'That's not being a sissy. That's just being sensible.'

'Whatever.'

The thought of drugs however pinged in Nick's brain. 'I know! Simon's chill pills.'

'His *what?*'

'Chill pills. Don't ask me what they are, but he takes them when he gets too stressed.'

'Valium? My mum takes those. *A lot.*'

Nick stopped himself from saying he wasn't surprised. 'I don't know what they are. But he took some before I put him under. They worked a treat. We could pinch some of them from him.'

'How?'

'The same way I got his phone, I guess.'

Amanda looked pensive. 'And you don't know what these pills are for? They're not for like serious psychological shit?'

'Jesus, Amanda. Simon's not a psycho, all right?'

She gave him a heavy-lidded look of disbelief.

'I mean, sure, he has his issues,' he relented, 'but he's not like super crazy or anything.'

Amanda shook her head. 'I'd rather not risk it. Who knows what they might do to me. You're sure you can't find a bit of weed from somewhere?'

'I'm open to suggestions.'

'Okay. We've got a few days, right? And this Daniel person that Simon's latched onto as my hitman is in jail, right? We'll try again tomorrow. Maybe when we've both had a good night's sleep, things'll be easier.'

Nick nodded. He wanted nothing more than to take a couple of painkillers and hit the pillow. Amanda stood up and walked to the door. She peeped down the corridor then stepped out.

'See you tomorrow, gold star boy,' she said with a sultry smile and closed the door behind her.

Nick leaned back in his chair and groaned.

17

Amiens, France – Thursday, 11th August, 2016

The next morning, Nick knocked on Simon's door. Simon opened it, distracted and flustered, and returned to his half-packed suitcase on the bed.

'What are you doing?' said Nick in surprise.

'It's no use. We should just go home,' muttered Simon, shovelling a shirt into the case. 'We don't know what we might unleash. She could be even worse. She could be the devil!' He looked up with wild eyes. 'It's the only explanation. You can't go backwards. It all must lead to perfect empathy. We've been wrong. I've been wrong. What if she turns out to be some kind of female Hitler? Some kind of Ilse Koch or Irma Grese.'

'Who? What are you talking about?'

Simon continued stuffing his case until Nick pulled him away.

'Simon! For God's sake, what are you doing? What are you talking about?'

Simon stopped with a hefty sigh and sank onto the bed. 'I was wrong. About this whole thing. We shouldn't save Catherine. She ought to die just as fate had originally planned.'

'Why?' Nick couldn't quite keep the fright out of his voice. 'I thought you wanted to save her.'

'I did, but now that I've thought about it, we really shouldn't.' He got up and began pacing his room. 'If the theory of perfect empathy is correct then Amanda must be an improvement on Catherine, but then what does that say about Catherine? What was she going to turn out like?'

Nick stared at him, unsettled by Simon's frame of mind. 'Perfect what?'

'Perfect empathy. It means we're all living multiple lives in order to see the world through different points of view, able to understand what others are feeling. With each life, we improve, we become more compassionate, until finally we reach perfect empathy.' He continued to collect his belongings from the dressing table, bundling them into his arms, dropping his hairbrush and his deodorant, not noticing, dumping the rest into his suitcase. 'Have you seen my phone? I can't find it anywhere. I could have sworn I had it last night. Maybe I left it in the restaurant. I hope someone turned it in. Do you think they would have? It's an old one. I can't imagine anyone would want to steal it.'

'No, Simon. No, I haven't seen it. Just stop! Will you?'

Simon jolted to a halt, eyes staring, nostrils flared. 'What?'

'You're acting like – I don't know. You're unnerving me, okay?' Nick pulled out a chair and patted it. 'Just sit down for a moment. Please.'

Simon shook his head. 'Don't patronise me, Nick. I'm being perfectly clear. We need to leave. Isn't that what everyone wants? This study's over. And Amanda's right. We really shouldn't be messing about with the past.'

Nick felt panic rise up into his throat. If Simon went home and found his father alive then Nick could kiss goodbye to the life he'd known before. There'd be no chance of him and Amanda turning things back to the way they were. 'Don't I have a say in this?' he exclaimed. 'What if I want to save Catherine?'

Simon looked at him in surprise. 'Why do you want to save her?'

'Because – because maybe I think she deserves a shot at life? Because maybe I think Amanda deserves a bit of come-uppance?' he said scrambling for reasons.

'But what if she turns out worse than Amanda? If perfect empathy–'

'Stop going on about this perfect empathy! Simon, it's nonsense. It's a theory. You're really going to let Catherine go the gas chamber because of some *theory*?' He began to discreetly unpack the suitcase.

Simon's eyes darted around as he thought. 'What if it's right though?'

'What if it's wrong? Where did you get this theory from?'

'That's not important. What if it's right? What damage will we do by unleashing her on this world?'

'Can you really see Catherine becoming some mass murderer or dictator? Hell, she can barely tie her own shoelaces by herself.'

Simon pushed him out of the way and started repacking his case. 'You don't know her. She's stronger than that. Who knows what the trauma of war might do to her.'

Nick watched him in alarm. Simon disappeared into his bathroom and returned with his shaving bag and shampoo. 'Simon, stop, please.' He tried to take the bag away from him, and they had a short tussle until the contents spilled over the floor.

'Fuck's sake, Nick!' cried Simon, falling to his knees. He picked up half the items and left the rest to roll under the bed.

'If perfect empathy is correct, then how do you explain me?' Nick asked.

'What do you mean?'

'Well…' Nick desperately sought for a convincing argument. 'We couldn't find any past lives for me, could we?'

Simon got to his feet, twiddling his razor between his fingers.

Nick tried to ignore the threat it posed. How much damage could a safety razor do? He didn't want to put it to the test. 'If I'm on my first life then I should be completely apathetic, right? I should be a serial killer or a dictator or something. But I'm not that bad, am I?'

Simon's face twitched.

'Am I?'

'No, you're okay,' mumbled Simon.

'So, where have I got my empathy from? And for all her faults, Amanda isn't that bad.' Simon glared at him, and Nick hurried on. 'I mean, she's not perfect by any means, but there are people more selfish than her, more vain than her, more self-serving than her who still aren't as bad as Hitler and whoever else it was you said.'

'Ilse Koch and Irma Gr–'

'I don't care! Why did you want to save Catherine in the first place?'

Simon hung his head and played with the corner of the rug with the toe of his shoe. 'I felt – I felt sorry for her.'

'Because she is a victim. She's just a girl, a naïve, innocent girl caught up in a horrible war that will end with her being starved in a concentration camp before being sent to her death in a gas chamber and buried in a mass grave. Is that what you want for her?'

Simon's lip quivered and he bit it aggressively. He shook his head.

'Maybe she doesn't grow up to be Mother Theresa. Maybe she grows up to be a flawed human being just like the rest of us. Is that so bad?' Nick paused, daring to hope he was finally getting through. 'Now, you said it yourself, we've been given this opportunity to save her, so let's do that. Let's save her.'

Simon lifted his eyes. The wildness had left them, only to be replaced with damp remorse. He sat on the bed with a bump and let his shaving bag drop to the floor. 'I don't know what to do, Nick,' he whispered.

'I do,' Nick replied with more confidence than he felt. 'Let's get on Daniel Barrow's case and send him to find Catherine.'

'But he's in jail. And I looked it up. Most of the British Union supporters were detained until the end of the war.'

Nick suppressed a satisfied smile. 'Well, let's see, shall we?'

18

London, England – Sunday, 26th May, 1940

Daniel was playing cards with the Blackshirt lad the next morning when another surly-looking man was thrown into their cell. Ginger had left earlier, leaving behind a trail of insults and boozy body odour. Daniel's shoulder was as stiff as a door, and it hurt even to pick up his two cards, but on a positive note he'd cleaned the lad of twelve cigarettes and ten shillings. Their new cellmate looked shifty, unkempt with dark, shady eyes. A thief, Daniel surmised, he'd known enough of them in the past.

'Get in there, you dirty bugger,' said the bearded pig with a shove. He slammed the cell door shut with a clang that spiked through Daniel's head and was just locking it when another guard walked over.

'Wait oh!' he said. 'Looks like someone's got a reprieve.'

The bearded guard turned scornful eyes on Daniel and his cellmates.

'Daniel Barrow?' said the other.

Daniel looked at him in surprise. 'Yes?'

'Yeah, up you get. You're out of here.'

Daniel exchanged bewildered glances with the lad then began to collect his winnings.

'Hey!' cried the lad. 'Come on, you're out of here. Leave me some.'

Daniel tossed down his two kings and flicked a cigarette at his chest. 'You win this hand.'

'Hey!'

Daniel got off the bed and sauntered over to the cell door. He met the bearded guard's disparaging gaze with lofty insolence through the thick metal bars. He raised an eyebrow.

The bearded guard sneered at him and opened the door.

Daniel walked out, brushing down his clothes. He couldn't think why they were letting him out and not the lad, but he wasn't going to hang around and ask questions. He took his comb out to smarten his hair. It was thick and sticky after a night on the cell's dirty mattress, and he felt like a walking urinal.

The second guard walked him up to the light of the main hub of Canon Row Station. 'Terribly sorry for the mix-up. You know how it is at these protests. All gets a bit chaotic.'

They rounded the corner to the front desk, and Daniel saw the reason for his amnesty. A young man, a couple of years older than Daniel's twenty-three, stood drumming his long fingers on the desk. Broad-shouldered and tall, he still carried a slight plumpness from his youth. His face was honest and open, blue-eyed and apple-cheeked. His blond hair had been oiled back but was already jumping up into its natural curls. It was Daniel's boss and best friend, Fletch Willoughby.

'Daniel!' Fletch's greeting was awash with concern. 'Are you all right?'

'I'm fine.' Daniel lit a cigarette and turned a scornful eye on the policemen. He blew a cloud of smoke over at them.

Fletch took his arm and propelled him towards the door. 'Mistakes happen, as we all know. And no harm done. If anything, I should think you've had the whole experience and will do an even finer job in your write-up.'

The desk sergeant waved them out. 'We'll be sure to pick up a copy.'

Fletch pushed Daniel out of the door into the drizzling rain.

Daniel grinned as they strode down the street. 'Did you see the looks on their faces? Two-faced bloody bastards.'

'Will you shut up and put on your coat, please?' Fletch said with unusual vehemence.

'All right, all right. What's biting your arse?' Still grinning, Daniel clamped his teeth down on his fag and shrugged his coat on, turning his nose away from the repugnant smell that clung to the wool weave.

'And button it up. That shirt you're wearing has caused us enough trouble.'

Daniel felt a surge of pleasure in his chest at the word 'us'. They were a team, him and Fletch. And that wasn't a term he'd been too familiar with in his life.

'What did you tell them?'

Fletch sent him a sidelong look as they swung around the corner into Westminster Station. A ghost of a smile floated across his face. 'That you were undercover doing a story on how very anti-British those Blackshirts are.'

'And that was it? They let me go?'

'It took some convincing, believe you me. I had to go find your staff records. Then I had to find a copy of a past edition in which you'd written a reasonably receptive piece just to prove you're a journalist.'

'That couldn't have been easy.'

'It wasn't, I can assure you. The last piece you wrote that was relatively anodyne was a story on the mistreatment of working horses in London.'

They jogged down the steps to the platform and jumped on the train about to head out.

'That was last year,' said Daniel. 'The butcher round from my flat still drives his horse everywhere like they're in a chariot race. Poor old thing's got bones sticking out everywhere. It had a cough for about two months over the winter.'

Fletch took hold of a hand grip and sighed. 'If only you would treat people with the same compassion that you have for animals.'

Daniel shrugged. 'Animals never knocked my teeth out when I was ten or made me sit on the front step in February in nothing but my shorts and shirt.'

Fletch's eyes softened, and Daniel held up a warning finger.

'Don't. I don't want your pity.'

'I know.'

There was a brief silence as they rocked from side to side with the motion of the carriage, Fletch no doubt pitying him and feeling ashamed of his own comfortable upbringing, while Daniel relived those long hours sat on the icy stone step, grit biting into his buttocks until eventually he was so numb it felt like he was hovering just above the step.

Daniel cleared the memory with a quick shake of his head. 'So, I guess I'd better write the story since the bobbies are so keen to read it.'

'You can give me your notes, and I'll write it.'

'Come on, Fletch. You need me as a voice to balance out all the other giddy noise.'

'Maybe all that giddy noise is what we need right now. There are tens of thousands of troops stranded on a beach in France at this precise moment, and everybody with a bathtub and a pair of oars is heading over to pick them up. We're calling it the "Dunkirk Spirit". People need something to get behind. They don't need the doom and death that you put out.'

Daniel shrugged. 'You're my editor. You could edit it.'

'There's editing, and then there's completely rewriting,' snapped Fletch. 'Just go home, have a bath, and bring me over your notes so I can get on with it.'

Daniel remained silent. He didn't like pushing Fletch this far. He'd overdone it. His blood was up from walking out of Canon Row with those wretched pigs blowing kisses after them. He hadn't meant to test Fletch.

In truth, Fletch was only the assistant editor. The editor of *The Northern Gazette* was actually Fletch's father, Harold Willoughby, but the man suffered terribly from the blues and wasn't much use even on the sporadic occasions that he was in the office. The responsibility of keeping the family business going had fallen more and more to Fletch until now most of the staff turned to him as a matter of course. Many probably weren't even aware that Harold Willoughby worked there at all.

Daniel had known the Willoughbys for eight years. Back then, Harold had been an ambitious and determined man, only given to infrequent bouts of despondency. Fletch was fresh out of prep school and being made to do a stint in the mail room where Daniel was working. Daniel had never had much time for toffs, but Fletch was different.

In many ways, thought Daniel, looking at his friend swaying beside him on the train, Fletch had saved him. If he'd stayed a moment longer at his last home, he was certain his foster-father would have beaten him to death. Daniel had been an ill-educated and angry fifteen-year-old boy when he'd arrived at *The Northern Gazette*. Fletch had helped him, emotionally and academically and, eventually, professionally.

He gave Fletch a soft punch in the arm and smiled.

Fletch smiled back. 'You're welcome.'

19

Amiens, France – Thursday, 11ᵗʰ August, 2016

Nick slipped into Amanda's room with a couple of lattes he'd picked up downstairs. Amanda was sitting cross-legged on her bed in a black and red kimono painting her toenails. Nick tried not to look at the tampons she'd slotted between her toes to spread them.

'How did it go?' she asked.

Nick placed the Styrofoam cups on the bedside table and straightened up with a sigh. He realised he was more apprehensive about her reaction than he was about the consequences this new development might have on his future. 'Slight problem. Daniel's out of jail. He's a journalist. His boss bailed him out. Said he was undercover at the protest.'

'You mean he's not a fascist?'

'Oh yes. I think he's definitely that. But he's not in jail anymore.'

'But he's still in England?'

'Yes.'

Amanda shrugged. 'Then just keep him there.'

'Mmm,' agreed Nick noncommittally. He'd tried to egg Daniel on, at the protest and in the jail, but he hadn't felt like Daniel had 'heard' him. That surely was good news for them though. They shouldn't have to manipulate him at all. What man in his right frame of mind would go to France of his own accord with the Nazis pillaging and plundering the place? The important thing was that Catherine was exploitable. All they needed to do now was access her and keep her from running from the Gromaires' attic.

'Shall we get started?' Nick said. 'I brought coffee.'

'Caffeinated?'

Nick felt the wrong answer here would receive the sharp end of Amanda's tongue, and he wasn't sure which it was. 'Er – yes.'

She rolled her eyes and got up off the bed and tossed her nail file onto the dressing table. 'Nick, we're struggling enough as it is to put me under. The last thing I need is caffeine.'

'Oh. Yes. Of course. How silly of me. I'll–' He picked up both the cups. 'I'll just drink them both.'

Amanda picked up her iPod and selected a track before setting it into the dock. Nick felt like he'd been transported into an aquarium. The room was suddenly filled with the mournful cries of whales and dolphins.

'Whatever,' she said irritably. 'Remember, you need to go slow too.'

Five minutes later, Amanda had arranged herself on the chaise longue. The morning sun filtered through the window to highlight a rectangle of her face that curved and bent to the contours of her cheeks and nose.

She was a woman who could manipulate the lines of light with her beauty, Nick found himself thinking.

Amanda's eyes opened. 'Nick? Let's get on with it, shall we?'

He took her down the steps of consciousness slower than before and walked her down the corridor to the doors of May, 1940. Amanda's responses became more and more subdued.

'Now, open that door. It should open very easily,' he added.

Amanda didn't respond.

'Have you opened it?'

Still Amanda didn't respond.

'Amanda?' He looked around, unsure what to do in this situation. 'Amanda?'

Amanda's eyelashes lay undisturbed upon her cheeks.

Nick's heart began to pound. 'Catherine? Amanda, are you having me on?'

Not even a nose twitch.

'Can you hear me?' Nick suddenly felt very alone. Just him

and the baleful moans of blue whales ten thousand feet down in the ocean's depths. What if she never woke up? He didn't have the experience to know the difference between hypnotised and comatose. How was he going to recover the Taylor fortune then? At least they were in her room and not his. Maybe he should go and get Simon. No. He stopped himself even before he moved a muscle to get up. Getting Simon would ruin everything, and for all he knew Amanda was simply playing one of her little games that only she found amusing.

'Amanda,' he said in a louder, firmer voice. 'Tell me where you are.' He shook her shoulder, none too gently, and Amanda's eyes shot open.

'What the fuck, Nick?' She scrambled up into a sitting position.

Nick let out an exhalation of relief that rivalled the whales on the iPod. 'Oh, thank God. I thought you were comatose. What happened?'

'The last thing I remember was you talking about doors. Very vaguely. Like you were way back at the top of the stairs and then…' Amanda's ears turned red. 'I think I must have fallen asleep.'

Nick stood up with a cry of exasperation.

'I only got three or four hours last night,' she said defensively. 'I thought if I was tired I would be more susceptible to regression.'

'We're wasting time.' Nick dragged his fingers through his hair and stared out of the window at the bright yellow glow of the morning. They were only booked in until the following Wednesday and it was already Thursday. 'Let's try again.'

They settled down, and Nick tried once more to lead Amanda down through the stages of consciousness. But he hadn't even got to the doors yet when Amanda sat up with an irritated tut.

'It's no use. Now I'm wide awake after you shouted at me.'
'I didn't shout–'
'I can't do it.'

'Then try.'

'I can't!'

'Well, you have to.'

'It's not something you can just turn on and off. You have to be in the right frame of mind, and you're not helping.'

Nick stared at her. He couldn't believe she was blaming him. He took a deep breath, remembering how he'd watched his grandfather calm down a particularly fractious actor on set who'd kept forgetting her lines.

'What do you suggest then?' he said evenly.

Amanda pouted in thought. 'Did you get those chill pills from Simon?'

'No. He had the box in his hand the whole time. I couldn't risk it.'

'Well, we need to do something because this sure as fuck isn't working.'

'We could steal them from his room. He said he was going down for breakfast then out for some fresh air.'

'Do you have his key card?'

Nick shook his head and thought for a moment. 'But I have a plan.'

They caught the concierge nibbling on a croissant behind his desk, but he quickly brushed the pastry flakes from his lips and greeted them with a bright smile.

'Monsieur Taylor, I trust you are enjoying your stay?' He turned appreciative eyes on Amanda who'd flung on a pair of shorts and a thin, skimpy blouse that very clearly showed she wasn't wearing a bra.

'Yeah, thanks. It's been a real hoot. But I've been an idiot and lost my room key card. Can I get another one?'

'I am sorry to hear that.' The concierge feigned concern with a small frown and tapped on his keyboard with greasy fingers. 'Which room are you staying in?'

For a moment, Nick was gripped with panic. He couldn't remember what Simon's room number was.

'Room 214,' supplied Amanda with a sultry smile.

The concierge gave her a knowing look and almost winked at Nick before he remembered himself. 'Of course. Please bear with me.'

They waited while the new card was programmed to open 214's door. Nick could barely believe how easy it was. Mind you, he was paying for all three rooms. How was the hotel to know who was sleeping in which?

The concierge handed it over with a smile. 'Unfortunately I shall have to add it to your final bill.'

Nick took it with a shrug. What did it matter? At the rate they were going he wasn't going to be paying for anything.

Simon finished his breakfast of croissants and jam and strong bitter coffee before returning to the lobby. He passed a grainy photocopied poster on the way advertising 'The great British artist Nick Taylor' performing live that Sunday night. For some curious reason they'd added Queen lyrics around it as well. Simon couldn't recall ever hearing him cover Queen.

He stopped on his way out of the revolving doors as his automatic patting of his pockets yielded no hard tell-tale lump of his inhaler. He turned back and headed for the stairs. Eyes down, he almost collided with Amanda coming the other way at the top.

'Jesus, Simon,' she exclaimed, clinging to the bannister. 'Are you determined to kill me?'

Simon felt red heat flood his face. Goodness, her breasts looked good in that top. 'I didn't see you.'

They stared at each other for a moment. Simon searched her face for a hint of her feelings. Had what he'd proposed – saving Catherine, risking her – hurt her? Had her faith in his devotion been shattered? Had her heart broken just a little bit to know he'd risk her life for someone he'd never met, would never meet?

Simon supposed a part of him was glad if that were true; glad that she might feel a little of the grief he'd felt when she'd crushed him back at university, how she continued to crush him. Like a bug. Then there was this whole fiasco with Nick. She didn't want either of them. The woman had a heart of ice. But dammit, she was beautiful. From the gemstone glitter of her eyes to the sultry pout of her mouth and delicate skin around her nostrils, she could be as villainous as the devil and still bring every God-serving man to his knees in servitude.

'I'm surprised you're still here,' she said with an arched eyebrow. 'Thought now the study's over, you'd be running back to your precious second-hand shop.'

Simon shrugged, tried to appear nonchalant. 'It's a pawnbroker's shop, not a second-hand shop. And I felt like I could do with the break. A few more days couldn't hurt.'

'Yes.' She gave him a sickly smile. 'You probably do need a break. You haven't been feeling well lately, have you?'

'What about you? Last I saw you were packing your bags back to London.'

'Was I?' Amanda frowned, pulling at her lower lip with her fingernail. 'Didn't you see me chucking Nick out of my room yesterday?'

Simon sent her a sour look. 'Did he outlive his usefulness?'

'We'll see. I might have been a little hasty.'

'Is that why you've stayed? To make up with your future sugar daddy?'

'We're the same age, Simon. Nick can't be my sugar daddy.'

'You know what I mean.'

'I'm keeping my options open, let's say,' she said with a coy smile.

'Well, I wouldn't count on it. Nick doesn't think much of your attitude.'

'Is that so?'

Simon clenched his teeth. She was goading him into saying too much. 'Excuse me.'

He tried to push past her, but she stepped into his path. 'Why the rush?' Her voice rattled a little higher than usual. 'We've barely spoken since our row over Catherine. Now that the whole mess is over, why don't we try to make amends? Drink downstairs?'

Simon gave her a suspicious look. She fluttered her eyelashes at him, bit her lip, transforming her from a womanly seductress into a young, vulnerable girl.

'I have to get my asthma inhaler.'

Again, she stopped him as he tried to get by. Her hand on his shoulder was warm, persuasive, a branding iron. She hadn't laid her hands on him since they'd been together. He thought he'd never forget her touch, but feeling it now brought it all into focus so quickly he felt quite light-headed.

'It's just a drink, Simon.'

He gave himself a mental shake then jerked his shoulder free. He couldn't forget what she'd done to him with Nick. 'Maybe another time.'

'Wait!'

Simon ignored her and rounded the corner into the corridor. He stopped in surprise at the sight of Nick walking away from his door.

'Simon! There you are. I was just knocking on your door.'

'I was at breakfast.'

'Of course. I forgot.' Nick gave a breathless laugh. 'Weren't you going for a walk, I thought I heard you say?'

'I forgot my inhaler.' Simon looked from Nick to Amanda who'd slithered round the corner after him. Nick seemed excessively jovial. Perhaps Amanda was making him nervous. 'Everything okay?'

Nick nodded with conviction. 'Absolutely.' He patted Simon on the back and headed for the stairs. 'See you later.'

'Hey!' Simon called after him.

Nick paused in the stairwell, shoulders tensed. Then he relaxed and turned around, a wide open smile on his face. 'Yes?'

'Was there something you wanted?'

'Hmm?'

'You were knocking on my door. Did you want something?'

'Oh!' Nick laughed again. 'It was nothing. I – I just wanted to ask…' He looked at Amanda. 'You know what? It doesn't matter.' He winked at Simon and sent a secret sidelong look in Amanda's direction that only he would see.

Simon nodded. Nick obviously didn't want to discuss it in front of Amanda. Fair enough. 'Okay then. See you later.'

Nick sent him a jolly wave over his shoulder as he descended the stairs. Amanda smiled tartly at him and followed Nick down. Simon watched them go with curiosity. He felt like his grasp of social communication and its complex subtleties was loosening with every interaction he had. He shook his head and continued on to his room to collect his inhaler.

With Simon observed safely on his way into the city centre, Nick and Amanda reconvened in his room.

'Did you get them?' Amanda said, closing the door behind her.

Nick rattled a blister strip of blue and white capsules for her to see. 'Couldn't risk taking them all. Hopefully he won't notice one pack gone.'

Amanda clapped her hands with an excited giggle like a little schoolgirl and took them from him. She read the text on the back foil. 'Never heard of the stuff. And we don't have the box to tell us how many to take.' She sent Nick an anxious look. 'How many does he take?'

'I don't know. Maybe two?'

'Are you sure?'

'No. I've never paid that much attention.'

'You need to be sure. If it's only one then two is double the dose. I don't want to OD.'

'You won't OD on two tablets,' said Nick, pouring her some water. 'At worst, you'll probably get high.'

Amanda popped two capsules onto her palm. 'Here goes nothing.' She swallowed the pills with the water he handed to her, and they stared at each other for a long moment.

'Anything?' asked Nick.

'No. Not yet.' She unzipped her bag and brought out her

iPod. 'Here. Put this on. Let's get going.'

Five minutes later, they were back in the depths of the Atlantic, and Amanda was stretched out on the chaise longue. Nick leaned forward in his chair and led her down the steps of consciousness.

'Now I want you to approach the first door. It will say the twenty-first of May, 1940 on it. Can you see it?'

Amanda's brow puckered. 'The writing's blurry. I can't see for sure.'

Nick paused. He didn't want her to open the door on some past life that they didn't know about, someone from Medieval England or something. 'Okay, go to the next door. This one will say the twenty-second of May, 1940.'

Amanda sighed, her lips parted. 'No. This one is blurry too.'

Nick rolled his eyes and tried to keep the impatience out of his voice. 'Try the next. This one will say...' He paused. They didn't want to go beyond Catherine's escape from the Gromaires' farm. 'This one will say the nineteenth of May, 1940.'

'It's foggy.'

'Well, open it anyway. And tell me what you see.'

There was a pause. Amanda's eyes darted sideways beneath her lids. Then a deep breath. 'I see cars and people.'

Good, well at least they weren't in Medieval England. 'What is your name?'

'Catherine Jacquot.'

Nick gave the room a triumphant smile. 'And what is the date?'

'I'm not sure.'

'Where are you?'

'In Paris.'

20

Paris, France – Monday, 27th May, 1940

Catherine walked through the cobbled streets, taking care to avoid the bustling crowds. The last lift she had received had been from a van of nuns who had stopped outside the towering Cathédrale Notre-Dame de Paris and told her to take the road south, and she would find the one hospital that they knew – Hôpital Cochin. Standing in the shadow of the majestic cathedral, Catherine wondered if this was a sign. It was not exactly the same as the Amiens version, but was similar enough to be its cousin. Many an hour had been spent with her father sitting in the gardens surrounding the Cathédrale Notre-Dame d'Amiens sketching on her art pad and marvelling at her father's apparent ease at drawing straight lines.

'I need a steady hand,' he had replied. 'What would my patients say if I could not draw a straight line?'

Catherine set off determinedly. Her body ached with fatigue and overexertion, and her feet stung from her sweaty shoes rubbing her blisters raw. Yet they did not matter. She knew she would find her father soon.

Her first impression of Hôpital Cochin was that of reassurance. Its sturdy four-square façade of yellow and red brick and the Tricolore above the entrance waving the sick and injured through its doors presented an aura of strength and dependability. She rounded an army medic lorry parked out front and stepped inside the building, only to be assaulted by a scene of chaos, noise, and the overpowering smell of body odour and disinfectant, the former winning over the latter. People stood, propped up against the discoloured walls, cradling their ailments with pitiful stares that went straight through her. The woman at the front desk was handing out forms and shrieking out instructions on how to fill them in to men in army uniform who crowded around her desk four-strong, while also assisting nurses who came through like a frantic relay team with papers, bottles of medication, and liquids of all colours.

Catherine tried to push her way through, but the soldiers blocked her way like a thick canvas wall. 'Madame?' she tried to shout over their heads, but the woman either didn't hear her or was ignoring her.

Catherine slipped away unseen into the corridors of the hospital. Soldiers lay on narrow beds pushed to the sides while others less fortunate had to make do with the odd chair or resign themselves to the floor, backs against the walls, heavy-booted legs outstretched ready to trip any inobservant nurse scurrying past. A pile of dirtied and bloodied rags and bandages lay in a heap in a corner, festering with flies. Catherine covered her mouth. She had to find the surgical ward. That was where Papa would be. Guardedly, she picked her way down the corridor, trying not to see the bloodied sheets covering the soldiers on the beds, trying equally not to be seen by any of them.

'Excuse me–' She tried to waylay a nurse, but the woman was halfway down the corridor before Catherine could get another word out.

It was hopeless. She stopped by a junction to another corridor, trying to decide which route to take. She noticed a young soldier lying on a bed just ahead of her. He lay staring up at the ceiling, his face dirtied and brown, blood fixed in three dried rivulets from his temple. Sporadic growth shadowed his upper lip and chin, and his brown hair was clumped with mud and, Catherine realised, probably blood. He was crying freely, the tears coursing clean lines down his face. His teeth chattered, and his neck muscles stood out like draped washing lines. Catherine looked away, not wanting to intrude on his suffering, but the fascination of seeing a man cry – even if he was young, perhaps in his early twenties – was too much. She'd never seen a man cry before. Not even her father.

When she looked again, the soldier had turned his head

towards her. His dirt-entrenched hand was outstretched; his blue eyes reddened and desperate.

'Mademoiselle,' he croaked.

Catherine hesitated.

His arm began to shake with the effort of holding it out, and Catherine quickly stepped forward and grasped his hand. The soldier closed his eyes, and, though his tears fell more rapidly, he seemed to momentarily relax as she squeezed his hand in both of hers. Then his body tensed like it had received an electric shock, and his fingers crushed hers until she gasped. He winced, squeezing two more tears out of his eyes.

'Tell me they won't take my leg,' he rasped. 'Don't let them take my leg.'

Catherine looked down the bed to where the sheet had fallen away to reveal a leg bared from the torn rags of his thick army trousers, a hundred different wounds criss-crossing the profusely swollen and bloody flesh. A tourniquet above his knee had stopped most of the bleeding, but every time he moved, a fresh pulse would seep from the wounds. She shuddered at the sight, wanting nothing more than to run away from the horror, but then she looked back at the man's face. He appeared not the brave man who had marched into war, but a scared boy, somebody's son, somebody's brother, in horrific pain.

Catherine wanted to cry, but instead she found herself nestling his hand to her chest and singing to him a lullaby. '*Dodo, l'enfant do, L'enfant dormira bien vite; Dodo, l'enfant do, L'enfant dormira bientôt…*'

The soldier closed his eyes and relaxed as she sang. His tears dried up as hers began. Still she sang to him, until suddenly she was interrupted by a stern incensed voice behind her.

'What do you think you're doing back here?'

Instinctively, Catherine dropped the man's hand and stepped away. A matronly looking nurse glared at her with unbridled hostility.

'I–' Catherine didn't know what to say. She looked to the soldier for assistance, but he'd turned his face away to stare at the wall. Catherine squared her shoulders. 'I'm looking for Dr. Jacquot. He will be in the surgical ward. He is my father.'

The nurse's eyes flittered over her, and Catherine resisted the urge to smooth down the dirty creases of her dress. A call from down the corridor made the woman sigh in impatience. 'Surgery is down there, take the stairs on the left to the third floor.'

'He is here?' Catherine exclaimed in delight, but the nurse was already gone, waddling down the corridor, shouting at the soldiers to move their trip-hazard legs out of the way.

Catherine turned to the soldier once again. 'I'm sorry. I have to go.'

The soldier slowly moved his head to face her again. His eyes were devoid of hope.

'What is your name?' she asked.

'Jean Paul. Jean Paul Bernard.'

'Well, Jean Paul, my father is a surgeon here, and I will tell him to do everything he can to save your leg,' she said, glowing with happiness. Just saying those words 'my father is a surgeon here' made her heart sing.

Jean Paul grunted and looked back up at the ceiling. Catherine touched his shoulder in a gesture of goodbye and practically skipped down the corridor to the stairwell.

Things were a little less chaotic up in the surgical ward. Catherine caught the attention of a nurse quite easily this time and asked to see Dr. Jacquot.

'He is in surgery now,' the nurse said. 'I will tell him when he is out.'

Catherine didn't care. She couldn't contain the broad smile stretching across her face. She could have forgiven the nurse downstairs to have misheard her or simply not listened to the name Jacquot, had sent her here just to get Catherine out of her ward. But here, a nurse in the surgical ward was saying the same thing. He was here! Her father was truly here!

The nurse smiled at Catherine, soft brown eyes just the sort you'd hope for and expect in a civil servant tasked with your care. 'Go sit through there.' She pointed to a room off the main corridor.

Catherine did as she was told. The room was vast, stretching far across to what must have been the end of the building, filled with two long rows of narrow iron beds just an arm's stretch apart from one another. Despite its size, it was unbearably stuffy and hot. It smelt of faecal matter, and a sickly sweet smell she couldn't identify. Every bed was occupied. Some with their heavily bandaged legs raised in slings. There were no doctors or nurses in here to care for them, and every now and then a sorrowful groan came from a mummified invalid.

Catherine sidled in and found a chair by the door. She didn't want to miss her father when he came out of surgery, and she couldn't trust the nurse to remember when she must surely be very busy. She sat on the cold metal chair and slipped the Fleur de l'Alexandrie out of her pocket. She cradled the necklace in her palm, allowing the gold chain to drape through her fingers. The sapphire glinted and winked at her in what seemed to Catherine a celebration of her endurance. How proud Papa would be when he heard of her adventures, of Duras, the Gromaires, and the half dozen others who had assisted her to Paris. He would pull her close to his chest and squeeze her shoulders, and she would feel the coolness of his dress shirt against her cheek and hear the dependable drum of his heart.

'How brave you have been, *ma cherie*,' he would murmur. 'But now we are together and you are safe...'

Catherine must have fallen asleep, but she jerked awake when she felt a hand shake her shoulder.

'Papa?' she gasped. Her voice was parched. She'd last had a drink of water when she'd left the nuns, and the smells and musty air of the hospital had coated her throat. The room was much darker, although dusk couldn't yet have settled outside.

It was the brown-eyed nurse. 'Dr. Jacquot is done. He will be through here in a minute to check his other patients.'

Barely a minute later, Catherine heard male voices approaching, but they were too indistinct, too numerous to gauge which was her father's. A doctor pushed open the doors with a couple of young white coats trotting behind him. He was broad-shouldered with thick brown hair, sharp intelligent eyes, and a square jaw. Catherine groggily scrambled to her feet. His gaze fell upon Catherine, and he looked her up and down in a fluid sweep.

'Are you the new nurse?' he demanded. 'Where is your uniform?'

It took Catherine a moment to find her tongue. 'N-no. I'm waiting for my father. He is Dr. Jacquot.'

The man's eyes flashed. 'I am Dr. Jacquot. What are you talking about?'

Catherine staggered back, making her chair's iron feet screech against the floor. She looked at the nurse for help. 'But she said he was here!' she cried. 'He must be here!'

His thin lips disappeared in impatience. 'I am the only Dr. Jacquot at this hospital. Goodness knows we could do with another, but sadly I am all we have.'

The strength and determination that had kept Catherine going over the past few days leaked out of her like somebody had pulled the plug. A huge painful ball rose in the back of her throat, and tears flooded her eyes.

The doctor marched away down the line of beds with his interns shuffling obediently behind like a litter of puppies following their master.

Catherine didn't know what to do – more than that she didn't have the strength to even think what to do. She could only stand there, a pathetic crying and dirty mess.

'Are you okay?' the nurse asked, placing a comforting hand on Catherine's arm.

Shoulders drooping, Catherine could only shake her head. 'He isn't my father. He was meant to be my father.'

'Your father is also Dr. Jacquot?'

Catherine nodded miserably.

'Why did you think he worked here? What has happened?'

'We were separated in Amiens. He is a surgeon there. But Duras told me that he would have been drafted to Paris. So now I'm here, and I don't know where he is.' Catherine sobbed quietly into her hands as the enormity of her situation occurred to her. She hadn't just lost her father. She, too, was now lost. She couldn't go home to Amiens. The Germans were there. 'I don't know what to do.'

'Have you tried the other hospitals?' asked the nurse.

Catherine shook her head.

'You should try them all. There are a few in Paris. Do you have somewhere to stay?'

Catherine gulped. She didn't want to burden the nurse any more than she already was. 'Yes,' she replied.

The nurse gave her a relieved smile. 'You have other family here?'

Catherine nodded, biting her lips together to hide her dishonesty.

The nurse hesitated, eyeing her warily, then patted her shoulder. 'I must get back to work. But it's good you have family here. Of course, there are shelters now available,' she said, fixing Catherine with a meaningful look that made Catherine blush with shame.

'Thank you,' she whispered.

The nurse turned away, and Catherine dragged her aching feet to the door. As she walked out of the stuffy ward, she remembered the soldier downstairs.

'Doctor!' she called back.

Dr. Jacquot turned around impatiently. 'What do you want?'

'There is a soldier downstairs called Jean Paul Bernard. His leg is very badly injured. Please do what you can to save it.'

Dr. Jacquot dismissed her with a wave of his hand like she was a bothersome fly. Out of the ward, she walked through the surgical reception where, through the windows, she could see the sky turning a dirty dusky pink. She must find a shelter before it got dark.

21

Amiens, France – Thursday, 11th August, 2016

Amanda drew in a deep breath as she regained full consciousness. She sat up and regarded Nick with a disconsolate twist to her mouth.

'Well, that didn't go to plan, did it?' she said.

Nick got up to pace the room. 'We could try again–'

'Nick, I think it's pretty clear we can't go back to the Gromaires' farm.' She shrugged. 'Maybe changing things means we can't go back before then.'

'We managed it with Simon.'

'Then maybe he has the magic touch. I don't know. We don't know the rules to this… this *thing* we've uncovered.'

Nick sighed, hands on hips. They had to be able go back to the Gromaires' farm and change things back to the way they were. The thought of not being able to made a ball of panic swell in his gut. This couldn't be his future. It wasn't right. It wasn't fair. He'd done nothing to deserve a life of poverty.

'What do you want to do next?' asked Amanda.

Nick looked about in despair, and his eye was caught by his great-grandfather's diaries stacked on his bedside table. In a couple of strides he was across the room, and he snatched them up. 'If we can't go back, then we go forward.'

'What?'

'We lead Catherine into Schneider's path.'

'And how do you propose we do that? Just send her wandering around France in the hope that the right Nazi picks her up?' Amanda's words dripped with sarcasm. 'Forgive me if that sounds a bit fluky.'

He sat down beside her and opened up one of the diaries. 'No. We use these. They're my great-grandfather's diaries.'

Amanda's eyes widened as she looked from him to the diaries and back again. 'You just happen to have Schneider's diaries with you?'

'Of course not. They were the package that arrived for me on Tuesday from Joe.'

Amanda continued to look at him in surprise. 'How long exactly have you known that your great-grandfather was involved in all of this?'

'Monday.'

'And you didn't say anything?'

'What was I supposed to say? "Oh, by the way, I think my great-grandfather killed your former life"?' exclaimed Nick. 'I only asked Joe to send them over so I could make sure it was him; there must be hundreds of Heinrich Schneiders in Germany. What are the odds it would turn out to be my ancestor?'

Amanda took the top journal and flicked through it. 'And does he describe Catherine's capture in here?'

'He does.'

'Did he kill her?'

'I don't know. He was kinda vague about it. I don't think she was exactly part of the plan. He didn't expect to find her at the Gromaires, but when he did, well... you know us Taylors, we're opportunists. He took her necklace and had to get rid of her. Quietly. Strictly speaking he should have handed the Fleur de l'Alexandrie to the boss.'

'Does Simon know Schneider is your great-grandfather?'

Nick shook his head. 'And he's not going to. Nor does he know about the journals.'

Amanda chewed her lip. 'Schneider finding Catherine in the Gromaires' attic is one thing; hoping he'll pick her out in the middle of Paris *and* steal her necklace is another thing entirely. There would've been thousands of Jews in Paris. We could direct her right into his path, and he might just bundle her into a lorry with a bunch of other Jews and send her off to a camp without ever setting eyes on the Fleur de l'Alexandrie.'

'For a start, I don't think they were rounding up French Jews just then. But also, the weird thing is, according to his journal before everything changed, he seemed to know Catherine.'

'How on earth would he know her?'

'Apparently, some time before the war, he attended a party thrown by Catherine's grandmother. Over at the family's château. Catherine was presented with the necklace in some sort of debutante ceremony. He was the photographer. So, he knew all about her *and* the necklace.'

Amanda considered this for a moment then shook her head. 'It's too risky. What if Schneider doesn't catch her? Or even if he does, what if he lets her live? If she lives, then I might cease to exist.'

'I doubt very much whether he'll let her live. Not if he plans on stealing the Fleur. He'll be stealing from Hitler in effect, and he wouldn't want to leave any witnesses.'

'But we can't know for sure. And we can't manipulate him. What are we meant to do – manipulate Catherine into begging him to kill her?'

'Well, what do you suggest then?' Nick snapped. It was all right for Amanda to sit there and choose not to use Schneider's diaries. Her life hadn't been turned tits up.

Amanda glared at him. 'What does he do in Paris?'

'The Nazis invaded on the fourteenth of June, 1940, according to this. He goes to various places, including a shelter set up at a theatre.' Nick ran his finger along the line of smudged looping ink. 'The Theatre de l'Opéra, where he picks up some Jewish physicist that the Nazis wanted. He sticks around for another day then heads south to Nantes.'

'That doesn't give us a lot of time.'

'We don't need much. We just need to persuade Catherine to go to this shelter and let fate do the rest. If Schneider knows her, he's sure to recognise her.' Nick looked desperately at Amanda. 'If he doesn't then I can manipulate Catherine into practically throwing herself and her necklace at him.' He wrung his fingers. Given how difficult Daniel was proving to manipulate, he was beginning to realise it wasn't simply a case of puppeteering, and something as unthinkable as giving oneself up to an SS officer would take some persuasion, even for someone as naïve as Catherine.

Amanda sent him an irritable look then got up to rummage through her bag for her cigarettes. 'It's a hell of a risk, Nick. Do you have a lighter?' she said, tossing her bag back onto the chaise longue.

'Think about that contract you signed—'

He was interrupted by a rap on the door. He looked at his watch. It was ten past twelve. 'Shit. I was meant to meet Simon at noon.' He looked around for somewhere Amanda could hide. There wasn't much cover and he didn't think she would lower herself to crawling under the bed. 'Quick,' he hissed. 'In the bathroom.'

She opened her mouth to protest, and Nick frantically gestured to her to be quiet. He bundled her into the bathroom and held the journals out to her. 'This is the only way,' he said.

Another knock came, but Nick ignored it. He waited for Amanda to make her decision, his teeth aching as he clenched them. Amanda gave him a challenging look.

'Think about that contract,' he said again.

She pouted then finally sighed and snatched the journals from him. Nick wanted to kiss her hands and weep. Instead, he closed the bathroom door and went to answer Simon's knock.

'Hey!' he said, opening the door. 'Sorry, I lost track of time.'

Simon peeked into the room. 'Have you got someone here? I thought I heard someone.'

'Television.'

'Could you understand any of it?'

'Subtitles.'

'Oh. You ready? I'm starving.'

Simon stepped into the room, and Nick spotted Amanda's handbag lying against the chaise longue out of the corner of his eye.

'Let's go.' He snatched up his key card and, with a last apprehensive glance towards the bathroom, shut the door behind him with Amanda locked in.

'You want to eat down in the bar or go out?' Simon asked as they descended the stairs.

'I don't mind,' Nick replied, thinking of his bank card that was sure to be declined wherever they went.

'Let's go down to the bar then. They do great paninis.'

They entered the lobby and crossed the foyer where the maître d' was chatting to some guests. They'd just reached the stairs down to the basement when M. Fourrier called out.

'Monsieur Taylor! A quick word if you have the time.'

Nick stiffened. Had his empty account somehow impacted upon his original payment back in the good old days when he'd been flush? 'Yes?'

M. Fourrier hurried over. He wrung his hands and spoke in a hushed voice. 'The Hôtel Sceau prides itself on being a respectable establishment.' He paused, but Nick and Simon looked at him blankly. 'We are a… *peaceful* hotel. Guests come here to relax and enjoy the sights and attractions of Amiens. We are aware that you have had some… *disagreements* with the *madame* in your party?'

'Oh! Yeah,' Nick said, realisation dawning. Heat flushed his face as he recalled Amanda chucking him naked out of her room. 'Sorry. That won't happen again.'

M. Fourrier gave him an awkward smile. 'I am grateful to hear it. Have a good day.'

Nick and Simon carried on their way.

'Nosy bastards,' Nick muttered once they were out of earshot.

Simon looked less than sympathetic.

'And they're one to talk about a "peaceful" stay. Their walls are made of paper.'

'Tell me about it,' Simon said. 'I know for a fact that my next door neighbours have gone to visit the cathedral today. They could barely contain themselves.'

The bar was busy with lunching guests, and the pair found a table tucked to the side.

Nick waited a couple of minutes behind his menu then tutted. 'Damn. I've left my wallet upstairs. You mind getting this?'

'Sure. What are you having?'

'Brie and cranberry panini looks good.'

'Great. Think I'll have the same. The sooner we eat, the sooner we can get back to work.'

Nick's spirits dipped another level. 'Yeah. Great.'

22

London, England – Monday, 3ʳᵈ June, 1940

aniel exited Blackfriars tube station and made his customary walk along the Thames Embankment to work. It was a beautiful early summer's day, and the noon sun was warm overhead. The river, awash with sparkling ripples, was bizarrely void of the usual paddle steamers and sailing barges. He wondered about their fate. Operation Dynamo was in its ninth day, and stories were winging their way back to Fleet Street – or, if you worked at the Northern Gazette as Daniel did, Temple Lane, just off Fleet Street – tales of fishermen and pleasure sailors answering the call for shallow draft boats to rescue the stranded Allied soldiers off Dunkirk Beach in northern France. Daniel was torn. On the one hand he was filled with admiration and pride at the hundreds who had risked their lives by making the journey across the Channel. On the other hand, he felt a sick satisfaction that the government should suffer such an embarrassing defeat.

His footsteps quickened at the thought of the story he intended to write. He'd spent most of the morning researching it through his British Union contacts and it filled him with such umbrage that he fairly trembled at the prospect of relaying it at his old Imperial typewriter. How would he start it? '*Darren Trawley and his brother-in-law Bill Hemmings didn't think twice when the call for boats like theirs came over the radio waves to sail to Dunkirk. They saved the lives of eight British and French servicemen, but had barely docked their boat back in Margate when MI5 arrested them, citing them a threat to national security. This is despite their blatant patriotism and all because of their once alliance to a now defunct political party. Is this truly what we so proudly label "Dunkirk Spirit"? Trawley and Hemmings left their comfortable homes to risk their lives for the sake of strangers, a true testament to the spirit of the brave men and women who made that same perilous trip. Are such men and women our comrades? Need we even ask the question? Yet our government has done exactly that. They have seen the name British Union Party, and have come away with an answer to the contrary...'*

It was disgusting. Britain claimed to be a democracy right up until the moment they were asked to believe in something they didn't want to. Had Oswald Mosley and his British Union continued to side with the Nazis then Daniel might well have understood their opposition and their mistrust. But when Hitler had posed a threat to the British, Mosley was the first to stand up and renounce his support of the Nazi party. He had made it clear that he was, first and foremost, British and that his loyalties would remain so even against those he'd previously seen as allies. It had taken great backbone to say such a thing; to, for all intents and purposes, admit that his advocacy of Adolph Hitler's policies had been misguided. Had the government taken a blind bit of notice of such humility? Not a chance! Now Mosley was being detained somewhere, and these two Dunkirk heroes had been arrested. What more did the British Union have to do to show they were on the same side in this war?

Daniel was still running these questions through his mind as he rounded the corner into Temple Lane. They would form the rest of his article. As someone who took great pride in making up his own mind, he would pose questions and let the readers come up with their own answers. Whether his copy would get past Fletch was another matter entirely. Journalists were obliged to preach the word of the newspaper's owner, usually some Tory lord, and to tell readers what to think, which made them no less propagandistic than German communications. Considering the rhetoric they were spouting about Hitler's persuasion techniques, Daniel found them laughably hypocritical.

He'd barely got halfway across the small lobby of *The Northern Gazette* when Fletch strode across from the front desk and propelled him by the arm.

'Mail room. Now.'

'What have I done?'

Fletch looked around at the dozen or so people in the room. 'Don't make a scene. I'll explain in a minute.'

The mail room was a cramped, stuffy room off the back concourse that smelt of damp newsprint and ink. Daniel had spent many an hour in here, sifting through post until his back muscles spasmed and franking outgoing mail until his palm was bruised blue. It had been long painful work, but, for all that, Daniel had fond memories of this room. It represented independence and freedom and, on more than one occasion, sexual gratification when Dorothy had still worked at Reception.

Now the mail room was run by Alfred, a simple lad from Whitechapel, who, at sixteen wasn't old enough to join his four brothers in the army. He sat on his stool, sifting through the morning's post and sorting them onto his trolley.

'You, out,' said Fletch, pointing at Alfred then at the door.

Alfred didn't need to be told twice. He scampered, knocking his trolley in his haste, and sprawling his neat piles of post. Fletch checked to make sure the door was secured. 'You've got to get out of here.'

'Is this some kind of challenge? You lock me in the mail room and then watch me escape? Are you going to time me?'

'This is serious, Daniel. Our Westminster source has tipped us off. You are now on MI5's radar thanks to that little prank you pulled the other day.'

'What? I didn't do anything.'

'No, but they're afraid you might. They're all a bit sensitive now Hitler is on the rampage.'

Daniel clenched his teeth. 'There's a story I've got to write; that's where I was this morning. A couple of chaps risked their hides rescuing troops at Dunkirk only to be arrested by MI5 when they got back. Why? Because they used to be members of the British Union. And now they're coming after the likes of me!'

'They're worried enough to have passed a new law to hold

"the likes of you" indefinitely.'

'On what charge?'

'They don't have to charge you with anything. That's the whole point of this new clause they've added.'

'I need to write this article. The people need to hear about this.'

Fletch clutched his blond curls in exasperation. 'The people aren't going to care. They are too frightened of Hitler to believe you aren't his pal anymore.'

'I was never his pal!' spat Daniel.

'Of course I know that; I know *you*. But they don't. They just see you as another fascist looking for a way to disrupt their world, and you can't really blame them. The British Union has hardly done itself any favours in the past.'

Daniel looked away. Fletch was right. Some of the party members hadn't exactly showered themselves in glory, and, of course, the British public had tarred them all with the same brush. 'So, what do you think I should do?'

Fletch sighed. 'You're fluent in French, aren't you?'

Daniel's back stiffened at the reference to his past. 'You know I am.'

'Well, Findlay's not exactly pulling his weight in Paris. His last copy focused more on complaining that his favourite theatre had closed to become a refugee shelter and the growing scarcity of good bourbon.'

'So?'

'So, you're going to Paris to replace him.'

Daniel stared at him in horror. 'You're sending me to a warzone?'

Fletch couldn't meet his gaze. 'It's Paris. The Germans won't break through.'

'Won't they?'

'Reynaud's adamant Paris won't be taken.'

'He's only been in office about a week. That's probably all pomp to get the people on his side.'

Fletch flicked through a heap of letters on Alfred's trolley indifferently. 'Paris wasn't taken in the last war.'

'Fletch, I'm not going to France!' Daniel cried. 'I'll leave here. I'll even leave my flat. I'll leave this job. I'll go somewhere else. Somewhere they can't find me.' He was hyperventilating when Fletch raised his hands in defeat.

'All right, all right. Don't panic. It was just an idea. I'm sorry. It wasn't a very good one. But you can't stay in the UK. They *will* find you. They're MI5, let's not forget.'

Daniel gulped. 'Then maybe I'll take my chances in prison.'

'They didn't pass a new law to lock you up for a couple of days. God knows how long you'll be behind bars. Certainly until this war is over, and that won't be for another year at least the way things are going.'

Daniel didn't fancy going to prison indefinitely, especially for something he hadn't done. He took a deep breath. There was no point panicking. The important thing was that they were a step ahead of MI5. He was still free. They had to keep their heads about them.

'Do you speak Spanish?' asked Fletch.

'Spanish? Not a lot. Why?'

'Spain is a neutral country. The family has some friends outside Bilbao. You can stay there until the heat dies down. Write us a few articles about bullfighting and flamenco dancers.'

Daniel stared at him, barely able to compute what Fletch was proposing. 'You want me to go to Spain? Is that even safe? What about the Civil War?'

'That ended ages ago. You'll enjoy it. Think of all that sunshine, the beautiful women. Consider this an assignment. There are other reporters here who would jump at the chance of spending a year soaking up the Spanish culture.'

Daniel hesitated. Weren't they overreacting just a mite?

'It's either Spanish flamenco bars or British prison bars,' said Fletch.

Perhaps they weren't overreacting. 'How do I get there? The Channel isn't exactly the safest place to be right now.'

Fletch's lips disappeared into a thin line. 'I'll think of

something. For now though, go check into a hostel, use a false name and for God's sake, keep your head down.'

23

Paris, France – Monday, 3rd June, 1940

The June sun beat down on Catherine's arms and bare head. She walked west across the city, weaving between the crowds of Parisian workers returning from their lunch break. She had visited all the hospitals in the city and asked so many distracted medical staff, 'I'm looking for my father, Dr. Benoit Jacquot. Has he been drafted to this hospital?' that she was sick of the sound of her own voice.

Hope had dwindled like a candle flame reaching the end of its wick as each time she was met with a pitying shake of the head until it had been snuffed out at the Hôpital Necker, the last on her list, and the same negative response. But then the receptionist had told her of a temporary hospital operating near Auteuil on the western outskirts of the city.

Catherine was filled with a strong certainty that this would be where she'd find her father. She didn't know why this temporary clinic would be different to all the major hospitals in the city, hospitals that were arguably more likely places to find a top Amiens surgeon, but something in her gut told her here Benoit Jacquot would be most needed, and he was always where he was most needed.

Catherine walked with purpose and direction, even enjoying the freedom and safety and normality that Paris presented, no matter how deceptive it might be. She wore a pale yellow dress given to her at the shelter she'd found on her first day and where she'd been for the past week. It was a horrid place, a modified school building that continued to operate for its original purpose, meaning all the refugees were crammed into the main assembly hall. Toilet facilities were limited as was fresh water, and simply the thought of any more Red Cross-supplied boiled potatoes and soggy cabbage was enough to turn her stomach.

Catherine took every opportunity to escape the shelter, to breathe air not permeated with rancid body odour and cabbage-induced flatulence, and to stretch her arms and legs without knocking into a miserable Belgian or a short-tempered Dutchman. Outside, apart from the odd group of soldiers pulling a small cannon or heading into a bar, Paris appeared to press on like nothing was the matter.

On her second day, she'd overheard two old men sitting outside a café discussing the advance of the Germans and one, in complete confidence and laidback certainty, had said, 'They did not break through into Paris in the Great War. There is no possibility they will get through this time. No chance! Our defences are too strong.'

It was a sentiment she was to hear a dozen times more from others, young and old, rich and poor. Not only would the French army successfully defend Paris's city walls, but there was a rumour that they were safe from the air as well. Apparently Hitler was an admirer of Paris's magnificent architecture and had no wish to destroy it. If there was any truth in it, then Catherine decided she would camp under the Champs Elysees from now on. It was all very reassuring to hear, but even so, the trauma of Amiens's fall still quivered within her, and she couldn't quite share the Parisians' faith.

She walked through the fifteenth arrondissement, catching the occasional glimpse of the top of the Eiffel Tower at road junctions where there was a gap between the yellow limestone buildings. She reached the Seine and walked along its promenade, taking relief from the shade of the strong arms and splayed green hands of the horse chestnuts that lined the way. People leaned upon the river walls and ate their lunches from brown wax paper wrappings, and Catherine noticed, not for the first time, men wearing *kippahs*, quite proudly showing their denomination.

Hesitantly at first, then with more conviction, she withdrew the Fleur de l'Alexandrie from her pocket and fastened it about her neck. The slight pull of the chain as she walked and the gentle thud of the pendant against her chest were more reassuring than any overheard rumour. Such a simple display of who she was allowed her to pretend that everything was normal, that perhaps Paris would remain a fortress of protection from the Nazis and that she could remain here until the war was over.

She watched with interest two dozen olive green flatbed lorries drive away from a vast, sprawling building proudly adorned with the sign Citroën. Catherine smiled to herself. Papa had always sworn his Citroën 7 was the best car ever to be made. 'The body of the car is welded to the chassis instead of being separate, unlike any other car on the road. This makes it lighter, so it can go much faster and use less fuel. It is a beautiful creature, *non*?'

Her father's words were clear in her mind, touched with pride and awe as he stroked the car's gracefully sloping wheel arch. She still had no idea what a chassis was, but that it was a car ahead of its time was very clear to her. Seeing all these lorries snaking away from the factory filled her with confidence. The French would overcome the Germans. They had just been caught flat-footed at the start of the battle. As she understood it, the only reason Hitler's armies were now in France was that the French had guarded the most likely border to be breached, the Maginot Line in the northeast, but the Germans had surprised everyone by breaching French territory through the previously thought unbreachable Ardennes Forest in the north, guarded only by trees and rugged undergrowth.

Catherine crossed over the Seine into the sixteenth arrondissement. She passed a school where the shrieks and laughter of children enjoying their lunch break drifted around the neighbourhood. She stopped to pick a stone out of her shoe, and, when she stood, she caught two young girls leaning against the fence staring at her. One pointed to the Fleur de l'Alexandrie that had been in plain view and held out her hand. Catherine smiled, even allowed herself a little chuckle, before shaking her head and moving on. The temporary 'H' signs for the hospital were becoming more and more frequent and a military medic's van had just passed her. She was moving in the right direction.

The van pulled up outside a building a few hundred feet ahead, and Catherine quickened her step. But the growl of the van's engines was suddenly drowned by the ominous wail of a siren. Catherine's heart jumped into her throat. She had no knowledge of the area; she had no clue where the nearest air raid shelter was. People around her looked more annoyed at having their lunch break interrupted than anything else, and they quickly but calmly hurried away. A group of children were marched out of the school by shepherding teachers, singing *la Marseillaise*. The boys swung their arms and legs like soldiers, and the girls trotted behind holding hands and gazing nervously up at the blue sky. Their voices were soon drowned out by the siren as they disappeared around a corner. Catherine ran, following others who had fled down a side street, but by the time she'd rounded the corner, they were nowhere to be found. She dashed back and saw others disappearing down another side street further along. But they too were gone by the time she got there. The noise of the siren grated on what was left of her composure, and, all of a sudden, she found herself quite alone in the street. The children and their singing had faded away. She ran towards the hospital, tripping over the cobbles. Her ankle turned and she fell with a cry. Then a familiar sound chilled her. Even above the long moan of the sirens that drifted across the city came the predatory growl of aircraft engines, closer and closer. She looked up and saw them high in the sky, dozens of black crows.

Catherine froze where she was sitting, then she shook her head. 'Hitler won't bomb Paris. He likes the architecture,' she whispered urgently to herself. 'Hitler won't bomb Paris…'

The air was suddenly alive with deafening sound. Whistling bombs were followed by the crash and thunder as they found their mark. The ground shook beneath her, as if in fear. Then the snarling bark of anti-aircraft guns firing back. Little puffs of white smoke appeared in the sky with a dull 'boof' as shells exploded short of their target.

Catherine dragged herself to the side of the street, her ankle screaming in pain, and tried to take cover in a doorway. The building shook, and the ground trembled as a bomb boomed nearby. Plaster rained down upon her, gritting her eyes. The choking stench of gunpowder filled the air as a great black cloud of smoke and dust began to gather overhead, turning the midday sunshine to twilight. Hitler didn't care about the architecture. He was bombing Paris! Catherine remembered the military lorries leaving the Citroën depot not half a mile from where she now cowered. He would be targeting munitions factories. She realised she couldn't be in a more vulnerable position. She had to find safety.

She pulled herself to her feet, but white-hot pain exploded in her ankle, and she nearly buckled when she tried to put weight on it. Ahead, the medic van was parked on the roadside. The hospital would surely be the safest place to be. Suddenly there was a mighty bang, and a piercing white light flooded her vision. She was lifted off her feet and catapulted backwards, as if in slow motion, then thrown to the ground amongst a hail of rocks and smoke.

At first, she thought the air raid must be over. The planes and guns sounded so distant, overpowered by a shrill incessant whistling in her ears. She spat out the dust and grit from her mouth and wiped it from her eyes with a bloody hand. She lay in a heap of rubble, concrete chunks biting into her body through her thin dress. Her eyes watered against the thick dust and stinging smoke that hung around in one big, dirty, yellow cloud. Coughing, she held her dress over her mouth but it was of little use. Ahead, she could make out the fiery orange tongues of fire licking at the building where the medic's van had parked. The van was gone. In fact, much of the building seemed to be gone, or scattered on the ground. Bits of walls hung in mid-air attached to wire that stuck out like an arachnid massacre. It must have taken a direct hit.

Catherine's thoughts immediately turned to her father, and,

for a fraction of a second, she allowed herself to contemplate that he might be dead. But the thought was too overwhelming, too painful to process even for a second. Papa was a top-class surgeon. He wouldn't have been at some silly, little temporary hospital. His skills would be put to use where they would be most effective. Where, she didn't know, but it wouldn't be here. Couldn't be here.

The ground shook again, and, slowly, Catherine's hearing began to return. With it came the realisation that the battle was still ongoing, and she was still in great danger. But where to go? The one place she thought she would be safe was now a pile of rubble. She must find an air raid shelter. She must get underground. Underground! The Metro! Catherine clawed through her muddled brain for a memory of a Metro sign. Even thinking was difficult. The Metro. Shelter. Safety. Yes, there had been a sign! And only at the bottom of this street.

She coughed again, her lungs straining against the suffocating air as she struggled to her feet. Added to her ankle injury, her shins throbbed with pain, and she must have bruises over most of her body. She forlornly fingered the rips in her dress. Then, with a reassuring touch to her throat, she found the Fleur de l'Alexandrie still in company with her.

She hobbled to the pavement and used the walls of the buildings as a support as she made her slow progress. Overhead, although she couldn't see them, she could hear the growl of the planes and the continuous whistle as they dropped bomb after bomb on the city. Each one sounded certain to be coming down directly upon her. The buildings beneath her fingers trembled and shook with each impact, a fearful shiver as one of their compatriots took a hit.

She stopped where she'd seen the school children playing. The school building had been hollowed out. Desks and chairs lay tangled, metal legs bent, among the ragged slabs of concrete. She couldn't see anybody. After the shouts and laughter that had so completely filled it just a few minutes ago, the silence and stillness were chilling.

At last, Catherine reached the end of the street. Through the dust and smoke the words '*Metropolitain*' flanked by arched, wrought iron street lamps came into view. She paused at the top of the steps and looked back. Having survived the first bomb, she felt strangely calm. The siren sounded so morose, the anti-aircraft guns so panicked, even the planes diving and ducking somewhere above the smoky clouds sounded agitated. Yet she stood alone, just a girl, but a survivor. Again, she had survived. Again, she had defeated the Germans. She had defeated Hitler.

'What are you doing standing out here?' a voice shouted at her. A young man, his hand on his head holding in place his grey fedora, and a woman in a pencil line dress and matching gloves were hurrying to the Metro entrance.

Catherine beamed at them and raised her arms wide. 'I have defeated Hitler.'

'Are you crazy? You are going to get yourself killed!' the man said.

'She's in shock,' snapped the woman. 'Come here, *ma cherie*. Come with us.'

Catherine allowed herself to be helped down the steps. The man thundered on the locked doors until they were opened, and the three of them were hustled inside to safety.

24

Southampton, England – Tuesday, 11th June, 1940

Night had long fallen when Daniel and Fletch stepped onto the Royal Pier at the darkened Southampton docks. Both were subdued. Any attempt at conversation was drowned out by the hiss and hoot of the steam locomotive that pulled up beside them and spilled out hundreds of chattering French soldiers. The salty air was suddenly filled with the sweet aromas of tobacco smoke. Daniel didn't see what they had to be so jolly about. They were about to embark on a perilous journey across the Channel back into a warzone that they'd just been rescued from.

A cool wind blew off the water, and Fletch tightened his coat about him. Daniel chain-smoked, too nervous to feel the cold. Finally, they stopped short of the gangway to a majestic passenger liner, the *Puerto Rico*, its black hull rising ominously high above them in the dark.

'Well, she looks pretty tough, doesn't she?' said Fletch.

Daniel didn't respond. He took another couple of puffs of his cigarette then ground it beneath his boot. He watched the endless lines of soldiers boarding the ship, the dozens above on the deck, leaning over the rail, and waving their *kepis* down at them. They must surely be overloading the ship. There couldn't be enough lifeboats. He noticed they were all wearing lifejackets, and he suddenly felt vulnerable without one.

'Will they give me a lifejacket on board?'

Fletch frowned. 'I think theirs are all military issue.' He patted Daniel on the back. 'It'll be okay. There's some treaty or other that forbids anyone attacking passenger ships. You'll be fine. Just a quick stop to drop off these chaps then down the coast to Spain. You'll be there this time tomorrow.'

Daniel shook his head in trepidation. Was the risk he was

taking worth escaping a prison sentence? He cursed the government. He wasn't a threat to them. Now they were forcing him to risk his life and move to some country full of bulls and tapas, and in whose language he only knew how to say 'Do you speak English?', 'May I have a beer?' and 'Where are the toilets?'.

Fletch took a booklet and papers and a wad of pesetas from his pocket and handed them to Daniel. 'Documentation, some money to get you started, and there're a few francs in there too in case you run out of cigarettes on board. I'll wire Santino, and he'll sort you out something more substantial once you're in Bilbao.'

'Very "Dunkirk Spirit" of you, Fletch.' Daniel flicked through the papers and raised an eyebrow. 'Dañel Barrera?'

'First rule of deception: keep as close to the truth as you can.'

A dockmaster passed them, blowing his whistle and shouting, 'All aboard! *Tous à bord! Tous à bord!*'

'Well,' said Daniel awkwardly, 'that's my cue, I guess.'

'Yes.' Fletch darted a quick look around then withdrew another item, wrapped in a handkerchief, from his pocket. He unfolded the cloth just enough to show Daniel a small pistol, then pushed it into his hand and closed his fingers around it. 'Take care of yourself, you hear?'

Daniel tucked the gun into his belt, a wry smile on his face. 'Haven't I always?'

Fletch shook his hand brusquely and grasped his shoulder. 'I'll see you when all of this is over.'

Daniel paused. Up until this point he'd been too busy worrying about being killed by the Nazis to think about how long he might be away if he survived. It might be years before he saw Fletch again – *if* he saw Fletch again. He steeled himself. He wasn't going to get morbid. He'd left behind many people in his life, and not since he'd been taken from his mother had he felt any sense of remorse at the departure. He'd designed a most effective life that prevented others from getting close enough to potentially become emotional baggage. Fletch, he now realised, had come disguised. He represented neither parent nor lover. He was a friend, a dismissively underestimated figure, who needed scant maintenance, who asked for scant attention, who gave so much affection though cloaked by casual banter and the commandment of their jobs to be so often in one another's company. Fletch was the one person in Daniel's life that, he now understood, he cared about.

He took a deep breath and forced a cool grin onto his face. 'I'll bring you back a flamenco dancer.'

Fletch attempted a smile in return but failed. Instead, he patted Daniel's shoulder in finality. 'Go on, before they leave you behind.'

It took approximately half an hour for Daniel's stomach to turn nauseous. Packed inside amidst thousands of malodorous French soldiers and the choking fog of tobacco smoke, he pushed and shoved his way outside onto the hull where it was equally crowded, but at least there was a fresh cool breeze to settle his gut. And if he did throw up, he had a fair chance of reaching the rail. Inside, there would be some very unhappy Frenchmen needing a new polish of their boots if the worst came to the worst.

The night was dark. No moon. No lights on the horizon. No horizon even. The Channel an oily black. He squeezed through the jabbering soldiers to the rail and leaned his elbows on it. He sucked in a lungful of cool tangy air and rested his forehead on his arms. He'd forgotten or perhaps had suppressed the memory that he got seasick. The last time he had been on a boat had been on a similar voyage, except in the opposite direction when he'd been six. He remembered now how he'd hurled his guts out; once his breakfast had been disgorged, he'd dry-retched, choking on the bitter bile that made him gag all the more. His mother had watched over him, rubbing his back.

'It's okay, Daniel. It won't be long now.' Her soothing words had been spoken in French. 'Soon you will meet your papa.'

That journey had seemed to take forever, but at last they'd arrived at Portsmouth, and, holding his mother's hand, he'd stepped onto *terra firma*, weak from his maladies on board. His mother's eyes had sparkled with excitement. She took out a torn, much-handled envelope from her breast pocket, picked up their one suitcase and strode along the pier to seek directions.

On the train, he looked out of the window at the countryside swooshing by, the rolling fields in a patchwork of a hundred shades of green, at the funny little houses in hamlets and villages and people at every stop speaking a strange language.

'Oh, what a surprise it will be!' his mother breathed, almost to herself. 'It will save him the trouble of coming back for us.'

Daniel had heard the story a hundred times before, but this time it felt tinged with excitement and adventure. It wasn't just another boring tale recounted by Maman in his grandparents' back garden while she took down the washing, or in the big stone kitchen while she cleaned the dishes after dinner. This time he lapped up every scrap of information about his father so that he would be prepared when he finally met him.

'Your father was one of the officers at the British base where I worked in their motor repair shop. Captain Gabriel Montgomery. He was so handsome, so dashing in his camouflage uniform and polished buckles. He had a moustache, and he would twist the ends when he was thinking. You have his eyes. His are that same pale blue as yours. You will be just as handsome as he.' She sighed. 'We fell in love so quickly. Then I became pregnant with you. Gabriel was being sent up north to the Somme, but he promised that he would come back for us when the war was over.' Her smile wavered for a moment. 'The war has been over nearly four years now, but I received a letter from him only a couple of months ago saying that he still cared for us. Your father is a very busy, very important man. So, we will go to him.' Daniel's mother had fluttered the envelope at him, obviously one of his father's letters.

They disembarked in London and took a bus to Richmond.

His mother's request for directions were met with many a blank stare until she showed them the envelope and pointed at the writing. Then they would gasp in understanding and point, prattling away in English. Daniel's mother would nod along, smiling, until they'd finished and walked away. She would grasp his hand and walk purposefully in the direction they'd first pointed.

'What did they say?' Daniel would ask.

'I don't know, but they pointed this way,' she would reply.

Eventually they found Captain Gabriel Montgomery's home, a tall white townhouse with black wrought iron fencing at the front and a shiny black door. They paused for a moment, taking in the imposing building, and Daniel was sure he felt his mother tremble. But then she squeezed his hand, led him up the steps, and knocked loudly with the brass knocker.

A housekeeper answered the door, and Daniel's mother said in faltering English, 'This is the house for Captain Montgomery?'

The housekeeper opened her mouth to respond when a woman's voice called from behind, presumably asking who was at the door, for, moments later, she appeared – a tall elegant woman with coiffed blonde hair. Daniel felt his mother freeze.

'Yes?' the woman said, joining the housekeeper at the door.

'Captain Gabriel Montgomery – this is not his house?' his mother stammered.

'Yes, it is.'

His mother gasped as if she'd been physically assaulted.

'Who are you?' asked the woman.

'My name is Fabienne Deschamps.'

'You are French?' said the woman with a bemused smile.

'Yes.'

The woman's smile remained pasted on her face although Daniel noticed her glance down at her watch. 'What can we do for you, Madame Deschamps?'

Daniel felt his mother's hand tremble in his. Her grip on him tightened. 'Gabriel is – He is…' She searched for the right word, but before she could find it, they were interrupted by three young boys bounding up the short path behind them, laughing and hitting one another with their school bags. Daniel and his mother were pushed aside as the boys barged through into the house, still shouting and jeering at each other.

The woman rolled her eyes. 'Sorry about that. Er – *pardon*. Boys. *Les fils*. No. *Garçons*, that's it.' She beamed.

Then the wailing of a baby from somewhere up the stairs drifted down, and the woman tutted. 'Honestly, those boys. Sylvie, please would you see to Arthur, and tell those boys to keep quiet!'

The housekeeper disappeared with a demure smile, and the woman turned back to them, her pasted smile a little less composed. 'Sorry, where were we? Ah, yes, what can we do for you, Madame Deschamps?'

His mother didn't respond, and when Daniel looked up at her, tears had filled her eyes, and her lip trembled.

'Nothing. This was a mistake. *Pardon*.'

And she turned and pulled Daniel after her so that he tripped down the steps. Yet she hadn't stopped. Her grip on his hand was enough to half drag, half keep him on his feet. He looked behind at the golden-haired woman. Her smile had gone, and she looked mightily confused. Mrs Montgomery looked right at him, right into his eyes, and, before Daniel was yanked around the corner, he saw her hand fly to her mouth in surprise.

Daniel sighed. He'd never got to meet Captain Gabriel Montgomery. Nor had his father ever tried to find them. Daniel was certain that woman had recognised him somehow, had realised the purpose of their visit before they'd disappeared from sight. But who knew if she'd confronted her husband, or whether she'd tucked her little secret away. Either way, Gabriel Montgomery was a first-class berk in his eyes. His mother had spent the last of her money getting them to London, so returning to France had been out of the question, although Daniel now suspected money was only part of her excuse and that shame had a lot to do with it as well. Somehow they'd just stayed put. For eighteen years.

Daniel gave a mirthless 'hmph' and patted his pockets. Perhaps a cigarette would settle his stomach. He pulled out a Navy Cut, but the breeze blew out his match every time.

'Here.' A dark, curly-haired soldier beside him said in French. He sparked his lighter and cupped Daniel's hands. Daniel took a deep drag, and his cigarette glowed into life.

'*Merci.*' Daniel took his packet of cigarettes out again and offered one to the French soldier.

The soldier's gaze fell to the gun tucked into Daniel's trousers. He took a cigarette and lit it. He nodded to Daniel's gun, now safely hidden beneath his coat. 'I'm surprised they let you keep that. We were all disarmed when we arrived.'

Daniel blew smoke out and breathed it in again as the breeze rebuffed it into his face. 'I haven't come from Dunkirk.' It felt strangely familiar to converse in his native tongue, although it was many years since he'd spoken with anyone remotely approaching fluency. The lads in French class at school had been stuttering imbeciles, and even their teacher, Mr Knowles, had had a limited vocabulary and poor pronunciation.

'Where have you come from then?'

Daniel eyed the soldier with caution. He seemed harmless enough standing there with his baby curls, snug in his lifejacket, but looks could be deceiving. 'Here and there,' he replied with a shrug.

The soldier laughed. 'Very good, my friend. I'm Antoine.'

He held out his hand and Daniel shook it. 'Daniel. Where are you from?'

'Reims. Have you been there?'

Daniel shook his head. His geography wasn't great at the best of times, but he realised he'd taken extra care to blank out as much of the information he'd ever received on France as possible.

Antoine regarded him curiously then a smile of dawning realisation spread across his face. '*Ah*. You speak French very well for an Englishman.'

Daniel remained unruffled that his cover had been blown. He took a leisurely drag of his cigarette. 'My mother was French.' He didn't feel the need to tell Antoine that, officially, he too was French. It would only prompt more questions.

'Is that why you are leaving the safety of England to go to France?' Antoine asked.

'I'm not going to France. I'm heading to Spain after your lot have been dropped off. And believe me, London isn't as safe as you'd think.'

Antoine shook his head, suddenly sombre. They lapsed into silence, listening to the laughs and cheery voices of the Frenchmen carrying on the wind. Daniel turned to look at them.

'And judging by the atmosphere on here, it doesn't say much for England that everyone's happier to be leaving it for a country occupied by Hitler's armies.'

'The evacuations made them feel that they were abandoning their homeland,' said Antoine. 'De Gaulle's broadcast last night has roused their spirits; to resist occupation! Now they have the chance to show Hitler that France is no pushover.'

'That's fighting talk, Antoine,' Daniel replied, resisting the urge to snort in scepticism, 'but it's not enough to win a war.'

'Why aren't you with the British army?' His face suddenly lit with excitement. 'Are you a spy?'

Daniel grinned. 'No, I'm not a spy.'

'Well, you would say that.'

Daniel laughed and shook his head. 'I'm not in the army either.' He shuddered at the thought and took another drag.

'Why not?' asked Antoine. 'Surely you are all expected to serve your country?'

Daniel hesitated. He had been conscripted, only a year before, as one of Chamberlain's 'militiamen', but he'd failed his physical. At the time, he hadn't known whether to be ashamed or relieved he didn't have to play any part in this war. 'Joining the army or any military group is just glorified suicide. No, I like my life as it is, thank you.'

'But without armies, who is going to protect the life you love so much? Look what has happened to Poland. They had practically no army. I doubt whether the Poles are enjoying life right now.'

Daniel thought for a moment. He wasn't a coward, he was certain of that much. He wasn't afraid to die either. But he valued life, so why take unnecessary risks? However, Antoine did have a point. As the Poles had proven, it seemed prudent to have some sort of trained defensive front in case the Hitlers of this world decided they wanted a bigger slice of the pie. That didn't mean every young man should feel obligated to be part of that defensive front though, did it? Why should he fight for a country run by a government he had no faith in? Why should he put his life in the hands of politicians to whom he was nothing but a statistic? Thank God he'd never been called upon to do so. He'd never thought he'd ever be thankful for his gammy leg until the moment he'd failed his physical.

'I wouldn't suit being a soldier,' he said finally.

'The Navy maybe?'

'RAF perhaps, if I had to.' He quite liked the idea of flying. There was something free, something rebellious about skidding across the sky, dodging bullets, and diving at the target that appealed to his sense of self. Up there one wouldn't feel so shackled to the war ministry's whims.

'It is your duty to defend your country,' persisted Antoine. 'You should be proud to have that honour.'

Daniel snorted. 'That's what they do, Antoine, see? They feed you words like "duty" and "pride" and "honour" to colour your common sense. What they're really saying is, "When our governments get into a pickle, we want you to take the brunt of it; we want you to put your life on the line instead of us; we want you to get us out of this shambles. That's all it is.'

'It is a fight worth fighting though, no? You can't blame your government for what Hitler is doing.'

Daniel regarded Antoine wearily, struck by his naïvety. He mightn't blame his government for Hitler's actions, but he could certainly blame Churchill for sending four thousand men of the 2nd Division to their bloody deaths in an effort to waylay the Germans' advance on Dunkirk. He stopped himself from telling this to Antoine. The lad didn't need the guilt of all that bloodshed on his shoulders.

Daniel took a long drag of his cigarette until the heat of the embers burnt his lips then he flicked it into the darkness. 'You're braver than I am, Antoine. Your parents must be very–'

He was interrupted by a vicious jolt and they were all rocked to the side. Daniel grasped the railing to keep his balance and withstand the impact from the surrounding soldiers. His eyes met Antoine's as a dull explosion shook the hull, and the boat gave a groan like a dying whale. Antoine's eyes gleamed with panic. An alarm bell split the night, and another savage shudder slung Daniel against Antoine. The two of them hit the damp wooden deck. Desperate shouts replaced the laughter of just a few moments ago, and people scrambled for a foothold. The deck tilted, and Daniel had to clutch at shuffling ankles to keep himself from sliding across its slippery surface.

'Daniel!' Antoine's voice was filled with fear. His wide eyes looked to him for reassurance.

'Hold on,' said Daniel through clenched teeth.

He steadied himself to one knee, reaching out for Antoine, but another explosion rocked the boat, and they were hurled against the railings. A laceration opened above Antoine's eye and blood sluiced down his face. He put his hand to his brow, dazed by the blow.

'Hold on!' shouted Daniel as the deck suddenly slipped away from them. He made a grab for Antoine but the young man was already sliding, ricocheting down the deck. Daniel's fingers caught briefly in Antoine's lifejacket, he felt a tearing, but Antoine's momentum carried him away. Daniel watched him land upon the far railings below like a ragdoll before disappearing into the abyss.

Daniel scraped his feet against the perpendicular floor trying to find a foothold and pull himself up onto the railings, but there was no purchase on the smooth boards. He swung himself from side to side until he could loop his leg through the iron barrier, but as he did so he felt hands grab him, grappling against his clothes, pulling on him like a drowning man.

'Get off!' he screamed at the soldier who hung by one hand from the railings. 'Get off!' Daniel tried to shake him free, but the soldier grasped his arm and pulled harder on him.

The ship gave a mighty bang and lurched.

Daniel lost his grip on the railing. He found himself falling, almost in slow motion. All he could see in his mind's eye was Antoine's body flung against the railings, knowing his would be the same fate, that these would be the last moments of his life, that he was in for some serious pain if he survived. He fell through the darkness, waiting for the metal railings to cut through his body, the ship's alarm mirrored within him. But when the impact came, it was hard certainly, but then it buckled.

Daniel plunged through the water, deeper and deeper, colder and colder, his wild flails paltry against the downward force. Bodies plummeted into the depths around him, cannon ball flurries of white bubbles shooting downwards amidst the gloomy black and green. A dull shriek of twisting metal filled the deep; heavy creaks and groans as the *Puerto Rico* battled to keep afloat.

When his descent finally slowed, Daniel kicked out, feeling the drag of his clothes work against his ascent. His lungs screamed for air. His left leg wasn't much good for kicking, but, arms flailing and his right leg going like a piston, he slowly rose higher. His lungs shrunk painfully without oxygen. It was difficult to tell how far away the surface was, but the water gradually became less cold and less dark.

Daniel fairly spouted from beneath the surface, groaning for air, then choked on the mouthful of seawater he inhaled. The dull gloopy noises of the depths were replaced with the sharper, louder sounds of shouts, alarms, splashing, and the screech of twisting, tearing metal.

He trod water, blinking the sting of the salt from his eyes, catching his breath, trying to get his head straight and figure out what the hell was happening. The ship was sinking – that much was clear. It rose above him like a breaching whale, its hull rearing up partly on its side. A torpedo? A bomb? Were they under attack? He looked up, trying to see any planes overhead but he couldn't see anything but stars. For a crazy moment, he thought what a beautiful night it was. So many stars. You didn't get stars like that in London.

Daniel looked around. An inert body bobbed nearby, buoyant from the lifejacket that pushed up against his neck and cheeks.

'Antoine!' Daniel screamed. He swum furiously and grabbed Antoine by the lifejacket and shook him. 'Antoine!'

Antoine didn't open his eyes. Blood, diluted by the water, weeped from the wound on his face. He looked so peaceful, as if sleeping, his head resting to one side against the jacket.

Daniel shook him again. 'Antoine!'

A more intense sound of distorted metal filled the air and Daniel looked up at the ship. It was sinking fast. Desperate shouts were cut off mid-scream as those closer to the vessel were sucked under with it.

'Shit. Antoine, wake up!' Daniel shook him again, slapped him across the face. 'Come on!' Grasping Antoine's lifejacket with one hand, he tried to swim away, pulling the young soldier after him. But it was slow going, and the undertow of the sinking ship pulled them back. It wasn't going to work. Clumsily, he pressed his fingers against Antoine's coronary artery beneath his jaw. Antoine's head lolled to the side, revealing a great crushing dent in the side of his head. Daniel gave a whimper and forgot to tread water. He flailed, choking, to the surface again.

Antoine was dead.

Daniel closed his eyes and rested his forehead against the young soldier's. But then more frightened shouts spurred him into action, and he wrestled the lifejacket from Antoine. 'Sorry mate. Needs must.'

As he wrestled with the jacket, he came across Antoine's

papers in the soldier's breast pocket. Shame at what he was doing prompted Daniel to take them. He didn't even know Antoine's last name. Free of the jacket, Antoine began to sink. Daniel watched for only a moment, then, aware of the rush of water through his clothes as the ship sucked him closer, he looped his arm through the jacket and swam for all he was worth in the opposite direction.

Daniel didn't know how long he'd been in the water, but his entire body was numb; his legs could only pitifully tread water beneath him. If it weren't for Antoine's lifejacket, he would most certainly have drowned by now. The sea had calmed to a soothing lap, now that it was satisfied with the bounty it had swallowed. The ship was gone, the water was quiet. There were dozens of other men in the water, but they were all silent, like him, lost in their own thoughts, perhaps dead or unconscious from the cold.

'Oi, oi! Anyone there?' a Cockney voice drifted across the water.

An Englishman!

'Hello!' Daniel yelled. He waved, not knowing where the voice had come from.

Finally, he saw it. A lifeboat, a man holding a lantern over the edge, hauling people over the side.

'Over here!' shouted Daniel at the top of his voice, which then descended into uncontrollable coughing.

The lifeboat took torturously long to get to him, but then the sailor, in his wide striped collar and round white cap, finally grasped Daniel by the lapels of his lifejacket and launched him into the boat. After the chill of the water, a fresh wave of cold swept through him as he was exposed to the breeze.

He looked up at his saviour, teeth a-chatter. 'Thank you,' he stammered.

'You all right, mate?' said the Cockney sailor. 'Parlay-voo Anglay? What's your name, Pierre?'

'Daniel. My name's Daniel. I'm English.'

The sailor did a double-take. 'You part of the crew?'

Daniel shook his head.

'Well, whatever you are, we'll have you safely on land soon enough.'

'We're going back to England?' Daniel said. He wasn't sure if he was relieved or not. On the one hand, yes, it would be good to be back in safe, dependable England. On the other hand, he didn't much want MI5 to be there waiting to greet him when he arrived. Good ol' safe and dependable England wasn't such a comfort when you were banged up in a twelve by twelve.

'Nah, mate. We're closer to France. Le Havre probably.'

'I don't want to go to France though,' said Daniel in a sudden panic. 'I'm meant to be going to Spain!'

The sailor shrugged. 'Sorry. That's where we're 'eaded. Get that blanket round ya. And have a drink of this,' he said, unearthing a flask from within his uniform.

Daniel sat back and accepted the proffered blanket. The heat of the brandy in the flask flooded his body like a blue fire, immediately offsetting his shivers.

France. The one place where he really didn't want to go. Still. Le Havre was a busy port. There was bound to be someone there who would be going to Spain.

Surely.

25

Amiens, France – Friday, 12ᵗʰ August, 2016

S imon came to with a shudder, as if the cold Channel waters still chilled his bones. He glared up at Nick, his breath coming in small gasps.

'Bloody hell!' he wheezed. 'What the hell just happened? Why did you let me get on that ship? Are you trying to get me killed?'

Nick bit his tongue as a volcanic spurt of indignation rose inside him. 'No, of course not,' he snapped. 'How was I supposed to know the *Puerto Rico* sank?'

'Couldn't you have at least found a boat that got to France safely?'

Nick glowered at him then scraped back his chair and got up. 'I'm not an expert on World War Two history. I'm doing my best, okay?' He picked up Simon's inhaler from the dressing table and tossed it to him. 'Take a puff before you have a full-blown attack, will you?'

Simon took it grudgingly and gulped down a couple of puffs. 'It's just that I'm – or rather Daniel is Catherine's last hope. We have to do more.'

'We are doing everything we possibly can,' Nick exclaimed with a desperate flap of his arms. 'We're already putting your life and Amanda's at risk. No one can expect more.'

Simon looked at him in surprise. 'Don't back out on me now, Nick.'

'I'm not backing out on you. I'm just saying we're doing everything we can to save bloody Catherine Jacquot. For what I still don't know, but hers isn't the only life that needs living.'

'*I* need to save her,' said Simon. 'You're helping *me*.'

Nick gave his step-brother a grim look. Simon was his best

friend and the closest thing he had to a brother, but dammit, wasn't this pushing the boundaries of loyalties? He looked at his watch and headed for the door. With any luck, he and Amanda could lead Catherine into Schneider's path at the Theatre de l'Opéra shelter and have everything wrapped up and back to normality before lunch. Simon would be none the wiser. Nick wondered if he could grab a quick drink down in the bar before Amanda's session. A soaking of Merlot was sure to take the edge off his nerves. 'Next time,' he said. 'Catherine's life isn't the only one that needs living.'

Simon nodded reluctantly. 'We're doing the right thing, Nick. I know you have your doubts, but it is the right thing.'

Nick paused by the door, his back to Simon. The right thing? What was the right thing? Who got to say what was the right thing? Was the right thing not to change things back to the way they were? Even if it meant hurting some people along the way? That, surely, was the natural way of things. That was life. That was Nature. It was only human emotion that put the natural ebb and flow of life and death off balance. Would Simon still think this was the right thing to do if he knew that his father was alive and well in London? Of course not.

Hidden from view, Nick felt a sneer curl his lip. Simon made out he was all holier than thou when really, when it came down to it, he was just as flawed, just as biased, just as selfish as the rest of them. Simon would give up Catherine Jacquot in a trice if he knew about John Hayes. He would also forsake Nick's inheritance. Without a second thought. Nick and Amanda might be double-crossing Simon, but he would do the exact same thing if he were in their position.

Nick turned around, a reassuring smile on his face. 'I know, mate.'

After Nick had gone, Simon was left with a jumble of thoughts about Daniel. So he was French originally. That was why they'd never been able to find a birth certificate for him. And his name was Daniel Deschamps, not Daniel Barrow. Where did he get the name Barrow? What had happened to his mother? Why had he needed to go into care?

Simon went over to his laptop and sat cross-legged on the bed, waiting for it to load. Finally, he was able to load a genealogy website and typed in 'Daniel Deschamps'. Dozens of results returned, but mostly from Canada. Simon scrolled through the names and dates and locations, on the first page, then the second. A couple of French censuses popped up but they were much too old to match Daniel. His hope swaying, he clicked on the final page.

Nothing. Mind, that wasn't so surprising. Daniel would have been born in roughly 1916 or 1917. He already knew French censuses weren't microfilmed like British records were, and the 100-year confidentiality rule might equally apply to French censuses too.

He clicked on the Birth Records tab. Again, mostly links to Quebec, Canada. Then one caught his eye – '*Daniel Deschamps; birth 04/10/1916 Departement de la Sarthe Pays de la Loire, France.*'

Simon's heart began to thud. Fingers trembling, he clicked on the link. A page asking him to pay some extortionate fee for foreign records appeared, and he groaned. Instead, he contented himself by looking at the brief details in the link preview. It had to be Daniel, surely.

Simon's thoughts turned to Montgomery, the sleaze who'd lied to Fabienne Deschamps about not having a family. He'd had at least four sons, the youngest of which, Arthur, had been born after the war and after his affair with Fabienne. On a whim, Simon entered Arthur Montgomery into the genealogy search engine, born in 1922, give or take two years, father Gabriel.

The very first link went to one Arthur Montgomery, born in Richmond, London in 1922. Simon clicked on it and followed it to somebody's public family tree. There was a picture of a young man in army uniform, handsome and bearing a striking resemblance to Daniel. 'Arthur Montgomery; 1922-1944.'

Simon's heart sank. That crying baby he'd heard upstairs at the Montgomerys' Richmond home had not even lived beyond

Simon's own age. He had been killed in France five weeks after his twenty-second birthday. Listed alongside him were, in fact, four other siblings. Three older brothers and one younger still. The older ones, William, Henry, and Kenneth had, like their younger brother Arthur, all been killed in the war – another in France, one in Germany, and one during the Western Desert Campaign in North Africa.

Simon's heart twisted in remorse. Captain Gabriel Montgomery might have been a dickhead to Fabienne and Daniel, but no person deserved to see four of their sons die in battle. Their poor mother. She hadn't deserved any of that punishment.

The youngest son, Bernard, had not gone to war. He had lived, married, and had had three children of his own. Simon wondered about the two sons who had died in France. One had been in June 1940, around the time Daniel was on his way across the Channel. Might they ever have crossed paths? How would Daniel, the lone wolf, have taken to having five brothers?

Above the boys' names were their parents, Gabriel and Blanche Montgomery. Blanche's photo showed an elderly woman, still handsome with striking cheekbones, a whispered hint of the younger woman he'd met through Daniel. Gabriel's photo was black and white; of a much younger man, dressed in his officer's uniform and cap, intense pale eyes, a styled handlebar moustache that curled lavishly upwards at each end, a narcissistic smirk on his lips.

Perhaps Simon was biased after the fact, but Gabriel looked just the sort to cheat on his family then leave his mistress with a child to raise by herself. He had 'player' written all over him.

'Wanker,' Simon murmured.

26

Paris, France – Thursday, 13th June, 1940

Outside Theatre de l'Opéra ticket booth, the curving walls that had once advertised plays and operas were now feathered with displaced persons notices. Since the bombing ten days ago, the last shelter Catherine had been at had become impossibly crowded, and it became obvious that her father was not amongst those refugees. The government, along with the banks, had fled Paris just three days ago, and Catherine had salvaged a wad of ledger paper and pens from one deserted building. She had painstakingly written out posters in loud lettering: '*CATHERINE JACQUOT (Amiens), searching for BENOIT JACQUOT (Amiens, surgeon). Enquire at Theatre de l'Opéra.*'

A chilly wind blew in and ruffled the notices. A couple blew away. Catherine took a pin attached to a torn shred and found a space for her poster to adorn the wall where it was clearly visible. It partly concealed a colourful advertisement for *L'heure Espagnole*, the comic opera that her father had forbidden her from seeing earlier that year because of its frivolous nature. It was a French opera, although set in Spain. The thought of Spain both fascinated and terrified Catherine in equal amounts. The rich cultural cities of Barcelona and Madrid had always been a source of alluring fascination, but the strict Spanish Catholicism unnerved her. The Spanish Inquisition might have ended a hundred years ago, but it had been around so long before then that its prejudices against other religions, especially Judaism, felt ingrained in the common psyche. Catherine had heard talk amongst the refugees of trekking south to Spain, which had declared neutrality, neither siding with the Allies nor the Axis. Catherine held her doubts over such a stance, especially given

Franco's pro-Axis leanings. She would rather take her chances in her homeland, where she knew her government would not abandon her.

Catherine considered the weather. Thunder grumbled from within the black clouds gathering overhead. With the wind as strong as it was, she hoped that the storm would pass over Paris before the clouds burst. She had a dozen more notices to pin up, and she still had many more shelters to visit today. Steeling herself, she stepped out into the street. She pinned her hands to her sides to keep her dress from flying up. This one was too small for her – she'd been given it after the bombing had shredded her last dress – but apart from the length riding up above her knees and its tightness around her chest one couldn't really tell given how much weight she'd lost. Neither did it have pockets, which meant there was nowhere to hide the Fleur de l'Alexandrie away from anti-Semitic eyes.

She'd gone just three blocks when fat bullets of rain began to fall. The deluge was soon to follow. Catherine braced herself then relaxed. Actually, it wasn't so bad. It was really quite refreshing after the oppressive heat of the last week.

But it wasn't long before she realised, to her horror, that the rain had turned the fabric of her dress sheer. She couldn't run around Paris like this. She looked around for somewhere to take cover and dry off. A man in a rumpled suit and fedora hat, holding an umbrella, two-stepped through the puddles towards her, his face cracked with smiles.

'Here!' he called.

Catherine hesitated, then she recognised him. He was the man she'd met at the bomb shelter at the metro, the one with the stylishly-dressed wife who'd hustled her inside when she'd stood outside like a fool challenging Hitler.

Hugging her posters to her chest, she darted beneath the umbrella. He pointed to a side street.

'Look there. We can take cover beneath that awning.'

They hurried over. The man laughed as Catherine shrieked with every puddle they splattered through. She breathed a sigh of relief as they reached the protection of the canopy, and the man shook out his umbrella. She looked at her posters and gave a moan of despair when she saw the ink had run and ruined them.

'What are those?' the man asked.

'I'm looking for my father.'

'You're alone?' he asked.

Catherine nodded. Miserably, she stood with her back pressed against the cold wall and her arms hugging her chest. The wind blew the rain in, and she shivered. Paris looked dank and deserted in the downpour, and this side street was full of smelly, overflowing rubbish bins.

'Here, you're cold,' the man said.

Catherine gave an involuntary shiver as the man wrapped an arm around her. Unease prickled her skin. She didn't want to appear impolite. She edged away, and he looked at her in surprise.

'I'm sorry. I didn't mean to make you feel uncomfortable.'

Catherine was immediately filled with remorse, and she shook her head, trying to hide the heat that had crept into her cheeks. 'I'm sorry.' She stepped back and tried not to think about his fingers brushing against her bare arm. 'Where is your wife?'

'She's at home. Lucky thing. I was on my way back from work.'

'Where do you work?'

'You are very curious,' the man said.

Catherine blushed. 'Sorry. I didn't mean to intrude.'

The man smiled at her. 'You are most beautiful with your hair and your dress wet like that.' He curled his fingers through her hair and she stiffened, conscious again of her see-through garment.

'I – I have to go,' she stammered.

The man's grip on her hair tightened, and she gasped with pain. The smile on his face turned to a leer as he thrust her against the wall.

'No. Help me!' she screamed, but the rain muted her cry.

He yanked her hair again, and in her ear, growled, 'Shut your mouth.'

The smell of his breath made her gag. Catherine strained away from him. There was nobody in sight. The rain had cleared the streets more thoroughly than the threat of the Nazis. She struggled against him, but he was much stronger than her. She knocked his hat off, and it landed in a dirty puddle. The man slapped her across the face, making her teeth rattle and her cheek sting. Then his wandering hands suddenly stilled.

'What's this?' His fingers curled around her necklace, and Catherine gave a whimper.

'Please, just leave me alone.'

With a sharp jerk, he broke the chain from around her neck and slipped the necklace into his pocket. 'Stay still, and this will all be over soon,' he murmured into her hair.

His hand slid beneath her dress. The posters fell to the floor. Catherine pushed against him with all her might, but he had her off balance and she was half-forced to cling to him. She pushed and pulled against his jacket, and her hand inadvertently caught on his pocket. Her fingers closed around the sharp corners of the Fleur de l'Alexandrie. She lifted it out and struck him as hard as she could in the face. A couple of the star's points dug painfully into her palm. The man cried out and fell away, clutching his eye.

'You bitch!' he yelled, staggering backwards.

Catherine kicked him in the crotch. The man went down with a death groan. She didn't wait to see if he was all right. She ran out into the rain and didn't stop until she was back at Theatre de l'Opéra.

27

Amiens, France – Friday, 12th August, 2016

Nick and Amanda nursed a bottle of wine in silence down in the restaurant-bar. It wasn't yet noon, but Nick had never longed so much for the reassurance and comfort of a quality full-bodied Merlot. He took a slug and closed his eyes to savour the plummy sweetness cascading over his taste buds. He couldn't bring himself to look at Amanda. Just the sight of her brought back the terror of how close Catherine had come to losing the Fleur de l'Alexandrie. She was so vulnerable.

'We need to keep her safe,' said Amanda. 'The rate she's going she's not going to survive until Schneider's arrival.'

Nick opened one eye. 'It's only a couple of days longer.'

'But look at her, carousing around the city, getting bombed, nearly getting raped and mugged.'

'She'll be more careful from now on.'

'Will she? You'd think she'd be more careful since she nearly got blown up, but she hasn't. She's desperate. She's taking risks.'

Nick sighed. 'What do you want us to do about it?'

'Get her to stay put.'

'I've tried that already. It doesn't always get through. And who's to say she's any safer staying put in a shelter? She could be lured away by someone in there. As long as she's alone, she's vulnerable.'

Amanda pouted and took a sip of her wine. 'What about Daniel?'

Nick closed his eyes again. He really didn't want to talk about Daniel. It would only get Amanda worked up, and he'd get a barrage of abuse from her as well. He took another slug.

'What about him?'

'Presumably the little shit's in France now.'

'Yeah.' He ventured a look at her, noted her pinched brow. 'I didn't know the ship was going to be torpedoed, okay?'

Amanda glared at him. 'Don't get all defensive on me. I didn't say anything.'

'No, but you were thinking it.'

'You don't know wank about what I was thinking, Nick. I was thinking that now he's there, we may as well make use of him.'

Nick raised an eyebrow.

'Catherine's vulnerable on her own. So, let's lead Daniel to her. It would make your time with Simon a bit easier.'

'Aren't you worried he might save her?'

'Does he strike you as the sort of person to help a Jewish girl?'

'Not as such, but…'

'Catherine is a liability on her own. She needs someone to look after her, just for the next couple of days. Then you just manipulate him into handing her over to Schneider. We influence them both; make them believe that going to Schneider is the right thing to do. I mean, we don't know how much influence we can really have, so influencing two people will give us much better results than one.' Amanda beamed at him. 'Couldn't be simpler.'

'It won't be as simple as you think,' he warned her. 'Daniel's a lot less suggestible than Catherine, and even she's proving a stubborn thing sometimes. I've tried twice now to get him into trouble, and he hasn't taken a blind bit of notice.'

'So far you've got him arrested, on the run from MI5, and on a ship that was sunk by a German U-boat.' Amanda ticked them off on her fingers. 'I think you're doing pretty well actually.'

'That was all him! I didn't do any of that.'

'Well, then we shouldn't have to worry about him being much of a problem if he's that attracted to trouble.'

Nick downed the last of his drink and poured another.

'Aren't you meant to be meeting Simon at some stage?'

He grunted and hunkered deeper into his chair. 'Later.'

'You don't want to waste too much time,' she said doubtfully. 'I mean it's already Friday lunchtime—'

'I know, Amanda!' Nick exclaimed. He had precisely four and a half days to steer Catherine's necklace back into Heinrich Schneider's clutches to right his and Simon's family histories. What if they failed? What sort of life awaited him? A life of struggle and poverty. A life of revulsion from Simon when he learnt how Nick had tried to kill John Hayes to get his fortune back.

A wave of crushing shame swept over him. Maybe an impoverished life on the street was what he deserved for what he was doing. But it wasn't killing in the truest sense of the word, Nick argued with himself. Simon's dad had died in their original history. All Nick was doing was trying to set history back the way it was. So what if it took a victim or two with it? There might be loads more people who had died since they'd altered it to how it was now. Wasn't that how the butterfly effect worked? A butterfly flapped its wings, unleashing a chain reaction of mounting events that resulted in a tornado on the other side of the world. What if saving Catherine had unleashed a chain reaction that resulted in another Hitler? Another World War? He would be doing the world a favour by changing things back. Why should he feel guilt for the rightful death of one person and none for countless others of whom he had no knowledge? Did karma still occur if one wasn't aware of an effect caused by their original alteration? Did guilt have any real value beyond one's own selfishness? How could it if people only felt it when they were aware of the consequences of their actions and not when they were blissfully oblivious?

'You need to chill out, Nick,' Amanda said, looking him up and down with distaste.

Nick just wanted to go home; his dysfunctional home that he'd always taken for granted, had always resented for the shackles it imposed upon him. Right now he'd do anything for another ear-bashing from his grandfather about the future of Taylor Made Television.

28

Paris, France – Thursday, 13ᵗʰ June, 1940

Daniel walked through the Parisian streets, head down, collar up against the rain. He kept his pace leisurely and his demeanour relaxed even though his heart was beating like a drum. Paris was the last place he wanted to be, but nobody in the small fishing port where they'd all been dropped off was interested in ferrying him down the coast, especially when he didn't have enough money. Nobody wanted pesetas apparently. It was pointless going to Le Havre, the nearest main port, where a rescue had been in operation for the past couple of days, as the Nazis had already taken control of the area, and the last rescue boat had long since sailed. So, stranded in France, the only other thing to do was hitch a lift to Paris with the few francs Fletch had given him, track down the paper's French correspondent, Ron Findlay, and hopefully he could help get him safe passage down to Spain.

After asking directions to the eighth arrondissement, Daniel turned down Avenue de l'Opéra. He patted his pockets and pulled out a soggy box of cigarettes. He would have to let them dry out, and even then they would probably taste disgusting. He stopped outside a theatre where a man stood smoking. He looked incredibly scruffy for someone out at the opera.

'Pardon me. May I have one of those?' Daniel pointed to the man's cigarette.

The man regarded him with marked disinclination. Daniel pulled out his wallet and offered him his last remaining coins. The man snatched the money and, squinting his eyes from the cigarette smoke, dug through his pocket for his tin of tobacco.

Daniel rolled one for himself, all the while glancing around discreetly. This man wasn't the only scruffy theatre goer it seemed. People came and went, dragging their feet in shoes that were falling to pieces, dressed in clothes that looked and smelt like they could do with a good clean. He realised it must be a shelter of some sorts.

'Where have you come from?' he asked the man, giving him back the tin of tobacco.

The man passed him a box of matches. 'Brussels.' He looked Daniel up and down, almost in distaste at the cleanliness of his wardrobe, even after a six hour dip in the sea. 'And you?'

'Near Le Havre.'

The man's eyes dulled with sadness. 'They are there already?'

'Two days ago.' Daniel lit his cigarette and took a couple of savoury puffs. It was a bit stale and it didn't do much for his throat, which had started to parch these last few hours, probably thanks to his involuntary midnight swim last night, but it was too delicious to put out.

He gave a last glance at the building – Theatre de l'Opéra. Why did that ring a bell? He looked up at the black lettering above the curved marquee – *L'heure Espagnole* – and he snorted at the irony. It translated as *Spanish Time*. Oh, how he wished he was now keeping Spanish time. He nodded his thanks to the man and walked on.

Daniel's days spent in the mail room had not been in vain. Ron Findlay's address was imprinted on his brain, and it didn't take him long to find it. It was one of a dozen or so flats in a complex, secured by a wrought iron gate through which Daniel could see a pleasant-looking glitter-stone courtyard with a fountain, overhung with purple wisteria blossoms that were losing their bloom.

He pressed the doorbell for Findlay's apartment and waited. And waited. The last thing he needed now was for Findlay to be out, or worse, gone. God only knew Daniel wouldn't be hanging about with Hitler bearing down on them. Two older women walked across the courtyard, arm in arm, and unlocked the gate.

Daniel gallantly held it open for them, bowing a little as they passed through. They hardly saw him, tittering to each other about the inconvenience of the banks closing. Daniel slipped through the gate, crossing the courtyard in quick limping steps, and stole into the stairwell. Two flights up, he found Findlay's apartment, overlooking the road. He knocked, tried to be patient, but his agitation was such that he was soon hammering on the door.

'Findlay!' he yelled.

His throat and his chest tightened with the effort, and he had to stop to cough. He was definitely coming down with something. He raised his fist to beat on the door again when it was opened by a podgy man with bleary bloodshot eyes and a red bulbous nose from which broken blood vessels spread across his cheeks. His top lip twitched beneath a bushy moustache yellowed from smoking. By the looks of his deranged salt and pepper hair and creased linen suit, Daniel had disturbed Findlay's afternoon siesta.

'What?' the man grumbled.

'I'm Daniel Barrow from the Northern Gazette,' he replied, pushing past Findlay into the apartment. It was a pretty decent place, open plan with parquet flooring and panelled walls, a chandelier, and French doors that opened onto a Juliet balcony, but Findlay had let it go to rot. It was filthy and was filled with the pervading stench of sweet bourbon, cigar smoke, and rubbish bins that had outstayed their welcome.

'What are you doing here?' Findlay said, stumbling after him though making no attempt to stop him.

'I was on my way to Spain, and my ship was sunk. I couldn't get anyone to take me the rest of the way.' Daniel stopped himself from adding that he'd hoped Findlay might help him. With a sinking heart he realised Findlay probably needed his help more.

Findlay shuffled over to a drinks table and splashed some bourbon into a cut glass. He raised it at Daniel. 'Bottoms up.' He threw the drink back, smacked his lips, and gave a satisfied groan. He examined the empty glass then looked across at Daniel, as if noticing him for the first time. 'You want one?'

Daniel shook his head. 'No. I want to get out of here. Out of Paris. Out of France.'

'Calm down. You're safe here. The Jerries won't get through to Paris.'

'I wouldn't be too sure about that. They've bulldozed through everything north of here, and they're making short work of the ports. The Allies are not winning this war.'

Findlay looked unperturbed. 'Paris'll be fine,' he mumbled, and shuffled over to a chaise longue in the living room, leaving Daniel to himself.

Catherine Jacquot.

Daniel woke up the following morning with the name imprinted on his brain.

Catherine Jacquot.

It was like waking up with a song looping over and over in one's head.

Catherine Jacquot. Catherine Jacquot.

But who the hell was she? Had he conjured up the name in his dreams? Was she someone from his past whose name had only sprouted to the surface of his mind by his return to France?

He tried to shake off the name and concentrate on his day ahead. He felt even worse than he had the day before. His bones were achy, and his sinuses were blocked solid, and he couldn't shake off the chills. Mucus dripping down his throat had left an uneasy feel to his gut. All he needed now was to come down with influenza.

Findlay was passed out on the chaise longue looking much the worse for wear. Daniel prodded him with his foot, but the man only grunted in his sleep and went on snoring. Daniel opened the French doors in an attempt to get some fresh air circulating.

Already a plan was formulating in his mind. Since Findlay wasn't in any shape to help him, he would borrow some money, find a post office, and send a telegram to Fletch. He couldn't stay in Paris. He would find his way south, either the whole way to Spain or at least part of the way down to the coast where he could find a boat to take him the rest of the way.

A wave of nausea rose up inside him, and Daniel only just made it to the bathroom in time. The toilet bowl was stained black, and he tried his best to avoid touching the sticky rim or inhaling the stench, but it was difficult when you were puking your guts out, and it only served to make him retch all the more.

Finally, spent and weak with fatigue, he groaned, falling sideways to slide down the bathroom wall. He pulled the chain and wiped his chin with the back of his hand. Maybe he should stay put for a couple of days longer, just until he got over the worst of this.

'No pity for a chap who can't handle his drink.' Findlay stood swaying in the doorway then stumbled forward, unzipping his flies.

Daniel turned his face away, gagging, as Findlay pulled out his fat, blotchy penis right at his eye level and proceeded to urinate haphazardly into the toilet bowl. Daniel rolled away and climbed to his feet. He leaned against the wall for a moment as the room tilted on its axis, then went to splash his face and wash his mouth out at the basin.

'I need to borrow some money,' he said, following Findlay out of the bathroom moments later.

'I don't have any to lend.'

'Just enough to send a telegram back to Fletch and to bribe somebody to take me to Spain. I'll tell Fletch to reimburse you.'

'Who?'

Daniel stared at him in disbelief. 'Fletch. Fletcher Willoughby. Our editor?'

Findlay frowned as he held up a dirty crystal glass to the light then decided it was acceptable and sloshed some bourbon into it.

'Don't you ever eat?' said Daniel in disgust. 'Or work? Or clean?'

'The water of life,' said Findlay, raising his glass, as if that answered all his questions. He took a slug and smacked his lips together. 'So, who is this Fletcher Willoughby? I thought our editor was Harold Willoughby.'

'Harold hasn't really worked there for ages. Fletch is his son. He's been acting editor for at least three years.'

'Hmm.' Findlay looked only mildly impressed.

'So, can I borrow some money?'

Findlay opened his mouth to respond, but was interrupted by shouts and cries coming from below the open French doors. Three young men were fighting over a Swastika flag in the cobbled street. As it was raised up the side of the opposite building, one of them began singing *la Marseillaise* in a rousing baritone and was silenced with a firm punch to his jaw that knocked him flat.

'Oi, oi,' murmured Findlay. 'What have we here?'

He turned back into the apartment and switched on a wireless radio in the living room. They were just in time to catch the end of a special broadcast.

'…And it is with a divine faith in the people of Paris that I pray that they will receive their German guests with hospitality and benevolence…'

Daniel and Findlay looked at each other in shock.

'The Nazis have broken through,' Daniel said, as much to himself as to Findlay.

'No, no. It isn't possible.'

Daniel hurried back to the balcony. 'What are you doing?' he shouted at the young men in French.

'Hitler has taken Paris,' one of them replied with a rigid *Sieg Heil* salute.

The man who'd been punched to the ground was still climbing to his feet. 'The French will prevail!' he shouted, and received another kicking for his troubles.

Daniel swung back into the apartment. 'We've got to get out of here. Findlay?'

Findlay was nowhere in sight.

'Findlay?' he called then had to steady himself against the back of the chaise longue as a barking cough squeezed his chest. He heard a clattering from the bedroom where he'd slept the night before. There, he found his host looking more animated than Daniel had thought possible, shovelling clothes and other possessions into a suitcase.

'We need to get the hell out of here,' said Daniel.

Findlay unearthed three sealed bottles of bourbon from beneath the bed and squashed them into the case. But it was too full, and the clasps wouldn't meet.

'Ohhhhh,' Findlay moaned and opened it again. He took out the whisky bottles… then dug out some fine leather shoes, a suit, and a shaving bag, and repacked the bottles. 'Ha!' This time the clasps just met, and he clicked them shut. 'Right. Let's go.'

There was an underlying current of unrest on the streets as Daniel and a red-faced, puffing Findlay hurried east to the nearest train station. They soon came out onto Avenue des Champs-Élysées where crowds had gathered on the roadside. They pushed through and were just about to step into the road when they were hauled back. Daniel looked left, and his heart plummeted to his feet. From beneath the spectacular arch of the Arc de Triomphe marched a hundred or more Nazi soldiers towards them. To his one side, a middle-aged man sobbed, unabashed. To his other, a man of about his own age clapped and cheered.

'We'll go via François Premier and cut ahead of them to the station,' said Findlay and disappeared back into the crowd.

Twenty minutes later, Findlay looked like he was ready to have a heart attack from his exertions, and even Daniel wasn't feeling too great. His lungs seemed to have shrunk to a tenth of their usual size and burned each time he coughed.

'Oh, my darling theatre. What will become of you?' bemoaned Findlay, halting quite suddenly.

It was the theatre Daniel had stopped at the day before and bought a cigarette off the Belgian refugee.

'Let's stop for a break,' Daniel rasped.

They moved beneath the marquee to avoid the shuttling crowds. Findlay still tutted to himself, his moustache twitching; shaking his salt and pepper head.

'I've been waiting months to go see this,' he said, gesturing to the poster for *L'heure Espagnole*. 'Months! And just when I have the chance, they close the place down and turn it into a bloody refugee shelter.'

Daniel gave him a dark look then turned his attention to the poster. Obscuring part of it were papers pinned up of missing persons. It made him shiver to see the sheer volume of lost loved ones. The nearest one caught his eye: '*CATHERINE JACQUOT (Amiens) searching for BENOIT JACQUOT (Amiens, surgeon). Enquire within.*'

Daniel's blood cooled a couple of degrees. There was that name! Catherine Jacquot! He couldn't have made her up. Here she was. But how? Daniel tried to think rationally. Maybe he'd seen the poster yesterday, but it had only registered on a subconscious level. Perhaps she was some European celebrity that he'd vaguely heard of.

'Do you know of a Catherine Jacquot?' he asked Findlay.

Findlay screwed the cap back on his flask and wiped his mouth with his sleeve. 'No.'

Then again Findlay hadn't ever heard of Fletch Willoughby.

Daniel tensed as a lorry of Nazi soldiers bumped past. Bundled into the back, they gazed around them like they were on a sight-seeing tour of Paris, except with rifles slung over their shoulders instead of cameras.

Catherine Jacquot. Find her. Find Catherine Jacquot.

The voice in Daniel's head was so clear, it startled him.

'Come on,' said Findlay. 'Let's get moving.'

Daniel nodded. He looked again at the missing persons poster. He was unnerving himself. Best that they got on their way. 'Yeah.' He took a couple of steps.

Find Catherine Jacquot.

Daniel stopped short, and Findlay gave him an impatient

glance. 'Are you coming or not?'

Daniel opened his mouth to reply to the affirmative then hesitated. He always trusted his gut. Even when his brain told him it was counter-intuitive, his gut was usually correct. And right now, his gut was telling him to find this Catherine Jacquot person. In some way, she must be able to help them. Daniel needed to get out of France, and if his gut was telling him to find Catherine Jacquot, then she must be the key to his escape.

'Wait,' he said. 'I just – I just need to go inside. I need to…' He felt stupid even saying it. 'I need to check something. Just wait here. I'll be back in a couple of minutes.'

Findlay rolled his eyes and put down his suitcase again. Out came the flask.

'Wait here.' Daniel turned back to the theatre and hurried inside.

The first thing that hit him was the smell. Even with his sinuses blocked, the stench of unwashed bodies and blocked toilets was nauseating. He fumbled frantically for his handkerchief and held it over his nose and mouth. The lobby was crowded with dirty, disconsolate souls. A woman sitting against the wall listlessly fanned an infant lying in her lap. Two elderly men hunkered over a *tric-trac* board. Three young girls sat together, drawing on the back of a torn poster.

Daniel weaved through them to get to the main auditorium. He stood at the entrance in shock. Swarms of people slunk about in the semi-darkness, people who were dirty and tired and wretched. It was a world away from the eighth arrondissement and the life Findlay and his neighbours lived.

He approached a Red Cross nurse. 'Pardon me. I'm looking for someone here. Catherine Jacquot.' Daniel paused and licked his lips nervously. Saying the name again made it feel all the more familiar. He must have known her at some stage during his early childhood. But in what capacity? 'She left a notice outside.'

The nurse regarded him with tired, lacklustre eyes and

gestured limply to the masses littering the aisles and rows. 'Good luck,' she said.

Daniel ventured into the heart of the theatre, taking care not to trip over recumbent limbs stretched across the aisle.

'Catherine Jacquot?' His voice was hesitant and did little to penetrate the low hum of a thousand subdued conversations. He made eye contact with a tall, strong-looking woman. 'Catherine Jacquot?'

She shook her head.

'Do you know her? Is she here?'

The woman just turned away.

Daniel moved further amongst the people. 'Jacquot? Catherine Jacquot?' He raised his voice, losing some of his self-consciousness, and a few heads turned in his direction. 'Jacquot!' he shouted. 'Is there a Jacquot here?'

Still no one responded.

Daniel tried the other name on the poster. 'Benoit Jacquot! Is there a Catherine Jacquot here?'

'Do you have news of my father?' a timid voice said from behind him.

Daniel whirled around. Before him stood a girl, gaunt and dirty, but with clear brown eyes that were filled with hope. She couldn't be more than eighteen or nineteen years old, which put paid to his theory of having known her when he was a young boy, but she was quite simply the most beautiful creature he'd ever laid eyes upon. 'Catherine Jacquot?'

The girl nodded. 'Who are you?'

A disturbance at the top of the stairs stalled Daniel's reply. Half a dozen Gestapo stood framed against the light of the exit. A tall, broad-shouldered officer with an authoritarian manner stood talking to the Red Cross nurse.

Catherine gasped and staggered backwards into Daniel. '*Him*.'

'Do you know him?' he asked, catching her by her arms before she fell.

Catherine was too terrified to reply.

Take her to him. Take her to him.

Daniel hesitated. There was that voice again.

Take her to him.

The officer stood, hands on hips, surveying the auditorium.

Take her to him.

Daniel shook his head. He couldn't rid himself of that damned voice. Why would he do such a ridiculous thing?

Take her to him.

But he always trusted his gut. His gut was always right. His grip tightened on Catherine's arms.

Take her to him.

The officer's gaze swept over them. Then returned. His expression registered surprise then familiarity. He stepped towards them and tripped over a prostrate refugee.

Take her to him.

His gut was never wrong. Daniel sucked in a deep breath and slipped his hand into hers. 'We have to leave. *Now.*'

PART THREE

29

Paris, France – Friday, 14th June, 1940

Catherine pulled her hand free from Daniel's grasp. 'Who are you? How do you know my name? Where is my father?'

Daniel eyed the Nazi soldiers weaving through the refugees, kicking people out of the way, demanding papers be shown. 'I'll explain everything later. Right now, we need to go.'

The officer was side-tracked by one of his men querying some papers. Daniel spotted an exit beside the stage, just half a dozen rows down from the end of the line of seats where they stood. He took Catherine's arm, but she shook herself free.

'No. I don't know you.'

'My name is Daniel,' he snapped. 'Your father has sent me. Now can we go?'

Catherine's eyes narrowed. 'Daniel who?'

'Daniel… Deschamps,' he said finally. God, how peculiar that name felt on his lips. He hadn't called himself by his birth name since he'd taken the name Barrow after one of his foster-families when he'd been about twelve.

Catherine still balked, but he could see her fear rising as she kept a panicky eye on the Germans.

'You know my father?' she said, her voice high with jitters. 'Where is he? Please!'

The officer finished with his man's query, and his eyes returned to Catherine.

Daniel grabbed her arm, ignoring her gasp of pain. 'I'll explain everything later,' he hissed in her ear. 'If we stay here any longer, you and I are both dead. Now walk!'

Catherine capitulated, and they weaved through the people to the stage exit. Daniel could feel her shaking. He glanced back.

The officer had his chin raised, scanning the crowds for them. They reached the exit, and, again, Daniel looked back. His eyes locked with the officer's. The man shouted to one of his soldiers and pointed at Daniel and Catherine. Daniel pushed her into the darkened corridor and out of sight.

The corridor had no doors, no windows. It only led to a vast dimly lit room behind the stage that was littered with props and costumes and eerily staring mannequins. Gold light seeped through narrow basement windows that were brown with dust and dirt. Daniel barged through a couple of obese boxes filled with wigs and hats and tried to open the windows. The latches on both were stuck fast.

'Do you know any other way out of here?' he asked.

Catherine gave him a look of terror that he accepted as a 'no'. He grabbed a seventeenth century chair and swung it against the window. The glass shattered with a loud crash. He used the legs to knock out the shards still stuck to the frame then placed the chair beneath it. He gestured to Catherine. 'Come on.'

The sound of bootsteps entering the corridor came into earshot, and Daniel's breath evaporated. The window was narrow, too narrow for two adults to make a hasty getaway. He whirled around, his heart thudding against his chest, looking for another escape.

There was none. The room was wall to solid wall stacked with boxes and clothes racks. A line of mannequins queued along the far wall like they were waiting for a bus. This must be the very back of the backstage. The soldier's footsteps grew ever louder, and Daniel heard the unmistakable sound of a rifle being cocked.

He pulled Catherine towards a clothes rack beside the window, a jumbled wreckage of vestments hanging snugly together with ancient Greek costumes draped over the top. 'Here.'

Moments later, the soldier entered the room with a flourish, brandishing his rifle and swinging it from side to side. He immediately spotted the broken window and went to investigate. He peered through the opening at the street beyond.

Watching, Daniel hoped he'd presume they had escaped and leave. Instead, the soldier turned back and picked his way across the room, lifting each polished boot high over the rubble of costumes and props, kicking over other potential hiding places. His eyes beadily swept the room. A garment slipped from its hanger on the rack and fell to the floor, catching the Nazi's eye. A sneering smile pulled at one side of his face, and he approached with more certainty. He raised his rifle and pulled the trigger. Bullets tore through the costumes, sending bits of velvet and feather flying.

Two mannequins standing against the far wall, dressed in stolas and togas and wearing Greek tragedy masks, jumped at the deafening sound of the rifle fire. Behind his mask, Daniel darted a look across at Catherine. He could see the frantic rise and fall of her shoulders as she breathed, and he begged God that they wouldn't be detected.

The soldier kicked off a seventeenth century Renaissance costume that had landed on his boot, then chuckled. He picked up the deep burgundy, velveteen garment and held it against himself. He posed, laughing quietly then dropped the costume and carried on with his duties. He approached the line of mannequins, knocking over the first with the barrel of his rifle.

Sweat tickled Daniel's temple as it ran down his face. Trying to hold his breath, he had an overpowering urge to cough, to relieve his still tender lungs. He tried to swallow it down, but the sensation continued to build in his chest.

The soldier struck the mannequin beside Catherine, knocking its head off. Daniel's breath caught in his chest as the cough rose up. The Nazi raised his rifle to take a swipe at a frozen Catherine.

'Sturmann!' An authoritative voice yelled from beyond the darkened exit.

The soldier swore under his breath and turned to leave.

Daniel waited until he couldn't hear the bootsteps anymore

before succumbing to the coughing fit. He pulled off his mask, doubling over as the coughs shredded his lungs. His eyes streamed, and he retched from the effort.

Catherine rubbed his back, half supporting him. She took a small flask from beneath her swathes of clothing. 'Here. It's water. Don't worry, it's boiled. It'll help.'

Daniel drank greedily, revelling in the cooling relief that the water brought. He looked up at her as he returned the flask and almost laughed. She looked so comical with her dramatically morose mask on. 'Let's get out of here,' he rasped.

Through the window and over the railings that separated the basement from the side street, Daniel and Catherine blended in with the busy crowd.

'Where are we going?' asked Catherine, trotting to keep up with him as he limped ahead.

'Just round here,' he replied, pointing to the side of the building that led to the entrance.

'But that's where the soldiers will be!'

'Not the soldiers. Someone else.' He slowed as they reached the corner and slid close to the wall and peered round. Catherine was right. There were Nazis everywhere. And absolutely no sign of Findlay. 'Bastard,' he muttered.

Findlay might be a drunk, but he knew the city, and he had money to get them out of there. Daniel looked back at Catherine. Her clothes were dishevelled, yet, conversely, a pricey-looking bejewelled Star of David hung around her neck. Her eyes darted around. She would be of no help to him. What the hell was he doing saddling himself with someone – a Jew of all people – who'd only slow him down, make him a target?

'Do you know where the nearest train station is?' he asked.

Catherine nodded and pointed back the way they'd come.

'Let's go then.'

Daniel's heart sank as soon as the beaux-arts stone façade of the station came into view. Huddled within a large forecourt, that was bordered by an elaborately designed hotel, were crowded hundreds of Parisians, all pushing and shouting, carrying their luggage above their heads, desperate to get into the station.

He grasped Catherine's hand. 'Hold on to me. Tight.' He put his head down and barged his way through the masses. Catherine's fingers clung around his. The sheer strength of the crowd pushing forward, of bodies crammed tight together, had Daniel wheezing and coughing and sweating.

With one last unceremonious butt with his shoulder, he squeezed through to the closed entrance gate. He stretched forward and grabbed one of the flimsy steel bars and wrenched himself forward a couple more places.

'Let us through,' he said to the station guard on the other side.

The black-moustachioed man shook his head, avoided his eye.

Daniel opened up his jacket and put his hand to the pistol in his belt, revealing it to the worker.

The man's eyes flickered, and he swallowed.

'Let us through!' shouted Daniel above the racket. The effort of raising his voice contracted his chest, and he was wracked with coughs that seemed to slash his lungs and box his ribs. It was enough for him to lose his grip on Catherine.

In seconds, she was pushed back by the crowds.

'Daniel!' she shouted.

Daniel reached back, found her fingertips, but then she was pulled away. Daniel watched as the crowd swallowed her up. He turned back to the gate.

The station guard eyed him uneasily, his hand on the bolt. 'You coming through or not?'

30

Amiens, France – Friday, 12th August, 2016

Nick watched Simon apprehensively. His step-brother's breathing was becoming more and more erratic as he lay on the chaise longue.

'I don't know what to do,' Simon wheezed. 'He's letting me through, but Catherine…' His voice trailed away as the air in his lungs dried up.

Nick watched in alarm as Simon's face became paler, his lips a little purple. He didn't know what to do either. They needed Daniel to keep Catherine safe, but he hadn't been much help so far. They'd probably missed Schneider at the theatre now, and Nick didn't know where the officer would be until days later when he took up his station further south of Paris. They couldn't trust Catherine to find her way there on her own.

'Go back for Catherine,' he said to Simon.

Simon's brow furrowed. 'But I can get out of here. I can escape.'

'Go back for Catherine,' Nick said again, this time in a firmer voice.

'He's letting me… through.'

Nick watched in horror as Simon's lips turned from purple to blue. He needed to be sure Daniel went back for Catherine. 'Go back…' He squeezed his eyes tight and clenched his fists. 'Bugger this.' He snatched Simon's inhaler from the dressing table. 'Counting down from five. You're beginning to feel more aware of your surroundings. Four… you can feel your fingers and toes.'

Simon gave a strangled wheeze, and Nick panicked.

'Simon, wake up!'

Simon's eyes shot open, but immediately, his hands went to

his throat.

'Here, here, here.' Nick thrust his inhaler into his hand.

Simon pushed it away and tried to sit up. He pointed vaguely to his suitcase. 'Neb… Neb…' He coughed, and his eyes widened. His hand trembled at his throat.

'What? What? What?' Nick cried. 'You want your bag? What are you trying to say, Si?' He tried to push the inhaler into Simon's hand once more, but, again, it was batted away. 'What are you doing? You're having an asthma attack. Take your inhaler!'

Simon pointed frantically at his suitcase. Nick jumped up and flung it open. He rummaged through the clothes and shoes.

'What is it? What do you want?'

'Nebuliser,' Simon croaked.

'A what?'

Simon got to his feet and immediately fell down again, crashing against the coffee table and pushing it to the side.

'Oh, fucking hell, Si,' whimpered Nick, flinging items from the case everywhere. 'What the fuck is a nebuliser?'

Then beneath a hoodie, he found an oxygen mask of sorts attached to an odd, white plastic box. 'This? Is this it?'

Simon nodded. Nick scrambled back over to him, helping to secure the mask over Simon's face. But Simon fought against him.

'What are you doing?'

'Med… in cup… first,' said Simon, pointing to the clear plastic cup affixed to the mask.

'Where's the medication?' Nick pounced on the suitcase again and found half a dozen thin plastic bottles in a side pocket. 'This it?'

Simon nodded. His eyes rolled, and his head lolled.

'Oh shit, Si. Hang on, hang on. How do I do this? How much?' Nick managed to detach the cup from the mask and looked at Simon for guidance.

Simon held up four wavering fingers.

'Four bottles? Four mils? Four–'

'Drops.'

Nick's hands were shaking wildly as he squeezed in the correct amount of drops and reattached the cup and mask. This time, Simon didn't struggle when Nick pulled the mask over his face. In fact, Nick was alarmed to find he had to support Simon's head.

'Is that it?'

Simon leaned forward groggily and slapped down on the side of the white box. Nick looked. There was a power button on the side. He snapped it on, and the box began to whirr. Simon's mask fogged up, and his neck muscles tautened as he tried to suck in air.

Nick stared, his body tense, waiting for a sign that Simon was improving.

'Do you want me to call an ambulance?' he said doubtfully. He hadn't a clue what asthma was in French.

Simon shook his head.

After a long few minutes, his eyes began to steady, and a bit of colour returned to his cheeks. Finally, his throat muscles relaxed, and his breathing became more regular. To Nick's relief, Simon at last pulled off the mask.

'Are you okay?'

Simon gave a half-nod. 'Do you think we did enough?' he rasped.

'I don't know. You're the expert. Do you feel like you need more meds?'

Simon shook his head. 'Not me. Daniel and Catherine. He lost her. He was going to leave her. Why did you pull me out?'

Nick stared at him, stunned at the accusation. 'Your lips were turning blue, Simon,' he said tersely.

'But Catherine…'

Nick scrambled to his feet, needing to put distance between him and his step-brother before he thumped him. 'I wasn't going to let you suffocate just so I could find out if someone who's already dead managed to escape a train station.'

'But…'

'You ungrateful sod,' Nick spat at him and stomped out of the room, crashing the door closed behind him.

Simon lurched to his feet to go after Nick but barely made it past the bed before giving up. He stared at the door as it trembled in the aftershock of Nick's departure, and his breath shuddered. He hated slamming doors. He always opened and closed them as quietly as he could. Just as he had on That Day.

How cold and large the brass doorknob had been in his child-sized palm as he'd opened the interconnecting door to the garage. The exhaust fumes choked in his chest and stung his eyes as he stepped into the darkened room and he dropped his school satchel as he coughed. Before him stood his father's prized, red Peugeot 406 saloon, its back end nearest the door, ready to be driven out into the street. The engine hummed a low even sound that was almost soothing, but, in this confined space and puzzling circumstance, it also felt strangely ominous. Simon stepped forward and ran his hand along the gleaming red boot.

The feeble chirp of the shop bell sounded again, an increasingly impatient customer, somewhere far away from the garage, but Simon barely noticed it. His attention was caught by the hose jammed into the exhaust pipe. It was green with a yellow chevron pattern on it. Simon's first thought was what sort of cleaning technique his father was carrying out on his car this time. Some sort of enema? He knew what an enema was because James Dell's mother had had one for constipation, and they'd all had a good laugh about it at school. The thought of giving a car an enema made him smile.

He stepped closer to the car and out of habit looked at his reflection in the rear window. But it wasn't his own skinny twelve-year-old face looking back. Instead, it was a man's, with a strong jaw, filled out cheeks, dark hair, and intense pale blue eyes.

Simon staggered back in surprise at seeing Daniel in his memory. His heel caught the curling edge of the moth-eaten Persian rug that lay on the floor, and he tumbled backwards. His shoulder caught the corner of the coffee table before he landed on his bottom with a thump.

Simon grimaced, clutching his shoulder in pain. 'Son of a bitch,' he growled through clenched teeth.

Rubbing the point of impact, he climbed to his feet again and fetched his glasses. There. He could see a lot better now. That would teach him. Soon, the pain subsided to a dull ache, and his thoughts returned to the unnerving memory of Daniel's face in the Peugeot's rear window. He shivered, arms prickling, as a chill swept over him. He went over to his minibar and picked out a beer.

As he lay on his bed, nursing his drink, his thoughts turned inevitably to Catherine. She was more beautiful than in her picture. Seeing her through Daniel's eyes, she'd been real. Alive. He knew Daniel was just as smitten as he. He'd felt him lose his breath when he'd seen her for the first time, how his heart had skipped a beat. Somehow, Simon felt vindicated. He wasn't crazy after all. How could he be when he was sure Daniel felt the same way as he did? Simon wasn't the only one to be swept away by Catherine's beauty. He wasn't the only one now who wanted to save her. He was sure Daniel did too. Maybe not as much as Simon did, but then again Daniel had to think of his own safety. Simon was safe and sound in his hotel room in 2016 – apart from the attack by that lousy coffee table. Would Daniel go back for Catherine? Simon hoped he would.

Then it occurred to him that he could find out. He rolled off the bed and found his printout about Catherine. The picture of her and Benoit was becoming more and more worn from the constant folding. He held his breath as he read the caption: *"Catherine Jacquot, captured during the Vél' d'Hiv Roundup in Paris in July 1942, later executed at Auschwitz."*

Nothing had changed. Getting Daniel all the way to France and having him meet up with Catherine, escaping Schneider at the theatre, hadn't made a blind bit of difference. They had to do more. But not now. Nick was furious with him. Nick was taking it personally when he shouldn't be. Couldn't he see how desperate Simon was to protect Catherine? It wasn't personal. Maybe Nick had just been a little spooked by his asthma attack. Probably. Simon forgot sometimes that other people weren't as used to the drama as he was. He should probably go see if Nick was all right, apologise – not that Simon'd done anything wrong, but he had to keep Nick onside. Later though. Best if Nick had time to cool down first.

Amanda was waiting for Nick in her room, eyes bright with anticipation. 'So? How'd it go?'

Nick had to sit down. His legs were still weak and his blood still up. 'Simon had an asthma attack. A bad one.'

She gasped. 'Is he all right?'

'I think so, yeah. But it was touch and go for a while.'

Amanda closed her eyes. 'Oh, thank God. Without Simon, we don't have access to Daniel. And Catherine's so vulnerable on her own.'

Nick stared at her. Was the whole world going mad? Didn't she have any empathy for Simon? He could have died! He wondered how he was going to keep to their contract if this was what she was really like. Would it be worth it? Giving first dibs on acting roles to someone who was so selfish, so completely absorbed in her own problems and her own path to success? Mightn't be better to quit this whole thing, let Simon go home and discover his father alive and live a happy life? He considered which he would rather live: a life as a pauper or a life having to deal with Amanda's dramatics. Neither sounded particularly attractive. But Amanda's dramatics would be a lot easier to deal with if he lived in a nice house, as the owner of a successful company and a fat bank balance. He wasn't sure he could actually survive living below the poverty line. After all, he could always fire Amanda down the line if she grew too tiresome.

'I wouldn't be too sure about Daniel's help,' he said.

'Why? What happened?'

'We got him to the theatre. Schneider was right there. And

the bugger went and climbed out of a window and ran off with Catherine.'

'Why didn't you stop him?' Amanda was indignant.

'I tried, didn't I? But he's not as easy to manipulate as Catherine. He ignored all the attempts I made to get him to hand her over to Schneider.'

Amanda pouted. 'And now?'

'They tried to get a train out of Paris, but the station was in chaos. He lost her in the crowd. Last thing, Daniel was by himself and pointing a gun at the station master or security guard or whatever he was. Then I had to pull Simon out.'

'You didn't bring him out slowly? Are you crazy?'

'He was having an asthma attack. His lips were turning blue. I had to do something!' Nick glared at her. What was it with these people that they cared more about what had happened seventy-six years ago than what was actually happening now? To them. The ones who were alive. The ones who had a future.

'And does he seem okay? You know how pulling someone out of regression can cause this D.I.D. thing.'

'This what?'

'I don't know what it stands for,' snapped Amanda. 'A multiple personality disorder.'

'Well, it was Simon I left in his room,' Nick replied doubtfully. He hadn't appeared to be showing any evidence of being someone else.

'Better keep an eye on him, just in case.'

'What do you want to do now?'

Amanda chewed her lip. 'Where does Schneider go after the theatre?'

'I don't know. He doesn't say. Not until he takes up his post in Nantes. But that's not for another week.'

'So we'd better get Catherine back to the theatre before he leaves then.'

Personally, Nick doubted whether Schneider would still be there, but telling Amanda that wouldn't help. He nodded. 'Okay. Let's get going.'

31

Paris, France – Friday, 14th June, 1940

'Daniel!' Catherine was pushed back from the station gates, and her cries were lost in the clamouring of the crowd. She popped out the back of the square with an unceremonious stagger and a sinking feeling of thick dread in her stomach. She was alone again. Alone and in a strange place. She couldn't go back to the theatre.

Yes! Go back to the theatre.

No, she couldn't. Catherine shook her head to get the voice out. It was a ridiculous idea. There was that man there, that officer who had been at the Gromaires', who had shot Octave. If it hadn't been for the voice in her head, her gut instinct, it might have been her instead of Octave. She would most certainly have been taken away and had goodness knows what done to her. Her instincts had saved her then. She would be best placed to listen to them now. But to go back to the theatre to where that terrible officer was?

Go back to the theatre.

She stood on tip-toe and tried to see above the sea of heads for Daniel's dark hair. Daniel would know what to do. It was impossible to see. Why would he come back for her anyway? They didn't know each other. It was only through circumstance that he had helped her at the theatre. But Papa had sent him. Surely he wouldn't leave her when he'd only just found her? If the station guard let him through though then, of course, he would leave her. She had to stop relying on others to get her out of trouble.

Catherine squared her shoulders and raised her chin. '"I am the master of my fate; I am the captain of my soul",' she quoted aloud from the Henley poem they'd been taught in English class.

The desperate yells of the crowd were drowned out by a deafening roar as two German soldiers pulled up on motorcycles beside her. Catherine froze as the men knocked out their kickstands and jumped swiftly from their saddles, rifles unslung. They jogged straight for her, the sunshine bouncing off their grey steel *Stahlhelms*. Catherine's breath evaporated in her throat, and she closed her eyes, waiting for them to grab hold of her arms. She was knocked sideways as one bumped her shoulder, but no hands reached out to detain her. She opened her eyes in surprise. The soldiers had passed her by. They pushed into the crowd, their rifles held aloft, kicking, yelling for clear passage. She looked on in shock. Nobody seemed to notice her.

'Catherine! Catherine!'

She swung round at the call of her name. Daniel pummelled his way free of the crush and stopped in front of her, leaning his hands on his thighs to catch his wheezing breath.

'Daniel.' Catherine had never been so glad to see anyone.

'Trains are useless,' he gasped. He took a deep breath, gave a couple of coughs, and straightened up. 'But we've got to get out of the city.'

'I think we should go back to the theatre,' she replied.

'Are you mad?'

'I just have a feeling—'

'That would be suicide. No.'

A couple of gunshots rang out, and they both ducked. The crowd sank as one with a collective cry, leaving just the two soldiers standing.

'Disperse! Disperse!' they shouted.

People struggled this way and that, tripping over each other in their panic. They soon surrounded Catherine and Daniel.

'We've got to get out of here,' muttered Daniel, looking around.

Go back to the theatre.

Again, that voice whispered in Catherine's mind.

Daniel darted a look towards the station gates then at the two motorcycles resting idly beside them. 'Are you coming with me?' he said, gesturing discreetly towards the bikes.

Catherine looked at him in horror. And he thought going back to the theatre was suicide? 'You can't!'

'Watch me. But tell me now if you're coming with. I'm not going to sit around with the engine running waiting for you to make up your mind.'

'Where will you go?'

'South. Spain if necessary.'

'But my father–'

'Told me to keep you safe,' said Daniel. 'Come on. I'm not going to ask again.'

'But…'

Go back to the theatre.

Catherine hesitated. Daniel shrugged and casually walked over to the nearest bike. He looked over his shoulder towards the station gates. By the sounds of the soldiers' yells, they were still preoccupied with crowd control. Daniel slipped a leg over the leather seat and curled his fingers around the handlebars. He bounced up and down a couple of times, as if testing its strength.

He looked up and smiled. 'The fool left the keys in the ignition.'

Catherine cast an apprehensive look towards the soldiers. Neither were in sight, but as soon as he started up the engine they were bound to come running. 'Daniel,' she hissed. 'You mustn't. You'll be killed.'

'They'll have to catch me first.' He kicked back the stand and straightened out the front wheel. 'And I have no intention of being caught.' His foot hovered on the kickstart lever. He sent Catherine a challenging look. 'Last chance.'

Go back to the theatre!

Catherine bit her lips together, torn. Her heart told her to trust him. Her father obviously did if he'd sent him to find her. But the voice in her head was so insistent. What he was doing was so dangerous. Dangerous but ever so dashing.

She closed her eyes as Daniel kicked the motorcycle into life. Then without really coming to a firm decision, she hitched up her dress and climbed onto the pillion seat behind him. She barely had time to wrap her arms around his waist before they were bombing away from the square. She squeezed her eyes shut and pressed herself against Daniel's strong and comforting back, waiting for the crack of gunfire and the searing pain of bullets to perforate her body.

But none came.

Daniel swung the bike around the corner, and the station was lost behind them, safe from the soldiers' guns.

Catherine had never been on a motorcycle. She didn't know if the adrenalin buzzing through her body was down to the thrill of the ride or the fear of having just stolen a Nazi vehicle. Soon though, much of the fear quelled as the city made way for countryside. The roads south of Paris were no less busy than those they had left behind although mercifully free of Nazis. With the agility of the motorcycle, they were able to weave between cars and pedestrians and carts and bicycles and make better headway than most.

Catherine was aware of the stares that followed them – the looks of surprise and awe when they saw the German military number plate and Swastika on the saddle bags yet two French civilians astride. But it was still slow-going, and many times they were reduced to such a crawl that Daniel was forced to propel them forward with his feet.

The sun sank lower in the west, and the heat of the day subsided. Catherine became more and more conscious of how little fuel the motorcycle must have left, but they hadn't passed through any towns or even any villages or hamlets where they might fill up.

They came to a junction leading down to Orléans, but the traffic was at a standstill. Even pedestrians sat on the verge or leaned up against vehicles. Daniel brought the motorcycle to a stop at the top of the junction.

'What do you think?' he said over his shoulder.

Catherine considered the gridlock traffic leading south and

the relatively open road ahead leading east. 'It must be the better route to travel,' she said pointing to the Orléans road.

'But the road east is much clearer,' he replied. He wheeled the bike as far as they could go and nodded to a middle-aged man resting against a cartwheel out of the sun. 'Monsieur, what is the hold up?'

The man regarded Daniel with heavy-lidded eyes. His eyebrows raised a fraction when he recognised the motorcycle. 'You are playing with fire, my friend.'

'We are all playing with fire,' said Daniel.

The man gave a yellow-toothed smile. 'You don't want to go any further down this road. I'm told there is a roadblock outside Ablis. It's not clear whether it is a Nazi roadblock or a French roadblock. Either way, I think you will be in trouble for your transport.'

Catherine clung tighter to Daniel and tried to see beyond the line of stationary vehicles for military presence, but the roadblock must have been much further along. 'Let's go east. We can cut back,' she said in his ear.

'The fuel mightn't last that long.'

Catherine couldn't believe he might be considering chancing their luck at the roadblock. The man was right. It didn't matter if it was a German or a French roadblock, they would still be in deep trouble for travelling on a Nazi motorcycle.

'We cannot go down here,' she said urgently.

Daniel nodded. 'I know. Come on.' He wheeled the bike around and took a left. The road was much clearer, and they were able to pick up a little speed. Catherine closed her eyes and enjoyed the cool wind rushing through her dress and her hair.

With their shadows growing longer on the road ahead of them, they rode for the next four hours. As the sky turned from blue to mauve and apricot, Catherine knew they were travelling on borrowed time.

And finally, in what seemed the middle of nowhere, the motorcycle's engine stuttered. With a couple of coughs, the growl that had filled her ears these past few hours was suddenly muted, leaving just the fluting breeze and the ominous shuffle of refugees about them.

They rolled to a stop, and Daniel tried to kickstart the engine a couple of times, but they both knew it was useless. They dismounted and exchanged rueful looks.

'Well, it got us so far,' she said.

'Yeah.' Daniel sounded less than impressed as he gazed around them. 'Not a car or a village in sight.'

'We shall have to walk.'

'To where though?'

Catherine pointed to a drunken rusty sign on the verge. 'Le Mans. Twenty kilometres.'

'I'm not pushing this thing twenty kilometres,' grumbled Daniel. He sighed, giving the bike a last regretful look then wheeled it to the side of the road.

'Wait!' Catherine ran after him. She unbuckled one of the leather saddlebags. Daniel unbuckled the other. But all they pulled out were rain gear, a toolkit, a can of oil, an empty drinking flask, and some crushed biscuits. Daniel withdrew a handful of bullets, but other than that no emergency fuel can.

'It was worth a try,' Catherine said. 'At least we have some food.'

'Yeah. Save it for later.' Daniel pocketed the bullets and pushed the bike into the ditch.

Catherine looked sadly at the motorcycle lying on its side in a tangle of weeds and nettles then at the road ahead. It seemed to have no end. Just one long constantly moving caterpillar of refugees.

Darkness had fallen when Catherine really began to notice the slowing of their pace. Daniel's breathing was becoming more and more laboured the further they went, and his step faltered and tripped more and more often. She gave him the last of the flask water that she'd filled up at a small river, but it didn't seem to help much. His cough still tore through him until his eyes watered, and his shirt was stained with sweat.

'I think we should stop here,' she said.

Daniel shook his head. 'We must keep going.'

'We must rest. *You* must rest.'

'No.'

'Yes.' Catherine was indignant, and Daniel stopped to look at her in surprise. 'You need to rest, and I'm hungry. My stomach has been thinking about those biscuits since we found them.'

With her chin in the air, she flounced off the road, leapt across the shallow ditch and made for a tree fifty yards in, neighbouring a field of beet. She didn't dare look back, but when she heard Daniel's coughs not far behind her, she relaxed.

The biscuits long finished and the last drop of water teased from the flask, Catherine and Daniel settled themselves for the night. It was difficult to get comfortable. The tree's bark bit into her back, and tufts of needle-like grass pricked her bottom and thighs through the thin cotton of her dress. Crickets sang around them, perhaps gossiping to each other about the strange exodus of humans still trekking along the road. Constantly, silently, like ghosts in the night, the refugees trudged past, their footsteps and the wheels of their carts and bicycles crunching the stones.

Sometime during the evening, a battle started up somewhere on the northern horizon. Catherine and Daniel watched the dull flashes light up the distant sky, listened to the obscure pop and thud of guns and shells rolling in on the breeze like an approaching thunderstorm.

'If the Germans win this war, what will become of us?' she asked.

Daniel didn't answer.

'I'm Jewish, did you know that?'

'I know.'

'Does it bother you?'

Daniel was silent for a moment, and Catherine shifted position to get a better look at him. His face was pale in contrast with the shadow of stubble on his jaw. Beads of sweat on his forehead caught the moonlight like tiny pearls.

'At this point in time I don't think it matters who or what we are.'

They lapsed into silence. Catherine wondered where they would go from here and how long Daniel would last without medical care. That had to be their priority. 'We can't keep going like this.'

'There are people I know in Le Mans,' Daniel replied. 'They might help... if I can find them.'

'Who?'

Daniel didn't answer. When she looked at him again, his eyes were closed. His breathing was shallow and hoarse, and every now and then he gave a shiver.

Here was another person risking his life to ensure her safety. She thought of Duras and the Gromaires; how they had all sacrificed themselves so that she might live. How were the Gromaires coping with the death of Octave? She could still hear Agathe's screams. She could only imagine the depth of grief they must still be feeling while she sat here, comparatively content, comparatively safe, certainly alive. And of Duras? What of his family? Might he not have a daughter somewhere searching for him just as she was searching for her father? And all the while, Duras was lying dead on a road outside Beauvais; dead because of her.

Catherine blinked tears from her eyes. She felt so selfish. Why should she deserve to live when those who had tried to help her should die? Then again, what had she done to deserve to die? All she was trying to do was find Papa.

Daniel shivered again. What if he died too, risking his life for her? She didn't want to be the reason for another tragedy, for another family's grief. Perhaps the selfless thing to do would be to leave him here; to steal away in the night.

Catherine edged away from him, and he shifted, trembling, in his sleep. She stood up and looked down at him. He had rescued her from the theatre, from Paris. He'd brought her this far, away from the Nazis and their guns. He had done enough.

Papa would be satisfied Daniel had done whatever duty he had owed her father.

She watched as Daniel rolled onto his side, coughing in his sleep. His breath shuddered as a shiver ran through him. She hesitated. How vulnerable he looked.

She sighed and padded away, taking care not to trip over the uneven ground. Beside the road, she looked back at him. He seemed so small, so alone under the tree. She stepped into the ditch and pulled out a discarded suitcase then rummaged through it until she found a man's jacket. She walked back to the tree and laid it over Daniel's sleeping body.

Then she made herself as comfortable as she could against the trunk and settled in for the long night. It was time she helped someone else.

32

Amiens, France – Friday, 12ᵗʰ August, 2016

Nick gently drew Amanda back to consciousness then closed his eyes and waited for the onslaught of abuse.

'What the hell is going on?' she demanded. 'Why are Daniel and Catherine halfway to Spain instead of in Paris waiting for Schneider to arrest them?'

'They're not halfway to Spain. They're barely out of Paris.'

'I don't care. They're going the wrong way. Why aren't you manipulating them?'

Nick threw up his hands in frustration. 'Because I'm not God. These are people with their own minds. I did my best to persuade Catherine at the station to go back to the theatre, but she wouldn't listen. Why? Because it was a stupid thing to do! She's not stupid, Amanda. She might be innocent and naïve, but she's not stupid.'

'Then you are going to have to think of a way to outsmart her.' Amanda's voice was as icy as her eyes. 'How are we supposed to get the necklace to Schneider now? What if Daniel manages to save her? What will happen to me?'

'Daniel's half dead by the sounds of things.'

'It's probably just man flu. Maybe Catherine should leave him behind.' She chewed her thumbnail.

'She can't do this by herself.'

'She might. She's getting more independent.'

'What if she gets attacked by someone again and the Fleur is stolen?'

'But how are we going to persuade her to go back to Paris? Daniel's not going to agree to that.'

'Maybe we don't need her to go back to Paris,' said Nick. 'Schneider's next post is in Nantes. They're heading in the right direction.'

'But what happens if Daniel gets in the way again? We can't carry on chasing Schneider around France for the rest of the war. For God's sake, Nick, we've only got four more days to sort this out.'

'I'm doing the best I can, all right!' Nick shouted. 'Don't you think I've got enough on my mind without you reminding me of the fuck-up my life has become?'

There was a dull banging on the wall from the room next door and muffled shouts. Nick banged back and yelled at their neighbouring guests to mind their own fucking business. He stalked over to the window and looked out. It was another sunny day. The streets were busy with Friday shoppers. It looked just how he'd imagined this trip to be – fun, relaxing, new. Instead, it had turned into a nightmare; a nightmare more horrific than any he could have imagined. And Amanda was not making things any easier for him. What did she have to worry about? Her life hadn't exactly been turned upside down.

A wave of tiredness rolled over him. Maybe none of this was worth it. Maybe they should all just go home. Simon could have his happy ever after with his dad and... well, Nick would find a way of surviving. He was a resourceful guy, smart, he had an education, although he didn't really fancy putting his film and media studies degree to use. He could be a singer, busking on corners.

The image this prompted in his mind was seductive. He could just imagine strumming on his guitar, singing in the sunshine, people dropping money into his guitar case, a crowd gathering, watching him in admiration, clapping and cheering, someone stepping forward, giving him a business card, saying, 'Hello, I work with Universal Music. You're a natural talent. Maybe you'd like to stop by our studio?' And before he knew it, he would have an album out, it would go platinum, he would go touring around the world. He could just see himself coming back on stage for an encore to thousands of screaming fans then, afterwards, relaxing on his tour bus with a couple of foreign girls cuddling up to him...

Nick remembered where he was before he got too carried away with his fantasy. He turned and glared at Amanda. 'Maybe we should just quit this whole thing. The money isn't worth all of this drama. And that contract we signed? To hell with it. If this is the sort of histrionics I'm going to get from you in the future then quite frankly, I'd rather go begging on the streets.'

Amanda stared at him in surprise. 'What?'

'I said I'd rather beg on the streets than put up with you.'

Amanda was quiet for a moment. 'It's not as easy as you think it is.' Her anger had disappeared, replaced with bitterness. 'We mightn't have been on the streets as such, but it was bad enough. Living in a crummy little flat with walls thinner than here, the stairwell smelling of piss, the rotting windows letting in a draught. And the humiliation of Mum having to go cap in hand to pay for just the basics. It sucks, Nick. It's not carefree. It's not fun.'

Nick snorted. He wasn't some precious little princess like Amanda. He was tough. He was a man. Yes, he'd had a relatively comfortable life so far, but it hadn't been without its struggles.

'It was my fault, you know,' she said quietly.

'What was?'

'My dad. When we lost everything. When he... when he went to prison.'

'Your dad went to prison?'

'He's still there. Nobody knows. You can't tell anyone.'

'Not even Simon?'

'Definitely not Simon.'

'When does your dad get out?'

'Not for a while, or I hope not. He got thirteen years for fraud and money laundering. It was a Ponzi scheme he was running, one of those dodgy investment schemes.' Amanda stopped to heave a big sigh. 'I'd overheard him explaining it to my uncle in the living room one night, and he made it sound like he was being clever, not that it was illegal. Then I got into a "big dick" fight with this cow at school, and I told her what my dad did at work. Turns out her mum worked for some financial regulatory place, and she then investigated Woodbine Investments.'

Nick stared at her. He had no idea Amanda had such a shady past. 'How much had he defrauded investors for?'

'I don't know. The figure fluctuated depending on how sensationalist the media wanted it to sound. The more people gossiped about it, the higher the amount. As far as I know, it wasn't any more than two hundred mill.'

Nick's eyes nearly popped out of their sockets. Even given his cushy life, that was still a shitload of money. And Amanda had said it with such indifference. '*Two hundred million pounds*?'

'Hmm. But you know what? All those people who lost their houses, who lost their savings, their pensions – that's not what upset me the most. I was more upset that I was no longer going skiing at Christmas with Henry Radin-Smith's family.' Amanda turned sorrowful eyes on Nick. 'Does that make me a bad person?'

Nick hurried to sit next to her on the chaise longue. 'No, Amanda, no. Of course not. You were young. You didn't know any better.'

She gave a sniff. 'I was eighteen.'

'Oh.' Nick was caught short for a moment. Eighteen was old enough for some independent thought to occur. 'Well, even so, to have it all snatched away when you're used to a certain lifestyle is going to be tough, whichever way you look at it.' He rubbed her back and hoped she wasn't about to start crying. He couldn't believe her father was doing thirteen years for defrauding people of two hundred million pounds. They must have been rolling in it. 'Do you still speak to your dad?'

Amanda shook her head. 'Not in four years. Not since his hearing. The bastard didn't care about anyone but himself. He was a cheat and a selfish fuck.'

'It does you credit then. You shouldn't blame yourself for your first reaction to his betrayal. Anyone can see how remorseful you feel now about all those investors he cheated.'

'I'm not talking about them!' Amanda cried, slapping the arm rest. 'I'm talking about us, me, his family. He made himself out to be this smart, successful businessman and made us feel completely secure in the lives we led. And it was all a lie. He made me believe I deserved a life of a princess then it was whipped away from me.' She paused, her eyes sparkling with unshed tears. 'I'm a Cinderella story told backwards. I can't live like this, Nick. I can't! You have no idea how hard it is, how stressful it is to be constantly counting the pennies, making sacrifices to keep a roof over your head and food on your table – no more social life, not that it would matter when I look like I do with clothes that are rip offs or charity shop bargains. I can't even afford to get my hair done more than twice a year!'

'You look lovely.' Nick squeezed her shoulder.

'That's because I splashed out on a cut and highlights before we came over here. Which means I can't afford to do anything for another three months. Nothing. I can't pay for an overpriced cinema ticket; I have to rely on friends to buy me a glass of wine at the pub. Do you know how humiliating that is? Having to rely on everyone else to pay for "poor old Amanda whose daddy's gone to prison for stealing money."'

'I can only imagine.' Actually, Nick couldn't. It was simply beyond the realms of comprehension. He'd bought many a glass of wine for Amanda, and she'd taken it as her due, not that he'd cared. He could afford limitless glasses of wine. Until recently, of course.

'Imagine having just fifty quid a month to spend on yourself. That's fifty quid to cover anything that remotely comes close to being a luxury. Drinks down the pub, new shoes, a couple of items to restock your makeup bag, a bit of moisturiser or hairspray, a nice scarf, a trip to the cinema or lunch with friends. Try doing all of that every month on fifty fucking quid.' Amanda's lip curled in bitterness. 'I'm not being a spoilt bitch. And I know there are people who've had to live like this their whole life. But it's not as hard for them because they haven't spent most of their lives where holidays in St Moritz and an off-the-catwalk wardrobe is the norm. It's so much more difficult when you've had it, and it's all taken away. I haven't had years of practice being frugal and being budget savvy. It sucks! And it's stressful. We live in this giant capitalist world where there are signs everywhere shouting, "SPEND! SPEND! SPEND!", and I don't have the fucking money to do so. But they've made it impossible not to. You have to spend if you're to survive, so most of the time I'm stressing about money.' She turned watery eyes on Nick and grasped his hands. 'I don't want this to be the rest of my life. I refuse to let this be the rest of my life. What kind of life is that? Who wants to continue living when you can't even bloody afford to buy your own glass of wine? You can think me shallow or a gold-digger or whatever the fuck you like, but I know what kind of life I'm going to lead, and I'm going to do whatever I have to to get it.'

Nick squeezed her hands in return. Amanda had shown him a new side, an honest side, and he felt terrible for thinking so low of her. She really had had a tough time of it. 'I don't think you're a gold-digger,' he said softly. 'Or shallow. Not now, at least.'

33

South-west of Paris, France – Saturday, 15ᵗʰ June, 1940

The guns seemed much closer when Daniel awoke at dawn. His first thoughts were to get moving, but how terribly ill he felt. His whole body ached, from the thumping in his head down to the bruises on his feet. His face felt like fire, but he shivered uncontrollably. He couldn't believe his relief at seeing Catherine still beside him. She was already awake and looking at him, concerned.

'Morning,' he croaked.

'How are you feeling?'

'Like death.'

'The guns are nearer. They started up about an hour ago.'

A fountain of despair rose inside Daniel – the knowledge that in his current state he would never outrun the Germans. But he had to try. 'Let's get going.'

Catherine helped him up, and almost immediately he slid down the trunk of the tree to the ground again, the world spinning. There was simply no strength in his legs. Again, she helped him up. He wobbled, gritting his teeth in the effort to keep his feet. His left leg was even weaker than usual.

Catherine ducked under his arm and pulled it around her neck. 'Come on.'

Once they were on the road and moving, Daniel found it a little easier. His muscles, sore as they were, warmed up, but he was still desperately weak. Dizziness prompted spells of nausea, but with nothing to throw up, his body was wracked with dry heaves that sapped the last of his strength from him.

Despite Catherine's support, he crumpled to the side of the

road in exhaustion. 'I just need to rest.'

Catherine bit her lip and looked around at the steady flow of refugees. A car rumbled past, but it was so packed with people and belongings that the chassis fairly scraped along the road. A donkey and cart approached, and Catherine threw herself into its path, making the donkey throw its head in alarm.

'Get out of the way! What are you doing?' the driver cried, pulling up. Five faces, a woman and four young children, popped up from behind the driver's seat to see what the commotion was about.

'Please, monsieur, my friend cannot walk any further. He is ill. He's too weak.'

Daniel didn't know where to look. His instinct was to try cover up his weakness, to put on a show of strength, but that probably wouldn't help in this situation.

'We have no room,' snapped the driver. He flicked the reins, and Catherine stumbled out of the donkey's path.

'He could have made room,' she grumbled once they were out of earshot.

'Forget it. Just give me ten minutes.'

'We don't have time. You need a doctor as soon as possible, and we're still miles away from Le Mans.'

She was right, but that didn't mean he had to accept it. 'Help me up.'

On his feet again, Daniel felt shakier than ever. Every step was an effort. The day grew hotter. Twice he nearly fell to his knees had it not been for Catherine holding him up. He managed another mile before collapsing again.

'Water,' he gasped.

Again, Catherine went begging. But this time she managed to get only a small amount, hardly enough to quench his raw throat. He passed the flask back and closed his eyes. Catherine cradled his head in her hand. It felt so comfortable, so tempting to relax his aching muscles and go to sleep.

'Wake up, Daniel!' Catherine's voice cut through his haze.

He opened his eyes groggily. 'I am awake.'

'Don't go to sleep. We must keep walking.'

Daniel tried, but his legs just wouldn't support him. 'I can't.'

'You must.'

'Go on without me. I'm only holding you up.'

Catherine looked around desperately. She laid Daniel's head down on the stony ground then got to her feet. Although he'd said it, he was gutted to see her leaving. He'd have no chance alone. He was destined to die on the side of a road in France.

He watched her walk away then she stopped. She stood in the middle of the road, refugees skirting around her wordlessly, and she looked into the distance. Daniel followed her gaze. There were no carts, no cars or carriages in sight. He wasn't going anywhere soon, and even he knew staying here much longer would be the end of him.

'Catherine, forget it,' he said as she returned.

Her shoulders slumped in despair. 'We shall just have to wait a little while for some car to come by, that's all.'

'Mademoiselle,' a gravelly voice spoke behind them. An elderly man with a white bird's nest beard and rheumy blue eyes stood behind a wheelbarrow piled with suitcases. 'If you are able to carry these suitcases, then I will push your friend.'

The man, whose name was Jean Paul, dropped them five kilometres outside of Le Mans and carried on his way south. The water and fruit he had given Daniel had done little to make him feel better, but at least the rest had revived him sufficiently to walk, albeit with Catherine's help. The mid-afternoon sun was hot on their backs, and Daniel could feel the dampness of Catherine's dress beneath his arm. She must have been exhausted, hauling Jean Paul's suitcases all that way and now half-carrying him.

Despite a road sign telling them they were only five kilometres from the city, they were still surrounded by vast swathes of farmland. Daniel's dizziness was becoming more severe, when Catherine suddenly pointed ahead.

'Look, Daniel. A river!'

They staggered to the water's edge like desert-ravaged travellers. Catherine had to fill up the flask twice before he finally had his fill. The water was cool and fresh and life-reviving. His head pounded less, and the world spun a little slower. He watched Catherine drink: her long eyelashes sweeping low as she closed her eyes in exaltation, the larynx in her swan-like neck rising and falling with each swallow. Her skin was brown, but with her exertions now tinged a deep pink. She was probably completely unaware of how beautiful she was. She finished drinking and opened her eyes, caught Daniel watching her. She wiped a trickle of water from her chin with a bashful giggle. Daniel returned her smile, averted his eyes. But he had to look back again. Once more, they caught each other's eye, looked away again. Daniel felt like a teenager with his first crush.

They set off again, becoming more optimistic as houses and farm structures became more frequent, but then they'd peter out and their spirits with them. The open land gave way to high banks and tall trees that funnelled the breeze and shaded them from the sun. Despite the relief this provided, Daniel's strength ebbed, and they had to rest more often and for longer.

They reached an avenue of shady trees with tangled ferny undergrowth that threatened to spill onto the road.

'Let's rest a minute,' said Catherine with a sigh.

It was the first time she'd asked for a break, and as they settled down, he noticed just how tired she looked. Her face was red and shiny, her hair messy and clinging to her face in wet tendrils, and the collar of her dress was stained dark and dirty with sweat.

'Thank you,' he managed.

She gave him the water flask. It was light in his hand, and he knew there must only be a couple of swallows left. He shook his head and passed it back to her. 'You need it too.'

'No.'

'Yes.'

'No.'

'*Yes.*'

Catherine was first to capitulate. She took the flask and drank greedily. All too soon it was empty, and she craned her head back and sucked the last drops from its rim.

'How much further do you think?' he asked.

She smiled. 'Not far.'

But her smile faded too quickly to be genuine. He looked around at the cool abounding of soft ferns. They looked so inviting. 'Maybe we should rest here until tomorrow.'

Catherine shook her head. 'You'll be too weak to walk tomorrow. We must get to help by tonight.'

Daniel sighed. Of course, she was right. But his body moaned in protest. The pain had become secondary to the growing weakness and lack of energy he felt. To sleep, right there, right then, had never felt so enticing. He closed his eyes and took as deep a breath as his tender lungs would allow.

'Let's press on.'

Finally, the signs for Le Mans became more frequent, and a new fear rose in Daniel. Up till now he'd simply concentrated on staying alive long enough to get to the city. Now he had to find their destination.

Off the main roads, the stream of refugees dwindled, to be replaced by local traffic. Daniel and Catherine received stares of concern and confusion. Children stopped playing to watch them stagger by, women paused in their choosing of fruit and vegetables laid out in front of general stores to eye them suspiciously.

Daniel looked around in mounting apprehension as no landmark triggered any spark of recognition. They couldn't afford to get lost. He simply didn't have the strength to wander around Le Mans looking for some indiscriminate house. There was little point asking directions either since he had no idea of the address. All he knew was that it was in the west of the city, over the railway tracks, near the Sarthe River.

Of course, it would be furthest away from where they were travelling from, he thought wryly.

'Do you recognise anything?' Catherine asked as they

passed a sign for the train station.

He shook his head, and Catherine fell silent again.

At last, they crossed the railway lines, and Daniel stopped to look around. He tried to remember that day his mother had held his hand and walked with him to the station. He remembered waving goodbye. But the rest was a black abyss.

The day was beginning to cool, and as the heat left the air, Daniel's body too began to lose its last reserves of energy. His chest became tighter with each strangled breath he took. Another coughing fit doubled him over. He tripped over his bad leg and fell heavily upon the cobbles, dragging Catherine down with him.

'I can't go any further,' he said as she tried to pull him up again. 'I must rest.'

'But we're so close. We can't fail now.'

'I can't.' It was pointless. He didn't recognise anything. He was stupid for having thought that he could after all this time. He didn't know if they still lived there, or even if they were still alive.

'Then I will go for help,' replied Catherine lifting her chin.

They both looked around doubtfully for assistance when a gateway caught his eye.

'Wait.'

'I must get help, Daniel.'

'No, wait. That gate.'

With Catherine's help, he climbed to his feet. They hobbled across the road to the white limestone wall. It had been plain grey stone as he remembered it, but the archway with its rusty pheasant weathervane was the same. It was the gendarme's old house where he and his gang of friends had bathed in the horses' water trough on hot summer days. The laughter. The coolness of the water. Of splashing wars with the other boys and girls.

'Supper time, Victor!' he could hear the gendarme's wife calling from the house. 'You others get home before you're late for your supper.'

Still laughing, he'd leapt from the trough, grabbing his

clothes that had been laid aside to keep dry but had been splashed until they were soaked anyway and running out, barefoot, under the archway and turning right.

Daniel followed his six-year-old gaze and stumbled forward. There was the home of Monsieur… Monsieur… He couldn't remember the name, but he was the local mechanic and had a huge black drooling dog chained outside his workshop that he and his friends would dare each other to provoke. And there was the wall that bordered Madame Brossard's paddock of horses where he and his friends would wage war against a rival gang with their catapults. The paddock was no longer there. Instead, modern houses now dwelt there, but he was sure it was the same wall. There was the square where he and his friends would spy on Mademoiselle Mercier meeting her beaus under the Judas trees. And there was the old chestnut tree that he would swing from when he'd been bored or Maman had been cross with him and sent him out of the house.

Daniel stopped. His eyes travelled from the tree across the street to a grey stone house with a faded black door and old slate-tiled roof.

'We're here.'

The surge of energy that had accompanied the last twenty minutes of remembrance dissipated. Perhaps the knowledge that their gruelling journey was finally over was allowing his body to rest. He leaned on Catherine more as they crossed the road. He could barely lift his right foot to take another step – his left had given out long ago and dragged uselessly over the bumpy cobbles.

They mounted the front step, and Daniel lifted his arm to knock on the door. It felt like he was lifting a fifty-pound stack of newspapers. From somewhere within the house, a dog barked, and finally, footsteps sounded. The door opened, and a tall wiry man, well into his seventies, with a white handlebar moustache, stood before them.

'Yes?'

Daniel stared at him, unable to speak. He'd hoped he'd

recognise him straight away, but his memories were blurry and he couldn't say with any certainty who this man was.

'Monsieur Deschamps?' he croaked.

The man nodded, and Daniel smiled to himself. His grip on Catherine faltered, and the world seemed to somersault over; his brain gave a short surge, like consciousness fighting the urge to sleep.

'Monsieur Deschamps, my name is Daniel. I am your grandson.'

He didn't have the opportunity to even register the man's response, as consciousness lost its battle.

34

Le Mans, France – Thursday, 20th June, 1940

Darkness and dreams; whispers and a cooling touch upon his brow. Daniel was lost in a whirlpool of vague sensations, surreal emotions, weakness, and pain.

Fletch would come to him, stand beside his bed. 'I can't publish this fascist nonsense, you know that!' He slapped a newspaper down on Daniel's bed.

'Fletch! Fletch!' And when he reached out for the paper, it was no longer there, just the thin scratchy fabric of a blanket.

'You walked away from him,' a woman's voice spoke up from the shadows. 'Just like you walked away from me.' She stepped forward. His mother looked down upon him, her eyes awash with tears. 'Why did you leave me, Daniel?'

'You left *me*, Maman,' Daniel replied, and his voice caught in his throat. 'You let *me* down. Why did you have to be so proud?'

Fabienne Deschamps shook her head in sadness and walked away.

'*Maman!*' Daniel cried. He tried to get up, but he was too weak to even reach out his arms. Instead, he laid his head back, pressing it into the pillow and cried himself back to sleep.

Whispers in his room, voices beyond the door, every time the cloak of darkness pulled back, the sounds that drifted through left him shivering or burning up.

'You little bastard! I told you not to play with it!'

'Here, Daniel, drink this. There you go.'

'No wonder your parents didn't want you!'

'Daniel Barrow, yes? And you can read and write? Very well, you can help Mr Roberts in the mail room.'

'Daniel, can you hear me? Come, wake up.'

'Hello, Daniel is it? I'm Fletch, Fletch Willoughby.'

'Daniel, come back to bed, you old tiger.'

'Lift your head. There you go. Your fever is down.'

'You arsehole! You made me believe this was serious!'

Every now and then, he regained awareness enough to recognise Catherine in the soft lamplight, the coil of her dark hair hanging over one shoulder, felt the touch of her hand lifting his head and the taste of a sweet syrup that soothed his throat and chest.

At last, he opened his eyes and consciousness returned in its entirety. Catherine sat beside his bed, reading a book. He reached out a hand to make sure she was real, and she almost dropped her book.

'Daniel, can you hear me? Are you awake?'

He tried to respond but mucus plugged his throat. He coughed it up, gagging as it left its bitter taste behind, and Catherine was quick to provide a bedpan for him to spit into. She gave him some water to drink, and Daniel sighed in ecstasy at the cool pure taste of it.

'Catherine.'

She smiled at him and held her hand to his forehead. She swept his hair gently to the side. 'Your fever has broken.'

He tried to sit up but barely had the strength. Catherine was quick to help stack pillows behind him. 'How long have I been out?'

'Five days, on and off. You would wake up long enough to eat then go back to sleep.'

'I don't remember.'

'No. I don't think you were completely awake.' She smiled shyly. 'You were speaking English sometimes. You speak it very well. Mine isn't very good. I don't think my teacher at school was very good either.'

Daniel didn't reply. For some unknown reason, he didn't want to tell her the truth, that he was in fact English and had found her by chance, by some twist of fate in which her name had become stuck in his head probably as a result of this damned fever, and he had stumbled upon her notice outside the theatre in Paris, that he had persuaded her to escape with him on the pretext that her father had sent him. Telling her all that would ruin her trust in him, and, for reasons he couldn't explain, that trust was important. Ruining her trust in him would give her no reason to stay, and again for reasons he couldn't fathom, her presence gave him comfort – more than that: pleasure.

'I dreamed that my mother was here,' he said quietly, remembering the brutality of her words. 'Is she?'

'No.'

Daniel tried to laugh at himself. Of course she wasn't. How silly of him. They had all been hallucinations: his mother, Fletch, his foster-fathers, Harold Willoughby, the numerous lovers whose hearts he'd trampled upon. 'How are things going in the real world?'

'Your grandparents have been very kind.' Catherine's smile was marred with sadness. 'But Le Mans has now been taken.'

Daniel tried to sit up more. They were trapped. Hitler's control over France was spreading like a virus. How long would it be before he had control of the entire country? Was this their future? Would Hitler rule the whole of Europe? Daniel had no papers, nothing to prove he didn't belong in one of those awful camps. Catherine was certainly destined for one of them. Her chance of escaping was gone. Instead, she'd stayed with him and nursed him. 'Why did you stay?'

She shrugged. 'Where would I go?'

Catherine filled a bath for him. Every time he heard her steps approaching, departing, the whoosh of water being emptied into the tin tub next door, approaching, departing, he felt ever more grateful to her. When, finally, he sunk his weary body into the warm depths, the beginnings of life began to return.

Rays of afternoon sunlight varnished the wooden floorboards, and the faint tang of jasmine and the twitter of birdsong filtered through the shuttered window. It was a world away from his dingy bedsit in London with its windowless cupboard of a bathroom and the blare of horns and engines and whiffs of exhaust fumes oozing through the single window that overlooked the fire escape. It all seemed so far away. War seemed so far away.

With every minute, he felt more human and more alert. His mind ran overtime. He would have to make a plan for him and Catherine. Once he had his strength back. They must leave as soon as possible.

He thought of the people whose house they now stayed in, the people who had given him a bed in which to convalesce, who obviously did not mind the fact that Catherine was Jewish. In some ways, it made him proud that they were his grandparents. But in others, it frightened him to stay and find out who they truly were. His memories of them were hazy, but tinged with happiness. Pépère had been kind, but not someone to take advantage of. Daniel remembered how many a time he'd found himself on the wrong side of him. He remembered his grandmother even less. A quiet woman, who did not participate much in family discussions or take sides in arguments, who had never shown much interest in Daniel's affairs. After the move to Britain, his mother had spoken about his grandparents only rarely, had shut him down every time he'd asked when they might go back to visit them. 'Our home is in England now,' she would say stiffly, and that would be the end of the discussion. In his memories, they were good people. Getting to know them now and discovering they weren't the people he remembered would shatter his childhood love for them.

The water had cooled by the time Daniel decided he could put off the meeting no longer. He climbed out with much huffing and puffing, still weak from his illness, and dressed himself in the clean clothes Catherine had laid out for him. She was waiting on the other side of the door when he emerged.

'I was getting worried,' she said, smiling. 'I thought I might have to come in…' Her words dried up, and her cheeks pinked.

Daniel grinned. 'I wouldn't dare expose you to such a scenario.'

She helped him down the stairs and into the salon.

'Daniel, this is your grandmother, Marie, and your aunt, Lucille.'

A small woman in her seventies with dark hair not entirely grey, rose to her feet from where she was crouched beside an armchair. But Daniel hardly noticed his grandmother. He was captured by the sight of a large woman sprawled in the chair, who wore odd socks and childlike clothing, who wore a bib onto which a string of saliva flowed down her double chin from her hanging lower lip, whose eyes did not seem to focus.

'Daniel, you are up at last.' His grandmother's words were warm and relieved, and she clasped her hands awkwardly, leaning forward, but holding back.

Daniel averted his attention back to her, saw her indecision and, while still holding onto Catherine for support, he held out his other arm to her. 'Hello, Mémère.'

Mémère embraced him delicately, like a bird. Daniel continued to stare, over her shoulder, at the woman drooling in the chair. Her eyes lit upon him, and she gave a loud animalistic cry.

'Lucille, hush,' Mémère, disentangling herself, said not unkindly. 'Do you remember Lucille, Daniel?'

He shook his head. He had no memory of this person. None whatsoever. He couldn't even recall his mother ever mentioning her to him in the years after they left for England. 'Has she always lived here?'

'Of course. Where else would she live?'

'I – I don't know. I just don't have any memories of her.'

'You were just a boy. Your mind was filled with more important things,' Mémère said. 'Why don't you sit down? Catherine can make us coffee if she doesn't mind? And we can talk.'

Daniel frowned to himself and looked around even though he knew there was no one else in the room. 'Where is my grandfather?' He was sure a man had answered the door to him and Catherine, but that too might have been a hallucination. His grandfather could be dead.

'Pépère is still at work. He works at Monsieur Roseau's butchery.'

Jean-Philippe Deschamps arrived shortly before dinner. His face split into a wide smile when he saw Daniel sitting at the heavy kitchen table.

'My son,' he chortled and pulled Daniel into a rough embrace. His whiskers scratched Daniel's face as he kissed him on both cheeks. 'How are you feeling?'

'Stronger. Thank you for letting us stay; for saving me.'

'It is the least we could do.' He handed Mémère a brown paper bag that was stained with blood, and she opened it to reveal an assortment of gristly off-cuts.

'We are very lucky with your grandfather working at the butchery,' Mémère said, sawing up the meat. 'Rations only go so far, but we are able to get more meat than others, and we grow much of our own vegetables.'

Daniel again felt the weight of gratitude he and Catherine owed. This couple must already be struggling, what with rations, only one source of income from a man well past his prime, and the responsibility of a mentally handicapped adult. He recalled asking his mother time and time again when they were stuck in that dirty cold hovel of a flat in the East End of London, 'Why can't we go home, Maman? Why can't we go back to Pépère and Mémère?'

His mother would barely look up from her sewing machine. 'This is our home now, Daniel. We have made our bed.'

He remembered being utterly confused about that last statement. For weeks afterwards he would purposefully not make his bed in the morning in the hope that such an act would mean they could go back to France, but all it resulted in was a telling off from Maman.

And, ever since then, he had blamed her for taking him away from his idyllic life in Le Mans on a fool's errand to London, embarrassing herself on the Montgomerys' doorstep then being too stubborn to return to France, being too proud to go back to his grandparents and admit the father of her child already had a family and had played her royally.

Now, Daniel realised that perhaps there had been more to it than pride. There must surely have been times in that freezing flat, with that horrid landlord who always stank of booze and body odour, paying his mother "special" visits, with the long days worked at a tailor's shop, when pride would surely have succumbed to the comforts of France.

Daniel looked at Lucille sitting at the table, playing with her spoon and giggling to herself, at Pépère rubbing his eyes in tiredness, at Mémère preparing their meal with Catherine. They had enough to deal with. The last thing they would have needed post the Great War was another daughter and her fatherless child to care for.

Shame washed over him. So many times he'd thrown that theory of pride in Maman's face during an argument, for so many years after Social Services had taken him away he had hated her for ruining his life.

'How is your mother?' Pépère interrupted his thoughts. 'It has been so long since we've heard from her. She is well, I hope?' His expression was eager, desperate even.

Daniel gulped. He nodded. He hadn't seen his mother since the lady from Social Services had taken him on that first "holiday". 'She's fine,' he mumbled.

'What is she up to these days? She must be so busy. She never writes.'

'She works at a tailor's shop.' It wasn't a complete lie. She had worked there the last he'd heard. It was run by a French family who had taken pity on them when Maman had failed to find any work that didn't involve speaking English. For all he knew, she might still be there.

'And your father?'

Daniel hesitated. He had no material to embellish upon. Should he choose from one of his half dozen foster-fathers? With the exception of Ian Barrow, the third with whom he'd only stayed a couple of months before Ian's wife had taken ill, they had all been bastards, each a little different in their own right, but so boringly the same in their brutality. No. Best to keep it simple. 'He's dead.'

Everyone's faces fell, except for Lucille, who was obliviously in her own happy game of looking at her distorted reflection in her spoon.

Mémère stopped chopping. 'That's awful. I'm so sorry.'

'What happened?' Pépère asked.

Tears filled Catherine's eyes, and the sorrow with which she looked at Daniel was more raw than mere sympathy. He realised he'd made a mistake. He had made her think of her own father.

'Heart attack,' he said shortly. 'A long time ago.'

'We are so sorry,' Pépère said, reaching out to pat Daniel's hands. 'Has your mother remarried? Do we have other grandchildren?'

Daniel shook his head. 'Just me. Mémère, can I help with anything?'

'No, you must rest,' she replied, flapping a tea cloth at him.

But the offer did the trick. The conversation turned, and Pépère began telling them of the leg of venison, enough to fill a week's ration quota of half a dozen Frenchmen, that had been demanded by a Gestapo officer who had taken up residence at Château Garamond.

Dinner was delicious. It was the first square meal Daniel could recall having since leaving London. The conversation inevitably centred on the war.

'Hitler is nothing but a fascist psychopath,' Pépère said through a mouthful of beef stew.

'A psychopath, yes, but he has abused the true ideology of fascism,' Daniel replied. 'True fascism in a nation simply concentrates its efforts on the welfare of its own people. Strength from within, if you like.'

'Does such strengthening include the cleansing of a nation?' Pépère retorted. 'Does it include the killing and torture of Jews?'

'Hitler took it too far, don't get me wrong. But where is the fault in trying to build one's own state into a nation of power? Eradicating poverty, building infrastructure and industry. If we all concentrated on strengthening ourselves, we'll be that much closer to having a united Europe.'

'A united Europe or a Nazi-controlled Europe? Fascism may start out with empowering one's own patch, but it is inevitably followed by external expansion. No one is ever satisfied with their lot. France is no more Hitler's than Germany is ours, but that hasn't stopped him.'

'Perhaps if France had minded its own business, Hitler wouldn't have invaded.'

Pépère exhaled noisily. 'And let Hitler brutalise Poland?'

'It wasn't France's fight.'

'But we had an obligation to protect them.'

'And to what end? Look at France now. Cities demolished, millions of people displaced, and God only knows how many lives lost. That's one hefty obligation.'

Pépère looked at him, perplexed. 'Daniel, I can't accept that this is what you believe. Surely, you must understand the importance of loyalty to one's allies? We may have stepped into a fight that wasn't ours and one that we alone could not win, but our defence of Poland is what is important. We defend them as they would defend us.'

'Pff! With what? They have no army.'

'Perhaps not an organised resistance, but they do exist. They are here, they are in Britain. Their competence is neither here nor there; their dedication to the Polish cause and to Europe's cause is what matters.'

Daniel heaped a spoonful of carrots and parsnips, dripping with watery red wine gravy, into his mouth before responding. Pépère's loyalty to the cause reminded him of that lad, Antoine, on the boat. 'Your patriotism does you credit, Pépère. It is unflinching. But it isn't a patriotism I understand. I'm all for protecting my country, but going out of our way to throw stones at – admittedly – a bully like Hitler, who is picking on a neighbour, and then getting myself and my people beaten up in the process is not my idea of patriotism.'

'Where is the unity in standing aside and watching your neighbour be tortured and killed? It is pure selfishness.'

'And to step in when you are so ill-equipped is selfless suicide.'

'But you shall die with pride.'

'Will I? I will die knowing that I have opened up Hitler's brutality to my own people, the people to whom I owe my first loyalty. How is it patriotic to endanger your own country?'

'The danger would be inevitable. Bullies desire power, more and more power. Hitler wants only one thing: to rule Europe in its entirety.'

'What about Spain then? They minded their own business, and Hitler is leaving them alone.'

Pépère looked at him sadly. 'My son, I don't know what life you have led to bring you to such views, but when you find something or someone that touches you in such a way that you will put aside thoughts of your own safety so that they may be safe, then you will understand why we must protect Europe. How would you feel if you were Poland?'

Daniel remained silent. How could he explain to Pépère that he already knew what it felt like to be Poland? But whereas the rest of Europe had come to Poland's aid, he'd had no allies to help him, nobody to stick up for him during the holy hell of his childhood. All this loyalty nonsense was a farce, something to make those so-called Allies feel better about themselves.

Daniel retired to bed shortly after dinner, having exchanged brittle goodnights with Pépère. Catherine accompanied him up for which he was grateful.

'I'm not pro-Hitler, you must understand,' he said while Catherine helped him to change his sheets. 'Pépère twisted my words to make me look like I don't care.'

'You managed to give that impression all on your own,' Catherine murmured without looking up.

'But you know me better than that. I do care. Would we be here together if I didn't?'

Catherine tucked the sheet beneath the mattress and straightened up with a sigh. 'I barely know you. I didn't know you were a fascist until this evening. But you helped me in Paris. I am safe because of you. Yet I am a Jew and you are a fascist. How can that be?'

'Not all fascists are anti-Semitic. It only appears that way when we refuse to get involved in Polish Jews' conflict with Germany. To me, you are just the same as anyone else.'

'Can I trust you?'

Daniel stared at her in surprise. 'Of course you can.'

She nodded. 'I don't believe you are as selfish and self-seeking as you make yourself out to be.'

He couldn't meet her eye. He turned away and pretended to look out of the window. Unfortunately, it was dark outside so the lamplight practically turned it into a mirror. He looked at his scowling reflection. 'Well, I'm not as noble as Pépère would like me to be. What has the world ever done for me?'

Catherine joined him at the window. Her hand slipped into his. 'My father is a noble man. That is why he left me in Amiens. There were people that required his help more than I. He once told me that how you face life is like facing a window. You can choose to focus on your own reflection, or you can choose to look beyond yourself and see just how beautiful the world can be. It is hard at times, at difficult times, when it is darker out there than it is in here, where you are. And it is easier to focus only on yourself. But to do so is to shut yourself away from the world. We should always look beyond ourselves, even when the world is darker than where you stand.'

They stood in silence. Daniel tried hard to refocus his eyes, to peer into the darkness, into the "world beyond". He could just make out the beech trees that bordered the rear of his grandparents' property. With his mind's eye, he saw a little boy building a fort and searching for insects around their mulchy bases, saw him leaning against the scratchy trunk and watching his mother hang the laundry on the line. A ball swelled in his throat, and he shut his eyes to block out the pain of loss. How could he give himself to the world when all it had ever done was hurt and abandon him?

Catherine squeezed his hand, and he opened his eyes to look at her. His instinct was to kiss her, but something inexplicable prevented him from doing so. She wasn't one of his London broads. She was something so much finer, who deserved more respect than his advances would offer.

'I need to rest now,' he said.

The disappointment in her eyes was so fleeting he thought he might have imagined it.

She smiled, and her hand slipped out of his, leaving it cold and empty. 'Yes, of course. I'll get you some water.'

'Thank you.'

She walked towards the door, but Daniel stopped her. 'Catherine. *Thank you.*'

35

Le Mans, France – Friday, 21ˢᵗ June, 1940

Daniel felt much stronger the following morning, and he enjoyed a quiet day with Catherine and Mémère. He watched in admiration as Catherine cared for his aunt Lucille, tending to her when she ate her meals and showing interest in the scribbles Lucille drew on her slate board. Daniel didn't know what to say or how to act around his aunt. He was so out of his comfort zone yet Catherine was a natural and never seemed to tire of the woman's constant demands.

After dinner, with Lucille put to bed, they reconvened in the salon. Pépère frowned at Daniel's progress.

'Are you injured?' he asked, gesturing to his limp.

Daniel hesitated before responding. He didn't like people asking about it, and he liked even less having to explain. 'An old injury,' he said. When Pépère continued to look at him quizzically, Daniel relented. 'I had polio as a child.' It seemed such an inadequate explanation after all he'd gone through – the illness, the physiotherapy, and, of course, the visit from Social Services who had deemed his mother incompetent and had taken him away – yet it seemed to suffice.

'I'm sorry to hear that,' Pépère replied. He switched on the wireless. It was playing Edith Piaf's 'La Vie en Rose'. Pépère gallantly held out his hand and bowed to Catherine. 'May I have this dance?'

Catherine gave an embarrassed laugh. 'I don't know how.'

'Neither do I. But that has never stopped me before.'

She giggled and took his hand. Pépère whirled her round, then, looking composed, proceeded to slowly waltz Catherine around the room.

'He always had an eye for the young ladies,' Mémère said

without malice. 'I don't remember the last time he asked me to dance.'

There was a hint of sadness in her tone, and Daniel couldn't just leave her sitting there. 'Would you dance with me?'

Her face lit up then clouded with doubt. 'Are you sure you're able to?'

His leg hadn't stopped him dancing many a night away in London. 'Quite sure.'

'Then I would be delighted, Daniel!'

The two couples waltzed around the room, laughing as they collided, Daniel and Pépère throwing jovial insults at one another. Edith Piaf was followed by Charles Trenet's 'Hop! Hop!' accompanied by more laughter and hoots of delight from Mémère and the feigned howls of pain from Pépère when Catherine stepped on his toes. Daniel had to admit to himself, as different as this was to the dances he'd attended in London with girls in their finery and alcohol abundant, he was thoroughly enjoying himself.

Mémère called time at the end of the song. 'I'm too old for this. So are you, Jean-Philippe. Let the young ones dance now.'

Pépère wiped his brow over-dramatically and, laughing with Catherine, passed her hand to Daniel. Her face was flushed, and her eyes glistened. Her hair had escaped its tie and fell across one shoulder. She had never looked so ravishing to Daniel. After the verve of the last song, the tempo slowed to a romantic number. A cage of butterflies was set free in Daniel's stomach as he took Catherine in his arms. Her skin warmed his hand through the light cotton fabric of her dress where he held her waist. Her soft fingers curled inside his. For the first time in his life, Daniel felt nervous about dancing with a girl. She caught his eye and they both gave awkward laughs. And then they danced. The sweet tragic tones of Lucienne Boyer singing 'Parlez Moi d'Amour' enclosed them in a private world of soft touches and gentle gazes, in which they were the only ones to exist. Barely a minute in though, Lucienne Boyer was abruptly interrupted by the radio presenter.

'We interrupt this programme with a special broadcast. At six thirty-six this evening, Prime Minister Philippe Pétain signed an armistice with German Führer Adolf Hitler to cease all fighting. The agreement grants Germany governorship and full control over northern and western France in order to safeguard the interests of the German Reich. In the occupied parts of France, the German Reich exercises all rights of an occupying power, and the French government obligates itself to support with every means possible the regulations resulting from the exercise of these rights and to carry them out with the aid of French administration. A new French government has been established in the city of Vichy that will govern the unoccupied southern and eastern state territories of France. A demarcation line will be created in coming days that will officially partition these two governments…'

With a growl of rage, Pépère spat at the wireless. 'The coward! The traitor! How can he give his homeland to the Germans?'

'Maybe this will be the end of the fighting,' Mémère tried to compensate. 'No more loss of lives.'

'You think this is the end of it? France will never rest under German rule.' Pépère's face was red with fury. 'This demarcation line is no accident. Most of our food is grown in the north, where our coal is mined, our steel industry is located. *We* will be living under Hitler's rule here in Le Mans.'

Mémère's eyes welled with tears. 'Oh, Jean-Philippe.'

Catherine dashed over to embrace Mémère, and Daniel exchanged worried looks with Pépère. He had known their safety in Le Mans would be fleeting, but he hadn't banked on suddenly being in German territory. He and Catherine would have to leave before the demarcation line was set up.

Later that evening, Daniel and Pépère sat in the salon after Catherine and Mémère had retired for the night. Daniel tuned the wireless in to BBC World Service, and they sat, drinking brandy in silence and listening to the broadcasts in the hope of a different perspective on the evening's news. They didn't have to wait long. Charles de Gaulle, France's brigadier-general and Under-Secretary of State, self-exiled in Britain, soon came over the airwaves. In his precise impassioned voice, he began to speak.

'Honour, common sense, and the interests of the country require that all free Frenchmen, wherever they be, should continue to fight as best they may... I, General de Gaulle, am undertaking this national task in England. I call upon all French servicemen of the land, sea and air forces; I call upon French engineers and skilled armaments workers who are on British soil, or have the means of getting here, to come and join me.'

Daniel rose and switched it off once the broadcast had finished and topped up his and Pépère's glasses.

'Will you fight?' Pépère asked. 'When you return to England?'

Daniel shrugged. 'I've never had much time for war.'

'I don't know many men who do, but, when fighting is needed, they do the right thing.'

'What is the right thing in a war? To take another man's life?'

'It is the unfortunate consequence of war certainly, but when war is the clash of power, it will be the force with the most power that wins. And strength of men is power.'

Daniel sighed. 'War is nothing but a strategy game played by politicians who toy with the lives of gullible men. They're nothing but numbers to them. In fact, they're given numbers as individuals, then put into units that are also identified by numbers. It dehumanises them to the point where our governments don't see them as men at all, but mere game tokens to be sacrificed for the sake of strategy in a game of power and control.'

'It would appear so tonight, but it won't stop every Frenchman from fighting. To them France is primary, and they will sacrifice their lives for the honour of defending their homeland.'

'That's what the politicians tell them – it's an honour to

sacrifice your life, it's your duty to kill and be killed. And it's not just soldiers who believe it, it's entire populations!' Daniel gestured to Pépère through a haze of liquor. 'They're all gullible fools – a boy, who puts on a uniform and picks up a gun with the intention of killing other boys who have been fed the same lies by their leaders, who thinks that somehow that makes him honourable; that if he kills another that makes him a hero; that if he himself is killed that too makes him a hero. It's a hollow virtue in a propagandist delusion that they fall for to remedy their own lack of integrity and sense of worth.'

Pépère shook his head sadly. 'It's a mistake to assume that every boy or man who puts on a uniform and picks up a rifle is a fool. They all have their own personal reasons for signing up. For many, it isn't a choice. Conscription is mandatory for many, as you must know.' Pépère paused to take a swallow of his brandy. 'For those for whom it's a choice, their reasons are many and often don't seem much of a choice at all. Some seek a better life–'

'Ha! Better life!'

'One that risks their life certainly,' Pépère went on calmly, 'but which is a risk worth taking for the sake of a bed to lie on and food in their belly. There are those who truly believe in defending one's country and empowering their community, regardless of what the politicians and generals say.'

'Yet do their bidding,' Daniel countered.

'It's an instinctive thing in both man and beast to defend one's territory, to broaden that territory in order to enrich and empower their nation or herd. And to do so successfully, they subscribe to a leader.' Pépère took a lingering sip of his drink. 'And then there are those who seek purpose in life, who want to be part of something greater than themselves – boys who have not yet had families and children to provide them with that fulfilment.'

'I don't need to fire a gun to give me purpose, and *I* don't have a family or children. It's nothing but weakness on their part!' Daniel blurted.

Pépère smiled and tilted his glass towards him. 'And yet here you sit.'

36

Amiens, France – Saturday, 13th August, 2016

The smile of contentment that had been on Simon's face was quickly replaced with an anxious frown when he came round. He replaced his specs and got up to check the printout of Catherine's fate. He sighed.

'No change?' Nick asked.

'No longer caught at Vel' d'Hiv Roundup, but she still ends up at Auschwitz. I don't understand.'

'Don't understand what?'

'How she can still be destined to die. What about Daniel? How has he not saved her? What are we doing wrong?'

'The last I heard, he was telling his grandfather that he had no one that he cared about enough to risk his life for.'

'Yes, but… you can see he cares for Catherine. He's trying to save her.'

'No, Simon. *You* are trying to save her. Don't get confused. Daniel is only trying to save his own ass.'

'A part of him is. You're not there, Nick! You're not seeing what I'm seeing. He's falling in love with her.'

'No, *you* are falling in love with her. It's all you! And it's bloody disturbing, if you must know. How the hell do you fall in love with someone who's been dead seventy-six years?'

Simon's angry flush deepened. 'We have the chance to save them. Caring doesn't mean I'm in love with her.'

Nick shook his head and walked away. Nobody did denial like Simon. At the door, he turned back. 'Do you honestly think Catherine is going to come out of this whole thing alive?'

Simon lifted his chin. 'She could. With our help.'

'Fat lot of good it's done so far.'

'Then why not?' exclaimed Simon. 'Why hasn't Daniel

saved her yet?'

'I don't know!' Nick yelled.

'You're going to get them killed!'

Nick strode over to the coffee table, tripping momentarily on that damned rug, and snatched up the printout. He held it aggressively in Simon's face. 'They already get caught. Don't you see? They are already dead!'

There was a loud banging on the wall from next door. '*Silencieux!*' came a surprisingly clear shout.

Nick slammed the printout against Simon's chest and stalked out.

He returned to his own room and raided the minibar. He sat down by the window. It was a bright day outside; people walked and laughed in the sunshine, so ignorant of the anguish he was feeling. He gave an inadvertent sob. He sucked in his breath to stem the tsunami of emotion rising inside him. He didn't cry. He wasn't that sort of a man. Nonetheless, his eyes welled and he banged his fist on the coffee table making Schneider's journals jump. The tears came out in great wracking sobs. Guilty tears. Simon was his best friend. They were brothers. Yet Nick was lying to him, concocting a web of deception and betrayal that only seemed to become more entangled the further they pursued the past. He was keeping from Simon the one thing he knew would cure all of Simon's insecurities and hauntings. In fact, he was going one step further. He was trying to kill John Hayes all over again. What kind of a brother did that? He thought of his own parents, their absence; what he would do to be told that when he got back to London, one or both of them would be there waiting for him like nothing had happened. How many people had mourned a loved one and had begged God for their return, fantasised about it? And here, Simon had that opportunity. And Nick and Amanda were doing their best to take it away from him. What kind of rotten human beings were they?

Through the blur of his tears, he looked over at the door. It would be so easy to just be done with all of this. To go to Simon and tell him the truth. His moral compass pointed him in that direction. *Get up and tell him. It's the right thing to do. It's the good thing to do.*

Nick's face crumpled again as he was once more overcome with shame. He couldn't do it. He couldn't condemn himself to a life of poverty and struggle. An image of his online bank account arose in his mind, and a horrid feeling of dread crept over him. How was he to live in such debt? How could he have lost all he had? What had he done to deserve such a cruel twist of fate? He had nowhere to go back to in London, no job, no money, no prospects, no future.

Nick downed his drink then went to the bathroom and splashed some water on his face. His eyes were bloodshot and puffy, and his nose a little red, but it would have to do.

He found Amanda down in the bar chatting up the barman.

'You want a drink?' she asked, taking in his troubled expression.

'No. I think we should head back upstairs and get started.' Then as an afterthought, 'Thanks.'

'What's wrong? What've you–' She stopped mid-sentence and frowned at him. 'Have you been *crying?*'

There was no sympathy in her voice, just distaste, and Nick felt his cheeks flush hot. 'I'm fine.' He guided her away from the barman's inquisitive ears. 'It's Daniel. The bloody fool is falling in love with Catherine.'

'Oh my God, he's as bad as Simon. Can we never get away from him? First in this life and now in the last. He's like a fucking parasite.'

'The good news is I think Catherine is safe in Daniel's keeping until we can get her to Schneider. He's not going to let anyone rape or mug her. The bad news is I doubt very much whether he's just going to hand her over.'

'So, what are we going to do?'

'I don't know,' Nick said with a sigh. 'We'll just have to try.'

'Try? *Try?*' Amanda looked horrified. 'We have to do more

than try, Nick. If bloody Daniel whatever his name is decides he's in love with Catherine and escapes with her, then where does that leave me?'

'Come on, the odds of them getting away are pretty slim. France has just signed an armistice with Germany to break the country in two, and they're still stuck in Germany's half. They don't have any papers, and by the sounds of things Daniel's grandparents have got enough on their plates without having to harbour a Jew and a Brit.'

Amanda chewed her lip. 'This is too much of a gamble.'

'No, it's not. All we need to do is get them to Nantes, preferably on a train. According to Schneider's journals, he spent most of his time checking papers at the train station. Catherine and Daniel will walk right into his hands.'

'You've been saying that from the beginning. Catherine was meant to walk right into his hands at the theatre. We can't keep doing this, Nick. *I* can't keep doing this.'

Nick's blood went cold. 'What are you saying?'

'I'm saying I'm not risking my life for a career that you can't even guarantee me.'

'You can't back out now,' he spluttered. 'You'll have your career. Taylor Made Television is one of the biggest studios in the country.'

'It *was* one of the biggest. Now it doesn't exist. Who knows what it'll be like if you manage to bring it back from the dead.'

Before Nick could think of a suitable rebuttal, Amanda had flounced out of the bar and up the stairs to the lobby.

'Amanda!' He ran after her, taking the stairs two at a time. 'Come on, don't do this to me.'

'It's too much of a risk. No career is worth risking your existence for. I'm out, Nick.'

'No!' His knees were liquidating with every step, and he could feel his heart thumping into his throat. The stairwell began to list. Oh God, he was going to have a heart attack. 'We're so close.'

Amanda turned and glared at him. 'We're also closer to

273

killing me. No, thank you very much.'

She pounded up the remaining stairs into the lobby, and Nick watched her go in despair. This couldn't be the end of it. This couldn't be his life hereon in.

'Amanda, wait!'

'Not this time, Nick,' she threw over her shoulder.

He ran after her and dragged her to a stop. 'Please, don't do this. Think about what you're saying. You walk away from this now, you'll be going back to the sad poverty-stricken life you were leading before. You'll become a struggling actor forced to do commercials for constipation and the disappointed girlfriend in impotence ads. Is that what you want? I'm offering you a lifetime of top film roles. Isn't that worth some risk?'

'Not my life,' Amanda grumbled.

'Your life isn't in danger. Catherine and Daniel are sitting ducks. Either way, they are going to get caught and end up in a death camp. All we need to do is ensure Schneider gets to them first. We've got his journals, we've got control of their thoughts, we've got everything we need. A little more hard work and you've got a lifetime of money and success.'

Amanda pouted in contemplation. 'You honestly believe that?'

'Of course I do. I wouldn't be doing this if I thought your life was in danger. How could I do that to you?'

Amanda smirked. 'You keep talking like that, and we'll have time for a shag before we get started.'

Nick heaved a sigh big enough to revive a whale. 'Thank you.'

She brushed past him, trailing a fingernail across his cheek and headed for the stairwell that led to the rooms. Nick closed his eyes in gratitude and thanked all the gods he could think of. What's more he was getting a bonus lay out of the deal.

'Ahem, Monsieur Taylor, a quick word, please?' M. Fourrier, the hotel manager, spoke up as Nick walked past the front desk.

'Not now, I'm in a bit of a rush.'

'This will only take a minute.'

'Fine. What is it?'

'Monsieur, we have unfortunately had more complaints about disturbances in your rooms, not to mention you and madame arguing here in the foyer where I would like to encourage new guests to stay, not send them away.'

'Okay, sorry, we'll keep it down in future,' Nick replied and went to step around the man.

But M. Fourrier blocked his path. 'This is not the first time I have had to raise this topic with you. Unfortunately, I can no longer trust you to keep your word. I appreciate you are providing the entertainment tomorrow evening, therefore, I would kindly ask that you and your friends seek accommodation elsewhere from Monday.'

Nick stared at him in disbelief. 'You're kicking us out?'

'We are simply saying you might find other accommodation that is more suitable to your needs.'

'Suitable to our needs? What the hell? If your walls weren't so bloody thin, you probably wouldn't be getting these complaints.'

'Monsieur, you have been seen naked in the corridor shouting with the madame, slamming doors and just now arguing in the welcome area. Our walls are not the issue here.'

Nick gulped. If they had to leave, he wouldn't be able to conjure up a plausible excuse for them all to stay in France. They would have to go back home and there, Simon would discover his father alive, and that would be the end of everything. Taylor Made Television would never exist. Leaving on Monday morning gave him less than forty-eight hours to change history.

'You can't do this. We've paid until Wednesday.'

'We will refund you at the same time that we pay you for your music.'

Nick trembled in a mixture of panic and rage. 'What makes you think I'll do a gig for you now, huh?'

'If that is the way you feel, then I understand. But it will mean that we must ask you to leave tomorrow morning.'

Nick's breath caught in his throat. Tomorrow morning? He'd never get anything done before then. 'Monday's fine. I can do the gig on Sunday, no problem.'

M. Fourrier smiled. 'I am so pleased we have come to an agreement. Please enjoy the rest of your stay.'

Nick bit his lips together before he blurted out something he'd regret. The son of a bitch. How dare he act all high and mighty with him when Hotel bloody Sceau was just a crumby budget joint? It wasn't like they were trashing the rooms with electric guitars and throwing televisions out of the windows, and really they weren't making that much noise.

'Nick!' Amanda yelled from the stairs, and her voice bounced around the foyer. 'What the fuck? Are you coming or not?'

Nick hurried away without looking at M. Fourrier.

37

Le Mans, France – Sunday, 23rd June, 1940

When Catherine went to check on Daniel the following morning, she found him already up and dressed, hands in pockets, staring out of the window. She joined him there and smiled at the children playing next door.

'They have no idea what sort of future they have ahead of them,' Daniel said.

'Ignorance is bliss.'

'Is it?'

'Well, I look at you who knows what is coming, and I look at them who do not, and they look much happier than you do.'

Daniel gave a mirthless laugh. 'We have to leave today. It isn't safe here. We need to reach the free zone before this demarcation line is set up properly.'

Catherine gulped. She wanted to stay here with Jean-Philippe and Marie, where it was safe and where she had a bed to sleep in and food to eat. She could be of use to Marie, helping with Lucille and the vegetable garden. She pictured herself in a wide-brimmed hat, picking carrots and beans, straightening up and seeing Daniel chopping wood, of walking back to the house with a basket brimming with produce, passing Daniel, of him catching her around the waist and spinning her around until they were both helpless with laughter.

Catherine smiled sadly to herself. It was no more than a fantasy, she knew. Hitler would ensure none of it would happen. Daniel was right. If they didn't leave now, then it would soon get back to the Nazi authorities that Monsieur and Madame Deschamps were harbouring a Jew, and Catherine wouldn't be the only one in trouble.

'Where will we go?' she asked.

'South,' he replied with a shrug. 'We have to get to Spain.'

Catherine kept quiet. It had taken so long and so much effort just to get from Paris to Le Mans; Spain seemed an impossible task.

Leaving the Deschamps was hard enough for Catherine, so she could only imagine what Daniel was feeling. Walking away and leaving them to life under Nazi rule felt like a betrayal after all they'd done for her and Daniel.

She had said as much to Marie in the kitchen, but the woman had hugged her close and said, 'How can we leave, my dear? Jean-Philippe and I are too old to be running around trying to escape the Nazis. And we must think of Lucille. She needs stability and routine.'

Marie pressed a basket of food covered with a cloth into Catherine's hands and made her promise to take care of her grandson.

On the doorstep, saying goodbye in drizzling rain, Jean-Philippe handed back Daniel's gun. 'Fight for those you care about.'

Daniel nodded and tucked it into his trousers.

It was only a short walk from the house over to the train station. It wasn't anywhere near as crowded as the ones in Paris. There was a train due in an hour that would head south, so Catherine and Daniel sat on a bench on the platform where they were sheltered from the rain. They watched a steam locomotive roll noisily into the station. It pulled dozens upon dozens of freight wagons that all bore signs reading, '*8 horses; 40 men*'.

'They're old wagons from the Great War,' Catherine told Daniel, proud of herself for knowing such trivia. Papa had pointed out the sign to her when they'd seen a couple in a siding at the station in Amiens years ago.

Daniel barely acknowledged her. He was restless, fidgeting and frowning, watching the scores of people board the wagons, listening to the passengers argue with station officials when they weren't allowed to take more than one suitcase with them.

Then, when a station assistant walked past, Daniel called out, 'Where is this train going?'

'Poitiers via Nantes. It's as close to the Free Zone as we can get.'

Board that train. Board that train.

Catherine fairly leapt in her seat, the voice in her head was so insistent.

Board that train.

She hesitated. Nantes was southwest of Le Mans, headed for the coast, then they would have to trek back south east to Poitiers. They would waste time detouring that way rather than just waiting for the Tours train and heading straight down south.

Get on that train. Get out of there!

She looked around for signs of Nazi uniforms, but only civilians milled about on the platform. Nevertheless, 'Daniel, I think we should get on this train.'

'But the Tours train will be here in an hour.'

'I know. I just… My gut is telling me we should be getting on this train. We don't even know if the Tours train will come. This train's here. Let's get on this one and get out of Le Mans. The sooner we're on the move, the better.'

Daniel frowned, first at Catherine then at the train where people filtered into the covered wagons. 'Yes, but…'

'Soldiers might arrive before the Tours train arrives.'

Abruptly, he stood up. 'You're right. Let's get moving.'

They hurried over to join the throng, shuffling along the platform, tripping over the abandoned luggage, then stepping into the dark and dusty wagon. There were no windows. Only slivers of light filtering through the wooden slats caught the frightened faces as they whirled around, eyes agog. Stuffy and hot, the oppression only got worse as more people squashed in. Catherine and Daniel made themselves as comfortable as they could in a corner, sitting on the dirty floor. When the wagon was full, the door slid closed, leaving them in darkness. The hum of conversation evaporated, and they sat in apprehensive silence, broken only by the barking cough of a child.

At the mercy of strangers, Catherine had never felt more trapped.

The journey was long and torturously slow. At each town they stopped to squeeze more passengers on board. The door would slide open, blinding them as the sunlight poured in then slam shut again just as their eyes had adjusted to the light. On they would travel, jostled from side to side as they rumbled through the countryside, the rattle of the wheels on the tracks making anything but the most lethargic of conversation impossible.

Daniel broke off a wedge of bread from their hamper for them to share for lunch and a nectarine each. A young teenage boy with gaunt cheeks and a shock of black hair watched them eat, his eyes following every mouthful they took. The boy didn't appear to be accompanied by anyone, no adult touched him on the shoulder to ask if he was okay, to check that he wasn't hungry or tired, to ensure that he was drinking enough.

Catherine wondered when the boy had last eaten, but it was Daniel who passed him one of the huge apples they'd been saving for later. 'Here.'

The boy's eyes widened in delight and he grabbed the apple, stroking his dirty fingers over its smooth texture before plunging his teeth into it and ripping out a chunk. Juice dribbling down his chin, he crunched happily through the fruit.

Catherine caught Daniel's eye and smiled at him. He looked away, embarrassed.

By late afternoon, Catherine wished they could have a break from the train. Just five minutes to stretch her legs and get some fresh air. Her dress was damp through and her legs were cramping. The train slowed and tooted as they approached another station, and she groaned. How many more people could they fit in?

The door was pulled open, and the passengers were instead confronted by two Nazi soldiers, rifles slung over their shoulders. Catherine's heart leapt into her throat then plunged to her feet. Crying out in alarm, everyone pushed back from the open doorway. Catherine tried to make herself as unobtrusive as she could in their dark corner. She felt for Daniel's hand and he squeezed it tight.

The soldiers poked at them with their rifles. 'Off! Get off! Where are your identity papers?'

There was no hiding. They had to disembark with everyone else. From sheer instinct, Catherine's hand went to her throat.

'Hide your necklace,' Daniel whispered as they awaited their turn to jump to the platform.

Her fingers were trembling so much she couldn't unhook the chain. All too soon they found themselves at the entrance to the wagon. Daniel flashed her a desperate glance, and she tucked the necklace beneath the neck of her dress. They jumped down from the train and into the dusky sunlight. A breeze swept down the platform and a sign informed them they were at Nantes.

Soldiers bustled them into lines with the butts of their rifles while still more went from person to person, inspecting identity papers. Those who did not pass muster were jerked aside. Catherine and Daniel stood, sweating in anticipation.

'Daniel, I don't have any papers,' she whispered. 'What are we going to do?'

Daniel licked his lips nervously. 'I'm thinking.'

Nausea spread through Catherine's stomach as it tied itself in knots. She watched one of the soldiers slowly making his way down the line towards them. She looked around for an escape. They wouldn't have a chance of escaping through the station's front building, but at the end of the platform was a wooden fence sectioning off a patch of tangled scrubland and houses beyond.

Eventually a young soldier stopped in front of them.

'Papers, please?'

Daniel gave an uncertain nod and delved into his pocket. His hands were shaking so much he dropped the wad of papers. Both he and the soldier bent to pick them up.

The soldier grabbed them first. Beneath his *Stalhelm*, his

eyes travelled up to meet Daniel's in suspicious consideration. 'Corporal Antoine Joubert?'

Daniel gasped. 'What? No! No, those ones there. Dañel Barrera.' He pointed frantically to a second lot of identity papers. 'I'm Spanish.'

Catherine stared at him, trying to hide her surprise, but unable to comprehend why he would have two lots of fake papers.

The soldier ignored Daniel. 'You are with the French Army?'

'No! I'm Spanish, I'm telling you. Antoine Joubert was a friend – rather a person that I met, not a friend as such. He died. I was taking his papers back for his family.'

'Wait here,' the soldier said and walked back up the line to his supervising officer.

'What is he talking about?' Catherine hissed in Daniel's ear.

Daniel didn't reply for a moment. He was too preoccupied with watching the soldier and the officer. A puzzled frown furrowed his brow. 'It's him.'

'Who?' Catherine looked closer at the Germans. The officer looked bizarrely like the one they had run into at the shelter in Paris and before that at the Gromaires' farm. But in that uniform they must all look alike. It would be too much of a coincidence. The officer listened to the soldier, then his eyes roamed the crowds on the platform until they came to rest on Catherine and Daniel.

Catherine's heart skipped a beat. It was the same officer. He had the same steely blue eyes.

'I'd say now is a good time for us to leave,' Daniel murmured, his gaze not leaving the officer. He edged backwards through the passengers, holding Catherine's hand tight in his. The officer was still in conversation with the soldier, examining Daniel's papers.

'Daniel! Who are Antoine Joubert and Dañel Barrera?'

'I'll explain later. For now though…' They neared the back of the line, '…run!' Twisting around, Daniel barrelled through the last of the passengers and hurtled towards the fence. Catherine stumbled after him.

'Stop! Stop!'

They ignored the shouted commands, and Catherine winced away from the inevitable. Daniel half-assisted, half-pushed her over the fence then vaulted over it after her. A crack of gunfire split the warm air, and splinters from the fence stung her arm. The passengers on the platform screamed and Catherine looked back. The officer and his soldiers were trying to follow, but the crowding passengers cowering on the ground weren't making their passage easy. Rifles were raised and fired erratically. Catherine and Daniel ducked out of sight before any more bullets flew their way.

They stumbled through the unkempt undergrowth to the road on the other side of the station. A yell from the station entrance and a Nazi pointed in their direction. The soldiers jumped onto their sidecar-motorcycles and gave chase.

Catherine and Daniel fled through the narrow, cobbled streets, ducking between houses and through gardens. Finally, they were free of the sound of roaring motorcycle engines.

'I think we've lost them,' Daniel gasped.

They skirted the corner of a leather merchant's shop and came face to face with a black Admiral saloon car and a couple of motorcycles. The steely-eyed officer stepped out of the backseat in his long pristine boots and pointed at them.

'Catch them!'

Gun fire shattered windows around them. Running hard, Daniel began to falter, limping and gasping for breath. But it was Catherine who tripped over the cobbles and fell. Daniel ran back to help her.

'You okay?'

He didn't wait for an answer. He dragged her to her feet and pulled her after him down a narrow alleyway between houses. Backs against the wall, they tried to catch their breath.

Daniel leaned out to check if the coast was clear then whipped back out of sight when a motorcycle blasted past. He peered out again. 'Okay.' He sought out her hand and tried to pull her after him, but she resisted.

'Just a minute more,' she gasped.

'We have to keep moving.' He stuck his head out again, then pulled her after him. They stumbled across the empty road. They were obviously on the edge of the town. Against the sinking sun, a windmill's slowly revolving turbines shuttered the dusky light and threw shadows across the farmland.

In the dim oval expanse of the windmill, the rickety door stuck as Daniel pulled it closed after them. The last of the sun's rays sliced through the old wooden panels highlighting the dust floating in the air. It smelt of livestock and hay, although only the latter was present inside, piled high on a mezzanine and spilling over onto the hard-packed ground below.

Catherine rounded on Daniel and stared at him. A million questions raced through her brain, but all she registered was that he was a stranger. 'What happened back there? Who are you?'

Daniel sat down against the central pillar and eased his bad leg out. He patted his pockets and found his cigarettes.

'Who are you?' she demanded again, indignation turning to unease as she realised this man that she was alone with could be anyone.

Daniel delayed the moment of truth by lighting up and taking a long drag. He coughed. 'My name is Daniel Barrow, not Daniel Deschamps. I'm British.'

'You're British? But he said you were Antoine Joubert. You told him you were Spanish…'

'I'm a journalist from London. I was on my way to Spain with a false identity when my boat was sunk. Antoine Joubert was a soldier I met on board. He died. I took his identity papers to send to his family. The rescue boat brought me here to France.'

Catherine stared at him in bewilderment. It sounded like the truth, but there were too many other unanswered questions for it to truly be plausible. 'But Jean-Philippe and Marie. Are they not your grandparents?'

'Yes, but estranged. My mother and I left France when I was a small boy, moved to London to find my father.'

Catherine went very still as a thought occurred to her. 'You said you knew my father. My father doesn't know any British journalists.'

Daniel dropped his eyes. 'I'm sorry.'

'You lied?'

'It was the only way I could make you come with me.'

Catherine twisted her lips in anger. 'Why though?'

'Because if you'd stayed in that shelter you would've ended up dead.'

'But why do you want to help me? How did you know my name? I don't understand.'

Daniel shook his head and took a couple of quick drags. 'I don't know how to make you understand when I don't even understand it myself.' He hesitated and stubbed out his cigarette. 'All I can tell you is that I woke up one day with your name imprinted on my brain. Then I saw your notice outside the shelter, and to be honest, I thought that you might have been someone from my past, someone I didn't remember but whom my subconscious had dragged up now that I was back in France. I thought – I thought you could help me get out of France. But then when I saw you, I realised I couldn't possibly know you. Then that officer started over to you. I couldn't just leave you there.'

Catherine shook her head, for a moment diverted from her suspicions by the reappearance of Sturmbannführer Schneider. 'And then he was at the station as well. I can't believe I keep bumping into him.'

'It is him, isn't it?' Daniel said. 'The officer from the shelter. I thought I was imagining things.'

'And from the Gromaires' farm.'

'Where?'

'Before I got to Paris, I was staying with a family in Beauvais, and he arrived to look for French troops hiding on their farm. He almost found me instead. Sturmbannführer

Schneider, he called himself.' Catherine shuddered. She let the implications of Daniel's betrayal sink in. 'My father's dead, isn't he?'

Daniel pulled himself up to his feet and took her by the shoulders. 'We don't know that.'

'He would've found me by now.' Her eyes welled with tears, and she bit her lower lip to stop them overflowing.

'Not necessarily. He could be anywhere.' He pulled her into a rough hug. 'I'm sorry.'

As Catherine cried quietly in his arms, Daniel held her tighter and tighter. When finally her tears subsided, he brushed her cheeks dry.

'Please trust me. I know I've done little to deserve it, and my answers to your questions are flimsy at best, but it's the truth. I'm not the danger.'

Catherine pulled herself together. His answers weren't as flimsy as he thought. She knew how insistent and bizarre one's inner voice could be. She tried to smile her forgiveness, reached out and touched his cheek. It felt like an electric current passed between them, and each touch sent a surge through both of their bodies. Daniel took her face in his hands and kissed her, softly, comfortingly at first but then as arousal flared inside them both, with more passion and insistence.

38

Amiens, France – Sunday, 14ᵗʰ August, 2016

Amanda groaned as she regained consciousness. 'Nick! Come on, what the fuck is going on?'

'I'm doing my best,' he replied, teeth gritted.

'Really? Well, if this is your best I don't know if I want to gamble my future career on you as a producer. You're not filling me with confidence. Catherine and Daniel seem to be pretty damn talented at avoiding the Nazis in a country that's occupied by the bastards. And they don't even know what's coming. You know it all, and you still can't get it right.'

'It's not only up to me! Schneider has to do his part as well, and I'm not exactly able to manipulate him. He doesn't know what's coming either. He's probably thinking how very coincidental it is that he's stumbled across Catherine as much as he has.'

'Then you have to do more. At the rate we're going, Catherine and Daniel are going to be sitting pretty, and where does that leave us, huh? Nowhere! I probably won't even exist.' She paced the room, running her fingers through her hair, making her frock rise up to reveal honey-brown thighs.

'Look, either way, Catherine is not going to make it,' Nick said. 'She and Daniel might be slipping through Schneider's fingers, but she's still destined to die at Auschwitz. Your life is not in danger. What *is* in danger is the Taylor family fortune.'

Amanda shook her head. 'It only takes one move for them to be home and dry, and then that'll be it for me.' She snapped her fingers to emphasise her point. 'Then what? Are you going to persuade Simon you need to kill Catherine to bring me back? Will I come back as the person I am?'

For a moment, Nick thought of a kinder Amanda – just as

beautiful, but perhaps just a little sweeter, a little less demanding. Would that be such a bad thing?

'Nick!'

'No, of course not! I mean, that won't happen.'

'We can't rely on Daniel anyway. He hasn't done us much good so far, has he? Last time, you said he was falling in love with Catherine. He's not going to be much help handing her over if he's all starry-eyed over her. Next thing, you'll be telling me they've set a date for their wedding.'

'They only slept together. Daniel hasn't proposed.' *Yet*, Nick added silently. 'And you know what he's like. He's a complete womaniser. He'd bed anyone in a skirt.'

Amanda chewed her lip. 'This is pointless. We're leaving tomorrow anyway. I'm through playing Russian roulette with my life.'

'What?'

'I've had enough. Catherine and Daniel are defying expectations. You hand them to Schneider on a platter, and they still get away. They will escape, and they will survive if we meddle with things anymore.'

Nick stared at her, unsure whether she was just having another tantrum to make sure she was appreciated or whether she was being serious. 'Don't leave, Amanda. I can't do this without you.'

'I don't care.'

Nick remained silent, watching her warily, trying to gauge whether she was bluffing or not.

She crossed her arms and huffed. 'This is so wank, Nick! Why the hell couldn't you have manipulated them properly? Now, I've got to go back to doing it the hard way. Making all those blasted showreels that suck anyway, and when you do get an audition it's for some background prostitute which you have to shit all over your pride to try out for, and even then, the fucking director can't be bothered to look up from his phone.'

'Isn't this worth the chance then for a comfortable, proud future?'

'No! Of course not. I'd rather be alive and doing all that shitty work than dead.'

'Sometimes you have to take risks for the things that really make a difference.'

'Don't fucking patronise me. I've been taking risks. Fucking hell, Nick, what do you think this past week has been like for me? But those risks haven't paid off. I'm done. Seriously. We go home tomorrow and go our separate ways. I mean it this time.'

Nick's blood froze. She really was serious. A thought that had been lingering in the back of his mind all day edged to the fore. 'There is one other way.'

'I'm not interested. Get out.' She pointed at the door and fixed him with a beady eye like he was a recalcitrant dog that had crept into the house without permission.

'What about a life in which you didn't even have to work for that luxury lifestyle you want, hmm? Neither of us would have to. There wouldn't be any Taylor Made Television, no leading lady contract, but money that would allow you that yacht in St Tropez, that condo in Santa Barbara, those glittering parties with the rich and famous. Doesn't that sound tempting?' Nick babbled in one long breath.

Amanda looked at him suspiciously. 'How?'

'We don't send Catherine to Schneider.' He held up his hand when she opened her mouth to argue. 'Why do we want Schneider to capture Catherine anyway?'

'So he can steal her necklace and kill her.'

Nick faltered at her brutality. 'More or less. All we really need to do to ensure the security of Taylor Made Television is to make sure he gets the Fleur. But what we haven't realised is that neither of us really care about Taylor Made Television, do we? All we really want is the lifestyle it affords. We want the money. So, instead of manipulating Catherine into giving the necklace to Schneider, we cut out the middleman and simply get her to put it somewhere we can find it. It would have to be somewhere well hidden if we're to rely on no-one else finding it in the meantime, but doesn't that sound easier than trying to cross paths with Schneider in the hope that he'll catch her?'

Amanda's face lit up. 'Nick, you genius! Why didn't you suggest this before?' Then she hesitated. 'But we have to make sure Catherine dies. All the money in the world isn't going to do me any good if I don't exist.'

'That's not going to be difficult, is it? The place is crawling with Nazis. She's already destined for Auschwitz now, we hardly need to do much to ensure things stay that way.'

Amanda chewed her lip in deliberation.

'It's a lot easier keeping things the same than trying to change them,' he added.

Finally, she nodded. 'You're right. But where are we going to get her to hide the necklace? Seventy-six years is a long time. Buildings get demolished. Fields get torn up for car parks, trees get chopped down.'

'We just have to find somewhere in Nantes – we don't want to manipulate her too far away from where she is now – that hasn't been disturbed since 1940. There must be houses that old.'

'Yeah, but people live in them. Now *and* then. She can't just wander into someone's house and hide the necklace under the floorboards any more than we can wander in to find it. Besides, someone living in the house is sure to find it in the meantime.'

Nick thought for a moment. 'Nantes is a pretty old city, isn't it?'

'Fucked if I know.'

'Well, get your laptop out. Let's Google it.'

Amanda sent him a withering look but did as he said. They sat on the chaise longue, crowding over the laptop.

'Here we go,' said Amanda. '"*Nantes, a city on the Loire River in the Upper Brittany region of western France, has a long history as a port and industrial centre. It is home to the medieval Château des Ducs de Bretagne, where the Dukes of Brittany once lived.*" There! That's old. We could hide it there. No one's going to knock down a château.'

Nick pointed at the screen. 'It's been restored.'

Amanda sighed with impatience. 'But if it has a medieval château that means it was a medieval city, which means it will probably have conserved old city walls.'

'Yes! We could get her to leave the necklace in a particular part of the old city walls. No one's going to knock down the walls either.'

'Oh no, hang on. They already did, like in the eighteenth century. God, don't these people have any sense of historical preservation?'

They scrolled through more of Nantes's sights and attractions then Nick jabbed the screen. 'Here. That's where we go. It's still there. No one's touched it.'

Amanda looked across at him. 'It's a bit risky, isn't it? I mean anyone could find it in the meantime.'

'Not unless they were looking for it,' he said with more confidence than he felt.

'Okay.'

Nick took a deep breath. Abandoning their plan with Schneider meant this had to work. If it didn't, then it would be too late to go back and change things.

39

Amiens, France – Sunday, 14th August, 2016

Simon went down to the restaurant-bar for a drink. He needed one. It was only twenty past two in the afternoon, but it was the weekend, so he rationalised that it was acceptable. He needed the soothing warmth of alcohol to settle his feathers. The room was filled with people enjoying the Sunday bistro so he had to sit at the bar.

He ordered a whisky and drank it in silent contemplation of the day's events. Nick had lost his cool unusually quickly and quite unreasonably so. Weren't they on the same side? Simon was beginning to wonder. There was a niggling suggestion in his mind that perhaps, after that first fallout Nick had had with Amanda, he'd had time to cool off and was now having second thoughts about saving Catherine. Simon supposed those doubts were warranted. Jeopardising Amanda's existence wasn't a decision to be taken lightly. And, Simon told himself, it wasn't something he particularly wanted to do either. He wasn't a vindictive type. He wasn't doing all of this to 'remove' Amanda. He was doing it for Catherine. The poor girl hadn't done anything to deserve the atrocities that she was destined to endure – the trauma, the torture, the death when she was barely out of her teens. With this almost God-like power to change the past, how could they not try to save her?

Simon thought of his father and acknowledged the guilt he felt for not being there for him at his darkest hour. Saving Catherine made him feel that he'd at least been there for someone at the moment they most needed it.

But what of Amanda? Simon tried to tell himself that she could take care of herself, but she couldn't. She'd be helpless with Simon and Nick fiddling with her past life. Did she deserve such chancery with her own life? She hadn't done anything to deserve much else, he reasoned with himself.

Really? If he was honest with himself, he knew it was wrong. His justification was borne out of bitterness and the hurt she'd caused him. He knew that. She was flawed, certainly, but it wasn't grounds to hazard her life. No. Saving Catherine would provide no redemption for his father's death if it meant Amanda ceased to exist. It would probably only worsen his guilt.

Simon sighed, weary at the realisation. Either way he couldn't win. They were going home tomorrow. Probably the best thing to do would be to leave things as they were and never see Amanda again. That way she could never hurt him again. They would carry on with their lives, and let the past be the past. And the past included leaving Catherine to her fate. At least she'd found love, albeit briefly, with Daniel. He would still carry the shame of his father's death, but that too was the past. There was nothing he could do to change it, so he might as well accept it.

There were posters around the bar advertising Nick's gig that evening. Simon inwardly winced. He hadn't asked Nick how he felt about tonight's performance, hadn't asked him what songs he planned to sing, hadn't supported him in any way. Perhaps Nick's temper earlier was down to nerves. After all the help Nick had given him, Simon felt like a troll of a brother for not being there for him in return.

Simon downed the rest of his drink and slammed his empty glass down with finality. That was it. He would go up to see Nick, apologise for being a shitty brother, and tell him he was done with this whole drama.

Simon knocked on Nick's door and waited.

He knocked harder.

Still there was no answer. Nick might have gone out, gone to cool off somewhere. Or… Simon's gaze travelled down the corridor towards Amanda's door. He could leave it, come back later. But later, Nick would be performing. Simon wanted to be there for him before then, to support him before his gig. Knocking on Amanda's door wouldn't exactly be pleasant, but he owed it to Nick to show that courage, to show he was willing to go through unpleasant circumstances to make it up to him.

Before he could change his mind, he strode down the corridor to Amanda's room. He hesitated before knocking. He didn't want to catch them in bed, so he leaned his ear against the door, cringing in anticipation of the sounds he might hear. But no; no gasps or moans of a couple in the throes of lovemaking, just quiet talking. He couldn't help himself. He pressed his ear closer to the door. They might be talking about him.

'I'm walking along a road. It's dark. It's raining. I don't know if I should be doing this,' came the faint murmur of Amanda's voice.

'You must,' came Nick's reply. 'You must find a safe place to hide it. Daniel is not to be trusted.'

Simon jerked away from the door in surprise. What on earth were they talking about? He gasped as it dawned on him. They were doing a regression session. But what on earth for? Trying to steady his racing heart, he flattened his ear against the cold veneer of the door.

'Now, go to the second window along the left side,' said Nick, 'and remove one of the stones. Now hide the necklace behind it.'

Simon staggered away and stared at the door in shock. What were they doing? Was Nick going behind his back? Perhaps he was worried about the safety of the Fleur de l'Alexandrie and was ensuring Catherine put it somewhere only she could find it. But why go through Amanda? He could have ensured its safety through Daniel.

Daniel is not to be trusted. A fiery anger swelled in Simon's chest. They really were going behind his back. And Catherine wasn't the only one to know the necklace's whereabouts if it was hidden. Nick and Amanda would know too. The bastards were trying to grave rob her!

He raised his fist to pound on the door then paused.

Interrupting them now would only postpone their mission. Simon turned on his heel and stormed away.

Back in the privacy of his own room, he had to sit and catch his breath. He couldn't have an asthma attack now. 'Son of a bitch,' he murmured. He leapt to his feet again, his heart thumping in his chest. 'Okay, calm down, calm down.'

He scrabbled through the mess on his bedside table for his chill pills and sank a couple without water. He then tried to make himself comfortable on the chaise longue, but no position felt right. He closed his eyes and slowed his breathing, taking long forced breaths through his mouth and exhaling through his nose. He concentrated on relaxing his fingers and toes, then his hands and feet, his arms and legs, concentrated on the soothing tranquillity seeping through to his core. When his heart had steadied, he pictured the steps of consciousness, taking each one slowly and deliberately until he reached the bottom. He pictured the doors in the darkness, found the one with the plaque reading the 23rd of June, 1940. He opened it... and was greeted with a solid nothing.

Simon sat up with an impatient tut. It wasn't going to work. He was too anxious. He got up and fetched his box of chill pills again. He had only half a foil strip left. He frowned. He was sure he'd had more. He swallowed three more, even though it was far more than he should be taking in one go, and waited pensively. It wasn't happening fast enough. The minibar caught his eye, and he hurried over. He pulled out a miniature bottle of whisky. The liquid lit up his throat and stomach like a heatwave. He went and lay down on the chaise longue again and tried to clear his mind, to think of nothing while the pills and alcohol took effect.

Finally, a woozy haze took hold, and he closed his eyes again. He was much more comfortable this time. 'Right buddy, it's up to you now.' He took himself down the steps of consciousness and opened the door.

40

Nantes, France – Monday, 24ᵗʰ June, 1940

Daniel awoke in the night. He lay in the darkness, listening to the steady pitter-patter of rain outside and thinking of the woman beside him. She was like no other he'd met before. She was neither shallow nor cheap. She had worth. She wasn't a woman he could scorn.

A shiver ran over him, and he stretched out to snuggle against her warmth. But his arms only closed around flattened hay. 'Catherine?'

Her clothes were missing. She might have gone outside to relieve herself. He waited a couple of minutes, trying not to panic, reassuring himself that she had no reason to flee. What if she'd gone for a piss and been caught by a passing Nazi? His heart thudded in his chest, and his throat went dry.

'Catherine?' he called louder.

Only the light drum of rain and a distant grumble of thunder responded.

Daniel got up and pulled on his clothes and shoes.

Despite the drizzle, a dull dawn was rising. He hurried around the windmill, hissing Catherine's name. The place was deserted. He jogged down the road, keeping to the shadows, aware that curfew would not yet have been lifted.

Approaching the town centre, he slipped into a doorway and peered out into the gloom. 'Catherine, where are you?' He listened, but again he was greeted with silence. 'Bugger.'

He continued his search, every now and then stopping to call for Catherine. Where the hell had she gone? He couldn't wrap his head round why she might have gone wandering off. Did she still not trust him? Had she slept with him because she felt it was her only way of escape? Daniel pushed the thought away before the hurt could take hold. Perhaps she'd sleep-walked and got lost. It sounded ludicrous, but it was a very real consideration. He'd once dated a girl for a short while, and she'd had a terrible time with the condition. Somnambulism, it was called. She'd go out starkers, wandering around the streets of London. She'd left Daniel for a policeman she'd met on one of her 'wanders'. She'd called him dreamy.

Daniel's attention was caught by a whimper through a fence. He stopped and edged closer to the sound. 'Catherine?'

His heart nearly exploded in fright when a ginger cat jumped onto the fence from the other side. It meowed at him, looking quite pathetic in the rain, its fur in wet spikes. It shook itself then jumped down and ran down the alley.

Daniel took a deep breath to calm his heart then carried on. He turned a corner and saw five Nazis stumbling out of a bar, laughing uproariously and falling over each other. He slipped back into the shadows, but his heel caught on an empty glass bottle and it fell, shattering the quiet of the dawn.

The soldiers stopped laughing. '*Wer ist da? Geben Sie sich zu erkennen!*'

Daniel held his breath. The soldiers approached, apparently magically and terrifyingly sober. The cat reappeared, meowing and weaving itself in and out of his legs. He tried to shake it off, but it only purred louder.

The soldiers paused on the opposite side of the road to listen. The cat kicked the bottle and it tinkered against the wall. The soldiers unslung their rifles and crept across the deserted road. Daniel bit his lip and gave the cat a more decisive nudge. It pinned its ears at him and, flicking its tail, strutted out of the shadows into the street. The soldiers laughed when they saw it. One raised his rifle and took a pot shot at it. The sound reverberated around the houses. His aim was off, and the cat streaked away, but the bullet came unnervingly close to Daniel's hiding spot. He sucked in his breath and plastered himself further into the shadows.

The soldiers carried on their way, breaking into drunken,

patriotic song.

Daniel waited for their voices to fade before venturing out again. He looked up at the sky. Shit. It was getting lighter by the second. On the opposite side of the road was a bar in which he could see lots of grey-green uniforms drinking and laughing merrily. He backtracked and took another route that returned to the main street further along. He hadn't gone far when he heard a commotion up ahead – the sound of running bootsteps on the cobbles and raised German voices.

In this deserted, sleeping town, it could only mean one thing.

Daniel's heart sank. 'Catherine!'

He sprinted up the street as fast as his bad leg would allow, keeping to the shadows as much as possible. Up ahead, two Nazis ran across the street and up another. Daniel switched to a side street to run parallel to them. He cut through a connecting alley that rose to a blind rise.

The shouts drifted closer, and Daniel dived into a doorway. Over the blind rise, Catherine came running, her hair streaking behind her in wet tongues and her dress clinging to her body. A shot rang out, and Catherine gave a cry.

Daniel reached out and pulled her into cover. She screamed and fought to get away. He pulled her back and pressed his hand over her mouth.

'Sshhh! It's me!' he hissed.

Catherine whimpered, her eyes like saucers shining in the darkness. Her struggles subsided, and she gripped the arm he had across her chest. They both held their breath as the soldiers thundered past and out of earshot.

He relaxed his hold and turned her to face him. 'What the hell are you doing? Are you trying to get yourself killed?'

She looked bewildered. 'I – I don't know.'

He took a deep breath and hugged her to him. He couldn't believe she was alive and in his arms. 'Don't do that, okay? Are you hurt?'

She shook her head, and he cupped her face, gentler than

before. 'Stay with me. Come on. Let's get back to the windmill.'

They stepped out of the doorway and hurried up the alley in the direction Catherine had just come from. They bridged the blind rise and stopped at a junction.

'Which way is it to the windmill?' Catherine said.

Daniel hesitated. He looked left and right. He'd lost all sense of direction. Grey buildings rose up either side of them blotting out the dawn, so he couldn't even tell which way was east, which might have helped. Or not. He'd never claimed to be a sailor. He pointed right. 'This way, I think.'

They'd barely taken a step when a pistol hammer clicked back. They froze. Daniel blinked the rain out of his eyes, trying to see through the murk. A tall man in an SS officer's uniform stepped out of the shadows brandishing a gun. Daniel's hand went to his belt, and, with a sinking heart, he realised he'd left his pistol in the windmill. The SS officer circled them in slow deliberate steps then stopped in front of them. He smiled, and Daniel recognised him as the officer at the train station, the same one they'd seen at the shelter in Paris – Schneider, Catherine had called him.

The officer tutted. 'Running around after curfew. What are you up to, I wonder?' he said in perfect French.

They stared at him, speechless. What were they supposed to say? To be honest, Daniel wasn't even sure what they were up to running around after curfew. It wasn't his idea. Nevertheless, he kept a protective shoulder in front of Catherine.

'We were just going home,' she said.

Schneider nodded but was obviously not taken in by her excuse. 'Home? You do not think I believe you are from Nantes, do you? I believe this is what they call fate.' He smiled at Catherine. 'Mademoiselle Jacquot, do you not recognise me?'

'You were at the shelter in Paris,' she replied in a small voice.

The officer laughed. 'Yes! That is correct. But we met some years ago at your grandmother's Château de Pierrecourt. My name is Heinrich Schneider. Perhaps it is easier for me to remember as you were the centre of attention on that occasion, and I was not. I was simply the photographer at your grand party, the day your grandmother gave you a very special gift. Do you remember?'

Daniel felt Catherine tremble against him.

'She gave you a necklace – the Fleur de l'Alexandrie. A very precious gift, no? Your grandmother certainly told everyone about it. First Napoleon's, then Louis the XVIII's – or was it XVI?' Schneider smiled again. 'The sort of gift one takes care of. One I trust you still have.' He held out his gloved hand and clicked his fingers. 'Give it to me now.'

Catherine's hand went to her throat – her *bare* throat, Daniel noticed.

'I don't have it. It got lost.'

'Don't lie to me, girl!' Schneider snapped, his charm vanishing as quickly as a magician's trick. 'I have no time for liars.'

'I don't have it.'

'Nonsense! I saw you at the train station. You were wearing it there!' He pushed his pistol to Catherine's temple and Daniel's heart skipped a beat.

'Just give it to him, Catherine,' he hissed. 'What are you doing?'

Catherine looked at him helplessly. 'I don't have it.'

Schneider's leather glove closed around Catherine's throat, and she gasped as her jaw was raised up. 'Don't play games with me.'

Daniel couldn't help himself. He wrenched Schneider's hand away. 'Don't!'

Schneider growled and swiped him across the face with his pistol. Daniel's teeth rattled, and he went down like a stone. He scrabbled to his feet on the slippery cobbles, but Schneider was ready. He raised his gun and pulled the trigger.

The sound was what hurt first. Daniel's eardrums reverberated. At first, it only felt like he'd been punched, then slowly a burning sensation crept in. He put his hand to his shoulder then looked at it. Blood, diluted by the rain, slipped through his fingers.

Catherine cried out and went to hold him, but Schneider grabbed her and pulled her away like a ragdoll. He clicked back the hammer on his gun again and pointed it right between Daniel's eyes. Daniel looked up at it in a daze.

'I hid it!' Catherine cried. 'I hid it! I'll show you, but first, please let him go.'

'Does this look like a negotiation?' Schneider replied.

'Well, you want the necklace. She knows where it is. You don't,' said Daniel.

Schneider smacked him again with his gun, and the metallic taste of blood filled Daniel's mouth.

'Show me where it is or I will shoot him dead,' Schneider growled.

Catherine gulped then nodded. 'Come.'

'Catherine!'

Daniel's words went unheeded. Catherine tripped away with Schneider gripping her elbow.

41

Amiens, France – Sunday, 14th August, 2016

S imon was startled out of hypnosis by the slamming of the door. Amanda and Nick were in his room. Amanda strode over and shook him.

'Wake up, you little shit.'

Simon pulled himself away, scrabbling for his glasses. 'Get off. What are you doing? How did you get in here?' The room swam and Simon's head throbbed in protest at the interruption.

'What are *we* doing? What are *you* doing?'

'I – I–' Simon was still too shocked to make a comprehensible sentence. It took him a moment, as he cowered on the chaise longue, to re-piece recent events back together. He looked up at Nick, who appeared just as pissed off as Amanda. 'You double-crossed me. Why?'

'We had to change things back,' Nick said reluctantly. 'I knew you weren't going to help. We needed Schneider to catch Catherine, to take her necklace.'

Simon's mouth fell open. So, it hadn't all been coincidence. 'But *why*?'

'Because Schneider is his great-grandfather,' supplied Amanda. She sneered at him. 'Your *step*-grandfather, if I'm not mistaken.'

Simon blinked, uncomprehending. 'But your name's Taylor, not Schneider.'

'Taylor is the anglicised version of Schneider,' Nick replied.

'Schneider was meant to capture Catherine at the Gromaires' farm and take the necklace,' Amanda continued. 'That's what the Taylor family fortune stems from.'

Simon stared at Nick. 'Is that true?'

'Yes. But we were only trying to change things back to the

way they were supposed to be. Then bloody Daniel kept interfering, so instead we tried to get Catherine to hide the necklace somewhere where we could find it.'

'Until you bloody interfered on your own,' Amanda added.

'You were double-crossing me. I heard the two of you doing a PLR session,' Simon said. 'You were going to grave-rob her.'

'Oh, don't get all moralistic with us,' Amanda spat. 'You were willing to get me killed so you could save her. You're one to talk.'

'If you weren't such a bitch then maybe I'd be more bothered about it. I cared about you.'

'And where is it written that just because you're fucking obsessed with me that I have to be the same about you? You're pathetic, Simon. You always have been.' She paused and gave him an evil smile. 'Thank God I got rid of your baby. I don't think I could cope with having a child as pathetic as you.'

Simon stared at her in shock. His baby? She'd been pregnant with his baby? He tried to think back; vaguely, he remembered the 'bug' she'd had towards the end of their short-lived relationship, the constant vomiting. It had to have been morning sickness.

'You got rid of it?' Nick exclaimed. 'You told me you lost it. You miscarried.'

'Oh, what does it matter?'

'Of course it matters! There's a big difference between losing a baby and aborting a baby.'

'You knew?' Simon said to Nick.

There was a banging on the wall from next door, but none of them acknowledged it.

'You were pregnant with my baby,' Simon murmured. For a moment, he pictured himself in a delivery room, cradling a newborn, cooing at it, holding his finger out for it to curl its tiny hand around. 'You bitch.'

'It was my choice.'

'Yes, but... you never told me. We could have worked something out.'

'And what – stayed together? Trust me, Simon, that was never going to happen.'

He winced on the inside, then a deep, red anger curled around the hurt, suffocating it. 'You know, I thought long and hard about what we were doing – or what I thought we were doing here, saving Catherine, jeopardising you,' he said. 'I don't have anything to gain from saving her, not really, not like Nick had something to gain from having Schneider capture her. I thought about what it might mean, you dying, I mean. Who deserved to live more? You or her? And I couldn't decide. It's not like I'd ever know Catherine. I don't know what sort of woman she'd grow up to be. So I looked at it another way.' He looked up at Amanda and smiled at her narrowed eyes and half snarl. 'I asked myself who deserved to die more. And there the answer was obvious. You do nothing but take, take, take, Amanda. You're a parasite, a lazy, controlling, self-centred parasite. You've got nothing to offer. I honestly don't know what I saw in you.'

A deep growl rose up from Amanda, and suddenly she launched herself at him, scratching at his face and neck, shaking him, screaming like a banshee.

'Hey!' Nick shouted.

He pulled Amanda off, and she stumbled back. Her heel caught on the dog-eared rug. She fell backward onto the side of the coffee table. There was a sharp thud then she hit the ground.

'Oh, stop playing the drama queen, will you?' Nick snapped when she didn't move.

Simon jumped to his feet. 'Amanda?'

He gasped as a dark pool seeped out from beneath her head onto the carpet. 'Amanda! Shit, Nick!' He fell to his knees beside her and gently tapped her on the cheek. Amanda's eyes didn't flicker. Intense sapphire blue irises stared ahead like the glass eyes of a waxwork. Simon scrambled back to his feet and away. He looked at Nick. Nick stared at Amanda's lifeless form, unblinking, his lips pale.

'Is she – Is she–'

Simon took a deep breath and knelt down again, not too near. He took her wrist and felt for a pulse. There was nothing. He tried her throat just in case. Nothing. 'She's dead.'

Saying the words felt surreal. These sorts of things didn't happen to ordinary people like him. And Amanda, of all people, wasn't one to just *die*. She had too big a personality to be so simply shut off.

'Oh my God. Oh my God, Simon! We have to call an ambulance,' Nick said, pulling his mobile out of his pocket. 'What's the emergency services number here in France? Is it 999 like ours?'

Simon leapt up and snatched the phone away. 'Don't be so stupid,' he hissed. 'We can't call the emergency services.'

Nick stared at him. He was trembling. Even his teeth were chattering. 'Why not?'

'Because she's dead. She hit her head, Nick. She's not coming back from that.'

Nick's eyes grew larger as if this was breaking news to him. 'If we call anyone they're going to ask questions.'

'But it was an accident. We'd just tell them it was an accident. It's the truth.'

'And if they speak to the guests next door? They'll tell a different story. They heard us arguing.'

'So what do we do? Get rid of her body? How do we do that when we're in a hotel?'

Simon's heart hammered in his chest. Nick was right. Maybe they could simply check out and make a run for it. But then they'd be on the run forever. Interpol would be on their tails. They could never go home. They'd have to stowaway on a ship and start a new life in South America or somewhere. Or... Simon paused. 'We could save Catherine.'

'What? What the hell are you talking about? Amanda's dead, Simon! And you want to carry on with your vigilante hero mission?'

'If we save Catherine, Amanda ceases to exist.' He pointed at her. The pool of blood was expanding at a rapid rate. He hated to think what the wound must look like.

Nick didn't reply. His eyes darted from Amanda to Simon and back again. 'Her body would be gone? All of… *that*?' He gestured to the blood.

'Presumably so. It would be like it never happened.'

'But how do we do that when we don't have access to Catherine anymore?'

'We still have Daniel.'

'Yeah, but he's bleeding to death in some alley in Nantes and Schneider's taken Catherine.'

'Do you know where he's taking her?'

'Yes. *She* is taking *him* to an abbey ruin just outside of town. That's where she hid the Fleur.'

'Then we just send Daniel there. Oh, shit.'

'What oh, shit?' Nick looked at him in alarm.

'What if Daniel kills Schneider? What will happen to you?'

'Joe was born before the war. Don't you remember Schneider telling Gromaire he had a son called Josef who knew not to lie?'

Simon snorted. 'Well, he learnt pretty well as an adult.'

'What happens if Schneider kills Daniel? What will happen to you?'

'I think we're long past that question, don't you? I'm going to have to take my chances.'

Voices next door made them both jump.

'Come on, let's get on with it then,' said Nick.

Simon looked steadily at his step-brother. 'It would mean no Fleur de l'Alexandrie for the Schneiders. No family fortune to inherit.'

'What good is that if I'm in some lousy French prison?'

'Okay. We need to have a plan though. We can't just hope they make it safely to Spain. I mean Daniel's injured. We don't know how badly.' Simon chewed his lip as he thought. 'How far is Nantes from the coast?'

'I don't know.'

Simon stepped over Amanda's body and fetched his laptop

from his bed then set it up at the dressing table. He searched for Nantes on Google Maps. 'It's not far at all. Look.'

'What good is getting to the coast going to do them?'

'Evacuations, Nick. Dunkirk couldn't have been the only one. There had to be loads of Brits needing to be evacuated. If we can find one, we can get them back to the UK.'

'Daniel's not going to be that keen. MI5 will be waiting for him. He probably won't even listen to us.'

'He might be more amenable now he's got a hole in his shoulder.'

Nick shook his head. 'I don't see how there could have been any evacuations at this point. Hitler has taken over. He's not going to just let a whole load of people sail away.'

Simon turned back to his laptop and searched for '*WW2 France evacuations*'.

'"*Operation Ariel*",' Simon read the top result, '"*was an evacuation of north west French ports between 15-25 of June, 1940.*"' He clicked on the link and scanned the article, cross-referencing the names of ports with his map of France. Cherbourg and Saint-Malo would involve travelling north again and, according to Google Maps, would take thirty-eight hours to walk to the latter. 'What day is it?'

'Sunday, fourteenth of August.'

'No, not now. *Then*. Hitler and Petain signed the armistice on the twenty-second of June, 1940. What was that – a couple of days ago?'

'Um… I think so. They left Le Mans the day after, then got up to some nooky that night. It's now dawn of the following day.'

'So, the twenty-fourth.' Simon checked the dates of Operation Ariel again. '"*between 15-25 of June 1940*". Shit. They'll never make it in time.' Not unless they found a train or hitched a lift with someone. He scanned the rest of the article for any other ports. *Brest. La Pallice. Saint-Nazaire.*

Brest was even further away than Saint-Malo. La Pallice was another hundred and forty kilometres south of Nantes. Simon's breath disappeared when the results for Saint-Nazaire popped up. It was sixty-five kilometres away.

'Saint-Nazaire,' he said, pointing to the screen. 'They could go there. They have time. It's going to be tight; they'll have to steal a motorbike or hitch a lift, but they should make it before the last boat.'

Nick peered at the screen then nodded. 'Let's hope they get a space.'

Simon stood up and returned to the chaise longue, again stepping gingerly over Amanda's body. The blood around her head was still expanding. He hoped the floors and ceilings weren't as thin as the walls. He lay down and tried to make himself comfortable. Eyes closed. Deep breaths, in through the mouth, out through the nose. He waited for the sound of Nick coming to join him. The room stayed silent.

'Are you coming?'

Nick stood over Amanda's body, where it blocked his path to his chair. 'Oh, Jesus. I can't do this.' He turned and ripped the top blanket off the bed and billowed it over the body.

'Hey! That's my bedding.'

Nick came and sat down. 'If this works, then it won't matter.'

42

Nantes, France – Monday, 24th June, 1940

Daniel lay against the wall of the alley, dipping in and out of consciousness. His shoulder hurt like the dickens. It was a cool dawn, but sweat drizzled down his face. Schneider and Catherine had disappeared from sight. He looked at his shoulder. His jacket was stained black and there was a little hole where the bullet had pierced the fabric. He fingered his clothes aside to get a better look at the wound. Considering the pain he was in, it didn't look all that bad. He'd expected a huge hole and shreds of flesh and bone hanging out. That's what it felt like. But no. He twisted his right arm across his chest and over to feel for an exit wound. Yes, there was a hole in the fabric on the other side as well.

Daniel slipped off his jacket. He unbuckled his belt and looped his left arm through it, under his armpit, then positioned it over the wound. He took a couple of deep breaths in readiness then yanked it tight. He fell sideways and hit the cold wet cobbles with his cheek, teeth gritted in an effort not to cry out with pain. His sweaty, rain-soaked fingers slipped over the buckle, but finally he had it secured. He put his jacket back on then staggered to his feet.

He set off in the direction Catherine and Schneider had gone but soon slowed his pace as he passed more and more streets. They could have gone down any of them.

She's at the ruined abbey. Go to the ruined abbey.

The voice in his head was as loud as it had ever been. It wouldn't shut up. It must be the loss of blood. He must be losing his senses. His instinct had spoken to him before, had led him to Catherine at the shelter. It hadn't been wrong. But there had also been occasions when it had been wrong. It had wanted him to give Catherine over to Schneider before. He carried on jogging up the street. What was an instinct like this anyway? It didn't know anything for certain. It was just a hunch. Why his gut was telling him Catherine would be at the ruined abbey, he didn't know. He knew the place, of course. They had passed it on their way to the windmill. Perhaps that was it. The one place he was familiar with – its familiarity in comparison to the rest of Nantes – was calling him. He thought he knew the way. He knew the direction at any rate. But why would Schneider take her there?

Go to the ruined abbey.

He reminded himself that it was actually Catherine taking *him* there. She'd said she'd snuck out and hid her necklace. God only knew why. But that would be a reasonable place to hide it, he supposed. And they had left the alley and gone in the abbey's direction.

Go to the ruined abbey.

'All right, all right. I'm going,' he murmured to himself.

He took the next right then had to whip back out of sight again. Across the road was a bar, its Nazi patronage still going strong at this early hour. Daniel was about to backtrack and head down the next right turn, when he spotted a couple of bicycles propped under the wide bistro window outside. Catherine and Schneider had got a good head start on him. Schneider had a gun. All Daniel had was the element of surprise, and he would need to get ahead of them for that to work. He didn't have time to go to the windmill and fetch his gun. Catherine could be dead by then.

He took a deep breath then darted across the road. He plastered himself against the walls and slid closer to the bar. The German voices from within grew louder and more nerve-wracking.

Daniel ducked down and untangled the nearest bicycle from the one resting against the wall then quickly wheeled it away.

The noise to the bar suddenly grew louder and then softer again as the door slammed.

'Oi, you!'

Daniel froze, then slowly turned around. A Nazi soldier, looking somewhat worse for wear, staggered over to him, an unlit cigarette dripping from his lips.

'Where are you going?'

'To work,' Daniel replied.

'Work?'

'I'm a farm labourer.'

The soldier looked him up and down with heavy-lidded eyes that weren't quite focusing.

Daniel held his breath, hoping the soldier wouldn't comment on the blood stain and hole in his jacket.

'Do you have a light?'

Daniel patted his pockets with his right hand. His matches were in his right breast pocket, but he couldn't quite reach them with his right hand. Pain shot through his shoulder as he tried to move his left arm. He clenched his teeth, pretending to smile at the soldier as he torturously rummaged through his pocket and withdrew his matches.

'There you go.'

The soldier took them, and Daniel let his arm fall limp with a whispered gasp of relief. The soldier lit his cigarette, the glow highlighting the young man's Arian features and strong unshaven jaw. He offered them back, and Daniel shook his head.

'Keep them.'

The soldier smiled and gave him a half-hearted Nazi salute. 'Thank you, my friend. Have a good day.'

'You're welcome. You too.'

Save Catherine. You must save Catherine. She's at the ruined abbey. Take her to Saint-Nazaire evacuations. Take her to Saint-Nazaire evacuations.

The voice in his head repeated the commands over and over until finally he reached the abbey. The ruin was set back from the road in a small overgrown field that Daniel supposed had once been the well-tended abbey grounds. The abbey itself was no more than a shell with only three pale grey stone walls still standing, although even that was being generous. Most had crumbled down to window level. The wall facing the road was non-existent with just a skeletal archway remaining. Only the wall at the head of the abbey, rising above the rubble, still held grimly to its original majestic height. Grass and brambles grew within the walls, where fallen stone blocks hid waiting to turn unsuspecting ankles.

Daniel discarded his bicycle in a bush and, back hunched, limped through the half-light to take cover behind the crumbling stone wall at the head of the abbey. It was just light enough to see, but also to be seen. He slunk around to the far side and peeked through a crumbling window frame.

He whipped back out of sight when he spotted Schneider and Catherine standing towards the rear of the ruin. He peeked again, careful to keep in the shadows.

'Come on, where is it?' Schneider demanded, pushing Catherine ahead of him with his pistol.

'I don't know. It's somewhere here,' Catherine replied, stumbling forward. Her hands slid over the uneven stones, upturning the loose ones.

Schneider growled. 'Hurry up!'

'Here! Here it is!' Catherine held up the Fleur de l'Alexandrie and it twinkled in the half-light.

Schneider took the necklace from her and held it up. A smile spread across his face. He pocketed it then turned his attention back to Catherine. He cocked his pistol and took closer aim.

She stumbled back and fell over a hidden stone block. The gun went off and a stone in the wall behind her exploded. Slumbering birds in nearby trees flapped into life. Daniel fell back from sight.

Slipping on the dew-wet grass, he hurried along the outer wall and around the back. The bottom wall had half fallen, creating a pile of rubble behind itself. Daniel picked his way up the mountain of stones to the top. Schneider was just below him, his back to Daniel. Catherine sat on the ground, at the mercy of the German officer.

'Please, no, please. Take the necklace. You have it now. It's yours.' She stopped when she spotted Daniel, and she gasped in recognition.

Daniel launched himself off the rubble, but Schneider saw the look on her face and turned at the same time. A crack of gunfire. Daniel landed on Schneider and knocked him to the ground. He grabbed the officer's wrist and slammed it against a stone, sending the gun tumbling from Schneider's grasp. They both scuffled after it, foraging through the tangled undergrowth. Daniel's fingers touched upon the smooth metal, but Schneider kicked it away then punched him in his wounded shoulder.

Daniel fell back with a cry of agony. Schneider dived on top of him and punched him hard in the shoulder again, then one in his mouth that sent Daniel's teeth rattling.

Daniel looked up through the glistening of tears to see Schneider pick up a stone block and lift it high above his head. He closed his eyes, waiting for the inevitable, then started as another gunshot rang out. He opened his eyes. Schneider stared at him in surprise. The stone block fell out of his hands and tumbled to the side. The officer gasped, almost gagging. A thin trickle of blood oozed from his mouth.

As if in slow motion, Sturmbannführer Schneider fell beside Daniel and lay still. Where once the officer had hidden her from Daniel's view, Catherine now stood, still aiming the gun. Trembling, she dropped it and rushed over to him.

'Daniel, are you okay?'

'I'm fine. I think.' His shoulder throbbed with pain, and Schneider must have caught him in the gut because that too was beginning to smart. He tried to sit up, but his abdomen really did hurt. He looked down, puzzled to find his white shirt now stained red.

'You're hurt!' Catherine's hands went to the wound and pressed on it.

Daniel hissed through his teeth in pain. He lifted his shirt.

Blood pulsed out of a hole in his belly. Suddenly, the world started to tilt, and his head began to fill with muzziness.

'No,' Catherine cried. She scrambled over and pulled Schneider's jacket clumsily from his body and pressed it against Daniel's abdomen. Soon her fingers were soaked in blood. 'Hold this here. I'll go get help.'

'No, Catherine, wait!' Daniel reached out to halt her departure. 'Don't go. It's too late.'

'It can't be! Papa is a doctor; I know I can help. It's not too late.'

Daniel's grip on her arm tightened, and he pulled her back. 'Don't leave me alone.'

The strength in his arm faded, and he let his grasp fall. He swallowed with difficulty. This was it. He could feel death calling his name. He surprised himself. He wasn't frightened. He didn't feel panicked that his life was being cut short. All that wasted potential. Daniel smiled to himself. What potential? He'd done nothing but cause trouble in his short life. Then he looked up at Catherine. Her tears fell onto him, little drops of cool, soothing love. He felt a surge of regret. He would miss a life spent with her; a love that he'd only just found, only just realised existed, one he would not get to enjoy.

Catherine nestled him into her lap, cradling his head.

Saint-Nazaire. Evacuations.

'You have to go,' he whispered.

'No.'

'You have to leave here, Catherine.' He looked into her eyes, holding her gaze. 'There's a bicycle on the roadside. Take it. Head for the coast... Saint-Nazaire. They're evacuating people from there... taking them to England. You must hurry.'

'I won't leave you.'

'When you get to England...' Daniel had to stop. His head spun, and his tongue felt lumberous in his mouth, too slow and big to form the words. 'Go to London... Find Fletch Willoughby at *The Northern Gazette newspaper*... Fletch Willoughby... He's a good friend... He'll take care of you...

Tell him...' Daniel paused, struggling for breath. He shivered, suddenly freezing cold. 'Tell him... I'm sorry... I couldn't manage a flamenco dancer.' He smiled at Catherine's confusion. 'He'll know what you mean... I love you.'

As the world spun away and darkness closed in, Daniel heard the echo of Catherine crying out his name.

PART FOUR

43

Amiens, France – Sunday, 14ᵗʰ August, 2016

Simon awoke with a groggy headache. He lay on the chaise longue, looking up at a ray of gold that lit the darkened ceiling. Sunset. Why was he napping at this hour? The last mists of slumber burned away, and he sat up like a whack-a-mole and switched on the lamp beside the chaise.

'Nick?'

The room was quiet, empty. Had he deserted him? Simon's gaze swung to the floor where Amanda's body had lain. His bedding lay rumpled on the floor. He got up and snatched the blanket away. He blinked at the space it had covered. The bare rug. The green and red floral pattern.

Amanda was gone. The pool of blood had gone. Not gone as in scrubbed clean and leaving a faint brown stain, but gone as in had never been there in the first place. Simon held up the blanket to check for bloodstains. It too was clean.

His knees trembled, and he sat down with a bump. He held his head in his hands then rubbed his cheeks and raked his fingers through his hair. They'd done it. They'd saved Catherine. They'd eliminated Amanda. He stared at the rug, remembering that glassy stare and parting of her lips as if she'd been paused midsentence. Did this make them murderers? It had been an accident. No one had purposefully pushed her back to make her trip and hit her head, but eliminating her from existence made it feel that much more calculating.

He took a moment to think of her in a positive light, to mourn her loss, to feel remorse. But nothing came. He tried to force it, but it was fake. He felt nothing. No grief for Amanda no longer being a part of his world, no real heartfelt regret that her life had been cut short.

Instead, a wave of shame for not being able to feel those feelings washed over him. What did that make him? Weak and selfish. He thought of Daniel and how he'd sacrificed himself to save Catherine. Sure, he'd had Nick helping him, but Simon was sure only geographically. The rest was Daniel. He'd jumped Schneider because he loved Catherine. *Had.* He looked at his hands. They were real. He turned to the mirror above the dressing table. He was still himself. Somehow, Daniel's death hadn't affected him. Who was to say Daniel had lived much longer without their meddling?

Simon wondered what had become of Catherine. She must have lived if Amanda had disappeared. But where? Had she made it to Saint-Nazaire and travelled to England to find Fletch Willoughby? Had she missed the last evacuation but still managed to escape Nazi persecution? Perhaps she'd made it to Spain.

He'd look it up later. Right now, he needed to find Nick. He left his room and hurried down the corridor to his step-brother's room. He knocked, but there was no answer.

'Nick?' he hissed through the doorframe.

He knocked louder but was again met with silence. Maybe he'd gone down for a drink. God knew he needed one too.

The concierge was at his desk in the foyer, and Simon hurried over to him.

'Monsieur, have you seen my friend?'

The concierge blinked at him. 'Your friend, monsieur?'

'Yes. Um, *mon ami*? Have you seen him?'

The concierge hesitated, giving Simon a wary look. 'I'm afraid not.'

But Simon wasn't listening anymore. Instead, he could hear music playing down in the restaurant-bar. Someone singing. Of course! It was Sunday night. Nick's gig. He hurried down the steps, relieved to have found him, if a little indignant that Nick had left him to sleep.

The room was packed, standing room only. On stage was Nick, guitar strapped around him, singing into a microphone.

The crowd cheered and sang along. Nick played along to them, letting them sing the chorus. Simon had to admit Nick had vastly improved since he'd last seen him perform. He both looked and sounded the part.

Nick finished the song and thanked the crowd to rapt applause. He unhooked his guitar from over his shoulder and put it away in its case along with a songlist that had been on the floor. Simon pushed through the crowd, ignoring the annoyed curses thrown at him. He reached the stage just as Nick was about to come down the steps.

The crowd began to chant, '*Encore! Encore! Encore!*'

Simon grinned at him. 'Well, you were certainly a hit.'

Nick grinned back. 'Thank you. I hope you enjoyed the show.'

Simon paused. Nick sounded different, but maybe it was because of the noise. 'Maybe I would have if you hadn't left me to sleep.'

Nick's grin faded. 'Pardon me?'

'We did it, Nick! She's gone.'

Nick looked at him blankly.

'Amanda's gone!' Simon continued. 'You don't need to play dumb. Catherine must have lived.'

Nick gave him an uncertain smile. 'I'm sorry, I don't know what you mean. But I hope you enjoyed the music.'

This time, Simon wasn't imagining things. Nick did sound strange. His accent was different. It almost sounded *German*.

'Excuse me. I have to go now.' Nick pushed past him and was ferried through the crowd by a couple of burly men.

Simon staggered back in shock. What the hell was the matter with him? 'Nick!' he yelled.

The hotel manager, M. Fourrier, climbed to the stage and took the microphone. 'Nicklaus Schneider, everybody!' He clapped, prompting another wild bout of cheering.

Simon's breath disappeared. He whipped round, trying to find Nick's blond head in the semi-darkness, but he was gone. Nicklaus Schneider? *Schneider*? And what was with the German

321

accent? Simon began to hyperventilate. He scrambled for his inhaler and took a couple of relieving puffs. But his brain still spun. He felt faint. Had they changed more than just Amanda's existence? Had they changed Nick's too? But how? Simon froze in terror. Was he still Simon Hayes? He took out his wallet and checked his driver's license. Phew. Yes. He was still himself. But what about Nick? Certainly, they'd known that the Taylor family fortune would most likely disappear if Catherine had managed to escape Schneider, but this was a whole different ballgame. Catherine escaping with her necklace wasn't meant to rearrange Nick's entire identity.

Simon thought back to the events of the ruined abbey in Nantes. Of Daniel ambushing Schneider, of Catherine shooting him.

'Oh my God,' Simon whispered to himself.

Sturmbannführer Heinrich Schneider had died. That must certainly have affected the Schneider family. Had he then failed to produce a family? How did Nick exist in his current identity then? Simon tried to wrap his head around it, but his mind felt like it was moving through sludge. He staggered through the thinning crowds and out of the restaurant-bar. No, Schneider had definitely had a family. At the Gromaires' farm he'd said he had a son called Josef.

Simon mentally slapped his forehead. Of course! Nick had said as much before he'd put Simon under. Schneider's son, Josef, was Nick's grandfather, Joe. But without Heinrich Schneider at the head of the family to cash in on the Fleur de l'Alexandrie and move to the UK, the family must have stayed in Germany. Nick's father had been a drummer in a German heavy metal group, so his conception must still have happened.

Simon locked himself in his room and sat down on his bed. Nick had never become British Nick Taylor of the Taylor Made Television empire, duty-bound to become a TV producer like his grandfather and great-grandfather. He had been brought up in Germany as Nicklaus Schneider, destined to become a musician like his father. Nick still existed, but it wasn't the Nick that Simon knew. And Nick didn't know him from a bar of soap.

He'd lost his step-brother and best friend.

Simon fell back against the pillows as a sword of grief pierced him. What a mess they'd created. He thought back to the moment it had all changed, of himself yelling 'Run!' to Catherine – it was a mess *he'd* created. He'd killed not only Amanda, but Nick too. His heart thudded in his chest, swelling, tightening. Blood roared from his head, and the room began to spin as he was gripped by the mother of all panic attacks. He tried to calm himself. In his head, he did his seven times table. The distraction and mundanity of it usually calmed him down. But tonight it had no effect.

He raided the minibar and downed a couple of whisky shot bottles. His eyes alighted on the Kronenbourg beer on the shelf. Beer! Yes! That was always good for mellowing out. He glugged one whole bottle then belched loud enough to be heard three rooms down. It wasn't working. Nothing was working.

He scrabbled through the junk on his bedside table and found his chill pills. There were a lot more there than he remembered. He cracked open three and swallowed them with the last of his Kronenbourg. He lay back and looked up at the ceiling. He wasn't going to die – *but who was he?* Every time he tried to reassure himself, another panic-stricken question or possibility jolted back into his head to boost the panic. He closed his eyes. Sleep, just sleep. It'll be better in the morning. Sleep, sleep, sleep. Sleep.

44

London, England – Monday, 21ˢᵗ March, 2005

Simon trailed a hand along the sleek lines of his father's red Peugeot, rounding the back to the driver's side, stepping deliberately in his scuffed and dirty football boots upon the cement floor, his eyes following the green and yellow-chevron hosepipe that looped from the exhaust pipe up towards the driver's window. He couldn't really see inside. The interior was foggy, and only the light from the open doorway to the flat penetrated the gloom of the garage.

He reached the driver's door, looking curiously at the hose jammed between the window and frame. A little crack allowed some of the fog to seep out. His eyes refocused from the hose to the interior where he could make out the shape of a person, their head resting to the side.

'Dad?'

Fear gripped Simon, crystalizing his bones, as he realised what was happening. He fumbled with the handle. It always stuck. He yanked it open and pulled the prostrate body from the vehicle. It slid to the floor in a cloud of dirty fumes.

Simon staggered back in surprise. It wasn't his father at all. It was a young man with dark hair and an unshaven jaw. There were bloodstains on his shoulder and his stomach. His skin was pink, his lips dry and cracked, a cherry tinge. Simon couldn't help but stare at the man, so obviously dead despite the unusual colour of his skin. Then he remembered the first aid lessons they'd done at school.

He placed his hands in a cross and laid them upon the man's chest and began chest compressions.

'One-two-three-four; one-two-three-four; one-two-three-four,' he whispered aloud. Like a train on the tracks. 'One-two-three-four; one-two-three-four; one-two-three-four.' Who was this man and what was he doing in their car? 'One-two-three-four; one-two-three-four; one-two-three-four.' Where was his father? 'Dad?' he shouted. 'One-two-three-four; one-two-three-four; one-two-three-four. DAD!'

Chest compressions were tiring, and the heavier he breathed, the more choking the air became. The fumes in the garage made his head spin. He didn't know how long he had to keep doing this for. When was enough enough?

'Come on, Daniel,' he murmured. His rhythm broke in astonishment. Where had that name come from? 'Come on… mister.'

Without warning, the man's eyes shot open and he sat up with a heaving gulp of air.

He woke with a gasp and sat up in surprise. He looked around his hotel room. Everything was still. He patted his body, lifting the blankets to check himself. The phone trilled beside his bed, and he automatically answered it.

'Good morning, Monsieur 'Ayes,' said a pleasant French voice.

'Who?'

'This is M. Fourrier. This is your check-out call. You are required to vacate your room by eleven o'clock.'

He looked at the clock on the wall. It was almost half past ten. 'Er – yeah, okay.' He replaced the receiver and gingerly got out of bed. He rubbed his face, scruffed his hair. Everything seemed so foggy, like he'd been on an extreme bender the night before. Maybe he was still drunk. He must be. A coin of lucidity dropped into his mind like a penny in an arcade game.

'Catherine!' He whirled around. The room was empty, as he already knew. He rushed to the bathroom, but she wasn't in there either. He stood in the centre of the room, his blood roaring in his head, his heart beating out of his chest. He didn't know where he was. He didn't know where she was. Calm. He had to think. Where had he seen her last? The ruined abbey,

Nantes. That's right, yes. Before he'd passed out, he'd told her to go to Saint-Nazaire, to catch a boat to England; to find Fletch.

But where was he? He searched the room for clues. On the bedside table, his fingers paused over an asthma inhaler. What the hell was that? It lay on a notepad beside the telephone. On the headed paper read: 'Hôtel Sceau, 12 Rue Martin Bleu Dieu, 80000 Amiens, France.'

His fingers trembled. He was in *Amiens*? He went to the window, edging closer, peeping out. There didn't seem to be any unrest. He couldn't see any soldiers. His hand went to his shoulder. There was no pain. To his stomach. No pain. How long had he been out?

Snatching up the inhaler, he stuffed it into an overnight bag, which presumably belonged to him, zipped it up then hurried out of the room.

Downstairs, a man at the front desk smiled at him. 'Goodbye, Monsieur 'Ayes. We hope you have enjoyed your stay.'

Monsieur 'Ayes? Was this another pseudonym? He must have amnesia. He walked through the revolving doors and out into the warm sunshine. A signpost across from him pointed him in the direction of Cathédrale Notre-Dame d'Amiens, Somme River, Musée de Picardie, Zoo Amiens Métropole, le Gare d'Amiens.

He didn't think twice. He made for the train station. He kept his head down, darting inconspicuous glances around for soldiers. He had to find Catherine. She could be anywhere. She could be hurt. She could be in some ghastly prison camp. She could be – he couldn't bring himself to contemplate the worst. He had to believe she'd got out. But where to start looking?

Simon must have dozed off, must have taken too many chill pills, because when he came round he was on the train to Paris. His bag was beside him, packed with all his belongings. Dammit, where were his glasses? He must have left them behind. At least he was going in the right direction.

He gazed out of the window at the golden fields of wheat being harvested by monstrous combines, small hamlets that swished past before he realised they were there, vineyards, fields of dairy cattle; they all blurred together. Each passing field put more distance between him and Amiens and this crazy week; put more distance between him and Amanda's extinction, between him and Nick's radical change. Simon'd most likely never see him again, certainly never talk to him, hang out with him like they'd done all through their teenage years. An ache filled his heart. The last time he'd felt this way was when Amanda had broken up with him at university. He supposed it was a sort of heartbreak. Could one classify it as grief if the person was still alive? But was he? The Nick he'd known no longer existed. So, in a way he had died. Simon had killed him.

He tried to fend off the cloak of guilt that threatened to engulf him. Nick was still alive. He wasn't dead. *And* he was a musician. Wasn't that what he'd always wanted to be? So what if he hadn't grown up in a mansion surrounded by servants and gone to the best independent schools? He'd never been entitled to those luxuries anyway. The Fleur de l'Alexandrie had never belonged to the Schneiders. And who was he to say Nicklaus Schneider hadn't had a comfortable upbringing? He hadn't looked like he was starving. In fact, judging by the crowds, he was doing pretty well for himself.

Simon managed to assuage his guilt. Nick was better off. But it didn't stop him from missing his step-brother. Right now, all Simon wanted was to get home, back to the familiarity of the pawnbroker's shop, back to his own bedroom to sleep, his own fridge to eat and have a beer, his own living room to watch the Season 6 boxset of *Game of Thrones* that he'd ordered online before he left, back to normality.

He was jolted awake by a voice announcing they were arriving at St Pancras International. He was back in London. He sighed with relief. Even despite the very real threat that MI5 might well be waiting on the platform for him, it was good to be back on

British soil.

MI5 weren't waiting for him. Instead, a rather odd version of London was when he limped out from the station. He couldn't quite put his finger on it, but things seemed different. He must have been away a very long time. Perhaps Britain had been bombed after all. Perhaps this was the rebuilt version, a much more modern version. Futuristic, in fact.

He patted his pockets for his cigarettes. None, dammit.

'Excuse me, old chap,' he said to an oddly dressed man smoking outside the station doorway with a large satchel-type bag, covered in flags, resting against his legs. Taking in the fat messy braids and torn jeans, he guessed the man must be homeless. 'Don't suppose I could bum a fag off you?'

The man looked at him with an expression he could only interpret as horror. 'Excuse me?'

Daniel gasped, frozen to the spot by the man's accent. It was German without a doubt. He darted a look around. Was everyone here German? Was he not in England? Had England been taken over by the Nazis? If so, they looked pretty comfortable about it all judging by the commuters going about their business and not a single Panzer uniform to be seen.

He gulped and pointed a shaky finger at the man's cigarette. 'May I have a cigarette?'

The man's expression softened, and he even cracked a smile. He handed over a pouch of tobacco.

Fingers still trembling, he rolled himself a cigarette and returned the tobacco with thanks. The man lit it for him, and he took a deep calming drag. The smoke caught in his lungs, and he coughed and coughed until his eyes watered. The man grinned at him. Goodness, this tobacco was strong. It was like nothing he'd ever had before. Or perhaps he hadn't quite recovered from that terrible chest infection.

He walked through London, but with a wary step. His mind must still be hazy from his long sleep, or perhaps it was amnesia – a type of selective amnesia, given he could remember Catherine and everything they'd been through. It was more like the present didn't quite match his memory of how things had been. Thankfully, he heard some familiar accents. They were English, thank goodness. God only knew why there was a homeless German at the station. Perhaps he was a spy. If he was then he wasn't a very good one if he couldn't even feign a British accent. Daniel wondered if he should report the man. There was so much else though that demanded his attention. So many vehicles, none that he'd ever seen before. Most likely, that fellow, Henry Ford, capitalising on the war with his fancy new American cars.

He couldn't find his way to the newspaper office, so instead he headed back to his flat. Thank goodness he could remember where it was. And thank goodness it was still standing. Judging by the amount of new buildings around, London had been bombed pretty damn hard.

None of the keys in his pocket opened the lock, so he hammered on the door. 'Mrs Reynolds!' he shouted up to his landlady's open window on the third floor. No one appeared. 'Mrs Reynolds, I've lost my key.'

He stopped hammering when he noticed a new radio system installed in the wall. Good God, Mrs Reynolds must finally have decided to modernise things. He hoped that meant his flat would get some attention. He was constantly fixing the leak in his sink. He pressed the button next to Mrs Reynolds's flat number and waited. She couldn't be out. Mrs Reynolds never went out.

'Mrs Reynolds!' he shouted up again, then pressed his finger more resolutely to the button.

'What the hell do you want?'

He jumped back in surprise as Mrs Reynolds' voice blurted out of the wall. It appeared there was a speaker of some sort installed with the radio system. This was very modern indeed.

'It's Daniel Barrow from Flat 6,' he replied tentatively. 'Can you let me in? I've lost my key.'

'What the fuck are you talking about? Michael and Ariana live in Flat 6. Fuck off.'

Heat spilled down his face. 'Have you rented out my flat to someone else? You can't do that! What about all of my stuff? Mrs Reynolds–'

'Dude, I don't know who the fuck you are or who you think I am, but I'm not Mrs Reynolds, and you don't live here. Now fuck off and let me sleep.'

He stared at the radio system in surprise then staggered back and looked up at the windows. He was about to shout up to Mrs Reynolds just what he thought of her too, but the words faded on his lips. Whoever had answered the radio system had claimed not to be his landlady. And she had sounded a lot younger. Who were these people – Michael and Ariana – living in his home? Had Mrs Reynolds been killed in the bombings and her property sold? He looked around. Where was he supposed to go?

Fletch. He could go to Fletch's place. Yes, of course! He should have gone there to begin with. Catherine would probably be there if she'd made it across from France. He set off again, limping away in the direction of Fletch's flat, or at least he hoped it was.

An hour later, he had to concede he was hopelessly lost. Streets that felt familiar turned out to lead nowhere he knew. His eye was caught by a road sign: Gleeson Street. Now that felt very familiar. He turned down the narrow road. It was a little off the beaten track, with fewer cars and pedestrians. Houses and shops were squashed side by side, old carriage-houses had been modified into vehicle garages. He stopped outside one shop, struck by a sudden pull of déjà vu. In yellow letters across the window was the sign: 'Hayes & Son Pawnbrokers'.

A car tooted and roared past, and Simon faltered on the kerb. He blinked. He was home. Oh, thank God. He pulled out his keys and unlocked the shop door. The familiar jingle announced his arrival, and he let it slam shut behind him as he weaved through the shop to the backstairs.

He stopped halfway up. He could hear voices in the kitchen.

Simon's fingers tightened around the straps of his overnight case. It was clunky but it would have to do as a weapon. He crept up the stairs, avoiding the third from the top as it had the most revealing creak. He paused again before rounding the corner into the hallway. Whoever was in his home weren't worried about being caught. They were chatting away; a woman and a man. He stopped short when he recognised the woman's voice.

'It'll be fine, honestly. Colin assured me there's little to no risk. We just need to take out a second mortgage, and we'll start seeing returns in less than a year. Six months he said it sometimes starts piling up. And just think what we could do with all of that extra income. Colin says we'd get our money back within eighteen months and from there it's all profit. You could retire early. We could go on a cruise, buy a house in France.'

Simon stared unseeingly at the opposite wall. It was his mother. What the fuck was she doing here? How dare she come into his home? His teeth began to chatter as anger flooded through his veins. And who the hell had she brought with her? If it was that bloody Joe Taylor then he was chucking them both out. They had no business here.

'I don't know. It just sounds too good to be true. And Olivia, I really quite enjoy my job.'

The man's voice was strangely familiar. It wasn't Joe though. Was she having another affair? Bringing him back here when she thought Simon was away? The dirty bitch.

'But Colin said the risks are minimal. And look at the way he lives. He's got houses in Chelsea and another out in Buckinghamshire. He was showing me photos of the family's holiday in Kenya, and it looks amazing! Woodbine Investments can't be doing too badly if they can afford all of that.'

'Oh, Olivia, I don't know.'

Simon's overnight case dropped from his limp fingers, and he walked, as if in a trance, down the hallway to the kitchen. His mother was leaning up against a counter, sipping a cool drink, while a man stood opposite, carving slices of beef from a depleted roast to put in a sandwich.

'Simon!' she exclaimed. 'How was your gig?'

The man looked around at him, and Simon stared. The black moustache had grown into an iron grey beard, and his curly black hair had also greyed and thinned, now cut shorter. But it was still him.

'Dad?' Simon breathed.

'Hi bud. Did you have a good time?'

A lump swelled in Simon's throat, and he plunged forward and flung his arms around his father. John Hayes laughed awkwardly, patting him on the back then disentangled himself.

'Careful. I could've cut you. Is everything okay?'

Simon nodded. 'Everything's fine.' He brushed away the tears. He couldn't stop staring at him. He'd wished with every birthday candle these past thirteen years for this moment, never really believing it could ever come true.

He held up his hand to touch his father's face just to make sure he wasn't a hallucination. John gave him an odd look and moved out of reach.

'Simon, have you been taking your pills, honey?' his mother asked.

Simon dropped his hand, nodded obediently. 'I ran out last night.'

His mother sighed. 'Well, you'll have to ask Dr. Yakov for an emergency prescription when you go see him later.'

Simon looked at her blankly, and she rolled her eyes.

'Oh Simon, you haven't forgotten, have you? Three o'clock? That was part of the deal, remember? You go to the gig if you promise to keep your appointment.'

There was a jingle downstairs as a customer opened the shop door. John tutted.

'Jesus, Simon. Did you leave the door unlocked?'

'I – I–' Simon was taken aback by his father's annoyance. This shouldn't happen in a reunion of this magnitude. 'I'll go see to them.'

'Then lock the door after. I want to have some lunch,' John

Hayes called after him.

Simon backed out of the kitchen, still unable to take his eyes off his father. He nearly tripped over his discarded overnight bag. He picked it up and paused outside his bedroom as he passed by to throw it inside. The case landed on the rug beside his bed, and Simon was about to turn away when his eye was caught by the 'decorating' in his room. Posters of Nicklaus Schneider performing with his guitar were plastered everywhere. Concert ticket stumps, newspaper clippings, flyers, artwork. Simon stared. It was really quite disturbing. There wasn't space on the walls for anything else. It was just *Nick*. Everywhere.

The desk bell pinged downstairs, and Simon hastily exited his room and shut the door. He paused for a moment, his forehead resting on the door. Nick's life wasn't the only one to have changed.

The bell pinged again.

'Coming!' He jogged down the stairs. 'Hi. Sorry to keep you waiting.'

The young woman looked over from where she stood by the counter, and Simon nearly fell down the remaining steps.

'Catherine?'

45

London, England – Monday, 15th August, 2016

She gave him a peculiar look. 'Er, no, but close.'

Simon had half regained his composure by the time he got to the other side of the counter. 'Sorry. I thought you were someone else.'

But when he looked at her to share a laugh at his expense, he still couldn't quite ignore how striking the resemblance was. Obviously, it wasn't Catherine, but the young woman, maybe in her early twenties, had the same thick dark hair coiled over her shoulder, curlier perhaps than Catherine's; she had the same strong nose, softened though by a constellation of freckles; her eyes, the same doe-soft shape, fringed with dark lashes, were instead shamrock green.

'H-how can I help you?' he stammered.

'Well, actually, I was on my way to the big jewellers' on the High Street, but then I saw your shop, and I didn't want to make a complete tit of myself, so I thought I'd stop in here first, just to see if, like, I'm not wasting my time or being stupid… you know.'

Simon raised an eyebrow at her. 'Um, not really.'

The young woman blinked at him then burst out laughing. 'Of course not! Oh, I'm so sorry. Here's the thing. My grandmother passed away a couple of months ago, and well, she left me something.' She dug through her bag and withdrew a silk drawstring pouch. 'It was given to her by her grandmother.' She untied the strings and tipped out the pouch's contents. A necklace spilled out onto the counter – a gold Star of David with a dazzling sapphire cut into its centre.

Simon's breath dried in his throat. Carefully, he picked it up, turned it over on his palm, stroking his fingertips over the finely cut gemstone. It felt so surreal to be seeing it, holding it in his hand, after seeing it so often through Daniel's eyes.

'The Fleur de l'Alexandrie,' he murmured.

'That's right! You know it?' she said in delight. 'Oh, I'm so glad. I wasn't sure if it meant anything or was worth anything. I mean, I've heard the stories, but you're never really sure when it's your nan who's telling them.'

'Your grandmother – what was her name?' Simon held his breath in anticipation.

'Catherine Willoughby. Hey, that was the name you said coming down the stairs? Isn't that weird?' She looked at him with delighted surprise. 'And when I said you were close, that's because I'm named after her, but I go by Kate, not Catherine. I'm Kate Willoughby.'

He looked at her, dazed. His mind was seventy-six years away on a cool dawn in Nantes. '*Head for Saint-Nazaire. They're evacuating people to England. Find Fletch Willoughby. He'll take care of you.*' His smile broadened at the realisation of what had transpired. 'A pleasure to meet you, Kate Willoughby.'

'And you are? I'm presuming you're Hayes or hopefully Son,' she said pointing at the sign on the window.

'Simon Hayes. Son. My father is the main name.' Saying the words in the present tense sent a flutter of colour into his world.

'So, Simon Hayes, what do you think this is worth?'

He hesitated. Of course, he remembered the valuation the newspaper article on its theft had given, but that was another life. He thought of everything Catherine and Daniel had gone through to avoid Heinrich Schneider, what it had cost them in the end. What it had cost *him* in the end.

'It's priceless,' he said at last.

Kate rolled her eyes. 'That narrows it down. So, if I went to the jewellers' on the High Street, I wouldn't be making a fool of myself?'

Simon shook his head. 'You'll probably want to take it to somewhere more established to get an accurate valuation.'

Kate's eyes widened. 'Really?'

'You're looking at a good few million, but—' He watched in sudden panic as she dropped the necklace back into the pouch, ready to leave. 'What that necklace has seen, the suffering, the love, the sacrifice – it's priceless beyond words. Nobody can put a price on what your grandmother went through.'

She zipped up her bag and smiled at him. 'Don't worry. I'm not going to sell it. Anyway, thanks for the help.' She held out her hand. 'It was nice meeting you, Simon Hayes.'

Simon took her hand.

It made him think of the first time he'd held her hand – at the theatre shelter in Paris when Schneider had walked in. She looked different in some ways, but in others she was just the same. It was like with everything at the moment – so much was changed, yet the heart of London, of Catherine smiling in front of him, was the same. He'd found her, or rather she'd found him.

'I have to go,' she said. She turned and left the shop, the jingle proclaiming her departure before he could say anything.

He watched her through the window, pausing at the kerb to look both ways, crossing the road, walking away. Walking away? What was he doing still standing there?

He skidded out from behind the counter, knocking into a shelf of knick-knacks then bolted out of the shop.

'Wait! Wait!'

John Hayes stood at the sink, eating his beef sandwich and looking out of the window. He spotted Simon chasing after a girl. She was pretty, from what he could tell from up here. They stood and chatted in the middle of the street. She laughed, batted him away. Simon held his hands to his heart, gave her a charming smile. He couldn't hear what they were saying, but by their body language, they were both obviously taken with one another. Then she nodded, and they both walked away down the street.

'What is that boy doing now?'

Olivia came to see, standing on tiptoes to peer over the window frame down to street level. 'Who's that?'

'Some girl he's just picked up on the street. I think she was in the shop.'

Olivia shrugged. 'Well, maybe it'll get him over that girl at the clinic. His obsession over her has lasted longer than they usually do. Oh, I do hope he doesn't forget his appointment later.'

Epilogue

London, England – Monday, 15th August, 2016

D r. Sol Yakov checked his watch. His patient was a quarter of an hour late. He obviously wasn't coming. He muttered a few choice words. He was glad it would all be over soon. He'd lost his love for the profession many years ago. The misfirings of patients' brains no longer fascinated him, their sufferings no longer stirred any empathy in him. Why should he try to help them when they didn't bother to turn up for their appointments?

He opened the patient's folder and flicked through the sparse notes. He'd better write up something coherent for Dr. Pepple for when he took over the practice. If this patient ever bothered to return. This wasn't the first time he'd left him hanging.

He picked up his Parker pen, slowly swivelled it between his fingers. It had been a gift from his parents for graduating med school. All those many, many years ago; back when he'd been young and eager. Naïve. Unsullied by the endless strife of his patients' pathetic lives. His hand shook as he pressed the pen against the thick stationery paper.

'*Simon Hayes has been a patient at this practice since March 2014 after presenting with symptoms of Dissociative Identity Disorder (D.I.D.) partway through his studies at university where he was studying Military History. He currently only has one other distinct identity – that of Daniel Barrow. This identity appears to be very charming, very successful with women, with abundant self-confidence – your stereotypical alter ego. Daniel is everything that Mr Hayes is not. However, there is also evidence to suggest Mr Hayes has created an imaginary world around his own identity. He often refers to the death of his father (his father is still living), his love affair with Amanda Woodbine, and his friendship with pop singer, Nicklaus*

Schneider. Given Mr Hayes's marked lack of self-confidence and his tendency towards certain obsessive behaviours, the inclusion of admired and important people in his own reality is not surprising...'

There was a knock on his door, and his PA came in bearing a steaming mug of coffee. What he really wanted was a beer. It was a stinking hot day, and he couldn't wait to be done with his last patient. Nevertheless, his PA was a very sweet girl and, he couldn't ignore it, very pretty too. He would hear from his office sometimes the dreary moan of patients awaiting their appointment unloading their troubles onto her, and as ever, her sweet reply: 'Oh, bless you. You poor thing.'

She had a fantastic figure – young and toned, breasts that just cried out to be caressed by a man's hands, and bronzed from her recent family holiday in Kenya. In many ways, he didn't blame Simon Hayes for inventing a love affair with her. He'd done the same on many lonely nights in his bed.

She placed the mug on a coaster and looked at him with sparkling sapphire eyes. 'Thought you'd like a drink since Simon hasn't pitched up.'

Sol Yakov returned her smile. 'Thank you, Mandy. That's very thoughtful of you.'

In fact, he didn't blame Simon Hayes at all. The young man had quite the imagination.

THE END

ACKNOWLEDGEMENTS

The Thirteenth Hour has been fourteen years in the making, so I hope you'll allow me these few moments to thank the many people who contributed to its creation. When I first came up with the idea for *The Thirteenth Hour*, it was for my dissertation project on a creative writing access course. I had spent most of my previous assignments writing about horses, a much-favoured topic as my backlist of novels will attest to! However, I wanted to challenge myself on this occasion and I turned my attention to another subject that has always captured my imagination: World War Two. I knew I didn't want to make it a straight-forward war story so took inspiration from two sources I had recently and coincidentally watched: *Inception*, the 2010 Christopher Nolan film, and a grainy VHS-recorded documentary from the 1980s found on YouTube called *The Reincarnation Experiments*. From these inspirations, *The Thirteenth Hour* was born.

Hypnotherapist, Nicola Mills, generously offered me my own past life regression experience to further the authenticity of the story, in addition to my more academic research using books such as *Life Before Life* and *Return to Life* by Dr Jim B. Tucker, and *Irreducible Mind* by Edward F. Kelly et al.

On my access course, I received instrumental advice from my tutor, Andy McDonnell on amongst other things literary, structure, feasibility and introducing me to the concept of Schrödinger's cat and the splitting of the atom, which would both play a part in the development of *The Thirteenth Hour*.

On my bachelor's and master's degrees, Judy Forshaw and Toby Venables took time out of their crazy teaching schedules to read the script when I adapted it into a screenplay, and thanks go to Steve Waters and all my university contemporaries for their invaluable feedback during workshops.

To Cambridge Writers, a writing group that has supported

me with all my novels over many years. Special thanks to Siobhán Carew, Mari Jane Law and Rachel Levy to whom I'm especially indebted for their constructive criticism, suggestions and encouragement.

To Michelle Foster, my incredible editor for many of my previous books, but whose premature passing meant she never got to cast her eye over this one. *The Thirteenth Hour* is poorer for it. However, the many literary lessons I've learnt from Michelle have, to the best of my ability, been applied here.

To my proof-readers: Isabelle Allott-Tsoflias, Graham Hunter, Michèle Isaac, Rachel Levy, Paul Westcott and Sue Wilson. Thank you for all of your hard work, correcting my grammar and rogue commas!

Lastly, my grateful thanks to innumerable people, too many to name, over the years for whose comments, research advice and suggestions have made this a better story.

Researching *The Thirteenth Hour* was a fascinating task and one of the hardest parts of writing the story was having to leave out so many historically important events and acts of courage, sacrifice and suffering. It also meant gathering information from a wide variety of sources, which I'm ashamed to say I haven't kept track of over the past fourteen years as well as I should. However, three absolutely absorbing books on the subject of World War Two that were my go-to references include *Fleeing Hitler: France 1940* by Hanna Diamond, *France: The Dark Years 1940-1944* by Julian Jackson and *The Unfree French: Life Under the Occupation* by Richard Vinen. These were instrumental in terms of historical fact, but to get the more personal details of the experience, the BBC's *WW2 People's War* has been a fantastic resource for learning the often tragic, often heroic stories of ordinary citizens caught in the crossfire of war.

Any mistakes are entirely my own and certain creative liberties have been taken.

Printed in Great Britain
by Amazon

46795254R00199